What the Critics are saying...

Five Stars! "...BRIANNA has gone to the top of the list of my favorite futuristic romances. I cannot express how much I enjoyed this book and I sincerely hope that there are more in the works. This is one universe that needs further exploration!" - *Nicole Hulst, eCataRomance Reviews*

Five Angels! "This novel is rollicking good fun, with a great plot, great characters, great back story-in other words, it's just plain GREAT!" - *Jean Fallen, Angel Reviews*

"Judy Mays has written an amazing and utterly superb story in BRIANNA...This extremely well written story is not only one of the best books I have read of hers, but may also be one of the top sci-fi romances ever. Her characters are absolutely amazing, and I fell for almost every one of them." - *Enya Adrian, Romance Reviews Today*

BRIANNA
CELESTIAL PASSIONS I

BRIANNA *CELESTIAL PASSIONS I*
An Ellora' s Cave Publication, November 2004

Ellora' s Cave Publishing, Inc.
1337 Commerse Drive
Stow, Ohio 44224

ISBN #1419950878

Second Edition.
First Edition ebook available from www.ellorascave.com.

Edited by Raelene Gorlinsky
Cover art by Syneca

Warning:

The following material contains graphic sexual content meant for mature readers. *Brianna* has been rated E-rotic by a minimum of three independent reviewers.

Ellora' s Cave Publishing offers three levels of Romantica™ reading entertainment: S (S-ensuous), E (E-rotic), and X (X-treme).

S-*ensuous* love scenes are explicit and leave nothing to the imagination.

E-*rotic* love scenes are explicit, leave nothing to the imagination, and are high in volume per the overall word count. In addition, some E-rated titles might contain fantasy material that some readers find objectionable, such as bondage, submission, same sex encounters, forced seductions, etc. E-rated titles are the most graphic titles we carry; it is common, for instance, for an author to use words such as "fucking", "cock", "pussy", etc., within their work of literature.

X-*treme* titles differ from E-rated titles only in plot premise and storyline execution. Unlike E-rated titles, stories designated with the letter X tend to contain controversial subject matter not for the faint of heart.

BRIANNA
CELESTIAL PASSIONS I

By Judy Mays

Prologue

"Spread your legs."

She complied.

"You' re very wet. Look."

When he placed the mirror beneath her, she was able to look down and see her honey dripping from between her swollen labia. He slid his fingers along her slit. She moaned and arched into his hand.

"Wider."

Cupping her own breasts, pinching her swollen nipples, she leaned back and spread her legs as widely as she could.

"Come into me, now!" she demanded.

Grasping her thighs, he thrust his cock into her and began to pump, slowly at first and then more rapidly, more deeply.

They both moaned.

Naked, Char lay back on his bed, hands clasped negligently behind his head. Still flaccid, his penis curled over his testicles.

With a bored grimace, he reached for the control and fast-forwarded. Soon two couples cavorted on the screen. Still, he remained unaroused.

With a mumbled curse, he swung his legs over the side of the bed and pushed himself to his feet. "I don' t know why I bother."

Discontent rippled through his mind. No woman had aroused his interest since...

But, she was certainly married now, and her husband would give him another scar to match the first if he ever got near her again.

Char raked his hands through his hair. Why was he lying to himself? Even with her, it had been the thrill of the chase, the pursuit of the forbidden.

Restless, he left his bedroom only to return a few minutes later with a glass of his favorite red wine. A solitary woman now amused herself on the video screen. His penis stirred.

"But she' s there, and I' m here, and self-appeasement doesn' t appeal to me today," he muttered to the empty room. "I want a woman who' s different, whose responses aren' t planned or choreographed. A woman who looks at me for *me*, not for my wealth or family name."

Could there be such a woman anywhere?

Laughing bitterly, Char tossed back his wine. "I' ve been everywhere."

The red light flashed above the intercom.

Setting his glass on the table, he punched a button.

"What?"

"We' ve lost them. We heard sounds of a struggle and then the audio went dead."

"I' m on my way."

Jerking his clothing from the chair next to his bed, Char slid into the form-fitting uniform. Then, tail lashing with barely controlled anger, he left his quarters and headed for the starship' s bridge.

Chapter One

The incessant screaming of the sirens burst across the base.

Brianna clenched the steering wheel tighter as she slowed to a stop at the gate. "Come on, Harry, ignore the sirens and raise the barrier."

The barrier remained down.

Harry stepped out of the guard box and walked towards her open window.

"Oh, shit!" She glanced back over her shoulder. "Stay down and don' t move."

The light wind blew a fine dust into her open window.

As the guard bent to look inside her SUV, Brianna forced a nonchalant grin. "Come on, Harry. I promise I didn' t steal any government secrets."

Harry grinned back. "Gotta follow the rules, Bri. Just need a quick look."

The shrill ringing of the phone pulled him back to the guard box. The look he gave her as he listened into the receiver told her she was out of time. Even now, two other soldiers were moving to close the gates.

"Double shit! Hang on. They' ve discovered you' re gone."

Stomping the gas pedal to the floor, Brianna smashed through the lowered barrier and roared off of the base.

* * * * *

Biting out a curse, the general hit the button on his buzzing intercom. This had better be important. "What is it?"

His aide' s voice was sharp. "Sir, the gates have been breached at the north entrance. A green Ford SUV registered to a Brianna O' Shea of laboratory area four, biomedical division, crashed through the checkpoint."

Wham! The violent slamming of the door reverberated up and down the corridor as Dr. Yens Gustovson burst into the office followed by the general's exasperated aide.

"Doctor, you just can't burst into the general's office!"

Gustovson ignored him and shouted, "She's got them!"

Silencing the incensed scientist with the slash of his hand, General Hawkins said, "That will be all, lieutenant."

After his aide left and he'd turned off the intercom, the general snapped, "Do I have to remind you this is top secret? Will you ever learn to keep your mouth shut?"

Gustovson slapped the desk. "You won't need to worry about secrecy if she gets away."

Hawkins steepled his fingers. "We never located a ship. This may work out after all. We'll soon have copters in the air, so they'll be easy enough to follow. With luck, they'll head straight back to their ship, and then we'll get that too. Don't worry, you'll get your ticket to fame and fortune back, Gustovson."

"What about O'Shea?"

The general shrugged. "Once we have them back, she'll be debriefed then fired."

"She'll go to the press!"

"And who'll believe her? *The National Enquirer*?"

Gustovson grimaced. "Just be sure of the troops you send after them. She has a lot of friends on this base."

The general drummed his fingers on the desk. "You may be right. Captain Douglas has a new platoon just in from Texas for woodland training. I'll send them. Lieutenant Simms," he ordered into his intercom, "have Captain Douglas report to me on the double and put his platoon on red alert. They pull out in fifteen minutes. Choppers ready?"

"Yes Sir. Major Richter has the potential routes mapped."

"Very good. Inform the major I'll be with him in a moment." The general rose. "Doctor, everything is under control. Would you like to accompany me?"

Gustovson curled his hands into fists, but he managed to keep control of his temper. "No, I'll wait in the lab. I have other things I can be doing."

The general nodded. "Very well, I' ll inform you when your specimens will be returned."

Once out of the general' s office, Gustovson hurried to the building' s foyer, where he waited as unobtrusively as possible until the man he wanted appeared.

As Captain Mark Douglas strode toward the elevators, Gustovson clutched his arm. Irritation evident on his face, the captain continued on, shrugging the hand loose.

The scientist was undeterred. "I need to talk to you."

Douglas stopped. "Make it quick. The general wanted me five minutes ago."

The scientist' s eyes darted around the foyer. No one was paying them any attention. "A mutual acquaintance has stolen some valuable specimens from the lab. A matter of national interest."

"Yeah, so what?" the younger man sneered, but he bent his head and listened.

"This person must not be permitted to make the existence of these specimens public. The damage to the base and the United States military will be irreparable. She must be stopped, and I know you' re the man for the job. You do understand?"

Watching the man' s reaction, Gustovson smiled to himself. Telling Douglas that Brianna had been spreading the rumors about him stealing things had been sheer genius.

Douglas contemplated the tiled pattern on the floor. There was only one person Gustovson could be referring to. After a curt nod, he spun away and headed to the elevators. The top brass had done a pretty good job keeping things hushed up. Even now that he was out of the loop, he still had a few sources. He had an idea about what was happening. A thoughtful expression on his face, he stepped into the empty elevator.

Clenching his fists, Douglas snarled mentally. It had been Brianna' s idea to go to the lab that night. Getting those papers was just an excuse to leave the party, wasn' t it? When he pushed her back onto the examining table, she was just acting, playing hard to get. If Gustovson hadn' t come in, she would have stopped fighting and spread her legs quickly enough. Women liked it when men got rough. He slammed his fist into the wall. Who' d have thought she' d spread those lies about him? You couldn' t trust any woman. The other guys still didn' t trust him even though nobody could prove he stole anything. Where did that bitch get off saying he had?

✳ ✳ ✳ ✳ ✳

Brianna's mind whirled as she sped north into the mountains. She must be crazy, stealing them from the lab, but she couldn't let Gustovson just murder them in the name of science.

Shivers of wonder raced up and down her spine and she smiled in spite of her present predicament. Aliens! She'd always known humans weren't alone, that there had to be life on other planets, but hermaphrodites! And tails that were really very long penises! Not even Hollywood could have dreamed that up. And how could they understand her when she talked to them? Where had they learned English?

Brianna glanced into her rear view mirror. "I hope you guys know where you want to go because I don't have the faintest idea what to do with you. I can't take you home. My parents would understand and agree with my actions 100 percent, but that's the first place the authorities will look."

One of the aliens tapped her shoulder.

Glancing back, she discovered they had inched up to her seat.

One of them pointed towards the mountain to their left.

"Left? Okay, that's as good a direction as any, I guess."

Switching to four-wheel drive, she turned onto the dirt road, a cloud of dust settling in her wake.

The taller alien turned to his companion. "Can you remember where the contact point is? Without our instruments, I'm blind."

Cindar dragged her gaze away from the window. "What happened to your sensor implant?"

"I don't know. I must've fallen on it when we were captured. My wrist's numb."

"Then the captain doesn't know where we are. We really do need to improve on this system. If we'd both had a transmitter, we wouldn't be in this predicament."

Miklan squeezed her hand and smiled. "As long as your locator is working, once we' re in range of the transport point, they' ll lock on to us. All we need to do is find it."

"No problem. I can hear the frequency in my translator, and it' s becoming stronger the further north we go. Besides, I recognize the trees along this road. The plant life on this planet is absolutely amazing."

His smile became a grin. "Advantage of being a botanist."

She laughed gently. "If I weren' t, we wouldn' t have enjoyed that afternoon on Deslossia so much. That was poison llacatian redfern you wanted to use for a bed!"

Hearing the soft, intimate laughter behind her, Brianna decided she had no regrets. These aliens were just as human as anyone else.

* * * * *

The pilot of the helicopter tapped Captain Douglas on the shoulder to get his attention, then shouted over the noise of the whirling blades. "She' s turned north onto an old logging road. It winds up the mountain to a small clearing in front of an old abandoned mine. I don' t think they know we' re tracking them."

Douglas looked up from the map he was studying. "Get us up there ahead of them. We' ll have a reception committee waiting."

"Roger, Sir. I' ll radio the other choppers."

Douglas allowed himself a satisfied smile. Brianna O' Shea would pay for ruining his career.

* * * * *

Yellow and blue lights lit the console on the navigator' s bridge station. After typing a command into the computer, she turned to her captain. "There' s been a great deal of activity at the contact point, sir. Our monitors picked up transports of some sort off-loading what are probably troops."

Char studied the navigator' s instruments. "Have the beam ready. As soon as you locate our people, get them up here. Lock in defense sequence 7-Yellow-7, just in case."

"Have we encountered a problem on this so-called *human* world, Captain Alalakan?" an oily voice asked.

Char stiffened slightly and turned to confront his tormentor. "We have a problem with a transmitter. Surely even Academy equipment sometimes fails?"

The shorter man laced his fingers together. "At times, Captain Alalakan, at times. But—we' re not under attack when it does happen."

Char arched a single eyebrow. "Attack? Do you hear sounds of attack, Bakom? I think you have an overactive imagination."

Acquiescing, the doctor bowed his head. "Possibly, Captain, possibly, but if we' d gone straight to Drakan as I requested, we wouldn' t be having this conversation, would we? However, if it' s needed, my medical training is at your disposal."

Char turned away. "So noted, but I doubt if it will be necessary. Now, if you will go back to your quarters, I' ll get back to captaining my ship."

Silence ruled Control as the door slid shut. Dr. Sendenton dem al' Lorilana walked over to stand beside the captain. "Don' t listen to him, Char. There could be a perfectly reasonable explanation why we lost contact with Miklan and Cindar."

Concentrating on his instruments, Char said nothing. Two of his officers were missing, and he was responsible. He was the one who' d sent them down to that planet.

After easing into the clearing, Brianna pulled to a halt. A single bird chirped. Then...silence.

She looked over her shoulder and asked, "Is this where you want to be?"

The alien on the left nodded affirmatively.

Sliding out of the SUV, Brianna hurried to the back and lowered the tailgate.

Slipping out, Miklan helped Cindar, who gingerly put weight on her left foot, said something low to her companion, and limped out into the meadow.

A forlorn feeling seeped through her body as Brianna watched her limp away. Even though the summer sun was warm, she rubbed her arms, trying to alleviate the sudden chill that enveloped her. She had never even gotten a chance to get to know them. What was it like, traveling in space? She turned as Miklan took her hand.

"Brianna," he began then added more in his musical language.

Tears formed in her eyes. "Thank you" in any language was easy to understand.

Pulling her into his arms, Miklan gave her a quick, hard hug.

A single burst of gunfire from an automatic rifle exploded into the air.

"You in the clearing, stand where you are and raise your hands. You' re completely surrounded. Surrender and you won' t be hurt."

Brianna and Miklan whirled as they heard snapping brush behind them. All around the clearing, soldiers with weapons pointed at them advanced slowly. Miklan shouted something, grabbed Brianna' s wrist, and began to run.

Brianna was jerked forward. "Hey! Wait a minute!"

"Halt or you will be fired upon! This is your last warning!"

Brianna whipped her head around. That was Mark' s voice.

A beam of clear, bright light appeared in the center of the clearing. Cindar stepped into it and promptly disappeared.

"Stop them!" Captain Douglas screamed. "Fire at will!"

Those words caused Brianna to stumble. *Fire at will! What' s the matter with him!*

When bursts of red light began sporadically sweeping the clearing, most of the soldiers dived back into the safety of the forest.

Brianna' s eyes were drawn back to the tall blond leader as he cursed vehemently. Horrified, she watched him pull his sidearm from its holster.

"You won' t get away, bitch!" he hollered after her.

"My God, he' s going to shoot at me!" She stumbled and tried to pull free of Miklan' s grasp.

Miklan ignored both her outburst and her attempt to jerk her wrist free from his grasp.

"I really don' t think this is a good idea." She glanced back again. Mark was aiming his sidearm at her.

Miklan shouted something over his shoulder and pulled her into the light.

Brianna swallowed and shivered involuntarily. However, she never learned exactly what matter displacement transportation felt like. Just before she stepped into the beam of light, a bullet ripped into her right shoulder. Unconsciousness blocked out the pain.

* * * * *

A bright red light began flashing on the screen. "They' re in range of the transport beam, Sir."

"They may need a diversion. Retrieve them, now! Begin the defense sequence," Char commanded. "Damn! I wish I could see what was happening!"

His communications officer shook his head. "Every frequency for the view screen is monitored by their satellites. The minute we activate it, they' ll know we' re here. The radio probes sent our way are becoming more numerous. So far, we' ve been able to deflect them. That' s a highly advanced civilization down there. The sooner we get out of here, the better."

"We have them," the chief engineer interrupted.

"Take us out of orbit immediately," Char snapped. "I want to get away from this planet now. Ademis, take charge. Lori, let' s go. They may need medical attention."

* * * * *

Blood spurting freely from the wound in her shoulder, Brianna collapsed to the floor. Falling to his knees, Miklan pressed his palms on the wound to staunch the bleeding.

"Quick," he ordered when the door slid open, "we need a doctor!"

As instructed, Kindis dem al' Eliana had waited near the transport station. When the exploratory party materialized, she entered the room and moved towards Miklan. "I' m a nurse," she said, nudging him aside.

Doctor Rodak don al' Bakom entered Transport as Eliana finished speaking.

Miklan tried to rise, but Bakom jabbed a hypodermic needle into his arm. He collapsed instantly. Bakom' s other assistant, Zator don al' Odam, silenced Cindar the same way.

"This is even better than I' d hoped. Leave them. We' ll take the specimen they brought back. Hurry, wrap it up before that damned Alalakan gets here."

The ship' s medical team arrived as Bakom and his assistants were leaving transport with a bundle of canvas.

"Hurry," he ordered, nodding towards Miklan and Cindar. "They' re unconscious. Get them to Medical as quickly as possible. My assistants and I are taking this specimen that was trapped in the transport beam to the facilities I have here on the ship. Tell your captain I' ll inform him of my findings when the examination is concluded."

The leader of the medical team did not think to question him. After all, Dr. Bakom was First President of the Academy of Science. Who better to examine a lifeform from a previously unknown planet? Granted the thing they were dragging out had a human outline, but getting Miklan and Cindar to Medical was more important than some unknown specimen. Miklan' s hands were covered with blood.

* * * * *

Char stopped pacing when Cindar and Miklan were carried into Medical. Both were hastily stripped and placed in medibunks.

"All of Cindar' s vital signs are normal," Lorilana' s assistant called. "I don' t understand why she' s unconscious. That' s never been a side effect of transport before."

Lorilana frowned. "Miklan' s the same. No wounds on either of them. Where did all this blood come from?"

Char stepped next to Lorilana and stared at his unconscious crew members with a worried frown. "Conjecture?"

The doctor shook her head. "I don' t know. Jaylin, did you notice anything unusual in transport?"

"No, Dr. Bakom had already stabilized them. He and his assistants took the specimen caught in the beam to his lab."

Char stiffened and turned towards Jaylin. "Bakom was there? What specimen? What did it look like?"

"I don' t know, sir. They' d already wrapped it in lab canvas when we arrived. It did seem to have a human outline, though."

He whirled towards the door. "Damn Bakom and his sex experiments! Lori, come with me. If the inhabitants of that planet are human, he may well begin a war."

"Jaylin, draw some blood and see if there is anything in their systems that shouldn' t be there. As long as their vital signs stay normal, let them sleep," Lorilana ordered as she followed Chardadon out the door.

* * * * *

Odam rolled Brianna from the canvas and lifted her onto the examining table. Heedless of the blood that began to seep from her shoulder once again, he raised her arms above her head and clamped her wrists firmly into place. Moving to the bottom of the table, he spread her legs and fastened her ankles to the clasps located on each side of the table. Then he began to methodically cut away her clothing. His thick tail began to jerk as her body was revealed.

"Are you sure this is wise, Doctor?" Eliana asked as they stepped next to the table where the woman lay. "Wouldn' t it be better to wait until we' re back at the Academy? Or at least until we care for her wound?"

A hungry grin settled onto Bakom' s face as he caressed Eliana' s buttocks. "No, my dear, we can' t wait. Alalakan will surely discover our little project and take it for himself. You' ve begun the program sequence on the computer?"

"Yes," she answered as her superior slipped his hand inside her shirt to pinch her nipple.

Bakom slipped the shirt over Eliana' s head and cupped her left breast. "Wonderful. Now, Odam, what do we have here?"

"I don' t know if it' s human," Odam said breathing heavily, his thin nostrils flaring as he stared at Brianna' s naked body, "but it' s certainly female." He stripped off his clothing.

Sliding his hand down the inside of Eliana' s pants, Bakom cupped her buttock, his fingers stroking, seeking. She shifted, spreading her legs.

Bakom continued his exploration as he turned his gaze to the woman. Eyes narrowing, he contemplated what fate had delivered into his hands. "Yes, she certainly is female. Now let' s see how she responds to mithrin."

Deep in her subconscious, Brianna returned to the previous day in Dr. Gustovson' s laboratory.

Brianna gasped when she saw what lay on the examining tables. "Aliens! Where did they come from?" Joy blossomed in her heart. She knew humans weren' t alone. There was intelligent life out there somewhere.

"Where they came from doesn' t matter to you. You' re only here to assist me, not to think. Gather your recording equipment and pay attention!" Dr.

Gustovson snapped as he fitted a headset equipped with an earpiece and a microphone onto his head. "Now, where was I? Oh, yes. The alien being designated Specimen A is approximately 6.5 feet in length and 200 pounds in weight. Face – slightly elongated, tapering to a pointed chin. Two eyes, color brown," he said as he lifted an eyelid, "somewhat large with thick lashes, set one on each side of small nose. One mouth with thin lips. No facial hair. The skin is very human-like, with a slight, ivory tint. The scalp is covered with short, fine brown hair – silky texture. One ear on each side of the head, lobeless and stretching upward to a point. The left ear seems to have some sort of growth on the inside. Whether this is characteristic of the species cannot be determined until an examination is performed on the second specimen.

"The neck is proportional to the body. Torso – slender with fine, almost invisible body hair, somewhat prominent pectoral muscles. Two arms, each jointed by an elbow. Arms ending with hands each containing five digits: four fingers and an opposable thumb. Two legs, bending at the knees, lower legs stretching to ankles; two feet with five toes each. Very human-like.

"Genitalia, one relatively small, slender penis. One scrotum..." Gustovson frowned. "No, it's too far back, and there's no connection to the penis."

He bent over the body and motioned Brianna closer. "Look! Vulva behind the penis! A hermaphrodite? Those aren't enlarged pectorals on the chest; they're small breasts! A species able to repopulate from single individuals. Amazing!"

Brianna shook her head. "But doctor. The penis is located in front of the vulva. It couldn't impregnate itself. The scrotum isn't connected. That can't be a penis; it must be the clitoris."

The scientist snorted. "Bah! Why so elongated?"

Not for the first time was she grateful that her immediate superior was practically asexual. "There's an opening. It must be the urethra."

Gustovson puckered his lips. "Well, you may have a point, but evolution is not kind to a species with a complicated sexual process. Here, help me turn it over. The scrotum is so far back, examination from behind should shed some light on the subject."

Carefully, they rolled the alien's body over.

"Hmm, the scrotum seems to be attached to the base of the tail. Interesting, the tail is completely hairless. But then, there is very little body hair. Even the pubic hair is very fine," Gustovson murmured absently as he probed the body. "This is indeed a puzzle."

He turned off his microphone.

As the doctor puzzled over the alien' s genitalia, Brianna lifted the tail. She ran her hand along its length—hairless and smooth. She bent it— somewhat supple, though it only curved forward. She smiled. Aliens with tails! When she reached the end of the tail, her smile became a frown. The tail thickened about eight inches from the end. Unlike the tails of most animals on Earth, this tail didn' t end with a tip but rather a knob—a knob with extra, loose skin over it.

"Doctor, look at the end of the tail."

Gustovson grabbed the tail and stared at the end. "What? Well, well, who would have thought?" Returning to what he considered his professional voice, he turned the microphone back on. "Tail, approximately 3 to 3.5 feet long with a two inch diameter, extending to a thick, blunt tip. Since the anus is underneath the base of the tail, as expected, the small opening at the end of the tail could be for seminal fluid. Conjecture? The creature doesn' t have a tail, rather a very supple penis. With as flexible as the penis seems to be, it is entirely possible for the alien to impregnate itself. However, the hermaphroditic theory will remain questionable until a complete dissection is performed."

He turned to Brianna. "Miss O' Shea, a dissecting kit."

"Uhhhhhhhhhhh."

Brianna spun back around and stared at the alien. Its eyes blinked a few times, then remained open. "Doctor, it' s alive!"

Gustovson spat a curse then rounded on Brianna. "Miss O' Shea, we are on the brink of one of the most amazing discoveries of the century. Perhaps we are even helping to save our world. Who knows what these aliens have planned. Now is not the time to be squeamish."

"Squeamish! This is an intelligent life form."

Eyes narrowed, Gustovson turned to face her. "Miss O' Shea, this is my laboratory. I can do damn well whatever I please. The only reason you have this job is because your father is an old colleague. Now, do as I say or get out."

Brianna was jolted back to consciousness by a sharp pain in her thigh. Moaning, she opened her eyes.

Three *people* looked down at her, two with unconcealed lust in their eyes and one with pity.

"How long before the drug takes effect?" Bakom asked.

"Only a few minutes," Odam answered. "I gave her a full dose."

Brianna couldn' t understand a word they said.

Her right shoulder was on fire, and she could feel blood seeping sluggishly from her wound.

Then a new fire surged through her bloodstream. Pain and heat enveloped her. Moaning, she arched her back. Her groin and nipples were on fire! She jerked against the bonds wrapped around her wrists. She had to touch herself!

The wound in her shoulder opened. More blood began to flow.

Sobbing, Brianna tried to close her legs against the fiery pressure in her loins.

Then someone grabbed her wounded shoulder. She fainted from the pain.

* * * * *

Halting before the door to Hold 3, Char palmed the door switch. Nothing happened. "That bastard' s crazy if he thinks he can realign the door codes."

Lorilana grasped his arm. "Mind your temper, Char. You don' t want to ruin your family' s plans."

He scowled, but nodded curtly. Taking an orange card from his belt, he slipped it into the door panel and punched in the override. The door slid open and they entered the Hold where they were greeted with the exact scene he had imagined. Both of Bakom' s assistants were naked, as was the humanoid on the table.

When Eliana stepped behind the table and Char got a good look at Bakom' s specimen, he felt as if someone planted a fist in his stomach.

A woman—a beautifully exotic woman.

Fiery red hair tumbled over the side of the table in an auburn waterfall. Pale skin, which any woman in his family would envy, glowed under harsh laboratory lights. Full breasts with rosy nipples rose and fell with harsh breathing. A narrow waist tapered to flared hips where a splash of equally fiery pubic hair curled at the juncture of her thighs. Long legs stretched to the end of the table.

Familiar, heavy pressure exploded in Char' s groin. However, the blood pooled under her shoulder and dripping to the floor immediately checked his ardor.

Striding to the table, Char grasped Bakom' s upper arm and jerked him around. "What the hell do you think you' re doing?"

Hate blazing from his eyes, Bakom snarled, "Release me, Alalakan. As an unidentified species from an unknown planet, this being falls under the jurisdiction of the Academy."

Lorilana stepped to Char's side. "She's too human in form to be subjected to the primary tests, and as a voting member of the Academy board, I'll testify to that."

Bakom glared at Lori. "That still puts it under Academy jurisdiction, Doctor Sendenton."

"That may be," Char growled, eyes narrowed, "but she's wounded and bleeding. She goes to Medical now."

"You have no right!"

Char crossed his arms over his chest. "I have every right. As captain, I have complete command over everyone on this ship. Would you care to read the Confederation rule book?"

"Get out!" Bakom snarled. "I'm entitled to the privacy of my own quarters."

"These are not your private quarters. It's a cargo hold, and no humanoid will be transported to Drakan in the cargo hold of my ship," Char stated flatly. Shoving Bakom aside, he unfastened the woman's wrists. Lorilana had already freed her ankles. Ignoring the waves of fury rolling from the smaller man, he gathered the woman into his arms and turned away.

As his two enemies disappeared out the door with his specimen, Bakom turned his smoldering gaze on his assistants.

Both Odam and Eliana had wisely placed the table between themselves and the angry captain.

"Come, both of you," Bakom growled as he tugged at his belt. "I'm in need of comfort."

Chapter Two

The woman' s thick auburn hair cascaded over Char as he carried her towards Medical. Held in thrall by the sexual stimulant, she struggled in his arms, but the blood loss she' d sustained weakened her enough so that he was able to carry her easily.

"She' s weakening," Lorilana muttered in a worried tone. "I don' t know what we' ll do about replacing the lost blood. Simple fluids may not be enough."

Char said nothing. The agonized expression on the woman' s face didn' t hide its exotic beauty. Her face was rounder than those of his people, her lips fuller. Stunning green eyes fluttered open and stared unseeing into his. Thick, dark lashes rimmed those eyes while the well-shaped auburn brows above them contrasted sharply with her wan complexion. Even with blood seeping from her shoulder, she stirred him as no woman had in a long time. His glance drifted down to her taut nipples.

I want her.

Lorilana palmed open the door to Medical, calling in crisp tones for her assistants and various pieces of equipment. "First, mithrin antidote. I wish I knew how much he gave her," she stated. "I wish I knew what her metabolism was like. We' ve got to get this shoulder cleaned out. Jaylin, get that hair out of the wound."

Char' s voice was sharp. "Don' t cut it!"

He refused to acknowledge the inquisitive look in Lorilana' s eyes and concentrated on the woman. Lights flashed as the medibunk registered an occupant when he laid her down then stepped back out of the way. He ignored the blood smeared on his uniform.

Lorilana placed her stethoscope on the woman' s chest. "Heart rate, slow—too slow, I think. Breathing is awfully shallow. I think we can count on the integrity of the medibunk for basic information. It seems to fit within human parameters. The respiration and heart rate seem to be accurate, so everything else is probably correct also."

Char remained where he was. "Will she live?"

Lori placed her hand on the woman' s forehead. "I don' t know. If there hadn' t been so much blood loss, I' d say she had a good chance, but…"

"Doctor Sendenton, I think you should look at this."

"Not now, Jaylin."

"You really have to look at this," the young woman insisted.

Lori tsked and strode to the computer. "What is it?"

"I put a sample of the blood from Miklan' s hands in the computer and, well, see for yourself."

After looking at the screen, Lorilana glanced up at Jaylin then reread the data. "Impossible."

Char stepped forward. "What?"

Ignoring him, Lorilana removed a small slide from the computer terminal. Returning to her patient, she gently smeared blood onto the slide. Placing it back in the computer, she entered a command.

"Amazing. Exactly like Medirian blood. I don' t know who she is, but she' s definitely human. Jaylin, how much Medirian blood type O positive do we have in storage?"

Punching up the data, her assistant answered, "Three bags, and we do have two or three Medirians with that blood type on board if that isn' t enough."

"Set up an IV immediately." Lorilana turned to Char. "I think we can be fairly certain that she' ll live."

Char nodded once and turned toward the door. "Very well, I' ll be in Command."

* * * * *

Miklan regained consciousness slowly. Struggling, he sat up.

Lorilana placed restraining hands on his shoulders. "Lie back down, Miklan. There' s some sort of chemical in your bloodstream that we can' t identify. We have to keep you under observation until we analyze it."

"It' s a sedative of some kind," he muttered still struggling against her. "Let me up. We have to help Brianna. Bakom surprised us as we transported in."

"Lie back down! And that' s an order. If Brianna is the woman who returned with you, she' s safe. We have her right here."

He relaxed immediately.

Lorilana turned to her assistant. "Inform the captain Miklan is awake."

"Brianna saved our lives," Miklan explained from his bunk, "against her superior' s orders. She deserves our thanks and all the help we can give her."

Lorilana checked his pulse. "We' ve done everything we can, Mik. It' s up to her now."

Miklan' s eyes opened wide. "What did Bakom do to her?"

Lorilana stared at him. First Char, now Miklan? Who is this woman? "We reached her before he had a chance to do anything. The wound she carried when she came on board caused us the most worry."

The door slid open and Char entered Medical. Miklan tried to rise, but Char motioned him to remain in his bed. "Report."

"Cindar was gathering plant specimens and I was recording seismic activity when a group of soldiers stumbled upon us. From what I could gather, they were practicing nighttime warfare. We put up a struggle, which is how Cindar was hurt. At first they thought we were inhabitants of their planet—until they got a good look at us. When they realized we were alien to them, we were drugged unconscious. The next thing I remember is waking up on an examining table."

Miklan continued, briefly relating how Brianna had saved them from dissection.

"So, without this woman' s help, you would not have survived?"

Miklan nodded. "Correct. They planned to dissect us."

Lorilana gasped with outrage. "Dissection! For that alone, she deserves whatever aid we can give her."

"The Alalakans always pay their debts," Chardadon stated softly.

Again the door hissed opened. Bakom sauntered in, a contemptuous sneer on his face. "Will the specimen live?"

Char stepped in front of him. "You aren' t needed here."

"Oh, but I have every right to be here. That' s a new life form. Until it' s properly categorized, it belongs to the Academy of Science. As First President, I' m taking personal interest in it."

Lorilana put her hand on Char' s arm, silencing him. "She' s lost a great deal of blood, Bakom. We aren' t even sure she' ll survive. There' s nothing more we can do at this time."

Gazing at the readouts on the medibunk, Bakom grunted. "I expect to be notified if its condition changes. Remember, I' m personally assuming categorization of this creature. Don' t try to gainsay my decision. The law supports me." Turning, he left Medical, chuckling in a most satisfactory manner.

Lorilana' s hand remained on Char' s arm. "He' s right. The law supports him."

"Her experience will be worse than mine," Miklan muttered. "My captors didn' t plan to torture me before they killed me."

"The Alalakan clan owes her a debt which will be paid," Char stated firmly. "This is my ship. As long as we' re in free space, my decisions override all else."

"True," Lorilana said quietly, "but I can' t keep him from Medical. Nor can I keep manipulating the medibunk. Bakom' s bound to notice her condition is improving and keeping her sedated will interfere with her natural healing process."

"Move her."

Lorilana busied herself attending her patient. "As First President, Bakom can gain access to any place on this ship. He outranks everyone on your crew. However, there are two places where he dare not go."

He raked he fingers through his hair. "Meri' s quarters. If she didn' t have the baby, I' d ask."

Lorilana' s steady gaze locked on his face. "I wasn' t thinking about Meri' s quarters, Char. I was thinking of yours."

He stiffened. "Mine?"

"It' s the only other place Bakom dare not go. I know it would make for inconveniences," she continued trying to gauge Char' s shuttered expression, "but it' s the only place we' ll be able to protect her. We' ll put her in the small room off your community room. My staff and I will see to her care. You won' t even know she' s there."

Arms now crossed over his chest, Chardadon stared at the Lorilana. *I will have this alien woman. I will wrap all that fiery hair around my naked body until I explode with ecstasy.* Finally, he spoke. "Very well, but only you' ll attend her. Bakom could intimidate your technicians, and I don' t want an endless stream of people wandering in and out."

"Thank you, Char. You' re paying your debt and doing a great service for humanity. Bakom may not want to admit it, but that woman is as human as we are. Anything he would do to her would serve no good purpose and would not endear us to her planet."

After a curt nod, Char left Medical.

From his medibunk, Miklan had listened quietly to the conversation between the doctor and his captain. With the effects of the sedative wearing off, he was feeling much stronger. The satisfied smile on the doctor' s face caused him to comment, "That was as fine a job of manipulation as I' ve seen in a long time, doctor."

She laughed. "Those of our race who carry only male genes are usually easily manipulated. Char is more perceptive than most full males but, given the right incentive, he too is susceptible."

Miklan grinned. "And you have obviously found the perfect incentive."

Lorilana continued to smile but spoke more solemnly. "Char has completely immersed himself in his family' s many enterprises for the last seven years. Though he never said it in so many words, he' s no longer content. Perhaps if his brother Rodane had children, he could play the doting uncle..."

Miklan laced his fingers behind his head. "He hasn' t seemed that discontent to me."

Lorilana shook her head. "He' s no longer actively pursuing women."

"He doesn' t have to," Miklan muttered.

Her laugh filled medical. "Just because women fall at his feet and he takes most of them to bed, doesn' t mean he' s content. Besides, he' s been completely abstinent since we left Drakan."

Miklan shook his head. "He never cohabitates with members of his crew."

Lorilana crossed her arms over her chest. "At every one of our stops, he has avoided women."

Miklan' s eyebrows rose. No healthy Drakian of legal age practiced abstinence.

"This woman, though," Lorilana continued, "has roused his interest. He' s allowed her into his quarters. Normally, he' d simply post guards outside of Medical and deny Bakom access. He' s never given a damn about rules and regulations."

"So, you'll force the issue, eh?"

Lorilana stared at the grinning Miklan. "You're getting rather impertinent with your superior officer, lieutenant."

"Only because I can get away with it, Aunt."

* * * * *

Groaning, Brianna opened her eyes then gasped at the sudden ache in her shoulder. Befuddled at first, she tried to focus her eyes in the dim light. Frowning, she lifted her head and looked around. Where was she? The last thing she remembered, she'd been in that clearing with the aliens.

Her eyes widened. Aliens—and soldiers.

A memory of Mark pointing a gun at her appeared before her eyes.

Her temper flared. "That son of a bitch! He shot me! What the hell did I ever do to him? He was the one who tried to *rape* me!"

Again she looked around the small room. Nothing looked familiar. *Where* was she? She continued to search her memory.

A bright beam of light. Miklan! He'd grabbed her wrist and pulled her into that bright light.

She felt the blood drain from her face. *My God, I must be on a spaceship.*

Heart leaping into her throat, Brianna gasped and choked. Shivers raced up and down her body. A spaceship? Oh God! What was she going to do?

Gritting her teeth, she forced herself to slow her panicked breathing. Fists clenched, she reasserted command over her trembling body. "I will not panic. I will not lie here shaking and crying like some too stupid to live heroine in a bad romance novel. I can handle this. I *will* handle this!"

She sat up and immediately grimaced at the twinge of pain in her shoulder. How badly had she been hurt? Moving slowly, she carefully raised her arms and legs. They moved the way they were supposed to, although there was a definite tenderness in her right shoulder.

Except for the white bandage covering her wound, she was naked. "Where the hell are my clothes?"

Wrapping the blanket around her torso, Brianna swung her legs over the bunk and pushed herself to her feet. Moving carefully, she gained her equilibrium and worked the slight stiffness out of her legs. How long had she been unconscious?

Brianna pulled the blanket more tightly beneath her arms and walked to the door. Tentatively, she placed her palm upon the handprint in the middle. It slid open with a slight whisper, revealing an empty room.

When she stepped cautiously into the larger room, the quiet hiss of the door closing caused her to spin about. A handprint identical to that on the inside was also affixed to this side. Pressing her palm against it, she was relieved when the door glided open. At least she could get back in. But was it a refuge or a cage?

Turning once more, Brianna took stock of her surroundings. This room was much larger with sparse but what looked like comfortable furnishings. A table with ten chairs was to one side while a sofa, overstuffed chair, and a smaller table sat on the other side. A large plant, with pale blue leaves and flowers of a darker blue, stood next to a closed door to her right. However, the huge window on the opposite wall drew her attention. There were drapes of a sort, pulled open. And outside of the window was nothing, absolutely nothing.

Brianna staggered to the window, braced her hands against it, and gaped at the blackness. One tiny pinpoint of light could be seen far, far below, but it flickered out as she stared at it. "Oh my God," she moaned, "I *am* in a spaceship! Where's Earth? How do I get home?" Frozen in place, her thoughts a whirling maelstrom, she didn't hear the door slide open behind her.

Rubbing his chin as he walked into the room—he really needed to shave—Char's gaze was immediately drawn to the figure standing before the window. Stopping half way across the room, he stared at the woman who had danced erotically through his dreams for the last week. She stood with her back to him, a blanket covering her from her torso to her knees. Her fiery hair cascaded to her hips.

A mental picture of those soft flames wrapped around his body jumped into his mind.

"So, you have finally awakened."

Brianna tensed. She wasn't alone. She turned slowly and gasped in shock. The man who shared the room with her was completely naked. A picture of Miklan and Cindar as they lay naked and unconscious on the lab tables leaped into her mind. In many ways, this man was much like them. He had the same skin tone, almond-shaped eyes, thin nose, and lips. His ears were pointed and his hair, though longer, thicker, and a darker brown, looked just as silky. He stood taller than Miklan, only a few inches short of seven feet. There, however, the similarities ended.

A colorful tattoo of what looked like some sort of dragon rode high on his right shoulder. His well-developed chest tapered to a slender waist. His legs were long and also displayed more muscle than Miklan' s.

Most obvious, though, was the difference in his genitals. A long, thick penis rested in a nest of fine brown pubic hair. He had a tail. She could see it dangling between his legs. But it really was a tail, not an elongated penis. This man was definitely not a hermaphrodite!

As Brianna watched, his penis stirred and began to rise.

Fear blossomed, and she pressed back against the window. She jerked her gaze back up his body to meet dark eyes surrounded by thick lashes, eyes that did not attempt to hide their amusement — or interest. Beautiful white teeth flashed as both hands combed his hair behind his ears. Muscles rippled across his naked chest as he spoke.

"You' re a very beautiful woman."

She swallowed and clutched her blanket more tightly. The musical language was the same as Miklan' s, but the voice much richer, much deeper, much more…masculine.

More importantly, she couldn' t understand a word he said.

Her imagination fueling her growing panic, Brianna flattened herself against the window. What was he saying to her? Would he understand her like Miklan did? Why was he naked? What was she doing here? Had she been kidnapped for sex? Were all those lurid stories about alien sex in those trashy tabloids true?

He spoke again. "Come, make love with me. Wrap your hair around my body as I suck your beautiful breasts. When I finally enter you, you will scream with pleasure."

Brianna had no idea what he had said, but she sagged with relief when he turned away. She continued to watch him warily as he strode to a panel attached to the wall, punched a button, and spoke into what looked like an intercom, undoubtedly about her. Was he calling Miklan? Please, let Miklan come.

In a few minutes, the light above a door flashed. When it opened, a woman, at least a person that *looked* like a woman, walked in and began talking to the man. Brianna was unable to follow their conversation, but they were obviously talking about her. What amazed her was the nonchalance they both showed towards his nudity. Did these people just walk around naked? God, what had she gotten herself into?

"I thought you were going to insert a translator."

Lorilana shrugged. "I am, but I couldn' t before she woke up. I have to know it' s been inserted properly."

They both turned towards Brianna.

When Brianna realized that they had stopped talking and were looking expectantly at her, her chin rose. *I will not faint. I will not faint.* "Well, what am I supposed to say? You don' t expect me to go through the hysterical ' Where am I?' routine do you? It' s obvious I' m on some sort of spaceship," she snapped. Voicing her thoughts was the only way she was able to control her panic.

"She' s got spirit," Lorilana said, trying to analyze Brianna through her words and body language as the younger woman clutched the blanket tightly about herself and kept glancing nervously at Char. "Char, I believe her culture is a bit more conservative than ours. Go put some clothes on. You' re making her nervous."

Thoughtfully, Char stared at the woman. His steady gaze induced more trembling, and when he took a step towards her, her face paled even more.

Lorilana grabbed his wrist. "Scientific experiments are my field, Char. Stop scaring the poor girl!"

He grinned. "Yes, Madam Doctor." Turning, he disappeared through the door behind him.

Brianna stared, intrigued in spite of her fear. He was handsome, for an alien. He had a great ass. And she got a clear view of his tail. An extension of his spine, it reached almost all the way to the floor. What in the world was the tail for?

A picture of that tail inching its way up along her naked thigh made her shiver.

Her common sense quickly asserted itself. *Shit, Brianna, get your mind out of the gutter. You could be a prisoner for all you know. What if there' s someone like Gustovson on board?*

Gathering her courage, Brianna turned to face the woman. She was older than the man, her features more androgynous. She was probably hermaphroditic like Miklan, and so much more approachable than the naked man had been. The slight wrinkles around her mouth and eyes gave hints at a person who smiled often. Her light brown hair was cut in a short, chic style. The robes she wore were long-sleeved and flowed to the floor. She was elegant and controlled in every line, but the unmistakable stethoscope embroidered on her bodice eased Brianna' s fears far more than her appearance. She had to be a doctor.

Motioning for Brianna to follow her, the woman led the way back into the smaller room. After they were inside, the woman palmed the door shut and spoke.

"Now that Char' s handsome face is out of the way, perhaps you' ll pay more attention to me."

Frowning, Brianna shook her head, tired of not being able to understand anyone. Pointing to herself, she said, "Brianna."

The woman motioned her over to the chair and spoke again.

"I know you' re frustrated, but we' ll remedy that in a few seconds." Reaching into her pocket, she withdrew a small case, opened it, and placed *something* on her fingertip. Pushing Brianna' s hair away, she placed her finger at the opening of her left ear and gave it a slight tap. The thing fell into Brianna' s ear and adhered itself to her eardrum.

"There, how' s that?"

Eyes widening, Brianna gasped, "What did you do?"

"I inserted a Medirian ghena into your ear. Don' t worry; it won' t harm you. It works as a translator for its host, but we have no idea how, even though the best scientists on three plants have spent the last fifty or so years studying it. Princess Merilinlalissa will be more than happy to tell you the entire story, I' m sure," the doctor said as she sat down on the bunk, "but right now you must have many questions of your own."

Clutching the ends of the blanket tighter to her bosom, Brianna asked, "Who are you? And where am I?"

"Doctor Sendenton dem al' Lorilana. Call me Lorilana. You' re on the exploratory cargo ship *Restoration*."

"Where are we?"

"For an exact location, you' ll have to ask the navigator or the captain. I do know we' re approximately four and a half months away from Drakan."

So far so good, she thought. "Drakan?"

"Our home planet."

"How far are we from Earth?"

"Earth?"

Brianna controlled her impatience. "Earth is the name of my planet."

"What an unassuming name," the doctor mused. "To be exact, again, you' d have to ask an expert. We' ve been traveling about a week, so it' s undoubtedly several million light years."

Brianna felt the blood drain from her face. *Several million light years!* "But...how do I get home?"

"I' m afraid it will be a while," Lorilana said gently.

Brianna swallowed and blinked back the tears that were threatening to fall. "A while? How long is a while?"

The doctor patted her shoulder, but Brianna shrugged it off. Forcing the feeling of helplessness and the uncertainty out of her mind, she blinked rapidly and struggled to swallow her tears. Crying wasn' t going to do any good. She had to get a hold of herself. And she definitely couldn' t let these aliens know she was scared! The first thing she had to find out was what they were going to do with her.

Taking a deep breath, she hugged herself tightly and gathered her scattered wits. "Are Miklan and Cindar all right?"

Surprise obvious on her face, the doctor simply stared for a moment.

"They are okay, aren' t they?"

"They' re fine. I' m surprised you were able to learn their names. They, of course, have translators, so understood everything you said."

"It' s not hard to understand someone pointing at himself and saying one word."

The doctor smiled. "Wonderful, you have a sense of humor."

"It' s either that or give in to hysterics, and I don' t think the gentleman in the other room would appreciate those."

Lorilana smiled at the younger woman. What a sly girl, introducing Char into the conversation so innocently. She was more interested in him than she wanted to admit. "You' re right. Your name is Brianna?"

Brianna nodded. If she was going to survive this trip with her sanity intact, she needed information. "Yes, Brianna Claire O' Shea. Who is that man? Is this part of his cabin? Why am I here? I' ve been wounded. How come I' m not in the medical section of the ship?"

Lorilana sighed. Brianna certainly got right to the point. "He' s Captain Alalakan don al' Chardadon. His family owns this and numerous other ships. And, yes, this room is part of the captain' s quarters, and as to why you' re here instead of in Medical... Well, there are complications with your presence."

Slumping, Brianna sighed. "The people on this ship hold me responsible for what almost happened to Miklan and Cindar. It would have been better if Miklan had left me behind."

Placing her fingers under Brianna' s chin, Lorilana lifted the younger woman' s head until their eyes locked. "Every member of this crew owes you a debt of gratitude for saving Miklan and Cinder' s lives, and they will not hesitate to tell you so, I especially, since Miklan is my nephew. No, not one member of the crew feels anything but gratitude towards you, Brianna. It' s the passengers who are causing the problem, one in particular, Dr. Rodak don al' Bakom."

"Why?"

"It' s a long story."

She jerked her chin free of Lorilana' s grasp. "I' m not going anywhere, and I deserve to know what' s going on."

Lorilana rose then sighed. "You do deserve a full explanation. I hope you' re comfortable."

"Just a second and I will be," Brianna said as she moved from the chair to the corner of the bunk and braced herself against the wall. "Tell me."

Lorilana slid down onto the chair. "Founded even before the scientists of Drakan discovered the power that allows us to roam freely about the galaxy, the Academy of Science was created to serve humankind. Its members concentrated on finding cures for diseases, discovering new strains of seeds to ensure larger harvests, and other ways to use all of our advances without harming each other or our environment."

After Brianna nodded, the doctor continued. "From satellites we' d launched early in our space programs, we mapped the planets in our solar system. After we achieved interplanetary travel, we sent an expedition to the planet that circles our sun exactly opposite of ours, Mediria, a planet whose surface is 90 percent water, and discovered it was inhabited. Medirians are able to breathe in both air and water and are almost as scientifically advanced as we are. What' s more, even though they didn' t look exactly like us, they are human."

"How can you tell?"

"Be patient," Lorilana said gently. "I want you to not only understand what is happening, but also why."

Brianna swallowed. That statement was entirely too ominous.

"The Medirians are a friendly people and greeted us with enthusiasm," continued the doctor. "Treaties were signed and trade established. As our space travel grew more advanced, we set up shuttle systems between our two planets. Now, it takes less than an hour to travel from one to the other."

"Since human life was found on another planet in our own solar system, the Academy concluded that it also might exist on others. Once the space drive was perfected, the Academy, which over the years had acquired a great deal of power in our government, mandated that we should search out human life on other planets. This mandate was formulated for the betterment of the human race. The Academy felt that humans from all planets could help each other improve life. And for years, that' s what we practiced. As time went on, during our explorations, we discovered three other planets with human life, two as advanced technically as ours and the other content with its pastoral life. You can learn the histories of these planets from the computer files at your leisure."

"About 150 years ago, the Academy began to change. A small group of members sought to revise some of the bylaws—only small things, at first. However, as their party gained in numbers, more radical changes were put into effect. All peoples living on the five planets whose races were known to be human were acknowledged as such. However, life indigenous to newly discovered planets would have to meet certain criteria."

Lorilana shifted in her chair. "Originally, these new criteria did not alarm many people. They were broad and everyone from the five plants easily fit into them. However, when we charted a new planet with what appeared to be human life, we learned just what had been enacted."

The doctor' s expression darkened. "Five years ago, a planet was discovered on the opposite end of the galaxy from yours. Its inhabitants were humanoid in form. When one of them volunteered to have a transmitter inserted, we discovered that they were extremely intelligent. They called their planet Wafhkte. The Academy scientist assigned to that particular ship asked if one of their number would be willing to volunteer to undergo a few tests. Since his people had been treated with respect, he who had received the transmitter volunteered under the condition that two of his people be present as witnesses."

"No sooner had he and the other volunteers boarded the ship, than all three were drugged. One of them was dissected immediately. Another was given an electronic brain scan that left him in a vegetative state. The last was given mithrin."

Brianna' s eyes grew wide with horror. What had happened to those unknown aliens paralleled too closely what had almost happened in Dr. Gustovson' s lab. In a small voice she asked, "What' s mithrin?"

Rising to her feet, Lorilana sighed. Rubbing her arms, she paced from one side of the small room to the other. "We Drakians are very open about our sexuality and are extremely hedonistic. We think nothing of strolling about our private quarters naked, even with guests present if they are close personal friends." Turning to Brianna, she continued with a weak smile, "I deduced that this is not considered normal behavior on your planet from your obvious discomfort with Char' s nudity."

After Brianna nodded, she resumed her explanation. "I know that you were a partner to the examination of Miklan, so you know that he is hermaphroditic, capable of self-impregnation. There is a reason for this, and, again, it is something you can research later. Approximately one half of our population is hermaphroditic, including me. But, as I know you saw with Char, the other half is single-sexed, roughly half male and half female."

With a weak smile, Lorilana continued. "Drakians enjoy sexual intercourse at a level we haven' t found duplicated on any other planet. Thus was mithrin, a very powerful aphrodisiac that works only on humans, invented. One of the Academy' s new criteria for humanity was the tolerance and acceptance of mithrin. Human beings, when under the influence of the drug, have sexual cravings and pleasures heightened. We didn' t think it would have any adverse effects on nonhumans since nothing happened to the test animals except for an increase in appetite for a short time. But it had never been tried on another clearly intelligent life form until the Wafhkte."

Brianna gripped her blanket so tightly, her hands hurt. "What happened?"

"The Wafhkteian became temporarily insane. Worse, he escaped and murdered about a dozen of his people, mostly females and their offspring. Others managed to overpower and restrain him until the mithrin wore off. Then he told them what had happened to his comrades. Our exploratory team barely escaped with their lives."

"But..."

Lorilana held up her hand. "Please, let me finish. Then I' ll answer your questions. The most horrific outcome of the entire incident was the fact that the First President of the Academy of Science released a report stating that the inhabitants of Wafhkte were not human, and what had happened on their planet was of no consequence. Needless to say, many members of the Academy and the Ruling Council of our planet were shocked. The human races on the other planets were appalled. Unfortunately, the faction who initiated these experiments is too firmly entrenched in the power structure of the Academy. Until we can oust them, their mandate for the identification of humans is still the rule. That' s where we come to you."

Brianna swallowed. "What do you mean?"

"Officially, Brianna, you' re not human," Lorilana said in a sad voice. "Until you pass the requisite tests, you will not be classified as such."

"Can' t I just take their tests and be done with it? Or am I not ' human' enough to even be tested?"

A poignant smile drifted across the doctor' s face. "You are certainly human, Brianna. Because of the wound in your shoulder, it was necessary to give you a blood transfusion. Hoping for some compatibility—after all, you look human—we analyzed a sample of your blood. You cannot imagine our surprise when we discovered that your blood is exactly the same as the Medirians. That by itself proves your humanity beyond a shadow of a doubt. Fifty years ago, this blood compatibility would have been enough."

Brianna' s stomach lurched. "Now what does it take?"

"There are a number of tests, but you only need pass 75% of them. However, you must accept an injection of mithrin into your body. The dosage is such that you would become sexually insatiable for anywhere from four to eight hours, and most if not all of the members of the examining team would have sexual intercourse with you. Once the dosage wore off, you would be subjected to a brain scan to determine intelligence quotients. Then you would be given a physical, which would include sexual intercourse without mithrin. If your responses are not satisfactory, you could be declared nonhuman."

Shuddering, Brianna blanched. "How could decent people let this happen?"

Lorilana' s voice was tired. "Decent people didn' t let this happen, Brianna. Almost everyone who would have denounced this policy was absent from the meeting that ratified it. We were tricked, very cleverly. You see, my husband was First President of the Academy of Science immediately before the Wafhkte debacle. The legislative sessions had been over for three days, and the Academy was in recess. My husband and I had left for our annual vacation, as had most of our allies in the Academy. While we were gone, Rodak don al' Bakom, the Second President, called an emergency meeting. My husband was deposed as First President, and the new Tests for Humanity were passed. Even though we' d received an emergency message, we arrived too late to prevent passage. All we could do was modify some of the tests and lower passage requirements to 75%."

Struggling to control the tremors wracking her body, Brianna asked, "Weren' t the other people on your planet against this new policy, or does the Academy make the laws?"

Again, Lorilana sighed. "The general population has no say in determining Academy policy, nor has Bakom tried to interfere with the laws of Drakan. And, as I said, ours is a very hedonistic race. Much of the population sees nothing wrong with sexual tests."

"But you don' t have to tell the Academy I' m here," Brianna said in a hopeful voice. "Can' t you just take me back home?"

"I wish it were that simple. Miklan chose to bring you on board because of the danger for you on your planet. Bakom knows you' re here and will do everything in his power to get you back."

"Back?"

"When you transported up, Bakom was waiting. He gave both Miklan and Cindar sedatives and spirited you away before our own medical staff arrived. We only knew about you because one of my staff mentioned a bundle Bakom and his assistants carried to their lab.

Mithrin had already been administered, but Char and I arrived before the drug was able to take any real effect. Since you were wounded, we were able to take you back to Medical where I gave you the antidote. After all, the Tests mandate a ' healthy' specimen be examined, and at that point we were unsure whether or not you' d survive. I couldn' t deny Bakom access to Medical, though, and he monitored your progress. As soon as you were judged to be healthy, you would have once again fallen under his control. That' s why you' re here."

"Here?"

"The Captain' s quarters. Bakom dare not come here. The Alalakans hate him with unbelievable passion. Char will keep you safe if for no other reason than to thwart Bakom."

The tears she' d been fighting began to slide down Brianna' s cheeks. "But what will happen when we reach your planet? I can' t stay on this ship, in these quarters, forever!"

Lorilana allowed her fatigue to show. "I know, Brianna, I know. But it will take months to get to Drakan, and that will give us time to devise a plan."

Eyes closed, Brianna leaned back against the wall. Tears ran silently down her cheeks.

Lorilana reached over and stroked her shoulder. "Don' t worry," she said softly. "We won' t allow anything to happen to you. If we ask, Princess Merilinlalissa' s family will grant you sanctuary on Mediria. Bakom has many enemies on the five known planets. We' ll keep you safe."

Brianna sniffed and wiped away tears with a corner of her blanket. "But when will I go home? Will I ever see my family again?"

The doctor' s eyes widened as she jerked her hand away. "Do you have a husband? Children?"

"No, but my parents will worry about me."

"Children would have certainly complicated matters," Lorilana murmured as relief flowed through her. "Too bad you' re not pregnant. Carrying a baby would certainly delay the tests if not cancel them completely."

Brianna said nothing. Her eyes remained closed as tears continued to run unchecked down her cheeks. She clenched the blanket more tightly.

Lorilana rose and stretched. She really needed to get some sleep. But first, she had to take care of Brianna. "Try to sleep. If you'd like, I'll give you a sedative. We can talk more when you wake. Just remember, you're completely safe here."

Eyes closed, Brianna remained silent. She *was* a prisoner. Who'd have ever believed it? All those tabloids and their disgusting stories about alien sex. They were true. A short burst of hysterical laughter escaped her lips. She didn't feel the needle gently inserted into her arm, nor did she realize when she fell into a deep sleep.

Chapter Three

Char swirled the wine around in his glass and stared out into the blackness of space. When Lorilana exited the alien woman' s room, he turned and walked to a finely crafted cabinet.

"You heard everything?"

He poured her a rose-colored drink. "Not enough to form an opinion."

Lorilana lifted the glass to her nose and savored the wine' s bouquet. Then she sipped. "One day, you simply must tell me how you talked the Deslossians into parting with so much vandanug wine. No one else can get anything nearly as good."

"And no one ever shall," he answered with a smile. "But about the woman, what opinion have you formed?"

Lorilana sipped more wine then sighed. "She' s simply someone who was trying to do the decent thing for another intelligent being and got caught up in something she never anticipated. I' m convinced she would have done the same thing no matter which species had discovered her planet first. By bringing her here, we' ve placed her in as much if not more danger than she was in on her own planet."

Char picked up his glass and tossed the rest of his wine into the back of his throat. "What will Bakom do if he manages to kidnap her?"

Lorilana' s voice was grim. "He will exploit having an unidentified species in his power. He' ll subject her to every sexual test that he can devise whether sanctioned or not. Then there will be an accident. Since she won' t survive, the Tests will prove to be inconclusive, and he' ll send another expedition to her planet to obtain more specimens. Their humanity will have to be acknowledged eventually, but we' ll have made an enemy of an entire planet."

Muttering a curse under his breath, Char set his glass down. "The other planets in our federation won' t countenance Bakom' s actions. They' ll demand an accounting that will be impossible to obtain since he' s President of the Academy as well as a member of our Ruling Council. Those members in his thrall will support him no matter what."

"It will mean an end to almost all of the interplanetary cooperation we' ve achieved up to this point," Lorilana agreed. "Bakom will turn back the tide of progress, just as he wants to."

Char' s fist slammed onto the cabinet. "He' s a damn fool. How can he begin to imagine that the other Federation members will allow us to go our merry way spreading havoc about the galaxy? The Gattans, Medirians, and Varcians are as technologically advanced as we are."

"No one understands how he thinks," Lorilana answered bitterly. "Our major concern now is what to do with Brianna. Even if Meri' s family gives her sanctuary, Bakom will get his hands on her somehow. I simply don' t know how to protect her."

His thoughts tumbling over each other, Char walked back to the huge window. Hands clasped behind his back, he stared out into the emptiness of deep space. He had to protect the alien woman. The honor of his clan was at stake. Not protecting her would bring great shame upon them, something he would not allow.

Char continued to ponder the blackness. Bakom considered the woman his. Judging by his past actions, he would do anything to have her back in his power. Therefore, she might be the key to Bakom' s downfall. If that meant using the woman as bait, well...

The peace of the universe was at stake. If Bakom weren' t curbed soon, he' d start a war that would reach all the way to her side of the galaxy anyway.

Char closed his eyes, remembering how smooth the woman' s skin had felt, how soft her hair. She was so exotic, so beautiful. His cock stirred. He wanted to lose himself in her glorious body. He wanted to feel her melt around him as he buried himself as deep as he could. But once they reached Drakan, the Academy would claim her. The law was on their side, and his clan would not, could not begin an insurrection over the fate of an alien woman. Their allies would never support them. How could he protect her, keep her in his possession? How could he thwart Bakom—legally?

Lorilana' s voice broke into his thoughts. "Maybe Dadon will have some ideas."

Char pulled his thoughts away from Bakom' s downfall and concentrated on Lorilana' s words. Dadon... Lorilana' s husband. Husband... Wife?... Marriage... Temporarily? The Academy could not take a wife from her husband even if she wasn' t a Drakian.

Before he had a chance to think over the ramifications of that particular thought, Char said, "Marriage. She' ll have to marry me."

Lorilana choked on the wine she was drinking. "What!"

He turned around and leaned back against the window. "Intermarriage among human species is recognized by the Academy. By marrying her, I will have the full weight of the Alalakan clan and the government to support her classification. Bakom' s Tests of Humanity don' t address marriage to an unidentified species. And, more importantly, he will never consider that I' d marry her. Once the council knows that you, Dr. Sendenton dem al' Lorilana, have no doubts as to her humanity, she' ll gain that status not only for herself but also for the inhabitants of her planet."

Lorilana shook her head. "Bakom will seek to block any such move by the Council, and have you given thought to what this will mean to you and, especially, to your family?"

He crossed his arms. "Father and Rodane will support me."

Lorilana set her glass on the table and stepped towards him. "Why are you doing this, Char? I understand why you want her in your bed. Her coloring alone titillates. But marriage?"

An unfathomable expression in his eyes, he locked gazes with her. "She saved two members of an Alalakan crew from certain death. For that reason alone, I won' t allow Bakom to use her as a sexual experiment. As my wife, both Drakian and Federation law protect her. If making her my wife is the only way to save her from Bakom, so be it." Then he smiled. "Besides, terminating a marriage is no difficult task. She can free herself whenever she chooses."

Lorilana leveled a gaze at Chardadon. *Termination. So that was his plan.* "As long as she doesn' t go beyond the first phase of marriage. If she accepts a clan tattoo, the marriage won' t be terminated as easily as you think. What' s more, Bakom will accuse you of marrying her just to spirit her away from him."

Char grinned. *I certainly hope so.* "He can try."

"He' s more powerful than you think."

Char walked back to his wine cabinet. "The Alalakans don' t underestimate Bakom' s power, Lorilana, but he' s become too impatient. If he had waited to begin his quest for power and control a few more years, he' d be much more firmly entrenched. As it is, his support isn' t as solid as he thinks."

"Maybe, but that' s months and years into the future. Bakom makes a very powerful enemy."

Char poured her another glass of wine and grinned when he handed it to her. "Lori, do you really believe he could hate the Alalakan clan any more than he already does?"

Her smile was weak. "No, but he' ll have reason to be more public in his condemnations. People will listen to him simply because he is First President of the Academy."

Char refilled his glass. "If he becomes too outspoken, there are certain indiscretions of his own which can be revealed, though we' d rather wait."

Lorilana changed her tactics. "What if Brianna refuses?"

He shrugged. "She seems to be rather intelligent. She' ll see that it' s the only possible way to save herself and her planet."

Her eyebrows rose. "Is that how you plan to broach the subject?"

Char lifted his glass and threw its contents into his mouth. Time to nip Lorilana' s romantic thoughts in the bud. She didn' t have to know just how much he wanted this woman in his bed, on the floor, or against the wall, for that matter.

He began to pace. "What do you expect me to do, Lori? She saved two of my crew from certain death. The clan owes her. As their captain, I owe her. I' m taking you at your word that she' s human. Can you think of another way to save her life? You' ve read the Alalakan reports on Bakom. You know what he' s capable of, all in the name of science. Do you really want him to get his hands on her?"

She sank down onto a chair. "No, I don' t, but this marriage idea… Events are moving too rapidly."

Char stopped pacing and stared out the window again. Was Lori right? Did he really know what he was doing? Marrying an alien? How would his parents react? How would the clan react? Thank goodness Rodane was already married. He and Crystas would provide the heir soon.

Straightening his shoulders, Char quashed his uncertainty ruthlessly. He would destroy Bakom! And he would use this alien woman to do so. First, though, they would pleasure each other in his bed.

He turned his attention back to Lorilana. "There' s no other way and no time to waste. The ceremony must be performed before we get home, the sooner the better. What' s more, it must be secret from everyone except the necessary witnesses. The longer we can keep Bakom from learning about it, the less time he' ll have to formulate plans. Right now he' s sure he' ll be able to take the woman as soon as we get to Drakan. The longer he thinks that, the better."

"Her name is Brianna."

Char frowned. "What?"

"You keep referring to her as ' the woman' . No one will believe in this marriage if you don' t even use her name."

He cocked his head and studied Lorilana intently. What plans was she formulating in that lovely head of hers? "Brianna, then. You will perform the ceremony, of course?"

Her smile was genuine. "I' ve been waiting years to perform this particular ceremony. I just wish it could be under different circumstances. What reason for this marriage will you give those not privy to your plans for Bakom?"

Char shifted his gaze away. "The only reason anyone who knows me would believe because it' s the least believable."

An elegant eyebrow rose. "And what would that be?"

He glanced back at Lorilana and grinned. "Why, that I fell madly in love at first sight, of course. Why else would the most eligible Alalakan left in the Clan marry a nobody from an unknown planet?"

"Madly in lust maybe," Lorilana answered with a chuckle.

He shrugged. "Lust, love, what' s the difference?"

Lorilana' s lips twitched. For such an intelligent man, Char could be such an idiot. Then she chuckled again. "Do you know how many mothers with eligible daughters have plans of action in place for the moment you return to your family' s estate? Do you know how many ' eligible' friends your sister-in-law has invited to the Solstice celebration? Or have those plans helped you formulate your own?"

"I must admit that the thought crossed my mind," he acknowledged with a grin. "As long as the...*Brianna* agrees, we' ll both be able to avoid difficult situations. Now, if you' ll excuse me, I must get back to Command. Are you staying here?"

"No, I' m tired, and with the sedative, Brianna should sleep approximately eight more hours. The guard you' ve posted, not to mention Meri' s Aradabs, will be sufficient protection."

"That and the fact the door is keyed to open only to you or me," Char said as he prepared to exit the room. "Do you want me to escort you to your room?"

She shook her head. "Go on. I want to make sure she' s resting comfortably."

Lorilana waited until Chardadon left. Then she slipped into the other room.

Brianna slept unaware of the conversation that had decided her fate. Her glorious red hair was draped about her, spilling over the side of the bunk onto the floor. The blanket had slipped to reveal firm white breasts with rosy pink nipples.

Lorilana regarded her dispassionately. This woman had touched Char in a way that she, for one, was glad. And the stubborn fool didn' t even realize it yet. "He' s lying to himself, Brianna," she said to the sleeping woman. "Oh, he thinks he just wants you in his bed. He may think of this as a marriage of convenience, but I think you' re more than an end to the meddling of Crystas and revenge on Bakom."

Bending, Lorilana tucked the blanket back around her patient' s shoulders. After brushing the hair from Brianna' s face, she smiled. Then she turned and left the room.

* * * * *

Dressed in a loose-fitting robe, Rodak don al' Bakom relaxed in the cramped quarters assigned to him. He' d shrugged off this insult to his status, more than willing to tolerate poor food and quarters to gain knowledge of his opponents. Captain Alalakan don al' Chardadon was no more than he' d expected, a member of a social group that reveled in what they considered their superior non-hermaphroditic sexual nature and four-syllable clan names. What fools!

Demanding transport on the Alalakan ship had been a stroke of genius, even if he had missed the Council voting session. The captain had provided the one thing he, Bakom, had been unable to acquire, a non-identified humanoid specimen for his Tests of Humanity. And Captain Alalakan could do nothing to stop him. True, he should have anticipated the captain bringing a halt to his initial tests, but even that was for the best. When he got the woman back to Drakan, he' d have the Academy' s entire staff and facilities to initiate and complete the testing, certainly a facility much more adequate than the cargo hold of even the most advanced interplanetary ship. He had to give the Alalakans credit. Their ships were the best.

Much as the captain's highhandedness irritated him, the theft of his specimen had been in his own best interest. The interfering Dr. Sendenton dem al' Lorilana would do her utmost to coddle the female back to perfect health, assuming the captain would somehow keep him from reclaiming her. Fools! He was just coming into his power. There weren't enough members of the Ruling Council willing to oppose him. As for the Federation of Planets? Bah! They were totally inept and ineffective.

He half reclined on his bunk, absentmindedly stroking his tail. That Aradab girl three years ago had been a nobody. What difference would one less brat make? How was he to completely catalog the effects of mithrin if he wasn't permitted to experiment! The Alalakan clan would pay. Before he was finished with them, they'd be no more than a third-rate transport company relying on him to keep them afloat financially. That form of revenge would be much more satisfying than destroying the clan completely. To have Alalakan don al' Jamiros and his two stiff-necked sons in his power was more heady than any aphrodisiac. The haughty daughter-in-law and wife would become his for the asking. And the daughter, Alalakan dem al' Sheala, young and nubile, was just discovering her sexuality; it would be a pleasure to introduce her to mithrin.

The imagined picture of the captain's sister naked before him dissolved into the much more real image of the humanoid specimen as she had lain on his examining table, her wrists tied securely above her head, her legs spread wide, and her thick, auburn hair falling about her body in waves. Bakom's pulse quickened as he imagined what he and others would do to her lush body. Damn Captain Alalakan for stealing his specimen. If only they were back on Drakan, he would be enjoying that lush body at this moment.

His tail moved sinuously as if it had a life of its own, and he moaned deep in the back of his throat. Gasps and sighs of pleasure deepened as his tail disappeared beneath his robes. He did not acknowledge the door opening with a quiet hiss.

Odam's breath quickened as he watched his superior. "The communication probe has been sent, Doctor."

Bakom turned his head. "Good!" he gasped as his hips jerked. His hands moved to his belt. "Would you care to join me?"

Odam didn' t need a second invitation.

$$* \quad * \quad * \quad * \quad *$$

Brianna struggled wildly against her bonds. She could feel hands groping and pinching her body. Something probed between her thighs. "No!" she sobbed.

"Shhhh, you' re safe."

The soothing voice penetrated her hysteria, and her struggles ceased when she realized she was held in strong arms. The hand tenderly stroking her hair eased the tension in her body and she relaxed. Sighing, she snuggled closer, seeking the safety of dreamless oblivion.

Cradling her against his chest, Char relaxed his hold but continued to murmur quiet platitudes and stroke her fiery hair—hair that clung to his hand and wrapped itself around his body with what seemed to be a life of its own. It was as soft and silky as that of his own people, but no one on his planet had any this thick or this long. And the color! Red such as he' d seen only once before on a planet halfway across the galaxy. Red that was a mixture of the rich, earthy auburn of the forest loams on his family' s estate, the shiny, burnished red copper of Gattan gold, and the deep, dark orange of the Varcian sun. The thick waves fell to her hips, and it fascinated him. Visions of the fiery locks wrapped around his aching erection appeared in his mind. He groaned and shifted as his cock stiffened, responding to his fantasies.

Brianna' s hair tangled about Char' s hand, and it was inevitable that he pull it.

While the sudden tug on her hair did not hurt Brianna, it did force her back towards consciousness. Once again she registered the soothing voice and gentle hands. Tilting her head back, she opened her eyes. Not yet fully awake, she smiled contentedly as she gazed into velvety, brown eyes. She closed her eyes as he continued to stroke her hair. *This must be how a contented cat feels*, she thought to herself, snuggling closer in his arms.

Then her eyes flew open. She wasn' t dreaming! Gasping, she sat straight up, pushing herself out of his arms and then clutching the fallen blanket back to her breasts.

With amusement and wonder, Char watched the pink blush that stole rapidly from her breasts to her face. He chuckled and said, "I' ve already seen you naked."

She lunged from his lap to stand half a room away. "I didn' t know you were there! You didn' t know I was..." she babbled. Then she stopped. She grasped the blanket firmly with one hand and threw her hair back over her shoulder with the other. Locking her eyes with his and raising her chin, she demanded, "What are you doing here?"

"I heard you cry out. You refused to quiet until I held you."

Her nightmare returned, vividly.

Compassion appeared on his face. "Bakom?"

She nodded.

"He can' t hurt you here, and no one else on this ship would seek to do so," Char stated firmly as he rose from the bunk. "I' m Alalakan don al' Chardadon, captain of the *Restoration*. My clan—and I—owe you a debt of honor that can never be fully repaid. We—I will protect you."

Brianna gazed into his dark eyes, searching for the truth. "Dr. Sendenton told me about the Academy and their Tests of Humanity," she said finally. "How do you propose to protect me from those?"

Char sighed and clasped his hands behind his back. Glancing into her expressionless face, he said, "I had hoped to explain under different circumstances, but—there' s one sure way to protect you, and I ask you to listen to me fully and think carefully before you answer."

After her curt nod, he continued. "Citizens of the five known planets are exempt from the Tests. There are a number of different ways to gain citizenship, but the one way that all the planets have in common is marriage."

Char waited for some reaction, but her face remained closed to him. Raking the fingers of both hands through his loose hair, he continued, "If you marry a citizen from one of the five planets, you' ll immediately be accepted as a member of that society. You' ll be acknowledged as human because no one would marry you if you were anything else."

"So," she interjected flatly, "I only have to find someone from one of these planets willing to marry me, and I' ll be safe from this Bakom person."

"Yes."

"And you and the doctor have already determined who this will be."

"Yes."

Her nostrils flared. "Am I permitted to know, or is yours a culture that delivers its brides to a preselected, unknown groom?"

Char cocked an eyebrow. He hadn' t expected anger. "We aren' t barbarians."

"Not barbarians!" she shouted, one arm flailing as the other clenched the blanket to her breasts. "One of your so-called scientists plans to inject a powerful aphrodisiac into a wounded, unconscious woman for the express purpose of some ridiculous sexual rite, and you say you aren' t barbarians! Exactly how would you describe yourself, Captain Alalakan don den del al' whatever Chardadon?"

He crossed his arms over his chest. "And your people are more civilized? One of my crew was scheduled for dissection."

Brianna chose to ignore that statement and his growing irritation as she began to pace the small room. "You' ve kept me locked in this room with nothing but a blanket to save my modesty. How do I know you aren' t seeking to lull me into a false sense of security until I am fully recovered so that you can then perform these sexual experiments, Captain?" she snapped as she turned to face him. "How do I know that' s not the true situation?"

Char' s eyes narrowed, but he kept a tight rein on his growing anger. Never had the word of an Alalakan, especially *his* word, been questioned so caustically.

Green fire sparkled dangerously in her eyes. "Why bother waiting?" she challenged. "Call this Bakom person and get with this damn testing over with. I' m tired of waiting!"

Char took a step towards her. "Woman, you try my patience!"

Brianna was past caring about physical danger. Her body had repaired itself, but mentally she was exhausted. Lorilana' s revelations about the Tests of Humanity had unnerved her more than she admitted even to herself. She needed an emotional outlet, and the captain had provided it with his plan of marriage.

"I *said* you would not be harmed," he growled, teeth clenched against his anger, hands fisted on his hips, tail lashing with agitation. "My word has never been questioned before."

She tilted her head back and glared into his eyes. "Then where are my clothes?"

He glared down at her. Clothes? What did her clothes matter? "Your clothes? Woman, what are you babbling about?"

Char' s now perplexed expression caused Brianna' s anger to completely conquer her fear. How could he be so obtuse!

"Where are my... Oh, forgive me!" She hit her forehead with the palm of her hand. "On your planet one doesn' t necessarily wear clothing when entertaining guests. Well, since you' ve decided I' m to join your society, I may as well get used to it. So what if *you' re* wearing your uniform? When in Rome..." she snarled and threw the blanket she' d kept clutched so tightly into his face.

Quick reflexes kept the blanket from becoming tangled about Char' s head. Flinging it onto the bed, he turned once more to the angry woman. Except for the bandage on her shoulder, she stood before him gloriously naked, her anger accentuating her beauty. She' d been nude when he carried her to this room, but then she' d been unconscious, pale and weak from loss of blood. This woman was vibrantly alive and breathtaking in her fury. His anger drained away, and his body reacted instantly. Desire pooled in his groin, and his erection surged against his skin-tight uniform.

Slowly Char' s gaze traveled down her body. Her breasts, which were much fuller than those of his planet' s women, bounced lightly as she expelled angry breaths. The muscles of her taut stomach clenched, drawing his gaze down to gently rounded hips, and curly, fiery pubic hair at the apex of long, shapely legs. Her slender feet were planted firmly on the floor, and her hands were fisted on her hips. And her magnificent, fiery hair draped over her shoulders and down her back to frame her from the top of her head to her hips. Fury and defiance radiated from her flushed body.

Char stepped closer as his gaze moved slowly back up her body to her face. He wanted her more than he had wanted any other woman in his entire life.

Brianna raised her chin higher and stared unflinchingly into his face. Then her eyes widened with shock when she saw the passion burning in his.

Slowly, Char lifted his left hand and brushed his fingers lightly against her cheek. "No woman on my planet looks so vibrantly alive," he said softly. "You rival the Gattan with your flamboyant beauty. Make love with me."

Brianna wanted to pull back, but his delicate caress trapped her— and tantalized her senses. Her anger and defiance melted away to be replaced with uncertainty, fear, and...passion.

As she trembled beneath his gentle caress, Brianna cursed silently. Damn it, she'd let her temper get her into trouble again! *His shoulders are so broad, and he's so tall.* She shook her head to clear her senses. *My God, she was naked!* And she'd thrown away her blanket! Stupid! Stupid! Stupid! *His eyes are so brown...like rich chocolate.* She swallowed and wrapped her arms around herself in an attempt to hide her nudity, but his intense gaze wouldn't let her step away.

He traced delicate whorls on her cheeks. "I want to protect you."

Brianna closed her eyes. Her breath quickened, and her nipples pebbled. She had to step back, had to get away from him. *His touch is so gentle.*

His fingers slid under her chin and stroked her neck. After another nervous swallow, she opened her eyes to find his face closer, his chocolaty-brown gaze locked with hers. She was tall, a shade over six feet, but he towered above her.

Char trailed his fingers down the length of her arm until he reached her hand. Lifting it to his mouth, he kissed her palm and then cradled it against his chest. Leaning forward, he brushed her lips with his.

Brianna's breath quickened. She lifted her free hand to her lips.

With his tongue, Char traced a gentle line along her jaw and down the side of her neck. Then, after he captured the hand she still held to her lips, he kissed her palm and pulled it to his chest. Both her hands now nestled there.

Her mind a jumble of uncertainty, Brianna tried to pull away. But her body had no doubts. Her last relationship had ended months ago, and Char's caresses had elicited an immediate reaction. Physically, she wanted him, wanted him to continue to caress her, to kiss her, to plunge his long, hard cock into her body.

Lifting his hand, Char traced her jawline back to her ear where he threaded his fingers through her hair and cupped the back of her head. Exerting gentle pressure, he pulled her closer until her tense body rested against his. Lowering his head, he nibbled and nipped her ear and neck until her body relaxed. As shivers ran down her spine, Brianna sighed and turned her mouth to his.

Settling his right hand in the small of her back, Char pulled her closer and nuzzled and sucked her lips.

With a low moan, Brianna opened her mouth, and his tongue swept in to mate with hers in a kiss that became more carnal as it lengthened.

She slid her hands upwards and clasped them behind his neck.

Char cupped her buttocks, lifted her hips, and pressed her rhythmically against his aching erection.

Sighing, she tilted her head as he kissed a passionate trail down the side of her neck.

Sweeping her into arms, Char lifted her high so his mouth could fasten on her nipple.

Brianna moaned as the logical part of her mind struggled to regain control. What was she doing? She had to stop this right now. *God, this feels so good.*

He sucked her other nipple into his mouth.

As jolts of heat stabbed her groin, Brianna ignored logic and listened to her body, a body that was aching to be loved. Lost in a sensual thrall, she did not fight her passion. This alien' s practiced caresses and deep, soul-searching kisses overpowered all resistance. Never had any man made her *feel* like this. She melted in his arms.

Carefully, Char laid Brianna on the bunk and stretched out beside her, his mouth returning to hers, his hands beginning their quest to know her body more intimately. His lips left hers, trailing hot kisses across her neck and collarbone until he reached her breasts. Once there, he laved and sucked first one then the other, until she sobbed with desire. His fingers slid between her thighs to play in the slippery folds until he found the hard nub hidden there.

She thrust her hips against his hand as his fingers began a slow, circular play. She tugged at his uniform.

Char reveled in her passion and gave himself up to his own.

Her hands skimmed down his body and brushed against his erection. Then she caressed the hard length of him. With a moan of frustration, she tugged at his one-piece uniform. He lifted himself off of the bunk until only their mouths were touching, his hands jerking the fastenings of his uniform open.

Lost in their mutual passion, Brianna' s reason, fear and defiance melted away. All that existed for her was the aching need between her thighs and the hard body next to hers.

Later, after she' d had time to ruminate over all that happened, she came to the uncomfortable conclusion that she' d have given herself to him unconditionally, would have wrapped her legs around his hips and urged him to thrust his rock-hard erection deeper and deeper into her achingly hot body — if they hadn' t been interrupted. As it was, her hands had found their way inside his tunic to the bare skin of his chest, skin that was stretched smoothly over taut muscles, when her brain registered the sound of the door sliding open.

Fully aware of the door opening, Char chose to ignore the intruder. Lorilana was the only other person who could enter his quarters without tripping the alarm, and he knew she' d discreetly withdraw. She was, after all, fully aware of his plans. Brianna' s reaction, however, took him by surprise.

Tearing her mouth from his, a horrified Brianna pushed him away and scrambled from the bunk to the far corner of the room. Trembling from both frustrated passion and newly awakened fear, she turned her shocked gaze to the woman who stood in the doorway, desperately trying to hide her nudity with her long, flowing hair.

Noting Brianna' s near panic, Lorilana refrained from the teasing banter that usually accompanied a situation such as this. Instead, she noted how Char' s fists clenched the sheets as he struggled to regain control and composure. He rose stiffly and turned, making no attempt to hide the erection that strained so blatantly against the uniform that sagged about his hips.

"Your timing, Lorilana," he said hoarsely, locking his gaze with hers, "is impeccable as usual." Turning his head, he directed a long, passion-filled gaze at Brianna. Wincing at the fear in her eyes, he berated himself mentally. *Fool. You acted like a boy with his first woman. Now she' s terrified.*

Pulling his tunic back up over his shoulders, Char smiled at Brianna then winked. "Your breasts are the most beautiful I' ve ever kissed." Spinning, he left the room without another word.

Her body tight and unsatisfied, Brianna shivered. His voice was so sexy.

Lorilana chuckled.

A blush that began at Brianna' s breasts crept up her neck and onto her face.

Lorilana watched with amused fascination. "That," she said, "is absolutely amazing."

With Char' s presence gone, defiance replaced the confusion in Brianna' s gaze and her chin came up. "What?"

"Why, the way you change color, of course. No one on our planet or any of the other four can turn such a rosy shade of pink."

That comment demanded Brianna' s full attention. "Nobody blushes? Doesn' t anyone ever get embarrassed?"

"Of course," Lorilana answered as she walked over to the bunk and laid the neatly folded clothing she carried there. "We just don' t turn another color."

"I have *not* turned another color," Brianna snapped. "Blushing is a perfectly natural expression of embarrassment on my planet."

Lorilana smiled to herself. Any anger at the situation in which Brianna had found herself didn' t seem to be directed at Char. And it seemed as if he' d taken the proper steps to ensure his plan of marriage to her would proceed without any delay.

"I' m here to check your shoulder, and I brought you some clothing," the doctor said abruptly changing the subject. "I apologize for the delay, but your own clothing was destroyed. You must thank Princess Merilinlalissa. You and she are of a size."

Shoving all thoughts of Char and her passionate reaction to him into a tiny corner of her brain, Brianna hurried to the bunk. Clothing would make her feel much less vulnerable. "You don' t happen to have a brush here somewhere, do you?" she asked eagerly. "And is it possible to take a bath on a spaceship? Our astronauts can' t, but you' re certainly more advanced than we are."

Lorilana laughed. "Women are the same throughout the galaxy. There' s nothing like a warm bath to relax the nerves. Bring those things and follow me."

Brianna followed her to the door. After a quick glance to make sure Char was nowhere in sight, she stepped through the doorway. She hesitated when she saw Lorilana palm the door to his bedroom.

"Char' s returned to Command," she said. "He won' t be back for three or four hours, so you' ll have privacy. I must warn you, however, he' ll have his evening meal served here."

Brianna followed her into Char' s sparsely furnished room, which contained nothing more than a large bed, a nightstand, and dresser. Leading the way to a control panel located on the far wall, she motioned Brianna closer.

"The translator in your ear allows you to understand everything anyone will ever say to you, no matter what the language. Unfortunately, you don' t gain literacy in a language with the translator, so pay close attention. The door to the bathing room hasn' t been keyed to you yet, so you' ll have to override the lock from this panel. Flip this green switch," she said and demonstrated, "and the door will open."

Stepping through the doorway, Brianna entered a small room that contained a combination bath/shower and toilet facilities. "Red for hot and blue for cold?" she asked.

"Color coding must be fairly standard throughout the galaxy," Lorilana said dryly as she removed the bandage from Brianna' s shoulder. "I don' t think you need any more bandages. Your wound is healing quite nicely. Enjoy your bath. I' ll be back in about an hour. Oh, Princess Merilinlalissa has expressed an interest in meeting you. She and her husband will also be among the dinner company tonight."

Lorilana turned to leave but Brianna' s voice caused her to pause as she reached the doorway. "Doctor, just whom have the captain and you decided I must marry?"

Lorilana looked back over her shoulder, surprise evident on her face. "From what I observed earlier," she said with wry amusement, "I' d thought Char had informed you."

"Well, he didn' t."

Lorilana chuckled. "Why you silly child, he' s going to marry you himself."

Chapter Four

The door opened with a quiet hiss, and a hand gripped Lorilana's forearm. "What are you and that damn Alalakan plotting?" Bakom snapped.

Lorilana drew herself to her full height of six feet, six inches and stared down at him.

Bakom flinched. Lorilana towered over his own six-foot height.

"Take your hand from my arm. I won' t answer any of your questions if you can' t behave in a civilized manner."

Gnashing his teeth, he snatched his hand away.

Lorilana waited, hoping Bakom would do something stupid. Any kind of physical attack on her, and he would lose support in the Academy.

Muscles tensed, Bakom clenched and unclenched his fists. After a deep breath, he said, "Forgive me, but as First President of the Academy, it' s unlawful to deny me access to a new specimen. This is an opportunity to study a new lifeform. Surely you can understand my excitement?"

Lorilana returned to her instrument panel and sat down, her back to Bakom. "Captain Alalakan is vehement in his belief that she be treated with all the respect due an honored guest for saving members of his crew."

"Then she should be housed in guest quarters rather than in the private quarters of the captain," he answered levelly. "Isn' t that the usual procedure on an interplanetary ship?"

Swiveling her seat, she faced Bakom. "I' m neither an expert on interplanetary travel nor the customs aboard such ships. You' ll have to ask the captain for his reasons."

His fists remained clenched. His tail jerked. "But you, my dear Dr. Sendenton, are a close friend of the family. Surely the captain' s confided in you."

Lorilana shook her head. "I' m sorry, I can' t help you. I may be an old friend of the family, but Captain Alalakan is a grown man who makes his own decisions and keeps his own council."

Bakom stared at her for a moment, face white, lips pinched together. When he finally spoke, his voice shook. "You will rue the day you allied yourself with the Alalakan clan against *me*, Dr. Sendenton dem al' Lorilana." Without another word, he spun about and stomped out of Medical.

Lorilana watched the door close. Turning her seat back to her panel, she flipped a switch and said, "Did you hear everything, Char?"

"Everything' s been recorded. Oh, and Cindar' s succeeded in her attempt to break the code to Bakom' s personal computer via his connection to the ship' s mainframe. All his medical records have been downloaded to your private files."

"I' ll start checking them immediately. By the way," she continued, "Brianna' s relaxing in your bathtub as we speak, if you' d like to continue your explanation as to why marrying you would be of great benefit."

Only silence answered her chuckling.

Char sat in his chair, elbows propped on the armrests, his fingers steepled beneath his chin. Set on its predetermined course and with its autopilot activated, the ship could navigate itself with only one man to monitor the computer' s activities, so he' d dismissed the rest of his crew with orders to report back in three hours. Then he' d be free the rest of the night.

Lorilana' s parting comment teased his senses. Closing his eyes, he drew a picture first of Brianna' s defiant nakedness, then her passionate responses to his lovemaking. He groaned at his body' s instant reaction. Today had been an accident. She' d been vulnerable because of the dream. When Lorilana had entered the room, Brianna' s shock at her own actions had been easy to read. Her planet was undoubtedly less sexually permissive. Women there probably didn' t fall right into sexual liaisons with men they just met. She might even be uninitiated.

Char raked his fingers through his hair. No, she was not uninitiated. Her kisses, her reactions to his caresses were too experienced, too…hungry. Her passion had matched his. She wanted him as much as he wanted her. Somehow, he would overcome her fears; then they' d share their passion until they tired of each other.

Cramped though she was, Brianna soaked contentedly in the small tub. Unfortunately, while the hot water relaxed her, it didn' t relieve her sexual tension. Char had primed her body for an earth-shattering orgasm and failed to deliver it. Leaning back, she closed her eyes and slid her hand between her thighs. Chardadon appeared in her mind' s eye. The clothing on his muscular form quickly dissolved as she remembered the first time she' d seen him, unashamedly naked. As her fingers stroked, her memory slipped back to the kisses they' d shared, his caresses on her body. Her breath quickened and her nipples hardened. She tried to spread her thighs wider, but the narrow confines of the tub wouldn' t allow it. Her hips arched. She threw back her head and shivered, both physically and mentally, with the delicate explosion of her orgasm.

After she caught her breath, Brianna scowled and opened her eyes. *You' ve got yourself into a real mess this time, Bri. Not only are you practically a prisoner on a spaceship, you' ve got the hots for the captain. And he has pointy ears and a tail!*

Water sluiced from her body as she rose. She turned a fixture to drain the water. As she did so, a blast of warm air blew down on her from what she' d thought was a second shower nozzle. "Well, that certainly cuts down on laundry bills," she muttered into the emptiness of the room.

Lifting the clothing that Lorilana had brought her, Brianna found a pair of brief panties that fit tolerably well, but nothing remotely resembling a bra. After pulling on a pair of loose-fitting green pants, she dropped the long, matching tunic over her head. Checking her reflection in the full-length mirror hanging beside the door, she was reasonably satisfied with her appearance.

The soft green color of her apparel complimented her auburn hair and green eyes. Draping gracefully over her breasts, the tunic hung well below her knees, but she certainly had the height to be complimented by the style. She frowned at her bare feet, but Lorilana had not provided shoes or stockings of any kind. Grabbing a comb and brush from a shelf next to the tub, she began the long process of comb-drying her hair.

A musical tone from the outer room caught her attention.

Still brushing the tangles from her hair, she returned to the other room.

The outer door slid open and Lorilana walked in. "My, what a difference a bath can make. You look positively radiant, my dear."

Brianna continued to brush her hair without commenting.

"Princess Merilinlalissa from Mediria wants to be introduced to you," Lorilana continued.

Before Brianna could reply, though, the door chimed again.

Lorilana motioned to the door. "The door will open only to Char' s and my palm scans," she said. "Anyone else who wishes to enter must be admitted. To release the lock, simply push this panel." She applied light pressure to a slight indentation and the door slid open.

A man stepped through the door, his eyes searching, memorizing every detail. After he' d thoroughly scanned the room, he concentrated on Brianna. His flat, hostile stare completely unnerved her, and she tripped backwards and collapsed onto the couch.

He wasn' t as tall as Char, but he was much broader. Muscles rippled on his bare chest and arms. His thighs bulged beneath a short kilt, and he wore sandals with straps wound around huge calf muscles. He carried no weapons, but he looked as if he didn' t need any. He was bald, with a prominent brow ridge jutting over deep-set, black eyes. His large nose looked more like a bird' s beak, while what was probably a very expressive mouth was drawn into a thin, stern line.

And, he was green—a deep, olive green!

Brianna was so shocked at his appearance that she didn' t notice the much slighter woman who followed him until she began to speak.

"Kahn likes to intimidate people when he first meets them, but he' s usually harmless."

Lorilana snorted. "Harmless enough to break a man in two with his bare hands. Princess, this is Brianna Claire O' Shea. Brianna, Princess Merilinlalissa."

"Her Royal Highness Lillalistross dem al' Merilinlalissa, Princess Hardan," interjected the green man' s gruff, gravelly voice.

The princess grimaced. "Go away, Kahn. You' re too intimidating, and there' s no one here to hurt me. You' ve been guarding the passageway all day."

Grabbing his arm, she tried to tug him towards the doorway.

Cocking an eyebrow, he gently removed her hands from his arm. "Yes, Princess," he replied. "I' ll be immediately outside." Bowing, he turned and left the room. The door slid closed behind him.

"Fine figure of a man, isn' t he, Brianna? What musculature! And he' s hung like a Deslossian stud bull," Lorilana said wistfully. "If I could only get him into my bed."

Gawking, Brianna wrenched her head around to stare at Lorilana. The older woman seemed serious!

Brianna' s mind whirled. *This can' t be real. I' m not on a spaceship. I' m in the twilight zone. No, I was in an accident and am lying in a coma, dreaming all of this!*

The princess' musical laughter drew Brianna' s attention back to her.

Brianna just stared. The princess was almost as tall as she was and built much the same way. Long, greenish-black hair cascaded down her back, reaching well below her knees. Her features were much more delicate than Kahn' s. Nor were there brow ridges above her dark eyes as there were on her huge guard. The princess could pass for human... if she weren' t the same color as a Granny Smith apple.

She gestured to Lorilana, "You may leave now, Doctor. Introductions have been properly performed, and I wish to know Brianna better."

Lorilana' s eyebrows shot up in surprise at the dismissal, but she acquiesced gracefully. Nodding her head, she left the room.

After the door slid closed once more, the princess grinned at Brianna and burst into merry laughter. "Now that we' ve gotten rid of Lorilana, what would you like to know?" she asked as she flopped down onto the sofa. Picking up the brush, she started brushing Brianna' s hair. "Let me do that, I' m used to long hair. I brushed my sisters' hair all the time back on Mediria."

"Why? What?" Brianna stuttered as the princess pushed her around and started to work the tangles out of her hair. "You' re green! Oh! I beg your pardon. I mean..."

Sighing quite audibly, the princess stopped brushing her hair. Placing her hands on her shoulders, she turned Brianna to face her. "Everyone from Mediria is green, of one shade or another. And, please call me Meri. I' m sorry if I seemed overbearing, but it was all a sham. Lorilana' s a wonderful person. However, if I hadn' t ' dismissed' her, I' d never have been able to speak to you privately. I' m sure you have questions you want to ask and asking them of someone less alien-seeming will probably be more comfortable for you. From what Lorilana told me, we' re biologically the same except for skin color." *I' ll tell her about the gills later. The sooner she feels comfortable with someone, the better.*

Hands clenched tightly in her lap, Brianna gazed solemnly at Meri for a few minutes. Then she smiled. The princess just might be the silver lining of the cloud she was under. "I think this is going to be the start of a beautiful friendship," she said and held out her hand.

The princess stared at her hand uncertainly for a few minutes and then held out her own. When Brianna grasped it firmly and pumped it, the princess began to smile. "I do believe you' re right. Now, what would you like to know?"

* * * * *

Grumbling, Lorilana stalked into Command and collapsed into the chair next to Char' s.

"I thought you were introducing Meri to Brianna."

"I did. Meri dismissed me."

He grinned. "I didn' t know anyone could make you leave if you didn' t want to go. I know very well that you planned to monitor that meeting."

"Why did Ademis have to marry a Hardan princess?" she said in a vexed tone.

He laughed outright. "Knowing our Meri, she planned to get rid of you at the outset."

"Humph."

"Put yourself in Brianna' s place. Wouldn' t you want the opportunity to question a seemingly neutral third party if you found yourself in similar circumstances? For all that she seems to be adapting well, she is, in essence, a prisoner."

Lorilana leaned back with a thoughtful frown on her face. "You' re right, of course. Although from what I observed earlier, you seemed to have calmed her down."

Char grinned devilishly. "She was anything but calm, Lori."

"And judging by the way your tail was lashing when you left, you were not exactly levelheaded either."

Still grinning, he asked, "Have you come to trade sexual innuendoes or is there something you wanted?"

"Will you ever learn, Char? I only have your best interests at heart."

He snorted. "Only if they coincide with what you think are my best interests. Now, why are you here?"

"I' ve come to listen to their conversation, of course."

One eyebrow cocked, he turned from the computer panel he was monitoring. "Do you really mean that?"

Lorilana had the good grace to show her embarrassment. "Yes... No... I don' t know. I' ve never been in a situation like this before. I feel that I have to know everything about Brianna to maximize our chances of success. We could fail, you know."

"No, Lori, we won' t fail. And we can' t monitor their conversation. That would put us on the same level as Bakom. Brianna is certainly as human as you and I. How can we treat her as anything less? And Meri would never forgive us. Do you want a Medirian assassin breathing down your neck?"

Lorilana snorted at Char' s comment. "Assassin indeed! As if the king of Mediria thinks I' m a threat to his family! Ha!" Then she sighed. "I just wish I could be so certain of success."

"Go back to your quarters and relax. We need tonight' s dinner to be a success, and you' re too keyed up. Brianna must agree that marriage will be the only way to save everyone on her planet."

"From what I observed," she said dryly, "she won' t need much convincing."

Char turned back to his console. When he refrained from commenting, Lorilana rose to leave.

"Very well. We' ll leave Brianna and Meri to themselves."

She left Chardadon to the silence of his monitors... and his fantasies of Brianna.

* * * * *

"Was Lorilana really serious about having sex with your guard?"

"I don' t think so." Meri resumed brushing Brianna' s hair. "Ademis told me that she and her husband are absolutely devoted to each other. While many married couples on Drakan are rather promiscuous, Lorilana and Dadon are not."

Brianna grimaced. She was, for all intents and purposes, being forced to marry a Drakian. *Isn' t that just Jim Dandy. I have to marry a man who won' t be faithful. But then, this is going to be a marriage in name only, right?* Shivers raced up and down Brianna' s spine when she thought of Char' s kisses. *Yeah, right.*

"Brianna? Are you all right? Brianna?"

She shook free of her fantasies and glanced back at Meri. "Yeah, sure. Ah…why did you marry a Drakian if there' s no certainty of faithfulness?"

"Ademis won' t be unfaithful to me. We love each other too much. Besides, he wouldn' t want to upset the Medirian royal family. We make nasty enemies."

Brianna snorted. "Lots of people say they' re in love but lie through their teeth."

"Lie through their teeth?" A mental picture of a person lying between a set of teeth passed through Meri' s mind.

Noticing the perplexed look on Meri' s face, Brianna sighed. "Never mind."

Meri put down the brush. Taking Brianna' s hand, she stood and pulled her towards the bedroom. "You' ll understand Drakan society better if you know how to operate the video monitor."

Once in the bedroom, Brianna let Meri push her down onto Char' s huge bed. She walked over to the control panel next to the bathroom door. "This blue button controls the video screen. The range of entertainment is limited to what' s stored in the ship' s computers, but there is a full complement of historical programming for all human planets plus all others that have been explored or discovered. There' s probably some basic information about yours in here now."

Brianna felt her spirits lift. "How do I turn it on?" *Television! She could survive if she had TV. Now, if only they had shopping malls too.*

Meri pushed the blue button. "The screen is voice activated. All you have to do is register your voice pattern, and the computer will run whichever program you select. This screen is like the one in my quarters, so I should be able to program your voice into it. There," she said, "all you have to do is identify yourself to the computer."

"How do I do that?"

"State your name and position."

"What exactly is my position?"

Meri stared at Brianna for a moment and then smiled. "You' re the ambassadorial liaison from a newly discovered planet."

A slow smile slide across Brianna' s lips. "Do planetary ambassadors in your Federation of Planets have diplomatic immunity?"

Meri' s grin was conspiratorial. "Of course they do."

Brianna stepped to the computer terminal next to the video screen. "Brianna Claire O' Shea, Ambassadorial Liaison from the planet Earth to the Federation of Planets."

"So witnessed and accepted as such by Lillalistross dem al' Merilinlalissa, Princess Hardan, Ambassador at large for the planet Mediria."

"Acknowledged and recorded," affirmed the computer' s disembodied voice.

"That will put a definite kink into Bakom' s plans," Meri commented smugly.

Brianna settled cross-legged on the edge of the bed. "Why does everybody hate this Bakom so much? Aside from the fact that I' m his next experiment, that is?"

Meri shivered. "Bakom' s evil, Brianna. He' ll stop at nothing to gain power first over his own planet and then over all others in the Federation. Three years ago, he kidnapped an Aradab girl from my planet. When confronted, he explained his actions away with his Tests of Humanity."

"I thought the five known planets' inhabitants were automatically classified as human."

Meri belly-flopped onto the bed. "They are. I' m sure you noticed Kahn and I do not look very much alike.

After Brianna nodded, she continued, "Unlike Drakan, which has only one race of people, we have three major races on Mediria. My planet is almost 90 percent water with only one large landmass and numerous islands of varying sizes. Kahn' s people have lived only on land for generations and have lost some of their ability to breathe underwater. My race is the most populous of the three. We' re comfortable on both land and in water and are able to breathe in either environment. The members of the third race live almost exclusively in the water."

"Are they green too?"

"Yes, but it' s such a dark green, they' re almost black. Other than their color, the Nessians, as they are called, look like my people."

Brianna stared at Meri. "You can breathe underwater?"

Meri motioned Brianna closer as she pulled her hair back behind her head. "Every person on my planet has gills. Even the Aradab, Kahn' s people, have residual gills. Anyway, since the Aradab don' t look like my people and the Nessians, Bakom decided to test one of them. He kidnapped a nine-year-old girl, Kahn' s sister."

"What happened?"

"Char' s family found out what Bakom was up to and rescued Paala. Char had Ademis bring her back to my father' s court. That was when I first met Ademis, by the way."

"I imagine Kahn' s family was relieved."

"My brother Davlalardrac took Paala home and returned with Kahn, Kahn' s youngest brother, and twenty cousins. They pledged themselves to my family' s service for all eternity," Meri answered with a wry grimace. "You can' t believe how tiresome that can be. My father couldn' t convince them to go home. One of Kahn' s cousins has also accompanied me on this trip. They decided that it would be impossible for only one of them to stay awake the entire time I was off planet."

"Was Bakom punished?"

"The Academy was censured on Mediria. Its members, with a few exceptions like Lorilana and her husband, are only allowed in certain sections of our capital city, and no member of the Academy is permitted anywhere near our planet without official clearance and an Aradab escort."

"That doesn' t seem to be a very harsh punishment."

"There wasn' t much else we could do without bringing public shame on Paala, but Kahn' s family exacted a much more subtle revenge."

"Oh?"

Meri grinned. "They decided that Bakom would have his subject for the Tests."

"What happened?"

"Kahn' s aunt volunteered to take the tests as long as they were videotaped for the benefit of the scientific community, were witnessed by scientists from both planets, and were personally administered by Bakom."

"Did he agree?"

"If he hadn' t, my father was going to declare him outlaw and kidnapper on Mediria. Under our laws, any Medirian anywhere in the galaxy would have had the right to execute him. He didn' t want to spend the rest of his life looking over his shoulder."

"What happened to Kahn' s aunt?"

Meri' s grin stretched from ear to ear. "You should ask what happened to Bakom. In most cases, any given drug will enhance an Aradab' s natural abilities in whatever physiological or psychological manner the drug is to affect them. Giving an aphrodisiac as powerful as mithrin to Kahn' s aunt was a huge mistake. She wore Bakom' s tail bloody!" Meri gloated. "It was six months before he healed."

"And Kahn' s aunt?"

Meri rolled onto her back, a wide grin on her face. "After she' d finished with Bakom, she asked for a real man. No one had the courage to try."

Laughing, Brianna fell back against the pillows.

After they both stopped laughing, Meri asked, "What do you want to know about Drakan?"

Propped against the pillows, Brianna asked, "How did they become hermaphroditic?"

"You can get the full story from the computer' s archives. Basically, however, about two thousand years ago, a plague swept across Drakan, killing almost three quarters of the total population. Very few of the survivors were male. Even back then, there was an Academy of Science. Its scientists convinced most of the population that the only chance for their species' survival was if everyone became hermaphroditic. About three-quarters of the survivors agreed. Everyone who so chose underwent a series of operations when he or she reached consensual age. Those who chose not to do so remained either male or female. Hence, three sexes on Drakan."

"Are children born hermaphroditic, or are the operations still required?"

Meri rolled back onto her stomach. "That' s the strangest thing about Drakians. They' re never quite sure what their children will be. Of course, a child with parents whose ancestors had never undergone the operations will be either male or female. It' s when the hermaphroditic and unaltered genes mingle that interesting things happen."

Brianna sat up and propped her right elbow on her knee and rested her chin in her hand. "What do you mean?"

"A female with unaltered genes will always have a single-sexed child no matter who or what the father was. Children born to two hermaphrodites can be male, female, or hermaphroditic."

Brianna' s eyebrows rose. "Two hermaphrodites could have a single-sexed child?"

Meri angled her head to and grinned at Brianna. "Yes, and it drives their geneticists crazy. The scientists on my planet feel that nature is reasserting herself. The Drakians are the only known human race to have three sexes. Among animals, if there is a third sex to any species, it' s always neuter. The Drakians meddled with natural biology. Every year, more single-sexed babies are born to them, and many which are still hermaphroditic display more female or male characteristics than their parents."

"What do they do with them?"

"They raise them, of course. Except for a small group of purists, Drakians are the most tolerant of all the human races. Most don' t even understand the concept of racial intolerance. They view every human being as a potential sexual partner."

"What about Kahn' s sister? I mean, she was just a child."

"Drakians love children. Even if Char' s family hadn' t stepped in, the Academy would never have allowed Bakom to experiment on her. He probably intended to keep her hidden away until she came of age. That' s why he' s such an evil man. Up until now, he' s been content to wait to bring his plans to fruition."

Brianna leaned back against the wall, closed her eyes, and swallowed. She' d been enjoying her time with Meri, but the reminders of Bakom' s evilness brought his plans for her back to the forefront of her mind. She hadn' t realized how long she' d been quiet until Meri was sitting next to her, rubbing her hands vigorously.

"What is it? Should I call for Lorilana?"

Shaking her head, Brianna pulled her hands from Meri' s. "I' m all right," she lied. "I guess I' m still a little tired."

Lips puckered, Meri stared levelly at her. "Posh!" she finally snorted. "You' re worrying about Bakom and his plans for you."

Brianna turned her face away.

Meri tsked, rose, and walked out of the room. In a few minutes, she returned with a glass full of an amber-colored liquid. "Here, drink this."

Brianna took the glass and sniffed its contents. "What is it?"

"Don' t smell it! Just drink it!"

Brianna took a sip. A delicately sweet flavor caressed her tongue. "Hmmm! This is good." She followed the sip with a swallow, then another and another until the wine was gone. She had just set the glass on the nightstand next to the bed when she felt a rush of warmth centered in her stomach rapidly spread throughout the rest of her body. Shivers raced up and down her back. "What is that?" she gasped. *It feels like a mini orgasm!*

Meri chuckled lightly. "Medirian argoth brandy."

"You could make a fortune selling this!" Brianna was glad she was sitting down because her legs probably wouldn' t have held her.

"Brianna, my friend, we already do. Now, I know just what you need. We have to get you out of these rooms."

"But it' s not safe. If Bakom spotted me, he could demand that I be given to him!"

Meri snorted. "As if he can issue commands to a Medirian princess. Besides, you have diplomatic immunity, remember? Anyway, we' re only going just down the corridor to my quarters. With Kahn outside, Bakom isn' t going to come anywhere near here. You need something to wear tonight. After all, you are dining with a princess. I' ll just send a message to Control so Char doesn' t tear the ship apart when he comes back and finds you gone."

Meri tapped a message into the console next to the viewing screen. When she finished, she grabbed Brianna' s hand and pulled her from the bed. "Come on," she said with a mischievous grin. "I put it on a thirty second delay. We want to be out of here before he gets the message and decides not to let you out of his quarters."

Brianna didn' t hesitate. She had not been looking forward to being alone with the intriguing alien captain. If he decided to kiss her again, she didn' t think she' d have the willpower to stop him — or herself.

Meri palmed the outer door open and Kahn turned to face them. "Brianna is my friend, Kahn. I want you to protect her as you would me. Bakom wants her."

His eyes widened and then narrowed. He nodded once and sketched a bow.

Hauling Brianna along behind her, Meri hurried up the corridor. They hadn' t gone very far when she stopped at another door.

It glided open silently, and she pulled her new friend inside.

* * * * *

Char leaned back in his chair, contemplating all that he' d heard. He hadn' t planned on listening to their conversation, but when Meri opened a direct channel for him to record Brianna' s declaration of ambassadorial status, he' d kept the channel open. Meri had been fully aware of this, for she could have severed the link any time she wanted. Her decision to take Brianna to her quarters had been her signal to him that any further conversation would be private. As it was, he was very thankful for the close ties his family had with the Hardan royal family. Meri' s conversation with Brianna had relaxed her and she' d talked freely. He was beginning to understand her.

Chapter Five

"There really isn' t much difference between these quarters and Char' s," Meri said as she walked across the room. "The basic proportions are the same, but I redecorated."

The door slid open and what could only be a relative of Kahn' s walked out. Somewhat shorter and less massive in bulk, she was obviously female. Her brow ridges were less pronounced and a topknot of black hair flowed down her back.

"This is Beti, Kahn' s cousin. Beti, this is Brianna. Bakom wants her."

A fierce look entered Beti' s black eyes. She nodded once and said, "Celene is no longer content with her sugar tit. It' s good that you have returned."

Meri chuckled and headed for another room. "Just like her father, concerned with instant gratification. Come along, Brianna, and meet the joy of my heart."

Obviously the equivalent of the room where Brianna had been staying, this one was furnished for a child. Meri bent and lifted a fussing baby from its crib. Her cries stopped when Meri opened the loose tunic she wore and presented her breast. Soon contented sucking noises filled the room.

Sitting herself in a comfortable chair, Meri looked up at Brianna. "This is my daughter, Celene. Isn' t she absolutely adorable?"

Brianna moved closer, curious to see what a half Drakian, half Medirian baby would look like. It was warm in the room, so the baby wasn' t wearing much more than a diaper. "She' s not green!"

Meri grinned ruefully. "And she has a tail. She' ll cause quite a stir on Mediria when she' s older. An ivory-colored Hardan princess with a tail! Grandmother will have fits."

Brianna sank into the room' s other chair and continued to watch the baby nurse. "She has gills."

"Thank goodness for that, but I would have loved her no matter what. So will my parents."

"Haven' t they seen her yet?"

"No. She was born right before we left Drakan so she' s just over seven months now. Ademis' parents wanted me to stay with them, but I refused. Char was kind enough to invite us along, and I was glad to accept. This was only supposed to be a two-month voyage, but Char' s little side trip has drastically changed things. I' m very thankful that I came along. Ademis would have missed so much, and I would have gone crazy without him."

"Did I hear someone talking about me?" said a voice from the doorway.

"Adem!" Meri exclaimed joyfully as she jumped up and bounced across the room and into her husband' s arms. The baby squalled once but quieted immediately when she found her mother' s other nipple.

Brianna watched her new friend' s reunion with her husband wistfully. *What kind of life will I have now, married to an alien?*

Meri shrugged herself out of her husband' s arms, took his hand, and led him to where Brianna sat. "Adem, this is Brianna. Brianna, my husband Ademis."

Brianna stared at him. She had thought that Chardadon was tall, but this man was at least another two or three inches taller. He was also broader and more muscular, though he was certainly not the equal of Kahn.

Ademis grinned at her perusal and bowed. "So you' re the woman who is tying Char' s thoughts into knots," he said as he put his arm around his wife' s shoulders.

Brianna felt her cheeks flush. Both Meri and her husband grinned wider.

"How do you do that?" Meri asked. "I' ve never seen anything like it."

"I can just tell I' m going to love your planets," Brianna grumbled as she got to her feet. "Isn' t there a race anywhere else in the universe that blushes?"

"I' m afraid not, fair lady," Ademis said as he took his daughter from his wife' s arms and lifted her high in the air.

She screamed with delight.

"You' d better burp her, my love," Meri said dryly, "or you' ll end up with her supper on your head again."

Brianna smiled at the picture in her mind.

"I didn' t expect to see you back so soon, Meri," Ademis teased, handing Celene back to her mother so that she could nurse more. "There are still a few hours left until dinner."

"Men!" Meri snorted as she caught Brianna' s eyes and shook her head. "It will require at least that amount of time for Brianna and me to get ready. You don' t expect us to wear just anything, do you?"

Celene chose that time to stop nursing and reach for her father. He grinned and took her into his arms. Meri buttoned her tunic and grabbed Brianna' s hand. "I knew she wasn' t that hungry. She' s just not used to not having me around. Having you here will be good for her. Now I can visit you and let Celene get used to being without me. You stay out of our bedroom, Ademis. We' ll come out when we' re ready."

"Married barely two years and already I' m being denied access to our bedchamber. I had friends who warned me this would happen when I married out of the true bloodline."

Meri laughed. "And I' ll bet every one of them was female. Char' s sister-in-law was livid when Ademis married me," she explained as they entered her bedroom where she stripped off her clothing and headed for the shower. "She' d already decided which of her full female friends would make the best wife for Ademis and wouldn' t listen when he said he wasn' t interested. She wasn' t completely convinced he wouldn' t terminate our marriage until Celene was born."

"Why didn' t Chardadon' s sister-in-law want you to marry Ademis?"

"She thinks full-blooded Drakians shouldn' t taint their bloodlines with ' alien' genes," Meri answered from the shower.

"She certainly won' t be thrilled with me, then," Brianna mumbled mostly to herself. "I guess she' s more of a barbarian than Char."

Meri walked out of the bathroom wrapped in a towel. "You called Char a barbarian? I' d have loved to see his reaction. What did he do?"

Brianna began to blush and Meri began to laugh. "I think this marriage may work after all."

Brianna groaned and flopped face down onto the bed. "Is there anyone on this ship who doesn' t know everything that' s happened to me since I got here?"

Meri grinned. "Of course, but those of us who will be closely involved with you have to know everything so we can help."

"I feel like a biology experiment!"

Meri laughed again. "By the time I finish with you, Char will want very much to experiment."

Brianna rolled over and stared morosely at the ceiling. "But what about what I want?"

Meri sat on the bed next to Brianna and began to brush her hair dry. "There' s nothing we would rather do than take you home, Brianna," she said in a quiet voice. "Unfortunately, since Bakom knows you exist, Char would face legal ramifications you wouldn' t believe if he took you back. Besides, Bakom knows where your planet is. If you weren' t here, he' d just send one of the Academy ships back as soon as he could summon one. Do you really want him going back and kidnapping some unsuspecting person for his experiments?"

Brianna stared at the ceiling. "That' s where they' ve got me. How could I let anyone else go through this? And what if they kidnapped a child?" With a sigh, she sat up, took the brush, and began working the tangles out of Meri' s wet hair. "I know you' re all thinking not only of me but also of everyone on Earth. But marriage! I don' t even know this Chardadon! What kind of man is he?"

Meri turned and took Brianna' s hands in hers. "If you' re truly against this marriage, we won' t force you into it."

Brianna withdrew her hands from Meri' s, rose from the bed, and walked across the room.

"I know this is the best way, but how much of a marriage will it be? What will be expected of me? How will his family react? Will they understand why he' s married me? Will they want to protect me from Bakom, too?"

Meri sighed as she watched Brianna. She could understand her fears. She herself had experienced some of them, and she' d known that Ademis wanted her for a wife. Brianna had no such assurances. Marriage would make protecting Brianna easier but would present numerous problems if either she or Char wanted to end it at a later date.

"Char would never willingly hurt you. I know you don' t know him very well, but I do," she said as Brianna turned to face her.

The uncertainty and misery on Brianna' s face tugged at Meri' s heart. "None of us knows why Char suggested marriage," she began slowly, "but I have my own theories. He' s been piloting his family' s starships since he was eighteen. He' s never shown an interest in family life, but has certainly had his share of affairs with women from every human planet. None lasted more than a few months. The last few years, he has seemed less than satisfied with his life. He' s even gone so far as to meet some of the women his sister-in-law has chosen as suitable marriage partners."

Brianna sighed. "I bet she' ll really love me."

Meri smiled. "Don' t worry about Crystas. We' ll deal with her when the time comes. Anyway, as I was saying, after Miklan brought you on board and Char was forced to rescue you from Bakom, there have been subtle changes in his behavior. You' ve sparked his interest. Both Adem and Lorilana agree on that. You' re different. Drakians have always been drawn to the exotic. We Medirians fascinate them because of our long hair. All Drakians have brown hair, in various hues, that barely reaches much past their shoulders."

Brianna pushed a lock of hair back over her shoulder. "I' ll definitely stand out in a crowd then."

Meri nodded her head affirmatively. "Exactly! Your coloring is more exotic than any except the Gattan, and they stick to themselves. The fact that you saved two members of his crew, however, demands action from Char. Any respectable Drakian would show his protective instincts and sense of responsibility towards you."

"Yeah, but marriage isn' t based on protectiveness and a sense of responsibility."

Meri stared at Brianna and decided to be blunt. "Those aren' t the only reasons Char wants to marry you. He wants you in his bed."

Brianna' s blush rose to the roots of her hair.

"And, if I' m correct," Meri continued, "that' s just where you' d like to be."

Brianna blushed even more. The prospect of making love to Char was becoming more and more intriguing as the hours went by.

Growing up in a royal court made reading people' s expressions a necessity, and Meri was very good at it. She hugged Brianna and then held her at arm's length. "Would making love to Char be taboo on your planet?"

"To some people, maybe, because he's an alien, but not to many others."

"Are you virginal? Haven't you ever been with a man before?"

Brianna's scathing look answered that question.

"Well then, what's the problem?"

"The problem is that I think I'd like it too much!" Brianna practically shouted as she shook off Meri's hands and strode across the room to stare unseeing at a painting.

Meri gazed thoughtfully at her new friend. "I don't understand."

Brianna turned back to Meri. "Neither do I," she admitted with a sigh. "I feel so overwhelmed."

"Do you want to go through with this marriage?"

Meri watched the play of emotions race across Brianna's face and let out the breath she hadn't realized that she'd been holding when Brianna nodded and said, "It's the most logical thing to do for the good of everyone else on Earth."

"You had expected marriage to be based on more than logic?"

Brianna nodded again and returned to sit on the edge of the bed with her elbows propped on her knees and her chin cupped in her hands. "On Earth, people get married because they're in love."

Meri laughed brightly. Sauntering back across the room, she once again took up her brush and began to work on her hair.

"Brianna, you're a delight. You'll have Char completely wrapped around your fingers in a matter of days."

Laying the brush on a dresser, Meri unwrapped the towel and shrugged into a comfortable robe. "You're more afraid of yourself than you are of Char. That's something that can be overcome."

"Humph."

Meri walk over to the wall and pushed a button. A door slid back and revealed a surprisingly spacious closet. "Come here and help me pick out a dress for you. You want to look beautiful for your own wedding, don't you?"

"Wedding! What wedding?"

"Whose marriage have we been discussing for the last fifteen minutes?"

"But I thought..."

"You thought you' d have more time to get used to the idea. I wish that were true, but the sooner you' re married, the harder it will be for Bakom to fight it."

"But who...?"

"Lorilana will perform the ceremony."

"Don' t we need a priest or something?"

"On Mediria we have priests, as you must have on your planet since you' ve mentioned them, but on Drakan anyone designated as an elder can perform marriages. Lorilana has presided at hundreds."

"Oh."

Still talking, Meri disappeared into the closet, but Brianna stopped listening, immersed in her own thoughts. She was walking a fine line and her sanity, if not her life, was at stake. Brianna thought back to when she' d been in Chardadon' s arms. Maybe Meri was right. Why shouldn' t she try to have a little fun before she went home? Char was handsome, in an alien sort of way.

Shaking herself out of her revelry, Brianna rose from the bed and walked to the closet. "I guess I should just make the best of the situation. What have you got for me to wear?"

Meri emerged from the closet grinning. In her arms, she carried a length of silvery material. "This dress will be perfect. Here, let' s try it on you."

Brianna removed the tunic and pants she was wearing, and Meri dropped the dress over her head. "I don' t think it fits, Meri. I can' t get the bodice in place," she said trying to fit the dress over her breasts.

Meri laughed again. Adjusting the dress so that silver ribbons looped around Brianna' s neck and nestled between her breasts, Meri turned her to face the mirror.

Brianna' s shocked face looked back at her. "I can' t wear this! I' m half-naked!"

The silver ribbons that lay between Brianna' s breasts were attached to a stiff cummerbund fitted snugly underneath her breasts, helping to lift and support them. Shimmery, silky material cascaded from the cummerbund and draped gracefully to the floor. It was a beautiful dress, but, as she had said, with her breasts fully exposed, she was half-naked.

"Meri!"

"Here's the jacket. I didn't think you'd want to go without it," Meri said with a grin. "Although on Drakan, baring one's breasts is perfectly acceptable."

Brianna shrugged into the short-sleeved, high-necked, form-fitting silver jacket. Once buttoned, it hugged her body, accentuating as much as covering her full breasts.

Meri nodded. "I knew that dress would fit. The color is perfect on you."

"It would be more perfect if I had some shoes."

Disappearing into the closet, Meri returned shortly with a pair of soft, white boots. "I've never worn these. See if they fit."

Brianna slid her feet into the boots and stood up. "They seem to fit," she said as she walked around.

"Good, now sit down in this chair and let me do something with your hair."

Sitting in front of the vanity mirror, Brianna watched as Meri deftly gathered her hair and arranged the red mass in a coronet of braids on top of her head.

"It's a bit thicker than mine," Meri said as she struggled with a braid, "but this should work."

Guiding Brianna's hand to the back of her head, Meri said, "Just pull out this pin, and the braids will come down. Now, do you want any cosmetics?"

"Those I can manage myself. Why don't you get dressed?"

Meri nodded and disappeared back into the closet, emerging some minutes later with an armful of blue-green material. Tossing her robe onto the bed, she slid into the turquoise gown, not bothering with any undergarments. Before Brianna could comment, the door slid open and Beti entered the room.

"Your husband said he was tired of waiting and went to keep Alalakan company. Call when you are ready and he will come escort you to dinner. Celene is napping."

Before Meri could answer, Beti stepped back and the door closed once more.

"Is she always so abrupt?" Brianna asked as she rose from the vanity chair and wandered over to a chest where some animal carvings were displayed.

"Afraid so," Meri answered as she stood in front of the mirror and adjusted her gown. It hugged her body like a second skin to just below her hips, where it flared in graceful folds to the floor. The low-cut neckline displayed a great deal of cleavage.

Following Brianna' s gaze, Meri looked down at her chest and said, "Medirians are fairly broad-minded about how much bosom women display. Most of us swim topless anyway."

Brianna shrugged and lifted one of the carvings. "These are very beautiful. What' s this?"

Meri looked in her vanity mirror and said, "It' s a klanac. They are used to pull objects underwater where we' d rather not use machines."

"A seal with a seahorse' s head," said Brianna setting it down carefully. "And this?"

"A mahir, it' s the only large land animal native to our planet. The Aradab use it as a draft and riding animal."

"It looks like a cross between a deer and a horse, even if it is red. Do all of them have antlers?"

"Yes," answered Meri, brushing her hair back behind her ears. "I think I' ll let it hang free tonight."

"This dolphin is beautiful, though," Brianna continued. "Whoever carved it did an excellent job."

Meri' s head jerked around. "Dol...phin?" she gasped, half rising to her feet.

"Hmmm, and the killer whale is lovely, too, although on my planet they' re black and white instead of blue and white."

Meri sank onto her chair.

Brianna set the carving down and hurried to her. "Beti!" she yelled. "There' s something wrong with Meri!"

Brianna was chafing Meri' s hands as the door slid open, and Beti charged into the room.

"No, no, I' m all right!" Meri said as she struggled against their supporting hands. "Brianna!" she continued breathlessly as she hurried to the chest where her carvings were displayed, lifting the dolphin and killer whale, "are you saying that there are animals like these on your planet?"

"Of course. Millions of them, probably," Brianna answered slowly.

"The dols and the orcs," Beti whispered in a reverent tone as both women stared at Brianna.

"What did I do?"

Meri set the carving down, threw her arms around Brianna in an exuberant hug, and burst into joyful tears. "What have you done! You've brought news of what was lost to my people centuries ago, the dols and the orcs. You need not fear Bakom now. On my planet you will be almost deified. Come on," she said wiping the joyful tears from her eyes. "We must tell the others."

Beti had already left the room when Meri tugged Brianna's wrist and dragged her to the outer door. Beti stood talking with Kahn, and when they saw Brianna, both of them bowed deeply. Straightening quickly, Kahn palmed open the door and checked the corridor. Ignoring Meri's impatience, he motioned them out and allowed them to precede him to Chardadon's quarters where Meri pounded on the door.

Hauling Brianna into the room behind her when the door opened, Meri ignored the surprised looks on the faces of the two men and flung herself into her husband's arms babbling about a long-lost legacy, an ancient prophecy, and dols and orcs.

Brianna fisted her hands on her hips. "Will someone please tell me what is going on here? I finally get to where I think I understand things and now this!"

Char stared at the vision before him. Meri had been correct about his reaction; he was enchanted. The gown molded itself to her breasts and hips and its silver hue complimented Brianna's vivid coloring perfectly. Her braided hair crowned her head and the slight trace of cosmetics deepened the passion in her green eyes and the temptation of her lips.

"Well?"

Snapped out of his reverie by her sharp tone, Char said, "The dols and orcs, which were removed from Mediria hundreds upon hundreds of years ago, apparently swim in the waters of your world."

Meri calmed herself enough to continue. "Almost three thousand years ago, our planet was torn by racial strife. Mediria's three races did not live in harmony, and we had reached the point where our extermination of each other was close to being complete. That's when the matriarchs of the dols and the orcs sent representatives to the warring factions saying that they had had enough. Since we couldn't live in peace, they were leaving."

"You could talk to them?"

Meri nodded and continued. "You must understand; the dols and the orcs were an integral part of our lives. We revered and respected them as we did not even respect ourselves. When they left, part of us went with them."

"How did they leave?"

"That' s the greatest mystery of our planet. One day the sky was darkened by the arrival of a huge spaceship. We don' t know from where or from whom it came. Every single dol and orc on our planet was transported onto that ship. Then it disappeared. We' ve been looking for them ever since we conquered space."

"As has every other human species," Ademis added as he poured his wife a glass of wine. "Now that we know where they are, dear wife, what do you intend to do?"

"I want immediate transportation to Mediria for myself and Brianna. Finding the dols and the orcs is an agreed number one priority by all members of the Federation. Even your Academy of Science has agreed that the location of the dols and orcs is of prime scientific importance."

Chardadon poured a glass of wine and took it to Brianna.

Swallowing, Brianna accepted it. She hadn' t been this close to him since he' d held her naked in his arms earlier that day, and his presence made her anxious. Forcing herself to meet his steady gaze, she was immediately lost in the velvety brown depths of his eyes. The pressure he exerted on her fingers as he handed her the wineglass brought her back to herself, and she struggled to concentrate on Meri. Char did not move away, however, but moved slightly behind and to her side.

The door slid open and Lorilana entered as Meri was saying, "I don' t care what Bakom wants, this takes precedence over any argument he could possibly produce."

"And what argument is that, Meri? I seem to have missed an interesting conversation."

"The dols and the orcs are on Brianna' s planet."

Lorilana stumbled.

Brianna would have hurried to her side if she hadn' t felt the gentle caress of Char' s fingers on her elbow.

"Wait," he murmured.

Meri helped Lorilana to the couch, and Ademis handed her a glass of wine.

"Are you sure?" she asked after a fortifying gulp.

"Brianna identified the carvings in my room without any prompting from me."

Gathering the shreds of her composure about her, Lorilana said, "Meri, I' m very happy for you and your people. As far as Bakom is concerned, though, this will only slow, not stop him. He may not be able to hurt Brianna now, but there is an entire planet of ' specimens' for him to choose from."

Brianna surprised them all when she spoke. "Which is why this marriage must take place. As the wife of a prominent Drakian, and a worldwide heroine on Mediria, I' ll have a much easier time of gaining ambassadorial status. The people from a world with an ambassador to your Federation of Planets will certainly have more rights than one without," she finished quietly.

The others stared at her, Ademis and Lorilana in surprise, Meri with a conspiratorial smile on her face, and Char with an unreadable expression on his.

"You' re right Brianna," said Lorilana. "The honors granted to you by Mediria' s people should be enough to give Bakom pause. Being married to Char will put you out of his reach completely. It' s all the other people on your planet who are at risk. Bakom will certainly send an Academy ship for more specimens unless we can find a way for the Ruling Council to censure the action. Having both the Medirian royal family and the Alalakan clan on your side will give any intelligent being pause."

Brianna nodded. She could sense Chardadon' s presence behind her with every nerve in her body.

"I have to send a message to my father immediately," Meri said impatiently. "He must make preparations for our arrival and inform the Federation."

Chardadon remained silent. His plans were being changed as they spoke, but Brianna herself had removed the one obstacle he feared. Lorilana was correct about the honors Mediria would bestow upon her; one of them would be Medirian citizenship. That would put her effectively out of Bakom' s reach. Luckily for him, she had reasoned out Bakom' s probable actions towards her planet. The only question he hadn' t been able to answer in his mind was whether or not she' d be willing to sacrifice herself into marriage to save her people.

I have to take her home with me. I can' t leave her on Mediria. Meri' s father will have his assassins guard her too closely for Bakom to capture her if she remains there. If she' s on Drakan, Bakom will think he can get to her. Then he' ll start making mistakes. Without Brianna, Bakom' s downfall would take longer.

Lorilana' s next comment brought Char out of his musings.

"Then I may as well perform the ceremony now, Char, Brianna," Lorilana said in a no-nonsense tone. "We no longer need to hash out the problems associated with our old plan."

Brianna nodded nervously, and the next fifteen minutes passed in a blur. She remembered a cool kiss on her cheek, and then her senses returned when she felt herself lifted high off the floor and twirled around. However, it wasn' t Char' s arms in which she found herself. When she looked down, Ademis grinned up at her.

"Are you back with us now?" he whispered in her ear as he kissed her cheek. "You looked ready to faint. Marrying Char is not a bad thing."

"I' m not your daughter!" Brianna gasped as Ademis lifted her higher.

Ademis laughed as he set her back on her feet.

"I don' t know how Meri tolerates you," she grumbled as she regained her equilibrium.

"I tolerate him because I love him," Meri whispered in Brianna' s ear as she hugged her tightly. "I hope you find the same joy. Char' s a good man."

Brianna sighed. "Maybe, but I' d have liked to get to know him better."

"Those two seem to have fallen into friendship rather quickly," Lorilana said quietly to Char as she watched Brianna and Meri whispering together. "Who would have thought it possible?"

"They' re very much alike or hadn' t you noticed?" was all Char answered, well aware of Lorilana' s dissatisfaction with the marriage kiss he gave Brianna. The passionate kisses he wanted to give her would wait until she was ready for them. Who knows how she would react to his passion in front of witnesses.

"Until you pointed it out, no," Lorilana answered. "But you' re right. Anyway, I' m looking forward to Sheala' s birthday celebration at Solstice. Your sister-in-law doesn' t particularly care for Meri. I can' t wait to see her reaction to Brianna."

Char had poured two glasses of wine while Lorilana was talking. Handing one to her, he raised his glass and said, "I give you my new wife, Alalakan dem al' Brianna."

The others followed his lead and toasted Brianna silently as she stood, uncomfortable, the center of attention.

Meri set her glass down as soon as the toast was finished. "I want to send that message now, Char," she demanded.

Ademis sighed loudly. "I' ll take her to Communications. You will soon discover, my friend, you' ll have no peace if your wife is not happy."

Char smiled. "I' ll have your dinner sent to your quarters."

"That' s why I love you so much, Char. You understand what truly matters in life." With those words, Ademis guided his wife to the door and disappeared into the corridor.

"I must go also, though I will find my own dinner. This matter of dols and orcs requires thought and study. It will cause an uproar in the Federation and the Academy," said Lorilana as she too exited the room.

Brianna found herself alone with her husband. Why did everybody leave! "Is finding those animals really such an earth-shattering event?" she blurted into the rapidly expanding silence.

"Yes. At the request of Mediria' s royal family, every ship traveling through space has scanned likely planets for the dols and orcs. Yours was the first we' d failed to scan. There were simply too many orbiting probes that would have discovered us had we attempted to do so. Besides, no one thought the dols and orcs would be discovered on such a highly developed planet."

"Why were you there in the first place?" she asked looking directly at Char for the first time since she' d become his wife.

He shrugged as he took another sip of wine. "Partly to inconvenience Bakom because he demanded passage on my ship when an Academy ship was leaving two days after us. Partly because we' d picked up some type of radio signal from this section of the galaxy, and searching for new human life is one of the Federation' s mandates."

"Oh," Brianna said and dropped her eyes. *God, what do I do now?*

Char watched Brianna as she wandered nervously about the room. After combing his fingers though his loose hair, he said, "Brianna, I don' t want you to feel pressured; I expect nothing you' re not willing to give. And, if you wish, once we have toppled Bakom from power, we can dissolve this marriage. The decision will be yours."

Turning away from Brianna, Char walked to the sidebar and poured himself another drink. "I won' t force myself on you."

Does he really mean it? But I want…what do I want?

The memory of his kisses and caresses returned.

She shivered. *Be honest with yourself, Bri. You' ve been wondering all day what making love with him would be like. What have you got to lose?*

"Char."

Setting his glass down, he turned to face Brianna. She stood in front of the doorway to the bedchamber with her soft hair cascading about her. As he watched, she unbuttoned the tight jacket she wore and slipped it off. Her nipples hardened as she dropped it to the floor.

Char crossed the room until he stood in front of her, his gaze locked on her bare breasts. "Do you know what you' re doing? I want you, all of you. There won' t be any interruptions this time."

"I know," she answered in the same quiet voice as she reached behind her neck and untied the ribbons. The dress billowed to her feet, and she stood before him all but naked.

Char looked deep into her eyes. Reflected there, he saw fear, hope…passion?

Not giving her a chance to reconsider, he lifted her into his arms and claimed her mouth with a deep kiss.

Brianna wrapped her arms around his neck as she answered his hungry kiss with one of her own.

Reaching back, he palmed the door.

It closed silently behind them as Char carried his wife to her bridal bed.

Chapter Six

Brianna shivered with anticipation when Char dropped his arm from beneath her legs and let her slide slowly down his body. As she grabbed hold of his waist to balance herself, he slid his hands down her back and cupped her buttocks, kneading gently, lifting and separating.

Moaning, Brianna rubbed against the erection that pushed against her stomach. His hands were pure magic.

When his hands left her buttocks and he pushed her away, Brianna sobbed.

"Patience," he murmured. "We need to get the rest of your clothing off."

Slowly, he kissed and nibbled his way down her torso until he knelt before her. Kissing the inside of her knee, he removed first one boot then the other, pausing to kiss each ankle. Then, hooking a finger on each side of her panties, he inched them down her legs, pausing only long enough to drag his tongue across her pubic hair.

Moaning, Brianna grabbed his shoulders when her knees threatened to buckle.

Rising to his feet, Char swept her into his arms and laid her down on the bed. But, instead of falling down next to her, he stepped back and caressed her from head to toe and back again with his eyes.

Then, after making sure he had her full attention, he began to strip—slowly.

Standing at the bottom of the huge bed, his eyes never leaving hers, Char unbuttoned his tunic. Starting at his right shoulder, he slowly released one button at a time. Once he'd finished with the diagonal row, he shrugged. His uniform slid down both arms. When he pulled them free, his uniform sagged around his hips.

Fisting her hands in the silken bed covering, Brianna held her breath as Char lifted his arms above his head and stretched, his supple skin sliding smoothly over the taut muscles of his arms and chest. The dragon on his right shoulder seemed to shimmer with a life of its own as his uniform slipped lower. Only his erection kept it from falling.

Brianna's body demanded that she breathe. She gulped air, but her eyes remained locked on Char.

Chuckling he turned his back, sat on the bottom of the bed, and pulled off his boots and socks. Then he stood again, his back still towards Brianna, planted his hands on his hips and slid his uniform down. He wore nothing underneath.

Brianna eyes glided down the line of his spine. *God, what a great ass.* Her gaze came to rest on his tail which was much thinner than those of Miklan and Cindar. But then, his was only a tail while theirs were sexual organs. "What in the world do you do with that tail?"

Char turned and smiled a devilish smile. "Another time, when you're ready, I'll show you just how this tail can be used."

But Brianna's stomach muscles were already clenched. She forgot all about Char's tail when she saw the size of the erection that sprang from its nest of fine, silky curls. Brianna had had her share of lovers, and she'd certainly looked at more than a few *Playgirl* magazines. She'd even let her friends talk her into watching a XXX-rated movie once, but she couldn't remember ever seeing anything as impressive as Char's cock.

Oh my God. Just how long is it? Then she smiled. *Mine.*

Chuckling, Char crawled up to her side, rubbing his engorged penis along the length of her body. Before his mouth claimed hers, he said, "Like what you see?"

"Yes," Brianna moaned and wrapped her arms around his neck.

Char lowered his mouth and kissed the corner of her lips. Shivers of pleasure jolted through him when she bit his lower lip and thrust her tongue between his lips to mate with his.

When she shoved her hips against him, Char threw his leg over her thighs to immobilize her. Lifting his head, he looked down into Brianna's face.

Passion burned in her green eyes. Her face was flushed, her lips red. She lifted her head, seeking his mouth. "Please…"

Char's entire body clenched, especially his cock. How he longed to plunge himself into her, but he was going to take his time. No matter what the future brought, Char intended that Brianna would never forget this wedding night.

"Slowly, love, slowly. We want this to last." After a deep, soul-wrenching kiss, Char tore his mouth from hers and turned his attention to her breasts.

When Brianna grabbed his head and tried to pull his mouth back to hers, Char captured both of her hands in his and stretched them above her head.

Moaning, Brianna arched her back, lifting her breasts.

Burying his face between them, Char inhaled. Then he dragged his tongue down between them, nuzzling underneath her left breast where he proceeded to kiss and nibble the delicate skin.

Brianna arched and bucked. "My nipples, please, suck on my nipples. Now!"

Char chuckled against her chest. "If you insist." He nipped her left nipple then sucked it into his mouth.

"Ahhhhhhh!"

Brianna arched her back even more and pushed her breast further into Char' s hot, wet mouth.

She tried to wrench her hands free, but Char tightened his grip. "Easy. Not so fast. Let me pleasure you." He sucked her other breast into his mouth.

Rolling her head back and forth, Brianna struggled against Char' s grip. She had to get her hands on him, had to pull him on top of her so she could thrust herself onto his magnificent cock.

"More, Char. I want more. I need more."

As Char continued to suckle her breasts, he shifted his body and slid his fingers between her thighs.

Keening, Brianna arched her hips and spread her legs wider as his fingers probed.

Char groaned as he slid first one then two fingers inside of her, stretching her, preparing her for his cock. She was so wet! He stroked, dipped and delved until her moisture covered his fingers.

"Look at me," he commanded.

After Brianna opened her eyes and focused on him, Char raised his fingers to his mouth and slowly, separately, sucked each one. "You taste of sweet woman — and hot passion."

The muscles in her body clenched. When he slid his fingers inside of her again, her internal muscles clenched and tried to pull them deeper. He pulled them out. She was close to orgasm.

The reactions of Brianna' s body to his fondling was putting more of a strain on Char' s control than he had thought possible, something that hadn' t happened in years. The texture of her skin was different from that of any other woman he' d ever been with, not as smooth as that of the women on his planet yet silky in its own subtle way. Her hair, though! There was so much of it! The feel of it against his bare skin excited him to levels he' d never before experienced. Releasing her hands, he braced himself on his forearm. Lifting one of her long curls with the fingers that had just been sliding in and out of her body, he wrapped one thick curl around his swollen penis, rubbing the silken loops up and down, up and down.

Her body screaming for release, Brianna slowly regained control of herself by watching Char' s fascinated reaction to her hair. Eyes closed, head thrown back, he rubbed her hair against his erection.

Sliding down a little, she replaced his hand with hers. She wound her hair around his cock then massaged his foreskin and teased the naked head with a single curl. His hips jerked once, then twice.

Groaning, Char pulled her hand away from his cock and rolled onto her, murmuring soft words against her mouth. Finally, his two hands returned to cup the sides of her face. He settled on her hips, using his thighs to push hers closed, resting his throbbing erection on the soft hair at their juncture. Moving slowly, he rubbed his engorged penis against the soft, wiry hair, groaning at the sensations that raced through his body.

Body tingling, Brianna pounded his shoulders with her fists and bucked her hips against his. The feelings racing through her body were stronger than any she' d ever experienced. She needed more—now! "Damn it. Stop teasing me. It' s been too long. I need your cock—deep—now!"

Pulling her with him, Char rolled onto his back.

Brianna straddled his hips, her hair cascading about both their bodies.

"Ride me, Brianna. Ride my cock."

Moaning, Brianna positioned herself over him. Finally!

Slowly, Brianna slid down onto his long, hard length, panting, her internal muscles shuddering, as she stretched to accommodate him.

Beads of sweat broke out on Char' s forehead as he grabbed Brianna' s hips and eased her down onto his cock. Groaning, he arched up into her as she slid further onto him. How he wanted to ram himself into her, but she was so tight! He had to wait, had to go slow so he didn' t hurt her.

A low moan escaped from Brianna when she finally had Char' s cock completely embedded. Never had she been stretched so much or felt so full. She pushed herself up and then slid down again, slowly at first, then faster.

Catching her rhythm, Char surged upward. It took only a few strokes for her orgasm to begin. Again, his fingers found their way between her thighs to the sensitive bud hidden by red curls.

Brianna shuddered, sobbed, and collapsed onto his chest.

As her body pulsed around him, Char struggled against his own orgasm. The tight, rhythmic clasps on his still deeply embedded erection brought more sweat to his brow as he fought for control. With a final surge of willpower, he gained mastery over his body. Inhaling the scent of the heavy, auburn tresses entangling both of them, he caressed her body and murmured soft words into her ears. As she slowly came back to her senses, his mouth renewed its worship of her nipples. He gently rolled her onto her back, still buried deep inside.

"I trust you have no complaints," Char said softly as his tongue played with the hard buds, "but we haven' t finished yet. No Alalakan bride sleeps on her wedding night."

He began to move slowly then more rapidly, thrusting more deeply as her body' s movements matched his. This time he held nothing back and, when Brianna began to shudder again, he thrust deeply, exploding with his own release.

Some minutes later, Char lifted his weight from Brianna and carried her with him as he rolled onto his back, holding her close to his chest. She sighed contentedly and rested her head against his left shoulder, the fingers of her left hand lightly traced his dragon tattoo.

He placed his fingers under her chin and lifted her face until her eyes met his. He grinned when he saw the rosy blush. "Will you always change color after we make love?"

"It' s called blushing," Brianna mumbled and turned even more red as she tried to pull away.

"Stay," he whispered as he nuzzled her ear. "I won' t tease you anymore."

Brianna relaxed against him and shivered as his fingers caressed her spine. His gentle kisses were already eliciting a response. Her nipples hardened as he nibbled on her neck, and she gasped when his fingers began stroking the sensitive skin on the inside of her thigh.

"I' ve learned much about your body," he whispered in her ear. "Aren' t you curious about mine?"

You can' t even begin to imagine, Alalakan don al' Chardadon.

Smiling, Brianna rose to one elbow and traced delicate lines across his chest, marveling at the silky texture of his skin. Her fingers slid across his upper abdomen, stopped, and traced a knotted scar below his right pectoral. "How did you get this scar?"

Before he could answer, she lowered her head and nipped the masculine nipple closest to her. Lifting herself higher on her elbow, her hand moved to his erection without hesitation. The amused expression on Char' s face changed rapidly to passion when her head followed her hand. The sight and touch of her thick red curls draped over his thighs, and the things her moist mouth and tongue were doing to him were too much for his willpower. Uttering an unintelligible oath, he pulled her mouth to his, rolled her onto her back, and thrust deep.

Brianna reveled in his lack of control. She was both comforted and excited that her alien husband wasn' t as cool and collected as he' d seemed. In moments, though, she too lost all control as sexual tension built to the breaking point. Their shared orgasm was all-encompassing.

After she was able to breathe normally again, Brianna teased, "Will you always suffer from such a lack of control when we make love?"

Char' s answer was his laugher and a swift, hard kiss. Then, grinning, he clasped his arms behind his head. Propping himself back against the pillows, he indulged himself with admiring his alien wife. She seemed to have quite a temper, and the blush that seemed always ready to rise accentuated her coloring perfectly. The nipples, though, that appeared and disappeared behind long red hair interested him far more than the prospect of enticing her prickly temper.

Closing his eyes, Char settled himself more comfortably. He needed rest. The last few days had been extremely trying.

Brianna relaxed against his side. Soon the events of the day took their toll and exhaustion claimed her.

Char wrapped his arm around her shoulders and pulled her closer. Yes, this marriage had been a good idea.

He woke Brianna twice more with his passionate kisses, kisses that she accepted eagerly and matched with her own passion. Both were completely sated when he left their bed ten hours later to shower.

Char stood by the bed and stared down Brianna. He' d have liked to spend the next twenty-four hours with her as was the custom on Drakan, but he was captain of the ship. Sacrifices had to be made. She shifted once and settled into a deeper sleep. Carefully, he thumbed a lock of her hair from her face then dropped a kiss on the top of her head.

Again Brianna awoke to silence. Stretching and yawning, she sat up when she realized she was alone. Sliding out of bed and brushing the hair out of her eyes, she readjusted the lighting and walked over to what she knew was Char' s closet. Pushing the same two buttons Meri had the day before in her room opened the door. Entering, she searched among his things for something to wear. She was tired of being naked. His clothing would do until she found something else.

"Doesn' t he wear anything but uniforms?" she mumbled irritably as she searched. Opening drawers, she found several pairs of what looked like silk pajamas.

"If he' s ever slept anyway but naked since he' s been out of diapers, I' ll grow a tail myself," she muttered as she pulled on a pair. Luckily there was a drawstring, and she was able to tie them tightly enough to keep them from falling. Rolling both legs up about a foot enabled her to walk without tripping. In another drawer, she found some soft, white, pullover type shirts that laced up the front. She slipped one over her head and rolled up the sleeves. After she brushed the tangles out of her hair, she gathered it together at the top of her head and tied it with a lace she had taken from another shirt. Working quickly, she soon had her hair in a long braid and tied the end with another lace.

"That' s the best I can do with what I' ve got to work with."

Slipping into boots Meri had given her, she looked around the room. Beyond making the bed, there was really nothing to do. She left the bedroom for the outer chamber. The delicious smells wafting from the covered tray on the table reminded her that she hadn' t eaten for she didn' t know how long. Her stomach rumbled as she lifted the domed lid. A plate and utensils lay next to the tray. "Well," she said, mostly to break the silence in the room, "as long as they have knives, forks, and spoons, they must be civilized."

Using the two-pronged fork, she selected items from various plates. There was some kind of pinkish meat in a white sauce that smelled heavenly and tasted like chicken. What looked like blue potatoes, but tasted more like cauliflower au gratin filled one dish, while what could only be some sort of fruit was piled high on another. And the bread looked like bread. A pitcher of what turned out to be plain water sat next to the tray, as did three separate bottles of wine. She chose the water.

Some time later, Brianna pushed her plate away contentedly. "A good meal and a good night' s sleep, or day' s sleep anyway," she said into the emptiness of the room, "works wonders on one' s disposition." She snorted and grinned to herself. *And fantastic sex has a way of relieving tensions.*

She placed her dirty dishes on the tray and covered it with the lid since she had no idea what else to do with them. Opening one of the wine bottles and sniffing its contents, she decided a glass would be just what she needed to finish her meal. She had just taken her first sip when the door opened.

"Have you eaten?" Char asked, as he walked to the table and poured a glass of wine for himself.

Brianna nodded, unsure of both herself and him after the night they had shared. She was his wife, but she had known him all of twenty-four hours and said no more than a hundred words to him.

Char leaned back against the table and grinned. "My clothing looks much better on you than it does on me."

Her nervousness ignited her temper. "Well, if I had some of my own, I wouldn' t have to wear other people' s!"

Char grinned more broadly. He was beginning to love her prickly temper. It brought sparks to her green eyes and that lovely pink blush to her face. "I meant no offense. I promise to do all that I can to remedy your lack of clothing, but until we get to Mediria, there' s not much I can do. "

Brianna sniffed. She knew not having clothes wasn' t Char' s fault, but his nearness made her nervous. She had to do something to relieve the tension that was building.

Still grinning, he abruptly turned and set his glass on the table. Taking the two unopened bottles of wine, he placed them back in their cabinet.

Brianna settled down on the sofa with her legs curled under her. Continuing to sip her wine, she watched as he busied himself arranging bottles in his wine cabinet. He was obviously something of a connoisseur. The vintage of whatever she was drinking was excellent.

"What exactly is it you do?" she asked, "besides captain a spaceship? From what I've gathered, your family is very powerful."

Char turned and gazed steadily at Brianna. This was not a question he had expected. Was she a woman like his sister-in-law, only interested in the power and wealth the Alalakan name could bring her?

"Would you be disappointed if captain this ship was all I did?"

Brianna shook her head. "No, but I know absolutely nothing about you or your family. I'm trying to do my best to adapt, but I'm so confused about so many things."

Char hadn't realized how important her answer was until he felt his body relax.

Picking up his wineglass, he crossed the room and sat on the opposite end of the sofa, stretching his long legs before him. "The Alalakan clan has extensive business interests on all five human planets." He set his glass on the end table and unbuttoned the top of his uniform and pulled it away from his neck. "Father has basically retired from the business since he was elected to the Council, and my brother Rodane administers matters on Drakan. I oversee our various ventures on the other planets."

"Then you don't spend much time with your family." She edged away from him.

"At times, not as much as I'd like. At other times, too much," he answered as he toed his ankle-high boots off. "My sister Sheala turns eighteen this year at summer. That will be an enjoyable time."

Brianna relaxed and smiled. Talking about his family was safe. "How old are you?"

"Thirty, and Rodane is thirty-three."

"Then your sister is much younger."

Char grinned. "She was a big surprise to everyone, especially my mother."

Brianna grinned back. "She must be spoiled rotten."

Char's brow puckered. "Spoiled… rotten? Like rotten fruit?"

A sigh of frustration. *I'm going to have to explain half of what I say.* "No, I mean overindulged."

He clasped his hands behind his head and closed his eyes. "And how do you know that?"

No longer the object of his intense gaze, Brianna relaxed even more. "Because I was spoiled rotten—overindulged—myself. My brother is nine years older than I am and both sisters older yet."

His eyes still closed, he smiled. "And how old are you?"

Though he didn't see it, Brianna stuck her tongue out at him. "Twenty-five."

"A veritable sage I've married then." He opened eyes that glittered with amusement…and speculation.

Brianna eyed him uneasily. She was beginning to recognize that look. Casting about widely for a topic of conversation, she spied part of the tattoo on his shoulder revealed by his loosened uniform. "Is there some significance to that tattoo? What kind of animal is it anyway?"

He sat up, undid the last few buttons, and shrugged out of the top of his uniform, an action Brianna was not expecting but one that did not surprise her. He did seem to have a one-track mind. "A dragon, our clan totem. Almost every Alalakan has one."

"Why does it carry a sword?"

"That's my personal emblem. It represents fidelity to my family."

Brianna tore her eyes from his and concentrated on the dragon on his shoulder.

It was not a modest representation, nor was it like any tattoo she'd ever seen. The artisans on his planet were extremely skilled.

The gold and green of the dragon's skin glistened with a life of its own. The red eyes in its uplifted head seemed to follow her movements, and the half-furled wings looked as if they were ready to snap open. A sinuous tail curled up over his shoulder and dipped down to circle his upper arm. The sword clenched in the dragon's foreclaws looked sharp enough to pierce skin.

Brianna leaned over to admire it more closely. "It's beautiful."

"As are you," he said as his mouth found hers. Her glass fell to the floor as he pulled her against his torso, one arm about her waist, the other hand cupping the back of her head.

Stretched out on top of him, Brianna could feel his erection. His tongue began to probe the inside of her mouth. Her heart racing and bosom heaving, she tore herself away from him and fled across the room to stand next to the table, her back to him. What was wrong with her? He was her husband, right? What was she afraid of?

Char rose and walked across the room and stood behind her. Softly caressing her upper arms, he asked, "Why do you run from me, Brianna? We both enjoyed last night."

Her sob startled him.

Gently, he turned her to face him.

Tears rolled down her cheeks as she admitted, "Because I could care too much."

Folding her in a tight hug, Char said, "My dragon carries the sword of fidelity. I would never intentionally hurt you." *Use you to trap Bakom — but never hurt you.*

Lifting her head, Brianna searched his face. The openness and integrity in his gaze promised things he'd not yet said. Reaching up, she cupped his cheeks and pulled his mouth to hers.

Groaning, Char lifted her up on the table, pushing the tray holding the remains of her meal crashing to the floor. He made short work of the tie at the front of her pants. Brianna jerked her shirt over her head then yanked at his one-piece uniform, desperately trying to free his erection.

After Char had divested Brianna of the last of her clothing, he made short work of his own. Pushing her back onto the table, he lifted her legs, wrapped them around his waist, and entered her with a hard thrust.

At that moment, the door slid open. It was hard to say who was more surprised, Lorilana or the lovers on the table.

"Get out!" they both ordered simultaneously.

As the door slid shut, Brianna snapped, "You'd better get these damn doors fixed!"

Some time later Brianna sighed contentedly as she lay in bed, her head on her husband's chest. After a mutually explosive orgasm, Char had carried her back to the bed where he had made love to her again, much more slowly, until she was mindless with pleasure.

She smiled. Being married to an alien might not be such a bad thing.

Turning her head, she brought her hand up to trace the dragon on his right shoulder. Her light caresses woke him from his doze.

Char stroked her upper arm.

"Did you say all Alalakans wear a dragon?"

"Hmmm." The lack of sleep was finally beginning to take its toll on him.

She traced it again. *A tattoo. I always wanted to get one but never had the courage. This is a bit more than a rose on the ass cheek or a butterfly in the small of my back. Oh well, what the hell. When in Rome...* "Can I have one?"

Char stilled his caressing hand and began to laugh, first lightly, then more loudly. Brianna jerked herself out of his arms. "Well, you don' t have to laugh at me," she sniffed, unsure whether to be angry or burst into tears from what seemed like rejection. "If I' m not supposed to wear a dragon, just say so!"

Reading her emotions correctly, Char pulled her back down onto his chest. "I am not laughing at you, love, but at myself. The sooner a dragon rides your shoulder the better. Once you wear one, no one dare harm you."

She pursed her lips. "Does it have to look like yours?"

He yawned. "If you want, but most of us design our own."

Brianna wanted to say more, but his exhaustion was obvious. Reaching over to the nightstand, she dimmed the lights.

Soon his deep breathing filled the room.

"At least you don' t snore," she muttered as she eased out of the bed.

Returning to the other room, Brianna found where her shirt had fallen and slipped it over her head. It fell to the middle of her thighs so she didn' t bother with the pants. Her makeshift cuffs had kept falling down anyway.

The door toned. Brianna looked at it dubiously, but then she shrugged. Walking over to the opening mechanism, she palmed the door and stepped back as it opened to reveal Beti with her arms full of clothing.

Pushing past Brianna, the Aradab dropped what she carried on the sofa. Looking around the room, she noticed where the plates and tray had fallen on the floor. For the first time Brianna detected emotion on an Aradab' s face when Beti smiled briefly. She left the room with out a word, only to return in a few minutes with supplies to clean the mess.

She finally spoke before she left the second time. "Princess Merilinlalissa sent clothing. If you ever wish to come out, you will have something to wear."

After those few short words, Beti left, taking the dirty dishes and cleaning supplies with her.

Brianna shook her head, and then went to look through the things Meri had sent. Finally, clothes!

Sighing happily, she pulled on a pair of panties and soon found the green pants and tunic she' d worn the day before. Grabbing the brush that she' d laid on the end table earlier, she brushed and rebraided her hair. Then she began to sort through her borrowed finery.

Once she had everything sorted, she decided against putting it in Char' s closet before he woke. He needed his sleep. She could, however, take a quick bath.

Moving quietly through the bedroom, she sent a quick glance his way. He had rolled onto his stomach, and sprawled across the middle of the bed. His tail dangled over the side. Pausing, she reached towards it then stopped. He did need his rest. But, if it was the last thing she did, she was going to find out what that tail was good for.

Closing the door to the bathroom, Brianna shrugged out of her clothing and turned on the water in the tub. After it was adjusted to a comfortable temperature, she stepped in, being careful not to wet her hair. *Too bad I don' t have any bubble bath. Oh well, I don' t have room to stretch out anyway.*

Leaning back, she relaxed, enjoying the warm water, contemplating what design her dragon should be...and arguing with herself.

What were you thinking, Brianna, to ask for a tattoo? You just got married, for God' s sake – to an alien yet. Now you want to get his clan tattoo? You don' t even know if this marriage will last. What if you can' t get it off?

She shook her head. *Tattoos come off. It' s painful, but possible. And it will help protect me.*

Brianna leaned her head back against the edge of the tub and closed her eyes. *Oh, why didn' t I just call in sick that day!*

Her conscience answered. *If you had, Miklan and Cindar would be dead. Then their planet would probably want to make war on ours. Where would we be then?*

"If we were home, I' d get in there with you."

Brianna opened her eyes and stared at her husband.

"If you keep looking at me like that, I will climb in with you, and you will turn your lovely shade of pink when someone comes to dismantle the tub to get us out."

As Char had known they would, his words brought a rosy blush to her breasts and face.

Brianna exacted her own subtle revenge, however. As she rose from the tub, the water cascaded from her body.

His eyes narrowed as she turned coyly and turned on the air jets. Running her hands slowly down her body, she smoothed water drops from her glistening skin. When he stepped over to the tub and reached for her, she stepped out and slipped past him.

"No you don' t. You told me yourself that you had to get back to Control. Touch me and you know very well that you' ll be late."

Char' s eyes glowed. "Minx. I' ll exact my revenge for this."

As he turned to adjust the shower for himself, Brianna reached out, grabbed his tail, and gave it a good yank.

Char yelped. "When I get you..."

"You have to catch me first!" floated through the door as it slid closed.

Char could only laugh. No woman had ever had the audacity to pull his tail.

Brianna was in the process of placing the clothing Meri had sent to her in the closet when he walked out of the bathroom, naked as usual. He leaned against the closed door as he watched her bustle about. Then, walking up behind her, he wrapped his arms around her and pulled her back against his chest.

She squirmed in his arms. "Let me go. I haven' t finished rearranging your closet so there will be room for the things Meri gave me. Besides, you have to go to Control. I put a clean uniform on the bed."

"Married barely a day and already you sound like a wife," Char grumbled in an amused tone. But he did release her and don his uniform.

"Don' t you ever wear underwear?"

"Underwear?" he asked as he slipped his tail through the small sleeve in the back of his uniform. The sleeve was approximately two inches long and provided protection for the base of his tail. Brianna hadn' t realized it before she' d pulled it, but his tail was covered with fine yet thick hair.

"You know, small clothes worn under your outer clothing next to your skin, like the panties I wear."

"No."

She snorted. "Well, that cuts down on laundry bills."

Laughing as he pulled his suit up onto his shoulders, he fastened the seven buttons that rode diagonally across the inverted golden vee on his chest to the top of his right shoulder. He certainly cut a trim figure in the forest green and gold uniform that molded itself to his body. Her gaze was drawn to the distinct bulge at the juncture of his thighs.

"It will become much larger if you keep staring. Then, I promise you, I won' t get to Control at all."

Brianna' s face flamed, but she lifted it defiantly. "If a little look is all it takes, it' s a wonder your race conquered space at all."

Still grinning, he crossed the room and planted a swift kiss on her forehead. Her pert tongue was becoming a constant source of amusement. "Begin thinking about your dragon. I' ll send Lorilana to you."

Brianna sighed. "Is there anything she doesn' t do?"

"I wouldn' t trust anyone else to mark your flesh," he said as he left the room. "Think on the design. Lorilana is a very capable artist."

Brianna' s mouth snapped shut. "Mark my flesh! Will this *hurt*?"

Char' s laughter floated back through the closed door.

"Men!" she mumbled as she carried borrowed clothing into the bedroom.

She had just finished rearranging the closet to her taste when the outer door chimed. She left the bedroom and discovered Lorilana waiting outside.

"Char certainly didn' t waste any time readjusting the door commands, did he?" Lorilana commented peevishly as she entered.

Brianna blushed but chuckled all the same as she sat down on the sofa.

"You and Char seem to be getting along very well."

Brianna shrugged and said nothing. She didn' t trust her voice.

A devilish grin on her face, Lorilana sat down. "Char said you wanted me for something. From what I observed, he was doing just fine by himself."

Brianna' s face flamed red and she began to stutter.

Lorilana reached over and placed her hand on Brianna' s arm. "I' m sorry, my dear, but it was impossible to resist. Char' s never shown so much interest in a woman."

"He' s never been married before, either!"

Lorilana' s perfectly formed eyebrows rose. This girl had a temper. Backtracking, her tone became more neutral. "What would you like?"

"A dragon."

Lorilana froze.

"Char explained that a dragon will make it that much harder for Bakom to claim me."

Speechless, Lorilana nodded her head. The marriage itself and the discovery of the dols and orcs would keep Brianna out of Bakom' s grasp. Why did Char tell her she needed a dragon? "Did Char tell you how important the clan symbols of Drakan are, Brianna?"

Brianna thought back to the declaration of fidelity he had made to her. "Yes," she answered simply.

Lorilana was glad she was sitting down because she wasn' t sure her legs would have been able to support her. Char would compromise his clan for no one.

Lorilana voiced her concerns. "Do you understand what wearing a dragon means? You' ll be irrevocably Alalakan."

Brianna stared at the darkness outside the large window. "Char said having a dragon tattoo is the last step in becoming Alalakan."

Lorilana stared at Brianna until she wanted to squirm. "Very well. Did Char explain you are expected to design your own? Did he tell you a clan tattoo can' t be removed once it' s been applied?"

Brianna froze, her thoughts turned inward. *Can' t be removed? Do I really want to do this?* Gritting her teeth, she glanced back to Lorilana. *The tattoo makes me Alalakan. The entire clan hates this Bakom guy. If it keeps me from becoming a biology experiment, it' s worth it. Besides, you only live once.*

She nodded at the older woman, who listened silently as she then explained exactly what she wanted.

Lorilana said nothing about the implications of the design the younger woman outlined. Perhaps this girl from across the galaxy was what Drakan needed. She' d certainly make life more interesting.

✴ ✴ ✴ ✴ ✴

Brianna yawned again and tried to stay awake until Char returned. He' d sent a message and an excellent meal, but that meal combined with the dullness of the historical video she was watching slowly overcame her determination to stay awake.

Her eyes closed and she jerked them open.

Her head nodded and her eyes closed again.

She dreamed of Lorilana and dragons.

Brianna stood behind Lorilana as she lectured a green and gold dragon about clan etiquette, something about how the majority of wives or husbands didn' t adopt their new clan' s totem for at least a year after marriage. No tattoo meant a marriage was much easier to dissolve.

The dragon shouldered Lorilana aside. Grasping Brianna gently with its forepaws, it enfolded her in its soft, leathery wings.

The lights were completely dimmed when Char entered his quarters. He' d been forced to stay in Control much longer than planned because Bakom tried to tap into and manipulate the master computer to disguise the fact that he' d sent a message. The major programs hadn' t been affected, but there were small idiosyncrasies that had to be corrected. It had taken him and his officers hours to correct the damage.

The prospect of seeing Brianna again had taken most of the edge off of his anger. Burying his face in her hair and his hardness in her soft body would diffuse the rest. Moving confidently across the darkened room, he palmed open the door to the bedroom unbuttoning his uniform as he entered. The lights there were also dimmed, but the viewing screen provided enough light for him to see that his wife was sound asleep. A program detailing the early history of Drakan moved ponderously across the screen.

Char glanced at it skeptically. It would have put him to sleep, too.

Tossing his uniform on the room' s only chair, he made a quick trip to the bathroom. Then he joined Brianna on the bed. She was stretched out on her stomach with her hair strewn about her. Tomorrow, he' d indulge himself and brush it. At this moment, however, he was more interested in other parts of her body.

Pulling the hair away from his wife' s neck, Char kissed her behind the ear. Stretching out beside her, he kept nibbling until he received a response. Mumbling something unintelligible, Brianna rolled onto her back. The light from the viewing screen was strong enough to illuminate the dark triangle between her thighs and the rosy nipples of her pert breasts — and the dragon on her right shoulder.

Though not as large as Char' s, a fully rampant dragon of deep red and gold with fully extended wings rode her shoulder. As with his, the fiery tail trailed over her shoulder to wrap itself around her upper arm. However, Brianna' s dragon was in no other way like the regal, self-controlled beast that adorned Char' s shoulder.

Her dragon was ready for war.

Fully extended claws reached out as if to attack, crimson flames gushing from its open jaws. She could not have been more clear about her challenge if she had thrown down a gauntlet.

His laughter brought her closer to consciousness.

Brianna stretched and blinked. "Char?"

Covering her mouth with his, he brought her to full awareness with a passionate kiss.

Her hands caressed their way lightly down his back to cup his buttocks, pulling his erection against the softness of her thighs.

He needed no more encouragement to bury himself into her welcoming body.

Brianna woke to the sound of running water coming through the open door of the bathroom. Slightly stiff and sore, she grimaced with discomfort as she rose from the bed. Char' s lovemaking was fabulous, but her body needed a rest. Sitting cross-legged on the floor, she rested her arms on her legs, took several deep breaths, and then closed her eyes.

Char found her still there when he exited the bathroom ten minutes later. "Do you find the floor more comfortable?"

Brianna opened her eyes but didn' t rise, surprised he hadn' t picked her up, tossed her onto the bed, and begun to make love to her again. "It' s called yoga. On my planet it' s used as an aid for meditation."

Char came back out of the closet carrying not one of his customary uniforms, but a pair of loose white pants and shirt like Brianna had borrowed from him the morning after their wedding. This unexpected action broke her concentration, and she rose to her feet.

Smiling at the questioning look she sent his way as he pulled on the comfortable clothing, he said, "I' ve informed my crew that I' ll be unavailable for the next twenty hours. I have paperwork to do, and I' d like to talk to you, and we both know little talking gets done in bed."

Brianna smiled. She would enjoy spending a day with Char. "You never told me what you thought of my dragon. You just laughed and made love to me until I fell asleep."

Char' s ready grin appeared again. "You are going to be the cause of more talk on Drakan than any other woman has ever been."

She frowned. "Is there something wrong with it? Lorilana didn' t say anything, so I assumed it was acceptable."

"You have the right to any design you want," he said as he leaned over and traced Brianna' s dragon. "Yours is rather intimidating, though, with fire as your personal emblem."

Brianna leaned back in her husband' s arms, looked him in the eye. "Good! I have to warn you, I am not going to be a meek and quiet wife who putters around the house cooking and cleaning. If there' s something I want, I' ll have it, one way or another."

Grinning widely, Char hugged her again. "I' ve never cared for meek women who acceded to my wishes. My grandmother spoiled me, I suppose."

"Your grandmother' s still alive?"

"Both of them, actually. But, I' m referring to my paternal grandmother. She' ll adore your spirit."

"As if there was ever an O' Shea who wasn' t spirited," Brianna retorted in a lilting Irish brogue.

He stared at her. "Why did you do that?"

"Do what?"

"Talk like that?"

"That' s how my grandmother sounded when she talked. She came from Ireland."

"Is that one of the other planets in your solar system?" Char asked in a puzzled tone. "We monitored all of them and thought them uninhabitable."

Chuckling, Brianna shook her head. "Ireland is a different country on my planet. Don' t the planets in your Federation have different countries on them?"

"I do not understand your word *country*," he said as Brianna pushed out of his arms.

She shook her head. "Boy, are you people going to be in for a rude awakening. My planet doesn' t have one central government, Char. There are hundreds of different governments."

His eyes widened. "How can you survive such chaos?"

Brianna grinned. "Sometimes, I think it' s the chaos that helps us survive."

Char shook his head. "It' s something we' ll have to discuss eventually, I suppose." Then he grinned. "Now you' ll have something to occupy yourself for the next four and a half months. We' ll need a detailed report about the major governments of your world."

"It will take four and a half months? Can' t the ship go faster?"

Char grinned. "Space is vast, Brianna. Planets, except for those in the same solar system, are light years apart. Even with the most advanced technology, it takes months to journey from one planet to another. And your Earth is very far from Drakan."

Brianna frowned. "How do you keep from getting bored?"

Char' s grin became wicked.

She pushed his hand away. "How did you keep from getting bored before you had me to fondle?"

"Paperwork. Trading plans. Plotting courses to potentially inhabitable or inhabited planets."

Brianna bit her lip. "What are you planning about Earth? Are you going to conquer it?"

He broke out into very amused laughter. "Conquer? I don' t want to conquer your planet. I' m interested in making profits, not war."

"Profits." Brianna shook her head and began to laugh also. "I married a man who' s interested only in his business."

Char pulled her close again, growling low in his throat. "I' ll show you what business interests me most," he said in a husky whisper as he cupped Brianna' s full breast.

Her breath quickened, but she pushed him away reluctantly, her ready blush rising. "I' m too sore."

Char kissed her once more. "For which there is only one sure cure," he said as he scooped her into his arms. Instead of dropping her onto the bed, however, he carried her into the bathroom and deposited her in a steaming tub of water. "I realized last night. You tensed with pain when I entered you. I' m sorry I didn' t anticipate your discomfort. My father will be very disappointed."

"Don' t you dare tell your father!" Brianna sputtered as she began to rise from the tub.

Char' s hand on her shoulder held her down. "Stay and soak. There' s special oil in the water. You' ll feel better by this evening."

"Just in time for your benefit," Brianna mumbled as she settle back against the tub, her knees and head the only parts of her body visible.

He kissed the top of her head. "You haven' t complained yet."

She heard the door to the outer room slide closed. Grumbling something inaudible, she closed her eyes. The water felt heavenly.

Chapter Seven

Char checked another row of figures. This had been a very profitable journey in more ways than one.

The door chimed. "Come."

Miklan entered carrying an oblong-shaped computer disk in one hand and a sheaf of papers in the other. "We've cataloged all of Bakom's attempts to compromise the computer, Captain," he said as he laid both on the table. "As you surmised, no real damage was done. Surely he can't be stupid enough to think he'd be able to take control of the ship?"

Char shuffled through the papers. "That wasn't his intent, Miklan. It was a feint to take our attention away from what he was really doing."

"And what was that?"

Char tossed the papers onto the table and lifted the disk. "Send messages without our knowledge."

"Why?"

Shrugging, Char dropped the disk onto the papers. "Bakom has his own agenda, and I wouldn't even try to understand how his twisted mind works. But he wanted a ruling shoved through the Council that would guarantee Brianna would be given to him as soon as we reached Drakan."

Miklan looked troubled. "The message won't be received, I take it."

"I thought you had more faith in me than that, Mik. It ran into an asteroid."

Miklan's expression was skeptical. "An asteroid in deep space?"

Char grinned. "Who am I to explain the wonders of the universe?"

Miklan joined Char in laughter, but then he sobered. "How's Brianna? My aunt is very close-mouthed."

As if on cue, the door to the bedroom slid open, and Brianna walked out, naked from the waist up, struggling with something in her hands. Since all of her attention was focused on that object, she didn' t realize Char wasn' t alone until she' d crossed most of the room and looked up to meet Miklan' s appreciative gaze.

Miklan! Here! I' m half-naked! With a gasp of horror, she clasped the shirt she was carrying to her bare breasts and fled back into the bedroom.

Miklan' s appreciation turned to surprise. "She wears a rampant dragon."

Char frowned. No one was supposed to know about that dragon yet. "I want your promise you won' t breathe a word of what you saw to anyone. Brianna' s ultimate safety relies on your discretion. It' s too soon for Bakom to know."

After his lieutenant nodded affirmatively, Char continued, "Lorilana married us with Ademis and Meri as witnesses. Brianna wears the Alalakan dragon with full knowledge of the responsibilities that go with it." Then, he grinned. "She' s not comfortable with anyone seeing her naked. If you want to avoid her wrath, you won' t mention her lovely breasts."

Miklan had been staring at the door through which Brianna had disappeared, but Char' s last comment caused him to swivel his head back to face his captain. "Is that true? Is everyone on her planet so modest?"

Char chuckled. His people were so much more open about sexual matters. "I haven' t been very interested in talking about her planet up to this point, Mik. Brianna has other, more interesting facets to explore."

Miklan shook his head. "They must be remarkable *facets* if she wears a dragon already. I don' t think anyone has ever received a clan symbol so rapidly."

"Suffice it to say that her other assets are just as remarkable as her lovely breasts," Char said as he walked towards the bedroom. "Sit down. I know she wanted to talk to you. I' ll see if she can conquer her embarrassment enough to come out."

"Embarrassment?"

"I' ll try to explain it to you sometime, Mik, but I' m not sure I understand it myself."

"Why didn' t you tell me Miklan was out there?!"

Char sighed. Teasing Brianna now might not be a good idea. She was pale rather than flushed. Sitting down next to her, he said, "I' m sorry, but I had no idea you were going to walk out on us. You' ve been adapting so well, that I forget you haven' t been among us longer. I' d have warned you if I' d known you weren' t completely dressed."

"I know." Holding up the shirt, she said, "I couldn' t open this, and it won' t fit over my head. How do I unfasten it?"

"It' s Deslossian. Each is a unique carving and has the clasp incorporated into the design. Here' s how you open it."

Brianna watched as he snapped the clasp open then closed it again.

"Now," Char said, as he dropped the shirt over her head, "Miklan is waiting to see you."

She blushed. "I know. I want to see him too. I just wish he hadn' t seen me half-naked."

Char felt it was safe to tease again. "But then," he whispered in her ear as he cupped her breasts, "he wouldn' t know why he was so jealous of me."

Brianna shoved Char off the bed. "Get out of here. I' ll be out as soon as I braid my hair."

When he rejoined Miklan, Char was still grinning.

"I was beginning to think you weren' t coming out. Anything interesting happen in there?"

"You' ll get nothing out of me, Mik," Char admonished cheerfully. "Bri isn' t like our women. She values her privacy when it comes to sexual matters."

He shook his head. "What a shame, such vibrant coloring."

"She' ll be joining us shortly, so mind your manners. I' d hate to have to reprimand one of my officers because he complimented my wife on the beauty of her breasts. No one would understand."

"I sure don' t," Miklan muttered as he followed Char back over to the table and the computer printouts.

Brianna stared at the closed door. *I guess it' s now or never.* Taking a deep breath, she opened the door. Both men turned to look at her as she entered the room. Both admired her beauty, Char possessively and

Miklan abstractly. For all that Brianna was a beautiful woman, he was devoted to Cindar.

Meeting her halfway across the room, Miklan swung her into a tight hug and whirled around the room.

"And I thought the Irish were emotional," she muttered, "but you people have us beat hands down."

"Irish?" Miklan began as he lowered Brianna to the floor. She grabbed his arm to keep her balance.

Char sent an amused look to his wife. "Don' t ask."

She stuck her tongue out at him.

Miklan watched the byplay between them with surprise. *I wonder if Char realizes how she' s affected him.* "I want bride price," he joked. "If it weren' t for me, you' d never have met."

Brianna' s eyebrows rose. "Bride price?"

Since he didn' t know if she' d find the concept offensive, Char wasn' t sure how to proceed.

Miklan had no reservations. "On our planet, for those who want them, there are marriage brokers who' ll arrange meetings between prospective brides and grooms. The meetings aren' t always successful, but if they are, a fee is paid to the brokers."

Brianna snorted inelegantly, but to Char' s relief, the idea of marriage brokers didn' t seem to bring out her quick temper. He gazed at his second officer who stood with his arm draped loosely around Brianna' s shoulders. She' d obviously overcome her embarrassment. *Maybe she will be able to fit in.* "You may be right, Miklan. You just may deserve bride price."

"Men!" Brianna exclaimed as she shrugged Miklan' s arm from her shoulders and walked over to face her husband. "Sometimes…"

Once again Char surprised Miklan by grabbing Brianna before she could finish what she wanted to say and kissing her passionately enough to leave her flustered. Drakian society was very open in showing affection, but Char was never demonstrative before others. But then, he' d never had a wife before, especially one so exotically beautiful.

Nor did Miklan miss Brianna' s slow, languid smile before she turned her back on her husband, strolled back to Miklan, and tucked her arm under his. Unlike Char, he wouldn' t have been able to control himself. He' d have had her down on the floor before she had time to think.

"Don' t say anything else, Char," she said saucily as she steered Miklan towards the sofa. "Just go back to those dull accounts you were grumbling about. Miklan and I have much to talk about."

Miklan shook his head in wonder at Char' s fluid bow.

Brianna yawned. She was curled up on the sofa, hands resting on its arm, her head resting on her hands. Char was back at his paperwork. He' d tried to explain it to her, but since she didn' t understand the Drakian numerical system, it made little sense. Learning it was one of the goals she set for herself.

After they' d eaten and Miklan returned to Control, Char taught Brianna a great deal about the ship. She now understood how it was possible to have so much fresh water for bathing, how to order food and where it came from, and how to keep her clothing fresh and clean. She was somewhat dismayed to discover there were no robots or anything like that to clean their quarters and had received another one of Char' s puzzled looks when she mentioned *Star Trek*.

She yawned again.

Glimpsing her movement out of the corner of his eye, Char turned and smiled at her. "Go to bed. I' m almost finished here."

Brianna rose and stretched. "I' ll see what I can find on the viewer to learn about. Turn it off if it puts me to sleep again."

Slipping into the bedroom, she switched on the view screen and stripped off her clothing. Glancing at the screen, she saw the program was the same dull documentary from the night before. This was not television. When reactivated, the program took up where it left off.

Stretching out on the bed, she said, "Next channel."

This program started talking about the prices of something called Deslossian wool.

Brianna made a face. "Next channel."

Her mouth dropped open. Two naked people cavorted on the screen, one hermaphroditic and one female. She watched, mouth still gaping, as the hermaphrodite' s tail snaked its way between the woman' s thighs and entered her, her moans and gasps coming louder as the tail thrust in and out of her body.

The camera panned the woman' s body and then circled around behind her. There it closed on the hermaphrodite as he slid his elongated clitoris into her anus. Both participants moaned louder as they approached orgasm. Both had barely collapsed on the bed when a full male Drakian joined them.

The hermaphrodite rolled off of the woman' s back as the man began to caress her. She responded eagerly to her new partner. What astonished Brianna more than anything, though, was what the two of them did with their tails.

A sound in the open doorway made her look up. Char watched her with a speculative gaze.

Brianna glanced back at the screen, shook her head in amazement, and said, "Can you do that with your tail?"

Bursting into hearty laughter, Char stripped off his clothing. "Watch."

Fascinated, Brianna watched as Char curled his slender tail around his thigh then lifted it up between his legs and wrapped it around his erect cock. He pumped it twice.

Smiling, he unwound his tail and joined her on the bed.

Brianna inhaled sharply as he wrapped it around her thigh and probed between her thighs with the tip.

"I mentioned it on our wedding night, love," he said between nips and kisses. "Since my tail has proved to be so fascinating, it' s time you learn just what it can do." Char' s fingers joined his tail between her thighs. Both finger and tail slid into her.

Brianna gasped. Already wet from the X-rated video she' d been watching, she felt even more moisture between her thighs.

Char inserted a second finger and stroked her clit with the tip of his tail.

Arching, she spread her legs wider. This felt good!

"You' re so wet, love. How ready you are for me." He sucked a nipple into his mouth.

Brianna thrust her hips against his hand. "Please, Char. I need your cock inside of me."

Lifting his head from her breast, he smiled. "Are you sure?"

"Yes, oh God, yes. Now, Char. Now!"

Slipping his fingers from her wet folds, he slid them back further, spreading her moisture all the way to her anus. He pressed the tip of his finger inside.

Brianna gasped and bucked against his finger. "Char!

Rolling onto his back, Char lifted her and slid Brianna down onto his cock. As she shuddered with the fullness of his possession, he cupped her buttocks, massaged, then separated them. He snaked his tail up between his legs and gently probed her anus.

Brianna froze. "I don' t…"

He rolled his hips and pinched her nipples. "You wanted to know, love. Relax. I promise you' ll enjoy this."

He rolled his hips again, and Brianna moaned as she settled further onto his cock. She rose up and slid back down.

Char slipped a thumb between her thighs and rubbed her clit. "That' s it, relax. Open for me."

Shivering, Brianna sucked his cock deeper inside. "Oh, God, you' re so hard."

His tail caressed the crack in her ass.

Char thrust and rolled his hips again.

The tip of his tail slipped inside of her anus.

Brianna froze.

He grabbed her hips, lifted her, and dropped her onto his cock as he thrust upwards.

Shuddering, Brianna spread her thighs wider and tried to pull his cock even deeper.

He pushed his tail further inside of her.

"Now," he commanded as he thumbed both nipples, "ride me."

Shuddering, filled front and rear, Brianna rode Char' s cock and tail until she screamed with ecstasy.

Brianna woke blushing. Char' s tail was a sex toy without equal. That first bout of lovemaking with his tail up her ass hadn' t been the end of his tricks. Later, he' d used it to massage her clit while he pounded his cock into her. He' d even slipped it inside with his cock and stretched her more than she' d dreamed possible. Lord, but sex with Char kept getting better and better.

Nor was Char conveniently missing when she woke up.

"You wanted to know what I could do with my tail," he whispered into her ear as he pulled her close again and wrapped his tail around her thigh. "Do you have any more questions?"

Brianna bolted upright. "No!"

"Your face is as red as your dragon, my love," he teased as he pulled her back down onto his chest. "You did ask."

"I know," Brianna mumbled against his chest.

"And you liked it, didn' t you?" her murmured into her hair.

Brianna' s braid had become undone during the night, and her hair covered both of them. Once again he wrapped his tail around her leg. She quivered as the tip of his tail teased the cleft between her buttocks, but she didn' t pull away.

Char smiled to himself. Whatever inhibitions she had were rapidly disintegrating under his sensual onslaught. But as much as he wanted to spend the rest of the day in bed with her, he had work to do. With a determined sigh, he laid Brianna back on her side of the bed. Pushing himself away from her, he said, "I must resume command of my ship. Ademis and Miklan deserve a rest."

Her blushes subsiding, Brianna nodded. She could use some time alone. So much had happened in such a short time. Just last week she' d been back on Earth, blissfully unaware that Char existed. She acknowledged his farewell kiss with an absentminded peck.

He gave her a puzzled look but left their quarters whistling.

Rising, she took a quick shower. After donning a loosely fitting dressing gown, she walked to the computer console in the outer room and punched in the code for breakfast.

Brianna had just finished cleaning up her meal when the outer door toned. Checking the view screen as Char had demanded, she opened the door and admitted Meri. Kahn remained in the corridor but bowed deeply when he saw her.

"Well," Meri teased. "Char finally unwrapped his tail and let you out of bed."

Brianna' s flaming blush caused Meri to crow with laughter. "Already? It took two weeks for Adem to bring that tail of his into play. Char couldn' t have run through his repertoire of sexual tricks yet. What happened?"

Meri' s matter-of-fact discussion to the topic calmed Brianna' s embarrassment. "I was looking for something to watch on the viewer while he did some paperwork."

Meri grinned. "And you found the Drakian ' recreational' channel."

Brianna nodded.

Meri flopped onto the couch. "I remember the first time I found that channel. It was a wild night."

"Did Ademis walk in on you right after you found it?"

"Yes, he did," Meri answered thoughtfully as her eyes locked with Brianna' s. "Why that...!" Meri never finished her thought. Instead her laughter joined Brianna' s. "Brianna, we have married a pair of scoundrels."

"Yes," Brianna gasped through her laughter, "and we are going to have to make sure they learn their places."

Meri nodded affirmatively. "I think it' s about time we started comparing notes."

Brianna slipped her robe off of her right shoulder. "Do you have one of these? I don' t remember from that day in your quarters."

Meri' s eyes widened. "You certainly don' t do anything halfway, do you?" she said with wonder in her voice. "Most men and women who marry into Drakian clans take at least a year to accept their new totems. Many people were shocked when I had mine applied after only five months of marriage. You were married barely two days."

"Char explained that it would be another way to thwart Bakom."

"It will definitely do that," Meri answered. "But did he tell you you' re now irrevocably Alalakan and can' t leave the clan even if you want to?"

Brianna stiffened. *Can' t leave the clan? Bullshit. If I decide to go, I' ll go, and nobody will stop me.* But to Meri she said, "I understand what this dragon represents. I won' t do anything to embarrass the clan."

Meri nodded, a dreamy expression on her face. "The tales you' ll be able to tell your grandchildren. Claimed from a planet across the galaxy. They' ll be writing stories about you."

"Humph!" Brianna snorted. "Fat chance. His family will take one look at the fire coming out of my dragon' s mouth and wonder just who it is he married."

A puzzled look appeared on Meri' s face. "Fat chance?"

"Never mind."

Meri shook her head then said, "Don' t worry, Bri. Char' s family will love you, especially his grandmother."

"That' s what he said," she replied. "What does your tattoo look like? I wasn' t paying that much attention that day in your quarters."

Meri pulled her tunic off of her shoulder. "Well, it certainly isn' t as flamboyant as yours. Mine is exactly like Adem' s."

Directly above Meri' s right breast, a gleaming blue and white dolphin leaped out of a frothy blue-green sea. Slightly above and to the left flew a small green and yellow dragon.

"I don' t understand. I thought each clan had its own symbol. Is Ademis related to the Alalakan clan?"

"No, Ademis' is a small clan, headed by his uncle. He chose to show his alliance to the Alalakan clan by adding the dragon to his dol. I chose to honor him by doing the same."

Brianna pulled her legs onto the couch and sat cross-legged. "But, there aren' t any dolph...dols on Drakan, are there?"

"No, and there never have been. All clan symbols are creatures that don' t exist on Drakan. Legend has it that the totems appeared in dreams to clan leaders thousands of years ago."

"Does everyone on Drakan belong to a clan? How many are there?"

Meri frowned. "Didn' t Char explain this all to you?"

Brianna blushed. "We haven' t really had much time to talk."

Meri' s laughter was infectious.

Once they gained control of themselves, she continued. "I don' t really know how many clans there are, but I' m sure there' s a record somewhere. Many clans died out during the plague, and those that didn' t had their numbers decimated. Those individuals who chose to become hermaphroditic forswore clan affiliation, so only full blooded males and females belong to clans unless a hermaphrodite marries into it."

"So some ancestor of Ademis' dreamed of a dol thousands of years ago, and you end up marrying him," Brianna mused. "I' d have liked to see the look on your face the first time you saw that totem."

"Kahn' s grandmother saw it first. She had him back in my father' s throne room stripped to the waist faster than you would believe possible. That was the first time I saw Adem."

"Love at first sight."

Meri chuckled. "Marrying me was the only way the Aradabs and Nessians would allow Adem to leave the planet. They believe he will be instrumental in finding the dols and orcs."

"And he just happens to be an officer on the ship that brings me back from Earth."

"Strange, isn' t it?" Meri said. Then, "Brianna, are there dragons on your planet?"

"In myths and legends." Her eyes widened. "You don' t suppose…"

Meri shrugged. "I don' t know, Bri, but my people believe all things—past, present, and future—are intertwined. It' s very strange, given all the interplanetary travel in our corner of the galaxy, no ship before Char' s picked up any radio signals from your planet. Some greater power is working here that we don' t understand."

Brianna shook her head. "Greater power? Sounds more like a coincidence to me."

"I know it' s hard to believe," Meri said stubbornly, "but what other explanation is there?"

Brianna shrugged. "A lot of people on my planet would say everything happens by chance. This does seem to be more than coincidental, but it isn' t worth worrying about. What' s done is done."

"I guess so, but you must admit it makes a great story."

Brianna laughed. "Meri, you' re a hopeless romantic."

* * * * *

Much later, when Char returned to his quarters, he found a hot meal waiting, and Brianna bent over a sheet of paper.

Unbuttoning the top four buttons on his uniform, he rolled his neck and shoulders as he walked over to see what Brianna was doing.

"If that uniform is so uncomfortable, why don' t you redesign it? It' s not as if the president of the company will deny your request," Brianna said a bit absentmindedly.

Chuckling, he kissed the top of her head. "I thought I might find you still blushing in bed."

Brianna controlled her embarrassment much better than he had expected. She hardly flushed.

"Meri came to visit today."

Char grinned ruefully as he sat down to his meal. "Bringing you two together may have been a mistake."

Brianna grinned. "You have no idea how true that is."

He changed the subject. He'd already learned it was impossible to get the last word in with Brianna. "What are you doing?"

"I'm trying to make our alphabets parallel. I'll never learn to read and write your language if I can't figure out what's what," she answered in a frustrated tone.

"Are you making progress?"

"I thought so, but you have more vowels than we do, even if I use *y* and *w*." She put down her pen and stretched, grimacing at the sharp pain that stabbed across her shoulders.

"Have you eaten?"

She nodded. "I was hungry, and I didn't know when you'd be back." Leaning back in her chair, she closed her eyes. She hadn't realized how tired she was.

Char watched Brianna as he ate. From the symbols drawn on the papers strewn about the table, she had been working for some time. *Once we get back to Drakan, I'll send all of her work on to the university in Benishan. The linguists there will appreciate the head start she's given them.*

Rising after he finished his meal, he cleaned up after himself, and then neatly piled Brianna's papers. He stroked her shoulder lightly. "Brianna, come to bed."

Yawning, she opened her eyes.

When she didn't move, he swept her into his arms and carried her. She snuggled against him, curling her arms around his neck.

"I think you are perfectly capable of walking," he murmured. "You just like to have me carry you."

"It didn't...take you long...to...figure that...out," she answered between more yawns.

Char dropped her on the bed and pulled her robe over her head. Rolling over onto her stomach, she wrapped her arms around a pillow and snuggled down into it. Char admired her smooth back and long legs. He' d have liked to remove her panties also—he really didn' t understand why she wore them—but he decided to leave her be. She was very tired, and he hadn' t been allowing her much rest when they were in bed. She deserved a night of uninterrupted sleep.

Stripping out of his uniform, he went into the bathroom. Opening the cabinet, he took out a small bottle and opened it. Swallowing one of the capsules, he sighed as he returned the vial to its customary place. Now he, too, would be able to sleep without having to deal with the aching erection Brianna' s soft body would invariably create. Dimming the lights, he dropped onto the bed next to his wife and gathered her into his arms.

Chapter Eight
Two months later

Rodane joined his father in the library. "Char' s sent another message, Father. Oh, hello, Grandmother. I didn' t realize you were here."

Elegant white eyebrows rose. "Where should I be?"

"I' m not here to argue, Grandmother. You' re usually tucked away in your rooms with your nose in a book."

"And where else would I get a book but the library?"

Jamiros chuckled. "Leave off, Mother. Rodane admitted years ago that you could think and talk circles around him. Now what does Char have to say? Don' t tell me he' s haring off to another corner of the galaxy after supposed radio signals to keep Bakom from Drakan— again."

Rodane nodded. "It turns out the radio signals were real. He found another inhabited planet. And he' s bringing one of its inhabitants home with him."

"Is that such a good idea with Bakom on the same ship?"

"He didn' t have much choice. It seems she rescued Miklan and Cindar from what sounds like an alter ego of Bakom' s. She was wounded in the process and transported back to the ship by mistake. Bakom managed to get his hands on her for his damn Tests, but Char and Lorilana were able to rescue her before they had progressed too far."

"She?" Jenneta asked. "This alien is a female?"

Rodane nodded. "A very human female. It seems her blood is exactly the same as Medirian blood."

Jamiros leaned forward. "I didn' t know that was possible. Why is Char bringing her here?"

"Because he married her."

"What!" two voices exclaimed in unison.

"Preposterous!" Jamiros continued. "The woman is an unknown entity. What possessed Char to marry her? The clan will never accept it."

Rodane shrugged. "It was a rather terse message. However, Char did say that there was no other way to protect her from Bakom. Since Meri is on board, they' re busy devising plans to keep her from Bakom' s clutches. She saved Miklan and Cindar from certain death and almost died herself in the process."

Sighing, Jamiros nodded. "That explains it. Char has always had an overdeveloped sense of duty and protectiveness. The clan does owe her more than our gratitude for saving Miklan and Cindar. The marriage is undoubtedly to throw Bakom off-balance."

"Bakom doesn' t know about it yet, Father. Char' s keeping it secret."

"Very, very good," Jenneta murmured. "Bakom would never suspect that Char would marry an unidentified species simply to keep her from him."

"Char' s probably counting on the Medirians accepting her because of their matching blood. Once she' s safely out of Bakom' s clutches, Char will simply dissolve the marriage," Jamiros mused. "It makes sense."

Jenneta' s locked her gaze on her son and grandson. "I wonder if she' s pretty."

"What do the woman' s looks have to do with anything?"

Both Jenneta and Rodane stared at Jamiros in amazement.

His expression became sheepish. "I must be getting old."

Jenneta chuckled. "No Drakian gets that old."

Rodane snorted.

Jamiros frowned. "Does Char say anything else?"

"Bakom sent a message to the Academy directing them to make sure the Ruling Council reaffirms the Tests."

"That can be circumvented."

"Char should be arriving in two and a half to three months. He wants us to see what we can do to weaken Bakom' s hold on the Council until then."

Jamiros nodded. "Plans can be pushed forward."

"What are you going to tell Xdana?" Jenneta asked.

"Everything except that Char married the woman. Since the marriage is a sham, there's no reason to upset her or Crystas. They're too deep in their plans for finding him the perfect wife this Solstice."

Jenneta snorted. "You mean Crystas is busy finding Char the perfect wife. Xdana just agrees to keep peace in the family."

Rodane frowned. He really didn't want to talk about his wife. "I think you're making a mistake, Father. Mother won't be happy when she discovers you've kept Char's marriage from her."

"A marriage that will be dissolved, possibly before he even arrives home? I think not. Now, if you'll excuse me, I'll go tell your mother the important parts of the message."

Jamiros left the room, closing the door firmly behind him.

Rodane glanced at Jenneta. "Father is making a mistake, Grandmother. Even if this marriage is just a sham, this woman will be entitled to Alalakan clan status, among other things."

Jenneta pursed her lips and stared steadily at her grandson. "Tell me, Rodane, could Char deny Bakom access to this woman on his own ship if he truly wanted to?"

"Of course. Char is his own man. No one tells him what to do on his own…"

Rodane's eyes widened as what he was saying registered in his own mind.

"Exactly," Jenneta said. "Why then did he marry this woman? I think that this Solstice will prove very interesting."

* * * * *

Staring out at the darkness of deep space for what had to be the millionth time, Brianna contemplated her situation. She hated not being able to go anywhere, hated being stuck in the Char's quarters day after day after day. She felt as if she'd been there two years rather than just over two months. And whenever she said anything to Char about seeing another part of the ship, he just smiled, said it was too dangerous, and then made love to her.

To make matters worse, she was having a particularly frustrating day with her studies. She knew she was close to bringing the two alphabets together, but a few sounds just would not mesh.

Brianna glanced over her shoulder. Char was lounging on the sofa with a book.

Damn him! How could he be so relaxed when she was ready to climb the walls! She was sick of being locked up in this room working on this stupid alphabet! She was sick and tired of everybody telling her how sorry they were that she couldn' t go anywhere else on the ship. They weren' t the ones penned up here. She was!

Grinding her teeth together, Brianna stomped back to the table and glanced at Char again.

He looked up and smiled at her.

Brianna clenched her fists. What was he smiling about? Asshole. She was nothing more than his sex kitten. As long as she purred, he was happy.

Crumbling a handful of the papers scattered before her, she threw them up into the air. "I can' t stand this anymore! I' m tired of being penned up in this room, locked up like some kind of animal!" As she whirled to face Char, a wave of dizziness swept over her, and she grabbed hold of the chair to keep from falling. Then she burst into tears.

"Brianna!" Char' s book tumbled to the floor. He leaped to her side and tried to pull her into his arms.

Brianna pushed him away. "Let me go, you, you sex-starved kidnapper. Take me home. My family doesn' t even know if I' m alive or dead."

Spinning away from Char' s worried expression, she took one step and crumpled to the floor.

A sharp pain stabbed Char' s chest in the general location of his heart. When he picked Brianna up, her head lolled back against his shoulder. What was wrong with her?! *Nothing must be wrong with her. I need...*

Char shied away from his own thoughts, unwilling to venture into such uncharted territory.

On his way to the bedroom, he opened his com-link to control. "Dr. Sendenton to my quarters immediately!"

Banging his shoulder against the control panel of the bedroom door to open it, he entered and carefully laid Brianna on the bed. The outer door toned, and he had to leave her side. She still had not regained consciousness when he returned with Lorilana.

"What' s wrong with her?" he asked anxiously, hovering. "She just collapsed."

"I don' t know. Her pulse is normal and her breathing seems fine," Lorilana said mostly to herself. A thoughtful expression appeared on her face. "Wait in the other room, Char."

"But…"

"Go!"

Scowling, he obeyed.

Lorilana chuckled quietly. Things were getting interesting.

A foul odor brought Brianna back to consciousness. Coughing, she pushed the vial away from her nose. "God, what is that stuff?"

"Brianna? Does the female of your species follow a monthly cycle?

"Of course. Why do you ask?"

But Lorilana didn' t have to answer.

Brianna' s eyes opened wide, and her hand went to her upper arm. "Where is it? What happened to it?"

"What are you talking about?"

"The birth control patch, the small patch under my skin. It prevents conception."

A guilty look crossed Lorilana' s face. "We noticed it when we were treating you for your wound. Since it was a foreign object, we removed it."

"Oh my God! I' m pregnant."

Char paced his outer room while Lorilana remained closeted in the bedroom with Brianna. She couldn' t be sick. She couldn' t die, could she? Was there some kind of germ or bacteria she' d contracted?

The bedroom door opened and Lorilana walked out. "Go in to Brianna, Char," she said before his frustration could explode. Then she left the room before he could question her.

Clenching his fists and swallowing his anxiety, Char managed to stifle his frustration at Lorilana' s seeming callousness. Carefully shaping his face into a neutral expression, he entered the bedroom.

Still pale, Brianna lay back against the pillows and watched him warily.

He eased himself down on the bed beside her, gently brushing some stray strands of hair from her forehead. "Do you feel better now?"

"I' m pregnant."

Stunned, Char stared at his wife. Of all the possible scenarios that had flashed through his mind, the possibility of pregnancy had never occurred to him. *That can' t be possible. No species gets pregnant so easily. She hasn' t even been in my bed three months yet!*

"Char... Char?" The worried expression on her face brought him back to himself.

"You' re going to have a baby?" he asked stupidly.

Brianna gulped a breath and nodded affirmatively, now completely unsure of herself.

Collapsing back against the pillows next to her, Char stared at the ceiling. *Pregnant!* "Are you sure?"

"Almost. Lori will know for sure in a few minutes."

A slow smile appeared on Char' s face. *Now, now I have the perfect bait to trap Bakom. When the Council discovers he wants to "test" a pregnant female, they' ll censure him. He might even lose control of the Academy.*

When Char began to smile, Brianna began to relax. "You' re happy about the baby?"

Her question brought Char back to himself. He allowed his grin to widen then rolled over and kissed her soundly. Lifting himself up onto an arm, he looked deep into her eyes. "Yes, I' m happy about the baby."

Tears welled in Brianna' s eyes and rolled down her cheeks.

Char rolled onto his back taking Brianna with him. "Please, don' t cry, Brianna."

"But I' m so happy!"

Bemused, Char stared at her. "You cry because you are happy? Am I ever going to understand you?"

Brianna hiccupped. "I hope not." She sniffed. "You' re not angry?"

She thinks I' m angry? "Why would I be angry about having a child?"

"You weren' t exactly shouting with joy when you found out!"

"Oh no, you don' t!" Char exclaimed as he hugged her tight. "I refuse to quarrel with you."

Brianna relaxed. Char wasn' t upset. Smiling coyly, she began to purr as she moved sensuously against him. His eyes narrowed, but he continued to smile. "Are you sure you know what you are starting?"

"I know exactly what I am starting," she answered with a low, sexy laugh. Her hand began to massage the bulge between his thighs, a bulge that began to harden and lengthen with her first caress.

Char's breath caught in his throat. Though Brianna had always been a willing partner, this was the first time that she had initiated sex.

Her hands moved to the buttons on his uniform. Once she had them open, she began to rub his chest sensuously. Then her head dipped and she began to suck on his flat nipples.

Pushing himself to his feet, he stripped off his clothing and then divested Brianna of hers. Stretching out on his side next to her, he rested his hand gently on her stomach. His head followed and he kissed her gently. Grasping his hair, she pulled his mouth to hers.

Char woke Brianna with a kiss.

Smiling sleepily, she said, "Shouldn't you be driving the ship?"

Char shook his head. Another one of her odd expressions. "Ademis checked in earlier. When I told him you were pregnant, he told me to stay with you today. I'll take his shift later." He put his hand on her stomach. "When?"

"Lorilana thinks I'm about a month pregnant, but she's wrong."

He cocked an eyebrow. "Why is that?"

Char slid his hand down her belly and buried his fingers in her fiery curls.

Arching, she gasped, "I believe I got pregnant the first time we made love."

"The women on your planet know these things?" he asked and licked newly sensitive nipples.

"No!" Brianna began to squirm.

His fingers were working their usual magic between her thighs.

"Then how can you be so sure?" he countered as he kissed and nibbled his way down her torso.

"Because, I just know. Char!" Brianna exclaimed as his mouth replaced his fingers.

Threading her fingers through his hair, she arched into his mouth.

Heat exploded low in Brianna's stomach as Char stabbed his tongue into her.

"You taste so sweet," he murmured as he sucked and lapped. "Honey, Drakian honey." He nipped her clit.

"Oh God!" She squeezed his head between her thighs. "More, please, more."

Chuckling, Char parted her labia so his tongue could play with the sensitive bud hidden between them. He sucked, lapped, kissed, and nipped, all the while inhaling her lusty scent and relishing her unique taste. No woman had ever tasted so sweet.

Brianna closed her eyes as her stomach muscles clenched. Char's tongue was just as magical as his tail.

When Brianna tensed, Char slid up her body, sliding his cock into her until he was deeply embedded. He captured her open mouth and sucked her tongue into his mouth. After only a few powerful thrusts, her internal muscles gripped his cock. Oozing moisture surrounded him and he exploded.

As usual, Char regained control of himself first. He watched intently as his wife lay panting, struggling to regain her composure.

Once her breathing quieted and her heart stopped racing, Brianna shot a perplexed look at him. "Why haven't you done that before?"

"Because, after marriage, that's the first gift a Drakian husband gives to his wife when he learns of her first pregnancy," he answered with a chuckle. "Ademis wouldn't deny you your first gift."

Her face almost the same color as her hair, Brianna bolted upright. "You mean he knew exactly what you'd be doing?"

Char nodded, stretching and resting his hands behind the back of his head. "You'll have to get used to the Drakian preoccupation with sex, love," he said gently. "We aren't being cruel. It's just the way we are."

Her expression was resigned. "I know, but it'll take time. You'll have to be patient. Just don't ever expect me to be nonchalant about people around me being nude. And don't expect me to walk around naked if anyone else is around. It's not going to happen."

Char pulled her into his arms. "I am a very patient man."

Brianna relaxed against his chest, her fingers tracing his dragon as they often did. "Do you want a boy or a girl?"

His answer was immediate. "It really doesn't matter. I'll love it no matter what, and either a boy or a girl can become the Alalakan heir."

"The Alalakan heir?"

But Char was silent, the ramifications of what he' d just said dawning on him. *The Alalakan heir. That means I' ll head the clan now. But Rodane was supposed to…*

"Char?"

"What? Oh. The first child of a generation who produces a child of his or her own, in marriage, becomes the clan heir. Though my brother has been married a number of years, he and his wife have no children. You, my love, have made me the heir apparent to the Alalakan clan," Char explained, wonder now in his voice.

Brianna stared at her husband. "What exactly does that mean?"

"Eventually, I' ll take my father' s place as head of the clan. If this child you now carry presents us with our first grandchild, that child will eventually take my place."

"But if we have another child who marries and has a baby before this first one, then that one will take your place?"

He nodded.

Brianna shook her head. "Your clan is really going to love me. Not only will you be bringing a new wife from an unidentified planet, she' ll be pregnant. Your parents will probably want to throw me out on my ear."

Char answered with a kiss to her nearest nipple. "My parents will love you."

"Humph! How many men have said that and lived to regret it? Are there any special customs I need to know about?"

"Customs?" Char asked in a drowsy voice as he closed his eyes. "What do you mean?"

"I don' t know," Brianna answered honestly. "I still don' t know how your culture works. What' s expected of a pregnant woman?"

"That she look beautiful," was the sleepy answer.

"I can see you aren' t going to be much help," Brianna muttered in vexation. "Thank goodness Meri is here."

Staring at her relaxed husband, Brianna continued, "We have some customs on Earth you probably don' t know about. One is circumcision for male children."

Char settled into an even more comfortable position. "Circumcision?"

Brianna propping her elbows on Char's chest to watch his reaction. "Hmmm. That's when the foreskin is cut from the penis to help prevent infections and disease."

Char's eyes snapped open. "What!"

Brianna began to laugh. His reaction was all she'd hoped for.

"You are making that up!"

She smiled. "No, I'm not."

Char glared.

Smirking, she looked down her nose at him.

"On Drakan," he continued, "there's only one way to handle a tease."

Gripping her upper arms firmly, Char flipped her onto her back and buried his face between her thighs. Before she lost the ability to think, Brianna made a mental note to herself to tease her husband on a regular basis.

Chapter Nine
Two-and-a-half months later

Ademis appeared in the doorway and motioned for them to follow him. "Hurry! Bakom is occupied in his quarters, and Odam and Eliana are checking their equipment. The shuttle has docked at the front of the ship. Our luggage has been transported down. All we need do now is follow. I just hope this pilot of yours knows what he is doing, Meri. His docking struck me as a bit riskier than it should have been."

Meri grabbed Celene. Then she and Brianna hurried down the passageway.

Beti and Kahn were waiting at the end of the corridor.

They led the way to the forward airlock, where Char waited. "That pilot takes more chances than I like, Meri. Who' d your father send to get you?"

"It couldn' t be," Meri muttered as the airlock door slid open to reveal a tall figure. With a joyful shriek, Meri practically tossed Celene to Brianna and flung herself into the man' s arms.

"Damn," Adem muttered.

A string of expletives erupted from Char' s mouth.

Brianna stared at the man who hugged Meri so enthusiastically. "Who is he?" she asked her husband.

Char only cursed more.

The stranger released Meri. "Where' s the new Hardan Princess, Cousin? I hear she has a tail. Won' t that set dear Grandmama on her ear?"

At first, his attention was centered on Celene, but then he glanced at Brianna' s face. In one stride he stood before her and took her free hand in his. "Beautiful lady, my heart is yours. Come with me and I will fly you to the stars," he murmured seductively as he lifted her hand to his lips.

"Let up, Bandalardrac," Char snarled as he slipped Brianna's sleeve off of her shoulder to display her dragon. "She carries the Alalakan heir."

Sending a shocked glare at Char, Brianna struggled to hold Celene and readjust her dress as it fell halfway down her breast. "Char!"

"Don' t argue, Brianna," Char snapped in a voice she had never heard him use before.

Ademis lifted the cooing Celene from Brianna's arm and in an unenthusiastic tone said, "Hello, Ban."

Releasing Brianna's hand slowly, the stranger smiled, but his eyes never left Char. "As usual, Char, you find the finest of everything and have the good sense to know when you do." Turning to Meri, he continued, "I was told to get you down to the palace immediately. Shall I land in the central courtyard?"

"You wretch," Meri said in a relieved voice, "knowing you, you' d enjoy trying to land there just to annoy Father."

"Now, Meri," he said motioning them through the airlock and into the shuttle, "I don' t try to annoy your father. I don' t really think I could because he always laughs. I try to annoy Grandmama."

"There' s no time for a family reunion," Char growled.

Forestalling an argument, Ademis said, "Bakom is on board."

The other man' s eyes narrowed, and he became all business. "I have a special cradle for the baby next to the last two seats."

As Ademis strapped his daughter into her cradle, Brianna slipped into the seat next to Meri. "I' ll sit here."

As soon as Char was seated behind their pilot, Brianna turned to Meri. "Who is that? Why does Char dislike him so?"

"My cousin, Bandalardrac. He' s my father' s youngest sister' s son and definitely the rebel in the family. As soon as he learned to fly, he sold some of his mother' s jewels and bought a spaceship. Grandmama was livid!"

"Were they valuable?"

Meri shrugged. "Of course."

Brianna stared at the back of Bandalardrac' s head. "Why doesn' t Char like him?"

Meri squirmed in her seat. "It' s really nothing important."

Brianna looked at her friend with narrowed eyes. "Talk, Meri."

Meri glanced back at Brianna nervously. "Bandalardrac loves women, every woman. If I weren' t his cousin, Ademis wouldn' t let him anywhere near me. *I* wouldn' t let me anywhere near him. Over the years, he' s made a game of taking women away from Char."

Brianna shook her head. "So, Char thinks your cousin will take me from him. How could he be so stupid?"

Meri smiled. "Men aren' t the most intelligent beings in the universe."

Brianna glanced towards Meri' s cousin. "But I can understand why. Your cousin is one of the most handsome men I' ve ever seen. He' s half Drakian, isn' t he?"

Meri nodded. "My aunt went against Grandmama' s wishes when she married Ban' s father."

The object of Brianna' s curiosity piloted the shuttle with great skill. Only a few inches shorter than Char, Bandalardrac Hardan had the best of the Medirian and Drakian races combined in his features. Black eyebrows rode above vibrant, dark eyes, which were rounder than a Drakian' s. A hawk-like nose sat above full, expressive lips. Rather than being heavily muscular, though, as were some Medirians, his body was slim and athletic. Like his Medirian mother, he had gills and no tail. His skin tone, however, was neither Drakian nor Medirian but a pleasant mixture of the two, a warm tan with a subtle olive undertone, much like a person of Spanish or Italian heritage back on Earth. All in all, he was a very attractive man.

Brianna leaned back and closed her eyes. Damn, but alien men were sexy.

Brianna laughed and spun around awkwardly when she stepped away from the shuttle. As Meri had warned her, it was humid, but she didn' t really care. "I don' t care if it' s a hundred degrees. I' m finally out of that damn cabin!"

Char smiled at his wife. Brianna' s joy at being off the ship and under the open sky was infectious. Catching her in his arms, he lifted her up and swung her in a circle. "You may be giddy with your freedom, love, but the noon humidity during the Medirian summer would sap the strength of the strongest man. You' re conserving yours for two."

"I' ve been cooped up so long!"

"Cooped up?"

"Char!"

He laughed. "Very well. If you promise to go to the palace and rest for a few hours, I' ll take you to the merchants' shops."

She wrapped her arms around his neck. "Shopping! You' re the most wonderful man in the universe!"

"Ah, sweet Brianna," Bandalardrac interrupted, "you do not yet know me."

Brianna giggled at Char' s scowl. The words she whispered in his ear calmed him and eventually he began to grin. Sweeping her completely into his arms, he carried her towards the palace.

A brooding look on his face, Bandalardrac watched as Char strode away, but as soon as Meri touched his arm, a dazzling smile appeared on his face.

Meri voice was low. "Don' t, Ban. Please. Brianna' s become very dear to me. Bakom' s been enough of a worry. Don' t add to their problems."

Ban smiled at his cousin. "You know I' d never do anything to hurt you, Meri."

Meri smiled and gave Ban a quick, hard hug. "Thank you, Ban. I' ve never believed all of those stories about you."

He smiled back at her, mischievously. "That doesn' t mean I can' t pay court to the beauteous Brianna, if for no other reason than to aggravate Char."

"Ban!" Meri exclaimed, but then she began to laugh. "You' re incorrigible."

"I certainly hope so, Cousin. I certainly hope so."

* * * * *

Bakom sat in his quarters as the ship approached Drakan. Earlier, he' d heard the shuttle for the Medirian Princess dock and leave. Nor could he complain about Char delaying their arrival on Drakan because the shuttle docked with the *Restoration* as it passed close to Mediria.

He gnawed his lower lip. Alalakan was planning something, he just knew it. He' d managed to keep the specimen hidden in his quarters. She had to be a bed toy for him, to help relieve the boredom of the journey, and he didn' t want to share her. Why else would he guard her so closely?

Most of Bakom' s equipment and possessions were packed for off-loading, but he' d turned on his personal view screen once more. The picture showed his specimen' s naked body strapped on his examining table. He watched as Odam jabbed the needle into her thigh. Her instant reaction to the mithrin once again registered in the small section of his mind that remained dispassionately apart from the rest of him. Only humans reacted that quickly, but this was the first of many tests.

As usual, Bakom closed off the logical part of his mind to concentrate on the woman' s lush body. His own body hardened and his tail jerked, demanding release. He pounded his fist into his hand in frustration. To think the Alalakan had this to himself! At that moment the screen went blank, as it had on every one of his previous viewings. It marked Alalakan' s interference and theft of his specimen.

Eliana walked into the lab and saw him sitting in front of the darkened screen. A look of irritation crossed her face, quickly masked. "Everything is ready to be sent to the Academy once we dock at the space station."

Bakom turned to face his assistant. Eliana was hermaphroditic, as he was, but in her, the feminine attributes of his race had chosen to make themselves more evident. Her tail was shorter than normal and her breasts were larger. He was fairly certain that any children she bore would be single sexed. He also knew she never lacked for sexual partners. He' d enjoyed her himself often, though she didn' t make a point of seeking him out.

As she passed, Bakom reached out and grabbed her hand. Turning it over, he kissed her palm. Not bothering to consider her feelings, he unfastened the top of her Academy uniform. He licked his lips as her breasts spilled out. Using both hands, he stripped her tunic and loose pants from her until she stood naked. His breath quickened as he turned her around. Flipping the switch to his viewer, Brianna' s naked body once again lay before his passion-glazed eyes. He made short work of his own clothing, and then began massaging Eliana' s buttocks. His own tail caressed her leg and then stabbed between her thighs, seeking entry. His erect clitoris nudged the cleft between her buttocks. Lost in his own fantasy, he did not notice her less than enthusiastic response.

Eliana braced herself against the counter and grimaced. Dr. Sendenton dem al' Lorilana owed her plenty for this.

The com-link from Bakom's quarters flashed in the control room as the *Restoration* finished docking at the Drakian orbiting space station. Miklan finished his systems check before answering. Casting a glance over his shoulder at Lorilana, he said, "Here it comes."

Flipping a switch, Miklan said, "Control."

"I am ready to disembark," Bakom said. "I demand that the specimen be brought to me."

Miklan struggled to maintain a dispassionate tone. "I'm sorry, Dr. Bakom, but Brianna left on the Medirian shuttle with Princess Merilinlalissa and her party."

"What! I demand to speak with the captain."

"The captain accompanied the party to Mediria."

"I'll have Alalakan before the Council on theft charges. He had no legal right to take that specimen from me!"

"I'm sorry, Doctor. It's my understanding that the princess demanded her presence. During the course of our journey home, it was discovered that Brianna's planet holds a sizable population of dols and orcs. The princess overrode all prior claims because of this information, as outlined in the Federation charter."

Bakom sat back. The dols and orcs! "Why wasn't I informed when this discovery was made?"

"The Princess has a message she wished transferred to you after we docked, Doctor. I will download it now," Miklan said. Then he terminated their link.

Brooding, Bakom stared at the screen as he finished reading the princess' message. She'd made it very clear that her family didn't consider him fit to be First President of the Academy and wouldn't allow him to be involved with the recovery of the dols and orcs in any way. Any discourse with the Academy would be conducted through the Second President, Sendenton don al' Dadon for the simple reason that Sendenton had never kidnapped a child. The princess also advised him never to set foot on Mediria again. The girl's relatives would exact their revenge in their own way, and the royal family would make no move to protect him. She hadn't mentioned the assassins, but the implied threat was there.

Bakom snarled as he cleared the screen. The Aradab brat had been a worthless piece of humanity, and the entire incident had been totally blown all out of proportion. Now, though, he' d been blocked from getting his hands on that woman he so wanted. But that could be taken care of. He finished packing the computer away and began to make plans.

* * * * *

Brianna stared in wonder as she wandered through their suite. "It' s so lavish, Char. I' ve never seen anything like this."

"Nothing like this on your planet?" Char asked as he stripped off his clothing. The form-fitting uniform he usually wore on his ship was entirely too uncomfortable for the midday humidity of Mediria.

"Of course there is. *I' ve* just never been anywhere that was so opulent," she answered as she picked up the uniform he had carelessly dropped on the floor. "Who picked up after you before you were married?"

A languid grin stretched across Char' s face. "I ' picked up' after myself, of course."

"Then why do you always throw everything all over now?" Brianna grumbled as she folded the uniform and laid it on a chair.

"Because you enjoy taking care of me so much."

"Oh!" she gasped as his arms went around her. He pressed his erection against her back. He wrapped his tail around her thigh.

"Maybe I should just let you take care of yourself from now on," she said breathlessly. But Char never answered her. He was too intent on other things.

Pulling her dress up over her head, he placed wet kisses on the side of her throat while his fingers delved down the front of her panties into the rapidly moistening cleft between her thighs. Sighing, she leaned back against him. Soon his play was not enough. He scooped her into his arms and carried her to the bed, her afternoon nap completely forgotten.

* * * * *

"Not there, you damn fool," Bakom snarled as he supervised the loading of his equipment for transport back to the Academy. "That goes in the other vehicle." Still fuming over the way the princess and Alalakan had spirited his specimen away, he ran the princess's message through his mind repeatedly. The discovery of the dols and orcs gave the Medirians first right to contact the planet, which would preclude Academy rights. Collecting specimens from the planet would be next to impossible. He had to get the woman back from Chardadon.

"Odam, Eliana," he called as the last crate was secured.

"Yes, Doctor."

"Our specimen was stolen, and we must retrieve her."

"But, Doctor," Eliana said, "they're on Mediria."

"Ah, child," he said stroking her face, "still so naive and innocent. Odam, the usual contact."

"Yes, Doctor. Do you need us for anything else?"

"No. Use this time for yourselves. We've been on that damn ship for almost a year."

Bakom joined the driver and went with his equipment to the Academy.

Odam leered at Eliana. "I know of a tavern with private rooms."

Eliana snaked her arms through his. "That sounds wonderful, but first we must contact the doctor's friends."

Odam leered even more and pinched Eliana's nipple. His tail began to jerk. "Our contact will be there also."

"Well, then," she said catching his tail and stroking it, "let's hurry."

* * * * *

Three hours later, a cloaked Kindis dem al' Eliana glanced furtively about a dark alley. Hugging the wall, she soon encountered a shadowy doorway. Knocking twice sharply, she ducked inside when the door opened. After the door was securely shut, the lights flashed on. Miklan and Cindar had waited patiently for their late-night visitor.

Shuddering out of her cloak and throwing it onto the floor, Eliana said, "You better have a big bathtub full of hot water. I feel as if I'll never be clean again."

Cindar gazed at her sister with a puzzled frown on her face. "I know Bakom is a despicable man, Meli, but he is very fastidious about his person."

Judy Mays

"I am not talking about Bakom. One need only shut one's eyes with him," she snapped. "No, I speak of Odam. He never bathes and his breath is horrible! Your aunt, my dear brother-in-law, owes me."

Miklan grinned. "My aunt will be happy to reward you in almost any way you wish. Now, what information do you have for us?"

"Bakom has agents on Mediria with orders to kidnap Brianna."

Miklan frowned but nodded. "Char expected something like this, but I'll send a message immediately."

As Miklan disappeared through an interior doorway, Eliana began to strip off her clothing. "Where's your bathtub, Cindar?" she said dropping her clothing into a waste shaft. "I swear the last bed was full of Varcian fleas."

Cindar laughed as she led her sister to the bathroom. Varcian fleas were as big as small coins.

* * * * *

Brianna soaked in a large bubble-filled tub. Leaning back and stretching out her legs, she sighed contentedly. At last, a tub big enough! A new turquoise dress hung in her closet along with some other things she'd need in the next few days. By then, the other clothes she'd ordered during her shopping expedition that afternoon would be delivered.

Closing her eyes, she smiled to herself as she leaned her head back against a soft cloth. Char had been more than generous. After finishing her fittings, they'd gone to another shop and selected shoes, in another, underwear. He had shaken his head in a perplexed manner when she found the Medirian equivalent of bras. Maybe the women in Drakan didn't use them, but she needed support! She ordered two dozen in various colors.

It was in the last shop—the jewelers—that Char had been the most extravagant. There, he'd made most of the selections himself, choosing some of the most tasteful yet expensive jewelry she'd ever seen. Brianna hadn't thought about how wealthy his family was until she heard him tell the jeweler that price was no object. She fell into a light doze with a smile on her face.

Half an hour later, Char walked into the bathroom to check on his wife. As he thought might have happened, she was dozing in the tub. "Brianna," he whispered into her ear, "wake up. Dinner's in an hour."

Brianna opened her eyes and smiled.

"You better get out now, or I won' t be able to resist the temptation. The king will want to know why we' re late, and we' ll have to tell the truth."

Laughing, she stood up, wrapped herself in a fluffy towel, and stepped out of the tub. "You' re incorrigible." Cocking her head to the side, she added, "What are you wearing?"

He was wearing what she guessed was the equivalent of an Alalakan dress uniform. Cut along the same lines as the uniform he wore daily, it was completely white. A short jacket with a beautifully embroidered dragon on its lapel hugged his broad shoulders. All in all, he cut quite an impressive figure.

"My, my," she continued, "I' ll have to beat the women off of you with a stick."

He stared at her dubiously. "You aren' t going to hit anyone, are you?"

Brianna laughed. Removing the pins from her hair, she shook it as it tumbled to her hips. Recognizing the smoldering look that appeared in his eyes, she said, "You better go wait in the living room, Char, or we *will* be late for dinner."

After he left the room, Brianna sat on the vanity stool and perused the various perfume bottles and cosmetics in front of her. Sniffing the stoppers of each bottle, she chose a sensual, musky scent and applied it liberally to various places on her body. Choosing among the cosmetics, she highlighted her eyes and cheeks. Then she began to work on her hair.

Ten minutes later, she was sighing with frustration. Her hair had cooperated very well until she tried to fasten the elaborately jeweled turquoise comb Char bought her earlier that day. Still wrapped in her towel and holding the comb in place, she headed for the other room and Char' s help. Pushing the door open with her hip — they were the old-fashioned kind that swung opened and closed — she walked into the living room. "Char, can you get this fastened? I have too much hair to do it myself."

It was hard to say who was more surprised — Brianna or the people with Char. She recognized Lorilana, who was standing next to a tall, distinguished-looking man. However, he and the other three people in the room were complete strangers.

"She' s wearing a dragon!" the elegant woman next to Char gasped, her hand going to her throat.

"I made it very clear that I was married, Mother."

Her hands and hair dropping, Brianna flushed pink and choked out, "Mother! Your mother' s here, and you didn' t warn me? How could you do this to me?!" Turning, she fled into the bedroom.

Rodane stared after her. "What coloring! Was that dragon breathing fire? Grandmother is going to love her! Brother, in your position, I' d have married her myself! Is the rest of her that magnificent?"

"That, dear Brother, is something you' ll probably never know. You' ll have to excuse me for a moment. My *wife* needs me," Char said dryly. Picking up the comb Brianna had dropped, he followed her into the bedroom.

Four pairs of eyes turned to a very amused Lorilana.

"It seems as if you will have to do the explaining. Does she always turn colors like that?" asked the man by her side.

"She only turns red when she' s embarrassed, Dadon," Lorilana answered. "She calls it blushing. Also, her culture is more reserved than ours. Family members, except for small children, are almost always dressed in each other' s presence."

Jamiros crossed the room and poured himself a glass of wine. "A society along the lines of the Varcians, then."

"In some ways, yes," answered Lorilana, "but, in many other ways, completely different. The planet is unique unto itself as are the five we already know."

"Well, I' m his mother," said the elegant woman who had been so shocked at Brianna' s appearance. "I deserve an explanation." With those words, Alalakan dem al' Xdana strode purposefully towards the bedroom door.

"I wouldn' t recommend going in there right now," Lorilana called. "Char has become very protective."

"Not from his mother!"

The sight that greeted Xdana was far more intimate than she expected. She' d walked in on her youngest son many times when he was enjoying a woman, but she' d never seen the tenderness he was now displaying.

Char was seated on the bed with the woman on his lap leaning back against his chest. His right arm was wrapped snugly beneath her breasts, pulling the towel she wore tight to reveal what its loosely draped folds had hidden when she'd first walked into the living room, the slightly distended stomach of midterm pregnancy. Char's left hand was splayed gently over her belly, and he was whispering something in her ear.

Both of them heard the door open. A horrified look appeared on Brianna's face and she flushed scarlet.

Char's reaction was more direct. "Mother, *get out!*"

Speechless, Xdana quickly backed out of the room, wrenching the door closed behind her. She grabbed the back of a chair for support. "She's pregnant! Lorilana, is she really pregnant?"

Lorilana walked over to her friend and helped her to the sofa. Throwing an expectant look at the three equally stunned men, she began to chafe Xdana's hands. "Yes, and the baby is definitely Char's. You saw the dragon she wears. Char had me put it there two days after they were married."

All three men's eyebrows rose.

"Brianna has the spirit to go with the challenge that dragon represents," Lorilana continued. "He not only dotes on her, but he has also come to respect her judgments and insights. She's taught herself our numerical system and it making great progress with paralleling our and her alphabets."

Jamiros lowered himself onto a chair. "Well, that settles it then. She wears a dragon and carries the Alalakan heir. It's up to us to make sure the elders accept her into the clan."

"As if they will have a choice," Dadon murmured into his wineglass.

"The Alalakan heir," Rodane said in a soft voice. "I hope the baby is as colorful as its mother. A fiery-haired Alalakan."

The bedroom door opened and Char rejoined them. "My wife," he said in a biting tone that shocked everyone except Lorilana, "will join us momentarily. And, yes, she does carry the Alalakan heir. Are there any other questions?"

Char himself could not believe the tone of voice in which he addressed them, but he wouldn't tolerate any insults, even from his mother. However, his mind shied away from how much Brianna was coming to mean to him. Instead, he concentrated on his other purpose. She was the bait for his trap.

Xdana asked, "When' s the baby due?"

Char smiled to himself. His mother had finally hit on the fact that her first grandchild was on the way. "Brianna feels that she' s about four and a half months pregnant."

"Lorilana?"

"I think Brianna' s wrong, but she won' t listen to me."

"You' ve examined her?"

"As well as I could in Char' s quarters."

"What in the world was wrong with Medical? Don' t tell me the girl doesn' t understand modern medicine! Char, you must take the baby into account."

Lorilana sighed. "Xdana, Brianna' s world is almost as advanced as ours. It wasn' t safe for her to leave Char' s quarters. Bakom was on board, remember."

Xdana' s lips curled into a sneer. "Bakom. Jamiros, it is time to squash that bug."

Char smiled to himself. If anything would endear Brianna to his mother, it would be the need to protect her from Bakom.

Now completely dressed, Brianna stood in the bedroom in a quandary. She was still unable to fasten the clasp on the turquoise comb. Shrugging her shoulders, she decided that since they were family, someone out here would be able to help her. So everyone except Char and Lorilana was surprised when she appeared and said, "I' m sorry to be a bother, but I still can' t get this clasp fastened."

Laughing, Char crossed the room and fastened the comb. Then he took Brianna' s hand and presented her to his family and friends. "My wife, Alalakan dem al' Brianna of Earth. Brianna, my parents, Alalakan dem al' Xdana and Alalakan don al' Jamiros and my brother, Alalakan don al' Rodane. The tall gentleman next to Lorilana is her husband, Dr. Sendenton don al' Dadon."

Brianna gazed at the tall man next to Lorilana. He was even taller than Char, and laugh lines crinkled at the corners of his mouth and eyes. "You were named for him, weren' t you, Char?"

Bowing, Dadon said, "The Alalakan clan has added a flower of incomparable beauty to its garden."

Brianna began to smile. "Now I understand why Char was named for you. His parents realized that his tongue was going to be as flexible as yours."

Dadon smiled broadly.

Char smiled to himself — one down, three to go.

Rodane didn' t wait for Brianna to come to him. He stepped to her, lifted her off of her feet, and planted a kiss on each cheek. "I' ve been looking forward to the day I had a sister-in-law."

"So that you can come to me and complain about everything Char does that you don' t like," Brianna shot back breathlessly.

Laughing, Rodane swung her in a circle. "She' s perfect, Char. I think we should keep her."

"As if you have any choice," she whispered in his ear as she clung to him for balance.

"Here, Father," Rodane said as he set her in front of Jamiros, "your turn."

Grasping Brianna' s arm to help her regain her balance, Jamiros gazed at his new daughter-in-law speculatively. She had proved herself charming, but then that was to be expected of any woman Char chose. "Well, Daughter, what do you have to offer to the Alalakan clan?"

Brianna stepped back so she didn' t get a crick in her neck looking into his face. If this was what Char would look like in thirty or forty years, he was going to age very well. "Cranberry juice."

A confused expression appeared on Jamiros' face.

Brianna grinned. "Char has introduced me to Deslossian vandanug red. On Earth, it' s called cranberry juice. And we have lots of it, in different flavors."

Jamiros stared at Brianna. Then he began to smile broadly. "Vandanug red! Son," he said as he hugged Brianna, "I am very pleased to welcome your wife to our family and clan."

Everyone turned his or her attention to Xdana who sat as regally as any queen on the sofa. Silently, she stared back.

Sighing, Brianna looked first to Char for his nod of reassurance and then walked over to the sofa until she stood directly in front of her mother-in-law. "Alalakan dem al' Xdana," she began quietly, "I can understand your reservations. I' m from a world you didn' t even know existed, and I have, in a manner of speaking, taken your son from you. The circumstances were not as any of us would have wished, but," she continued in a more challenging tone as she slipped her dress from her right shoulder, "I wear an Alalakan dragon, and I carry Char' s child. I' m afraid you' re stuck with me!"

Everyone, including Char, stared in amazement. No one had so directly challenged his mother in years. More than one of them murmured, "Stuck with me?"

"Reminds me a great deal of a certain young lady," Jamiros interjected, "who told my mother that both she and the entire Alalakan clan could go hang because she was going to marry me no matter what."

Xdana began to laugh. Rising from the sofa, she gathered Brianna into her arms for a fierce hug. Then she turned to Char. "Son, you have brought us a daughter worthy of the Alalakan dragon. I' m more than happy to welcome her into the family. Any woman who would challenge a mother for her own son is worth having."

Char relaxed. Brianna met his gaze with raised eyebrows and a smile. And the evening hadn' t yet begun.

Chapter Ten

Brianna shifted her weight from foot to foot. Char and the rest of his family seemed completely at ease as they waited to be escorted to dinner, but the prospect of eating dinner with royalty had Brianna's stomach in knots. To make matters worse, the baby was turning somersaults. How was she supposed to make it through tonight? What if she used the wrong spoon or something? Did they even have spoons?

Just as she was ready to bolt back to her suite, Meri appeared. "You look lovely."

Leaning closer and taking Brianna's hand in hers, she whispered, "I'm sorry I didn't warn you about Char's parents, but I didn't know they were here until it was too late. Come on. I'm here to take you to dinner."

Char's mother raised an elegant eyebrow at Meri's informal attitude. The younger woman, however, was not intimidated. "It's a family dinner, Xdana. Don't worry about formalities."

The butterflies in Brianna's stomach calmed a bit. *A family dinner? Well, maybe it won't be that bad.* Brianna relaxed until Meri pulled her into the elegantly appointed throne room and a crowd of people turned to stare at her. *There have to be at least fifty people in this room!* "Meri!" she hissed as her friend practically dragged her towards the dais on the other side of the room, with the rest of the Alalakans trailing along. "Are all these people members of you family?"

"More or less."

"Just how big is your family?"

Meri glanced back at her friend and grinned. "Some of my great aunts and uncles and second cousins were too far away to get here in time. You'll probably meet them within the next few days."

Brianna swallowed, but before she could say anything else, Meri came to an abrupt halt in front of her parents.

An older version of Meri sighed, shook her head, and said in a vexed tone, "I had hoped marriage and motherhood would dampen some of your exuberance, Meri. I can see that I was wrong." Turning to

Char's mother, she continued, "Xdana, I apologize for my daughter leading you across the room at almost a dead run. I did try to teach her better manners."

Xdana laughed as she embraced her old friend. "At least," she said shooting a chagrined look over her shoulder at Char, "*your* child told you she was getting married. My wayward son, on the other hand…"

Taking Brianna's hand from Meri, Xdana said, "Carilinlalissa, Queen Hardan, I present to you my son's wife and carrier of the Alalakan heir, Alalakan dem al' Brianna of Earth."

Brianna was going to curtsy, but before she got the chance, she found herself in the queen's embrace. "Welcome to Mediria, my dear. So you carry the heir already. Wonderful."

Turning to the man at her side, Carilin said, "This is Brianna, darling. Now wipe that rather pompous look off your face. I'm not going to go through all that formal introductory falderal. The Alalakans have been friends too long."

"Now you know where Meri gets her impetuousness," Xdana whispered into Brianna's ear. "At Meri's age, Carilin was twice as bad."

"I heard that," the queen teased. "Since you don't know the proper tone to use with royalty, you're going to have to come with me and talk to Findal's mother."

A dismayed expression flashed across Xdana's face, but the queen already had a firm grasp on her wrist and was dragging her across the room much as Meri had done with Brianna.

Sighing, the king watched his wife stride away. "This means another lecture from Mother. You'd think after twenty-eight years of marriage and five children, Mother would realize that she's not going to change Carilin."

All the men around Brianna laughed. Meri nudged her father in the ribs. "Father, you haven't introduced yourself to Brianna. You're the king. She can't introduce herself to you."

"Now you're interested in protocol," the king grumbled in an amused voice. His smile widened as he acknowledged Brianna. "You may as well just call me Findal."

"But…you're the king!"

Findal's eyes gleamed with amusement. "Ha! A girl who knows the correct way to greet royalty. She'll satisfy the Patriarch himself."

Then he swept Brianna into a hug that was even more exuberant than his wife's. "Tell me, Brianna," he said after he put her back down, "are there really dols and orcs on your planet?"

"Yes, if your dols and orc look like the carvings Meri has." Brianna was definitely unsettled by the familiar treatment she was receiving. *Am I nuts? Or am I really dreaming? A green man with a crown on his head just gave me a hug!*

"Ha! It's true then! Everybody, it's true!"

Everyone in the room turned his or her attention to the dais where Findal had taken Brianna's hand in his. "I wish to present to you Alalakan dem al' Brianna, new wife to the Alalakan clan and carrier of its heir. As you can see, she is not a member of one of the five known human species. She comes from a planet on the far side of the galaxy which she calls Earth. Our dols and orcs reside there."

At first...silence. Then...chaos, extremely loud chaos. Everyone began talking or rather shouting at once. Findal pounded the ornate cane he carried on the floor. The booming noise eventually silenced everyone. "The location of the dols and orcs has been given to us as a gift by Alalakan dem al' Brianna, and she asks nothing in return. The Alalakans have given us the use of their largest ships to transport any dols and orcs who wish to return. This is a gift for which we can never offer adequate thanks."

The whispers of anticipation whipped through the crowd.

"Therefore, I have decided to offer Brianna the only gift that even approaches the honor she has brought to us. I offer her the Hardan name and ask her to join my family as my fourth daughter." Turning to Brianna, Findal said humbly, "Will you accept this small token of our esteem? Will you join our family?"

Breathlessly, the crowd waited. What Findal was doing was unprecedented. No one had ever become a member of the Hardan royal family except through marriage.

The Dowager Queen Mother fainted.

Completely out of her depth, Brianna looked to Char for guidance. By his expression and those of his family, she knew Findal's offer was completely unexpected. Looking about the room, it was the face of Meri's cousin, Bandalardrac that caught her attention. Emotions that clearly showed his approval, hope, and uncertainty flashed across what she was sure was a countenance that rarely displayed its true feelings. *God. What am I supposed to do?*

Char flashed her a supportive smile.

Sighing deeply, Brianna said humbly, "I will be honored to join your family."

Findal swept her into another hug. Laughing, he whispered, "I' d like to see Bakom try and get his hands on you now."

Locking her arms around his neck, Brianna planted a huge kiss on his cheek. It wasn' t every day that one was adopted by royalty.

Later that evening, Char leaned against the column on the right side of the dais contemplating all that had transpired, a smug smile on his face. This side trip to Mediria had worked out better than he could possibly have hoped. If Bakom tried to take Brianna now, he' d have every Medirian assassin in the galaxy after him.

Char watched as another member of the Hardan royal family cornered his wife. Too bad Findal' s mother revived enough to stay. The evening would have been more pleasant without her and some of the other members of the royal family. But Brianna had faced down the dissenters with dignity and aplomb. Though she didn' t say a word, the first outcry against her caused her to flush and raise her chin in the air. When he saw that dangerous sparkle flash in her eyes, he smiled and felt pity for the first person who thought he' d be able to browbeat her into denying the honor extended.

Char shook himself from his musings as his father joined him. "Your wife certainly is a success," Jamiros commented as Brianna and Meri were surrounded by yet another group of Hardan relatives.

"For more than one reason, it seems," Char commented lightly. The last group that had surrounded Brianna consisted of Meri' s unmarried male relatives.

"From what I observed with Findal' s Uncle Dardralarlac, those rakes should be very careful," Jamiros said in an amused tone. "Brianna has a temper to rival a Gattan."

Char grinned. "And won' t it be very interesting when the Gattan finally make her acquaintance?"

The grin quickly turned to a frown and Char' s nonchalant pose against the column snapped to one of alertness. Bandalardrac had joined the group around Brianna. Char tensed as the Mediria' s most infamous womanizer raised his wife' s hand to his lips. Before he could take a step in their direction he felt a hand on his arm.

"You won' t interfere," Jamiros said in a stern voice.

Char scowled but acceded to his father' s demand.

From various parts of the room, Alalakan eyes watched Brianna' s encounter with the most notorious rake on five planets.

Damn it, Brianna, if you mess up my plans... Unwilling to admit the true reason for his reaction to Ban' s presence at his wife' s side, Char concentrated on his plans for Bakom.

Unaware of the close scrutiny of her in-laws, Brianna laughed at Ban' s comments, but her attention kept wandering. Where had Char gone? Finally she saw him standing next to the dais, talking with his father. Sending him a blinding smile, she turned her attention back to Meri' s cousin.

Ban had stopped his one-sided conversation with Brianna soon after her attention had begun to wander.

"Oh, I' m sorry, Ban," she said looking up into his face. "Did you say something?"

Bandalardrac glanced over her head and caught Meri' s eye.

She smiled in commiseration.

Ban leaned closer to Brianna. "I was saying, the moons are lovely tonight. Come, and I will show you a view to take your breath away."

Her face brightened. "There' s more than one moon?"

"Three, but their radiance pales next to your lovely face."

Chuckling, Brianna shook her head. "Ban, you are a true rogue, and I think I will become very fond of you. But, I' ll stay here with Meri...and my husband."

Ban leaned closer. The fingers caressing her bare arm raised goose bumps. "He can never love you as well as I, sweet Brianna."

"Go bother some other woman, Ban," she said in an exasperated tone, "preferably one who isn' t married."

For an instant, the pain and loneliness in Bandalardrac' s soul was evident in his eyes, but he quickly regained control of himself. Smiling gaily, he bowed deeply and said, "I am ever at your disposal, newest cousin. Welcome to the family."

Spinning, he struck out blindly with no definite destination in mind, but he soon found himself nearing Char and his father. Changing direction slightly, Ban stopped before them.

"Jamiros," Ban said as he nodded his head stiffly in greeting. He turned his attention to Char. "You seem to have won, but if she ever comes to harm because of you... She is Hardan now, and Medirian revenge is swift."

"No swifter than Alalakan," Jamiros interjected enigmatically.

Char smiled. Brianna' s gentle set-down of Bandalardrac left him disinclined to accept Ban' s obvious challenge. Nodding slightly, he watched the younger man stalk away.

"I wouldn' t want to be the next person who crosses that young man," Jamiros murmured. "You may have trouble from him, Char. Your wife is a temptation to any man not already in his grave."

"I' ll watch him. However, I don' t believe he' ll do anything to besmirch his honor."

"Hardan honor?"

"No, Father, his Drakian honor, as you well know."

✳ ✳ ✳ ✳ ✳

The sun was streaming through the balcony doors when Brianna awoke. Char was not in bed, but she heard movement in the living room and assumed it was him. Stretching, she rose from the bed, went into the bathroom and turned on the water to fill the tub, adding a generous dollop of bubble bath. Back on Earth, she' d always preferred showers, but after being stuck in a spaceship for almost five months, soaking in a huge tub was too appealing to pass up.

In minutes the tub was full and, after pinning up her hair, she slid into the hot water. She was barely settled when Char appeared in the doorway naked, his erection making his purpose quite clear. She began to smile seductively as he crossed the room to stand before her.

"I promised myself I' d share your bath at the first opportunity," he said as he lifted a bottle and poured fragrant bath oil onto his palms. He eased into the tub and pulled her into his arms for a long, passionate kiss. Eventually his mouth broke away from hers. His nibbled down her neck to her shoulder to her breasts...her lovely, lovely breasts.

Arching her back, Brianna laced her fingers though his hair as he suckled first one nipple then the other. "More, Char, more. Now!"

Chuckling, Char licked her erect nipples once more. "Getting rather demanding, aren' t you?" He slid his fingers between her thighs.

152

She spread her legs wider. "Your cock. I want your cock inside of me."

"Get on your knees and turn around, love. I want to mount you."

Shuddering, she turned around and gripped the side of the tub. "Deep, Char. I want you deep."

"As deep as I can, love." Rising to his knees, Char began to massage her buttocks, spreading them and pressing them to back together. "You have the most beautiful ass I've ever seen, love." He trailed an oily finger down her cleft and pushed against her anus.

Brianna moaned.

He slid a thigh between her legs and pushed her legs wider apart, then slid his cock back and forth against her slippery vulva. Then, slowly, he pushed his cock into her.

Sighing, Brianna braced herself against the side of the tub as ripples of pleasure coiled up from between her legs. Char knew exactly where and how to stroke, pinch, and prod.

Soon his tail slipped between his thighs and hers to rub her clit.

Brianna moaned. God, but his tail was pure heaven. She swiveled her hips and pushed back each time his hips thrust forward. "Yes, oh yes."

As he thrust his cock as deeply as possible, Char continued to massage Brianna's buttocks, sliding a finger into and out of her anus. He felt his balls contract as her internal muscles pulled him deeper. When Brianna shuddered with release, he ground his hips against her buttocks one last time.

Some minutes later, Char sat back down in the tub and pulled Brianna down into his lap. Sighing, she rested her head against his shoulder and smiled. Raising her eyes, she met her husband's gaze in the mirror that hung across the room. "You knew that mirror was there the entire time, didn't you?"

He chuckled. "Watching your face as you climaxed heightened my own pleasure."

"Well, don't expect to have mirrors on all the walls and the ceiling in our home," Brianna said with mock seriousness.

A speculative look appeared in Char's eyes. "Mirrors on the ceiling?"

"Char!"

He laughed and hugged her to him. "I promise to leave all of the decorating to you," he teased. "Now, if you want to have breakfast before you attend your official adoption into the Hardan royal family, you better get out of this tub. You've dawdled enough."

Water streaming from her body, Brianna stepped from the tub. "And who caused me to dawdle in the first place, I might ask?" She grabbed the washcloth and dropped it on his head.

His laughter followed her as she walked dripping from the room. The angry shriek that came from the bedroom, however, had him out of the tub in a flash. A few quick strides and he stood dripping in the doorway where he found his wife confronting an unemotional Beti.

"How do people keep getting into our room?' she said angrily. "We better not have this problem at home."

While one part of his mind was extremely pleased that she referred to Drakan as home, another part agreed wholeheartedly with her. Casting an angry glance at Beti, he was silenced before he could ask any questions when she held up a key.

"Kahn and I will be your servants and protectors, Princess Alalakan dem al' Brianna. It is so commanded by the Matriarch of the Aradab," Beti stated.

Brianna gaped as she digested that bit of information. While she was doing so, Beti's gaze turned to Char. With a slight smile she added, "You are somewhat thin, Alalakan, but well-hung nevertheless."

"Char! Go put your clothes on. And you," she continued to Beti, "I don't want any servants or bodyguards."

Beti was undeterred by Brianna's outburst. "You are a Hardan princess. The Aradab guard the royal family. Kahn and I volunteered. We know your ways better than any others."

"But..."

"You are the key to the dols and the orcs. You will be protected at all costs."

"Char," she began in a pleading tone when he returned with a towel wrapped around his waist.

He shrugged. "Never try to argue with an Aradab. Moving a mountain one spoonful at a time is easier."

A smug expression appeared on Beti's face as she nodded her head once in Char's direction. Then she left the room.

Brianna stamped her foot. "You weren't very much help!"

Char dropped the towel from about his waist and walked naked to the huge closet where his clothing hung.

Brianna's anger was replaced with confusion when he returned. Instead of the customary green and gold or the formal white uniform he'd worn the previous evening, he was dressed far more casually, too casually. "How can you go dressed like that? You look like an Indian out of a Western movie. Are you sure that's proper clothing for the occasion?"

Char combed his hair back and fastened it behind his head with a silver clasp. "A what?"

"Indian—Native American—a race of people who live on Earth, sort of."

Brianna shook her head. She was being formally adopted into a royal family, and Char was dressed in what looked like a breechcloth. He wore no shirt but had metal armguards that reached from wrist to elbow. The colors of his dragon tattoo seemed to glow more brightly. Would she ever completely understand his alien culture? "Ah, don't you think you should put more clothing on?"

Glancing back, he smiled. "Your new family will find your choice of apparel far more intriguing than mine."

Her pique returned. She crossed her arms over her breasts. "I'm not going anywhere until this is settled. And if you think to sidetrack me with kisses or with threats to carry me into the throne room naked, I know very well that you'd never do it. Now, about this bodyguard business..."

Char sat down on a chair next to the bed and pulled on tall leather boots with metal knee plates. Stiff, brown leather rose above the knee plates halfway up the front of his thighs. "Brianna, if I knew of a way to send Beti and Kahn back home, I'd do so in an instant. Ask Findal. The Aradab sense of purpose has been a thorn in his side for years. Nothing, I repeat nothing, will sway them once they've made up their minds."

Rising, Char crossed the room to stand in front of her. "But I promise you that I will do my best to limit their presence. There probably isn't much I can do here, but once we get back to Drakan, I'll make sure they understand what privacy means."

She crossed her arms over her chest.

He cupped her face. "Don't you realize that I will do anything in my power to keep you happy?"

"As long as you think it' s for my own good. I' ve no doubts that there will be certain ' restrictions' placed on me, for my own wellbeing, once we reach Drakan," she answered him in a dissatisfied tone.

Pulling his unresisting wife into his arms, Char carefully rethought his position. *I need her to cooperate. To do that, she must be kept happy.* "Very well," he sighed, "I' ll do what I can."

Releasing her, he strode to the door, pulled it open, and called for Beti. When she appeared, he said, "While I cannot keep you or Kahn from guarding the doorway, you will not enter these rooms without approval from Brianna or myself. Is this understood?"

Beti shifted her gaze to the defiant Brianna who met her baleful stare without flinching. Sullenly, Beti jerked her head in agreement and disappeared from the room. Soon they heard the door to the outside hallway slam.

Brianna knew her smile was smug. "It' s about time I won one. Now, what the hell are you wearing?"

Smiling crookedly, he shrugged. "This is an ancient clan costume, which I' m wearing for the benefit of the Aradab and the Gattan. Both races hold very tightly to tradition. Your adoption into the Medirian royal family is unprecedented. Traditional Alalakan clan costume on my part underscores how honored I am that they have extended this honor to my wife."

Muttering something under her breath about weird alien customs, Brianna watched as Char walked over to the dresser and slipped on a signet ring she had never seen before.

"What' s that?"

Meeting her gaze in the mirror, he said, "My father gave it to me last night. It belonged to my grandfather."

A concerned look appeared in her eyes. "Your grandfather didn' t die while you were away, did he?"

He grinned. "No. My grandfather died four years ago. My father gave the ring to me because you carry the Alalakan heir. Someday, whichever one of our children presents us with our first grandchild will receive my father' s ring."

Pulling her against his chest, Char stared at her reflection as he caressed her stomach. Brianna was still naked, and he examined her closely in the mirror. Her breasts were certainly fuller than they had been, and her nipples and areolas were beginning to change from rosy pink to light brown. Brianna' s stomach, though, quickly drew his attention. Only a few weeks ago her stomach had been flat, but now there was a definite bulge that seemed to grow bigger on an almost daily basis. He felt a slight stirring beneath his hand.

In the mirror, Brianna' s contented gaze met the amazed expression in his eyes. "He' s very active, you know. That' s why I' ve been getting up so often during the night. He seems to think my bladder is a springboard."

Char wasn' t quite sure what a springboard was, but he got the general idea. "He?"

"Hmmm, it' s a boy. Women' s intuition, you know."

Char didn' t know, but after feeling his child move for the first time — shaking himself from his reverie and his uncertainty, Char reluctantly pushed his wife from his arms. "You will be receiving close family naked yet," he teased. "Lately you seem to want to spend all of your time with your clothing off."

Brianna' s head snapped up. "Over my dead body," she began, but at his the alarmed look, she softened and said, "It' s only another Earth expression. Don' t look so shocked."

"Then be careful what you say," he replied in a very disgruntled tone as she began to dress.

Meri had suggested that she wear something blue or green to her adoption ceremony since these were favored on Mediria. Naturally, Brianna chose to ignore this suggestion. She wore a bright yellow dress that left her right shoulder with its flaming dragon bare. Foregoing an elaborate hairdo, her hair flowed unconfined down her back. They' d just have to take her as she was, and she wasn' t adding any more syllables to her name."

"Ready?"

She turned to Char. "As I' ll ever be."

Opening a box, he placed one of the more unassuming pieces of jewelry he had bought, a red gold pendant, around her neck. For the first time, she saw the dolphin that had been carefully etched onto its surface. "You don' t want to antagonize any of the Hardans any more than necessary," he said in the teasing tone he used so often. "Findal' s mother will take one look at that flaming dragon and faint again."

Brianna sniffed. Tucking her arm in his as they left their suite and made their way towards the throne room, followed by the ever-present

Kahn, she countered, "I became an Alalakan before I became a Hardan. I don' t care if she likes it or not."

Char couldn' t have been more pleased with her answer, and his satisfied expression showed it. Brianna' s quick jab in the ribs, though, took the smug expression from his face.

As Brianna adjusted the pendant, Char allowed his mind to wander. While he had never been to an official ceremony marking a royal adoption before, he was sure that it wouldn' t be all that much different from various other royal functions he had attended over the years. The changes in his wife, however, both physical and mental, were very intriguing.

Earlier, when he' d felt his child move, unfamiliar emotions began to nudge his conscience. Bakom' s downfall was still of paramount importance to him. However, he willingly admitted to himself that he was fond of his new wife. Sexually, he knew it would be a long time before he tired of her, if ever. But the child... Before, he' d accepted its existence in an abstract way. Now, however...

During the private conversation Char and his father had after dinner the previous evening, he' d agreed that his marriage to Brianna, under any other circumstances, would have been too impulsive to be accepted without comment by the Alalakan clan elders. However, the fact that she was pregnant and the Alalakan heir was due to arrive in a matter of months would ease her acceptance, though some members of the clan might oppose his own appointment as future leader. For years everyone had assumed Rodane would take the position after Jamiros decided to step down.

Char' s thoughts then settled on his older brother. As he' d explained to Brianna, on Drakan the oldest child did not automatically become his father or mother' s chief heir. That was reserved for whichever sibling presented the clan with the first child of that generation. That honor would now belong to him, not Rodane. This was not something Char had ever thought would happen and he hoped that Rodane wouldn' t be hurt by this unexpected change of events. *Rodane can have the leadership. I only care about destroying Bakom.*

His musings were interrupted by another jab from Brianna. Bandalardrac was standing before them.

"Ready, Cousin?" he said somewhat enigmatically.

Brianna missed the warning scowl the suave Hardan received from her husband. "As ready as I' ll ever be," she answered nervously. "I don' t have to do much of anything, do I?"

"Just stand there and look beautiful," Ban answered while presenting his arm. Then he added, "By the way, *I* approve of your dress selection."

A resigned expression on his face, Char followed his giggling wife into the throne room.

Brianna shifted in her chair again as the head prelate of the Medirian Church droned on. A hand squeezed her shoulder gently and she cast a smile back at Char. Then she looked out over the gathered assembly. There were hundreds of people in the throne room and every one of them was staring at her. She couldn' t wait for this ceremony to be over.

Findal leaned over and murmured, "Pompous windbag."

Brianna bit her lip to keep from giggling.

"He' s winding down now," Findal continued. "Then all we have to do is present you to the ambassadors and we can finally eat."

The prelate turned towards them. "Alalakan dem al' Brianna, Princess Hardan, I present to you the Matriarch of the Aradab."

A very intimidating gray-headed Aradab woman strode up to the dais where Brianna sat with the rest of the royal family. She leaned over and gently traced the dragon on Brianna' s shoulder. Then she nodded and returned to her seat.

The prelate continued, "Princess Alalakan dem al' Brianna, I present to you the Patriarch of the Nessians."

The Patriarch' s skin was so darkly green that it was almost black. Long, snowy white hair cascaded down his back while laugh lines wrinkled the corners of his eyes and mouth. The elderly man took both her hands in his, spread them wide, and lifted her from her chair to stand before him. "Behold," he said in a surprisingly booming voice, "the journey of the dols and orcs begins and ends with this woman. As was foretold ages past, the flame of the dragon will return our friends and heritage to us. This woman is the flame of our future."

Kissing Brianna on both cheeks the Patriarch whispered to her, "You carry a fine, strong son, Daughter of my Heart. The stars will hold no boundaries for him."

Chuckling at the amazed expression on her face, the old man nodded to Findal and turned to leave. Stopping before Bandalardrac, he said in a voice only those on the dais could hear, "Yours are the wings of the Flame' s salvation. Do not fail in this task, for we will all fall with you. Your own happiness lies on her world."

From where he stood behind Brianna, Char scowled. *What did the old man' mean by that? He didn' t want Bandalardrac getting any ideas. Brianna was his!*

Brianna didn' t have the time to mull over what the Patriarch said, for the Federation ambassadors were being introduced to the new Hardan princess. If Werdarartun don al' Sundosal of Drakan was surprised by the day' s proceedings, he hid it rather well. Shorter than Char and more stoutly built, the elaborate embroidery on his shoulder identifying his clan was totally unfamiliar to Brianna. While it was certainly some kind of animal, she had no idea what it was. She was fairly certain that Char, Jamiros, or Rodane had warned Werdarartun what to expect at today' s ceremony. However, his eyes widened when he saw Brianna' s dragon.

After staring at it for a few minutes, his eyes met Brianna' s and she recognized the gleam of approval in them. After a word or two welcoming her to both the Hardan family and Alalakan clan, and apologizing for his wife' s absence due to the illness of their youngest daughter, the Drakian stepped aside and Brianna finally got her first good look at the other human members of the Federation.

Tarlus Varnji, the Varcian ambassador, bowed his head and presented his wife Opala. Both were shorter than Drakians and Medirians. Their skin was dark brown, the irises of their eyes were yellow, and except for eyebrows and eyelashes, they were absolutely hairless. A bony ridge that resembled, of all things, an Earth-type Mohawk haircut rose from their foreheads and tapered to the base of their skulls, dyed a very bright yellow. Brianna did not miss the flicker of surprise in Opala' s eyes at the color of her dress, nor the pleased expression that immediately followed it.

After a few words of welcome, the Varcians stepped aside and Qjin, the Deslossian ambassador, was presented next. He was tall, lithe, and albino white, including the hair that flowed down his back. Like Drakians, Qjin had pointed ears. Like Medirians, he was tailless.

The epitome of relaxed dignity, he approached Brianna with a welcoming smile and executed a deep bow from the waist. Then he surprised everyone on the dais by leaning forward and lightly touching the dragon on her shoulder and saying, "A worthy dragon for a worthy woman."

As he left the dais, Qjin stopped and met the eyes of both the Patriarch of the Nessians and the Matriarch of the Aradabs. A swift, unspoken conversation seemed to pass among the three of them, and then Qjin joined his counterparts from Varce.

Shifting, Brianna squeezed her thighs together and tore her eyes away from Qjin. Damn, but she had to pee. One more ambassador, the Gattan, and she could finally go find a bathroom.

But the Gattan ambassador's appearance was more of a surprise than she anticipated.

Two inches under six feet in height and stockily built, Brendis Frierson had fierce blue eyes that flashed from beneath bushy white eyebrows. He was not a young man, but he carried his mature years easily. A loosely flowing brown tunic belted with solid gold covered his torso to his thighs, but the sleeves did not conceal the muscular power of his arms. He wore loosely fitting pants tucked into highly polished black boots, Cossack style.

His wife, Gileen Makasdotir, was dressed much as her husband, although her tunic dripped with bright jewels and embroidery. She was as stocky as her husband though not as muscular. Instead of trousers, she wore a dark red, ankle-length skirt. Soft brown boots completed her ensemble.

Both of them had shoulder-length gray hair that was combed behind pointed ears, hair with evenly spaced black stripes running through it. Stripes that did not stop at the hairline, but continued across their faces. Stripes that could be seen extending from the backs of their hands and on up their arms.

Brianna stared. "They look like white tigers," she said to no one in particular. "Does everyone on Gattan look like them?"

Brendis and his wife stopped before her, refraining from any type of bow, appraising her reaction to them. Sticking out his chin, he scowled. "You are upset by our appearance, Brianna, Princess Hardan. Why is that?"

Everyone in the vast throne room had held his or her breath. The Gattan were an extremely sensitive people who took insult very easily.

Brianna swallowed nervously and said, "Do you have cats on your planet?"

Though he wore a Medirian translator, the ambassador was obviously confused by her question. *"Cats?* I do not know this word."

Brianna swallowed. *Did I insult him? Have I said something wrong?* Taking a deep breath, she continued slowly, hoping desperately she wasn' t going to insult him. "On my planet there are animals we call cats, of many varieties and species. Your coloring is remarkably like a variety of cat we call a tiger."

Gileen stared at the dragon on Brianna' s shoulder and then locked eyes with the younger woman. "You can provide us with a picture of this animal?"

Brianna turned to Char.

He nodded. "While orbiting Brianna' s planet, we were able to record numerous transmissions from various sources, Gileen Makasdotir. Whether there is a picture of one of these tigers, I don' t know. Brianna hasn' t been able to catalog everything yet."

Brendis Frierson crossed his arms, planted his feet, and said, "We will see what you have now."

Findal sighed and signaled a servant. The assembled members and guests of his court tittered and shifted from foot to foot nervously. About five minutes later, the court librarian appeared with the Medirian version of a laptop computer. Nodding uncertainly to the group on the dais, the old librarian went directly to Findal, who waved the nervous man to Brianna.

"My new *daughter,*" Findal said, "requires pictures of her planet from those Captain Alalakan provided."

"What is it you wish to see, your highness? We' ve tried to continue your work, but in some cases we are not sure what a particular image represents."

Despite the obvious seriousness of the situation, Brianna rolled her eye at the title with which the librarian addressed her. "I' d like to see all the animals you have."

The librarian brightened immediately. "We feel that we have all of those, especially the mammals and birds, identified."

After a quick scan of the material, Brianna sighed with disappointment. Looking up at the unmoving Gattan in front of her, she' d said, "I' m sorry. There aren' t any tigers. There is a lion, though."

Turning the screen of the computer to face them, Brianna motioned the Gattan ambassador and his wife forward.

"This ' cat' can be found on your planet?" Brendis asked. "There is a ' cat' that resembles us?"

"Yes." Brianna was not sure exactly what, at this point, the Gattan was thinking.

Two faces slowly broke into wide smiles. Each Gattan took one of her hands and placed their palms against hers.

They have retractable claws!

"Welcome to the new Hardan princess," Brendis said. "We recognize the Alalakan dragon and its heir."

Not knowing what to say, Brianna remained silent.

Both Char and Findal rose and stepped forward to stand on either side of her. Taking the Gattans' hands from hers, each man matched one of his palms to that of the Gattan who faced him.

Then Brianna' s gasp echoed throughout the chamber when Brendis and his wife unsheathed wickedly sharp claws, and before the men could draw their hands away, slashed their palms deeply enough to make blood flow.

Brianna' s eyes flashed as she rose from her chair, unmindful of the computer sliding from her lap to be caught by the still-nervous librarian just before it crashed to the floor. "What' s going on? What are you doing?"

"She rises to their defense like a Gattan, Husband," Gileen said as she sheathed her claws. "The dragon she carries on her shoulder is warranted."

Brendis turned his attention back Brianna. "Fear not for your loved ones, Alalakan dem al' Brianna, Princess Hardan. We deem you worthy of your new position and the dragon you carry on your shoulder."

Crossing her arms over her chest, she demanded. "What gives you the right to decide my worthiness?"

Findal' s mother fainted.

Everyone else in the room gasped at her audacity. Even Char paled at her demand. Gattan blood feuds had begun over much less.

Brendis' s deep laugh filled the throne room. Gileen, smiling broadly, went so far as to hug Brianna. "A mate truly worthy of the Alalakan dragon. We meant no disrespect, child. Ours is a warrior race. Allowing us to blood their palms proved to us that your father and husband hold your honor and ours in the highest regard."

Brianna stood with her hands fisted on her hips. "What' s wrong with my own blood?"

Gileen smiled gently. "You carry a child. No Gattan would ask blood from a pregnant woman."

"Well, it would be nice if someone explained these things to me before they happened."

Char, who had wrapped his hand in a towel quickly provided by one of Findal' s servants, used his unwounded hand to exert gentle pressure on Brianna' s shoulder. She sat down—reluctantly.

Shooting a disgruntled look over her shoulder, she grumbled, "Is there anyone on this damn planet who doesn' t know I' m pregnant?"

The Gattans' laughter followed them from the dais.

Char leaned forward and whispered in his wife' s ear, "Probably not."

Chapter Eleven

Brianna inhaled deeply as a warm, salt breeze wafted in off the ocean. Loud shouts had her shading her eyes against the sun' s glare off the clear, blue water as Meri' s younger sisters burst out of the water. Both wore skimpy thongs and nothing else. Their brother exploded to the surface and surged after them. His own suit was little more than a small pouch that cupped his genitals.

Meri yelled something and Brianna blushed even more. Meri' s suit covered more of her body. The bottom half anyway. Her breasts were just as bare as her sisters' .

Celene shrieked happily and disappeared beneath the waves that swirled around Meri' s thighs. She didn' t surface.

Brianna shuddered. She' d never get used to them having gills.

A shadow stretched across her legs as Ban squatted beside her chair. "Enjoying your afternoon by the sea?"

Nodding, she pulled her gaze away slowly. If that little bag holding his cock and balls were any tighter, he' d burst the seams. Her lips twitched. That would be an interesting sight! *I wonder if I can talk Char into wearing one…just for me that is.*

Ban stood and shifted his attention to his cousins.

Brianna took the opportunity to admire him. A flat stomach gave way to six-pack abs. Damn, but he was built. But why was he wearing that short vest over his chest?

Her gaze continued upward.

He was grinning at her. "Aren' t our Medirian suits to your liking, Cousin?" he teased. "I think you' d turn heads even in Drakian' s jaded society if you wore one. Why not display those lovely breasts?"

She pushed herself up off the lounge. "If I didn' t know better, I' d think you and Char were brothers, you sound so much alike at times. I' m gong for a swim." Brianna sauntered away from him towards the waves that lapped the sand. Stopping once, she stooped to pick up a five-sided pink shell. Sighing with delight, she walked into the warm surf.

Meri' s youngest sister Jamilinlalissa was diving not far from shore. She suddenly surfaced next to Brianna and began to splash her. Joining in the fun, Brianna waded into waist-high water and was able to give as good as she got until Jami dove. Lacking gills of her own, Brianna was at a definite disadvantage. So when she felt the hands around her ankles, she took a big breath and prepared herself for the dunking she knew she was about to get.

Ban was standing next to Meri knee deep in the water when Brianna disappeared. When Jami surfaced, he called, "Be careful of your new sister' s temper, Coz. She may not appreciate being dunked."

Jami flung her long hair back over her shoulder. "I didn' t dunk her, Ban. I was trying to sneak up on you, but water' s too shallow."

Ban didn' t think. He simply dove, heading for the spot he' d last seen Brianna. Meri grabbed Celene and headed for the beach, calling to her brother as she waded through the surf, "Kav! Run for Father and Char. Something has happened to Brianna!"

As Kavlidardrac sprinted towards the palace, Jami dove and followed Ban. She soon surfaced. "There' s no sign of her," she sobbed. "Ban streaked by me, but I don' t know if he saw anything or not."

Holding her struggling daughter in one arm and her crying sister in the other, Meri was unmindful of the tears that streamed down her own face.

Brianna struggled against the strong hands that gripped both her wrists although she was intelligent enough not to fight the breathing apparatus her abductors placed over her face. Without it, she' d be dead. She could tell they were heading for deeper water. The surface kept getting farther and farther above her head. She had to slow them down! Thrashing her legs about, she was able to tangle them with those of one of her abductors.

Then Ban exploded into their midst.

Releasing her wrists, both of her captors quickly unsheathed long, wicked-looking knives. Ignoring her, they began to work in concert, circling Ban like a pair of hungry sharks.

He was definitely at a disadvantage. He' d obviously exerted a great deal of energy to catch them, and he was not carrying any weapons. Jackknifing between them, he grabbed her arm and pushed her up towards the surface.

Moving as quickly as she could, Brianna swam away, but not before she saw a knife slice through Ban' s vest.

Blood followed her upward.

Brianna was still far from the surface when she felt another hand on her ankle. Panicking, she began to struggle as she felt other hands on her waist. Those hands, however, quickly spun her around and she found herself looking into a face very similar to the Patriarch' s. As soon as she made eye contact, the woman who held her released her and pointed to the surface. Looking around and down, Brianna saw at least fifty Nessians, both men and women. Relaxing in the protective circle, she nodded and continued up.

When her head broke the surface of the water, she pulled the plastic bubble from her face. Taking deep breaths, she turned to face the Nessian who had surfaced next to her.

"Bandalardrac Hardan is down there!"

"Others have gone to his aid, Flame of Mediria."

More Nessian heads broke through the water, among them Ban' s and two strangers she didn' t recognize. The water around Ban was tinted pink. His back was turned towards her so she couldn' t see how bad his cuts were. The Nessians were rubbing some kind of salve into the wound. They also managed to get him to swallow some liquid from a flask, which was reviving him rapidly. Already he was treading water on his own.

The woman touched Brianna' s arm. "Others now come."

A motor launch neared. Swells surged as it circled their position, and Brianna was swamped. She went under. Supple arms lifted her up.

The water became even choppier as the launch roared to a stop. More water splashed into her face. Before she could protest, she was wrenched into the boat and wrapped in Char' s embrace. His kiss was fierce and demanding—and quick.

Soon Brianna was wrapped in a warm robe and settled into the launch' s spacious cabin.

She' d just accepted a mug of something hot from one of the crewmen when Findal appeared at the base of the companionway. Char, who half carried, half led Ban into the stateroom, followed him. Two Nessians followed them.

"I tell you, I' m fine," Ban snapped. "I' m not an invalid."

"Don' t argue with me, Bandalardrac," Findal commanded. "I want a good look at those cuts."

"Only the one on his shoulder will require stitching, O King," interjected the older of the two Nessian women. "Our salve will heal the others."

Findal held out a first aid kit. "Are either of you any good with a needle and thread? Embroidery was never one of my strong suits." Now that both Brianna and Ban were safe, his natural jocularity was returning.

The Nessians both shook their heads.

Brianna stopped blowing on her steaming mug and said, "I' ll do it." She set the mug on the table and took the kit from Findal. Setting it on the table, she began to sort through its contents. "I' ll try to be as gentle as I can," she said over her shoulder.

Taking her eyes from the needles she had been threading, she turned her gaze to Ban' s right shoulder to judge the angle and deepness of the cut. What she saw there caused her to stumble over the trailing edges of her robe.

Riding Ban' s shoulder was a blue-green dragon, massive wings straining as it rose from a turbulent ocean.

"He' s got a dragon," she stammered. "Char. He' s got a dragon. Why…." Before any of the men could answer, understanding dawned. "His father was an Alalakan."

Char nodded. "Ban' s father was my uncle, my father' s older brother."

"And you didn' t tell me!"

All three men exchanged sheepish glances.

Brianna glared from Char to Ban and back to Char again. Turning her icy gaze to Findal' s grinning face, she snapped, "Well?"

The king held up his hands. "Don' t blame me. I told them not to keep their relationship secret."

She turned her angry stare back on her husband and his cousin.

Char looked down and shuffled his feet. Ban smiled sheepishly. Neither spoke.

Findal grinned. "If you' re going to sew up that cut, Brianna, you' d better get to it. You can flay them both to ribbons with your tongue later. Ban will need all of his remaining blood to survive that encounter, I think."

Compressing her lips in a tight line, Brianna nodded.

The first stab of the needle into his flesh caused Ban to yelp. After that first jab, he gritted his teeth and swallowed his groans.

Char folded his arms over his chest and leaned back against the wall while Brianna ministered to his cousin, his thoughts roiling around his head. Bakom had almost gotten Brianna. If it hadn' t been for Ban... Why did he ever allow her on that beach? What was wrong with him! Medirians have gills. Water abduction was the most logical. He couldn' t lose Brianna, not now.

Char shifted his gaze to his cousin. What was he going to do with Bandalardrac? Why couldn' t someone else have saved her? Damn it, Findal was supposed to have assassins protecting her! But Ban! Char frowned. He owed Ban for Brianna' s life. Maybe he could use him. Yes, that was a good idea... But Ban wanted Brianna. She' d shrugged off his overtures at least half a dozen times already. What if he wore her down? What if she decided she wanted him? No woman had ever been able to resist Ban.

Char was drawn from his chaotic thoughts by a small gasp from Ban. Brianna' s last jab had been less than delicate.

After she finished with his shoulder, Ban relaxed visibly. "If that is gentle, dear Coz, I wouldn' t want to bear your ministrations when you' re not so careful," he joked lightly.

Brianna' s eyes flashed. "Do *not* speak to me now! I can' t believe that neither of you trusted me enough to tell me you were cousins!" Jaw clenched and head held high, she swept out of the stateroom.

Both Nessian women grinned broadly at Brianna' s outburst. "She is truly the Flame of Mediria," the elder said to the younger.

Char grunted as he grabbed a sponge and wiped the blood from Ban' s shoulder. Brianna may not have been gentle, but the stitches were evenly spaced, tight enough to hold the skin together, but still loose enough not to pinch the flesh.

"She' s even more magnificent when she' s angry," Ban murmured in a thoughtful voice as Char bandaged the wound. "Does that temper manifest itself very often?"

Char didn' t try to keep the curtness from his voice. "Often enough."

Ban' s devilish smile appeared. Brianna in a temper must be as prickly as a wet Gattan.

Findal turned to the Nessians. "Both abductors are alive?"

"We were able to save them," was the elder woman' s enigmatic reply.

"Good, I' ll take them back to the palace with me. Both the Patriarch and Matriarch are still there. Those two could make the water itself talk."

The Nessians bowed and left the cabin. In a moment, two splashes were heard.

Findal followed them. Char and Ban could hear him issuing orders for the launch to return to the palace.

Char locked eyes with his cousin and quietly said, "I owe you a debt I can never repay. Anything that is in my power to give you is yours."

Ban' s voice was mocking. "Don' t you mean the clan' s power?"

Char crossed his arms over his chest and stared into Ban' s eyes. "No."

"Even that ring on your finger?"

Without a second thought, Char slipped the Alalakan signet ring from his finger and held it out to Ban.

Ban started—and stared. "Do you realize what it would mean if I took it?"

Brianna' s worth it. "Alalakan don al' Bandalardrac, my father and my brother will support your claim before the clan elders."

Ban stared at Char. "You' re serious," he said with wonder in his voice. "You would actually do it."

Char said nothing. He just continued to hold the ring out.

The emotions that played across the younger man' s face were easy to read. Ban was finally being presented with the acknowledgment he felt he deserved and had never received.

Slowly he lifted the ring from Char' s palm.

Brianna stomped in and fisted her hands on her hips. "Now what are you two doing? I simply won' t tolerate the snide remarks you throw at each other any longer."

With a smile Ban tossed the ring back to Char. "Just admiring the Alalakan signet, Coz."

Brianna' s eyes narrowed. "And if I believe that, you have a bridge in Brooklyn to sell me."

Ban looked to Char for an explanation, but his cousin just shrugged. "One of the strange things she says every now and then. You get used to it after a while. Now, *Cousin*, I find it necessary to cozen my wife out of a bad mood."

Then, to Ban' s great amusement and enjoyment, Char swept Brianna into his arms and kissed her — thoroughly.

At first outraged, Brianna struggled against his tender onslaught. However, Char' s hungry lips and probing tongue eventually overcame her resistance. The tension caused by her abduction slowly dissolved and she lost herself in his embrace.

Char' s hands roamed freely up and down her back, then finally cupped her buttocks and pulled her tight against his hardness. He' d just slipped the robe from her shoulders when Ban' s voice broke his concentration.

"Would you like me to leave, Cousin?"

"Now!" Char growled.

Ban grinned. "I was talking to my other cousin."

"Oh, yes," was her breathless reply.

Laughing, Ban ducked into the companionway, pulling the door closed behind him.

Findal met him at the top of the companionway. "Char and Brianna?"

"Are occupied."

Findal smiled slightly, but then his frown returned. "You almost killed the kidnappers. We can' t get information from corpses."

Ban shrugged. "I wanted to make sure neither one ever touched her again."

Pursing his lips, Findal stared at his favorite nephew. "Admire her all you want, Ban. But she' s Char' s. You' d do well to remember that."

Ban leaned against the railing and stared at the churning waves. "Believe me, Uncle. That is the one thing I will *never* forget."

With a grunt, Findal turned away. "I' m going to see if those two will talk. Care to join me?"

"No, I' ll just stay here."

Ban stood at the bow of the launch and let the breeze blow through his swirling thoughts. Char had offered him leadership of the clan. For the life of a woman. Did he realize just how important Brianna had become to him?

Brianna' s bathing suit followed the robe onto the floor.

His mouth never leaving hers, Char lifted her into his arms and laid her on the room' s only bunk. He stopped plundering her mouth only long enough to strip off his own clothing. Lowering himself onto her, he entered her with one hard thrust. Once his cock was gripped tightly by her moist softness, he growled, "I thought I' d lost you."

Shuddering, Brianna kissed his chest, his neck, his shoulders and finally his mouth. "I knew you would come. Love me, Char. Love me hard."

"As hard as I can." He swiveled his hips then thrust as deeply as he could.

Brianna wrapped her legs around his waist so he could slide deeper.

Both moaned as their rhythms surged and melded as both gave and took comfort from each other. Their shared orgasm was quick and hard.

"This will never happen again," Char vowed when his breathing had slowed. "We' re lucky Ban was on the beach."

Brianna propped herself up on her husband' s chest. "That' s why he had your ring, isn' t it? You offered him all that the Alalakans represent, didn' t you? Can you do that?"

An exasperated expression appeared on Char' s face. "You are too smart by half. There have been precedents."

Brianna smiled a superior smile. "And what would have you done if he had accepted?"

"I fully expected him to," Char answered seriously. "I was surprised when he returned the ring."

Brianna settled against his side. "You' d have given him everything? For me?"

"Yes," he answered tersely, uncomfortable with his own actions. His eyes slipped away from hers.

Brianna didn' t badger him, but she wasn' t done talking. "I could have told you he wouldn' t accept the ring."

His eyes shifted back to her face as his fingers drew gentle whorls on her back. "Oh?" he answered in an amused tone. "More women' s intuition?"

Her fingers traced his dragon. "No. I' m just a good judge of character. Does Ban impress you as being ready to accept the responsibility that goes with being Alalakan heir apparent?"

Char sighed and shook his head. "But," he added, "that thought never entered my mind when I offered him the ring."

Her fingers traced the scar on his chest. "And he knows that, Char. I think that for the first time in a long time, Ban is ready to stop running from himself."

"That' s what he' s been doing with half the women on the five known planets?"

"Oh, you!" Hair streaming down about her body, she pushed herself up.

Ban chose that moment to open the door and walk in — without knocking. "We' ll be docking in a few minutes," he said with a devilish grin on his face.

Brianna whirled to face the door and froze when she saw Ban standing there.

Ban took a long minute to admire Brianna' s nude body — the full breasts with their darkening nipples, the fair skin that blushed a delicious pink, and the long legs with the fiery curls at the apex of her thighs, all surrounded by her streaming auburn locks.

Brianna jerked her gaze from Ban. She grabbed a piece of pottery sitting on the table next to the bunk.

Ban was quick enough to get out of the way of the jar that came flying through the air at him.

Char' s laughter followed him back up the companionway.

Once they were back in the palace, Char hustled Brianna to their suite and deposited her in a steaming tub. Over her weak protests, he reinstated Beti as her personal guard. Then, after changing into fresh clothing, he went in search of Findal.

The Medirian monarch had quickly secreted Brianna' s abductors in a small windowless room on one of the castle' s underground floors. Char arrived shortly after the Patriarch finished questioning the men.

"Well?"

Both the Patriarch and Matriarch raised their eyebrows at Char' s tone, but Findal waved it off. He' d have been just as angry if his wife or one of his children had been abducted. "Does the name Zator don al' Odam mean anything to you?"

A satisfied smile appeared on Char' s face. "Bakom' s senior assistant."

Kahn and another Aradab appeared and led the two fugitives away. The Matriarch followed immediately after.

"Bakom' s name was never mentioned, Dragon of the Alalakans," the Patriarch said as he held up a restraining hand. "You have no proof he was involved. Any accusations leveled against him will be disproved."

Findal nodded. "He' s right. Bakom will only deny knowledge of Odam' s actions."

Char' s expression did not change. "This is only one of many incidents. Bakom is beginning to make mistakes, and it' s only a matter of time until he makes one mistake too many."

The Patriarch clasped Char' s forearm. "Don' t make Bakom' s mistake and become overconfident."

"There won' t be any mistakes when the time comes, Wise One. My family has been preparing Bakom' s downfall for years."

"Not mistakes," the old man gently stated, "but miscalculations, perhaps. Brianna' s abduction could not have been part of your plan."

Rubbing the back of his neck, Char acknowledged the Patriarch' s gentle reprimand. "I was at fault. I knew that Bakom wanted her and had made arrangements for some type of abduction, but I made the mistake of thinking he' d use only Academy or Drakian allies. The possibility of Medirians using an underwater abduction never entered my mind."

Findal nodded. "We have our malcontents and criminals as do all of the planets. A submarine waited two miles offshore. Brianna would have been taken to it, and smuggled onto one of our smaller trading vessels and transported to Drakan. Her abductors knew nothing beyond that. We broadcast a scrambled transmission of the kidnappers' interrogation to Drakan' s central police. They assured us that Zator don al' Odam will be taken into custody immediately."

"Does my father know?"

"Yes."

"Good, he' ll coordinate things there," Char said in a satisfied tone of voice. Then he continued, his voice becoming flatter and harder, "What will happen to the two men who tried to kidnap my wife?"

The Patriarch regarded Char through narrowed eyes. "Put them from your mind, Alalakan. Their punishment is in our hands. Be content to know they will reside with the Aradab for the rest of their lives."

"We' re finished here," Findal interrupted. "How' s Brianna? She hasn' t suffered any ill effects?"

"I left her soaking in a tub demanding that Beti ' get the hell out of my face' I think were the exact words," Char stated with a wry smile.

Findal shook his head as he led the two men out of the chamber and up the hallway. "More Earth idioms," he sighed. "My daughters repeat things Brianna says to our linguists, and they become more and more puzzled. Do you know that there are times when the word *bad* means *good*?"

Char shrugged. "One begins to get used to them."

Once they reached the castle' s main floor, the Patriarch excused himself. He' d been scheduled to return to his underwater city that afternoon, but his departure had been delayed by Brianna' s abduction. At this moment, one of the royal launches awaited him at the dock. It would transport him about thirty miles offshore where he would take to the water and swim the rest of the way.

Findal and Char made their way towards the king' s office. "When will you leave for Drakan?"

"Father informed me that Bakom made an official protest to the Ruling Council and demanded the return of his ' specimen' . Now is the perfect time for you to inform your subjects that the dols and orcs have been found. We can' t keep Brianna' s adoption into your family secret, but everyone will be far more interested in the dols and orcs. With a bit of luck, her adoption won' t become common knowledge on Drakan."

Findal nodded. "We did not broadcast the adoption for that reason. Only those who follow the royal family closely will know about it. And even they will lose interest when we announce that we've found the dols and orcs."

"With a bit of luck, Bakom won't find out Brianna is now a member of your family," Char said. "The protest he's made to our Ruling Council will prove more than embarrassing. Identifying a member of the Hardan royal family as a 'specimen' will be as politically unpopular on Drakan as it will here."

Findal opened the door to his office and waved Char in. He dismissed the servants telling them to admit no one except his wife and to fetch his nephew, Bandalardrac.

If Char was surprised at Findal's orders, he masked it very well. Once the servants were gone, he continued, "I know my father and Rodane filled you in on our plans, so I won't go over them again."

Sitting down behind his desk and motioning Char to a comfortable chair, Findal nodded. "I'm sorry Carilin and I can't attend Sheala's Solstice celebration, but it's best that we remain here. Meri will be our official representative, and both Jami and Vani have manipulated invitations from Brianna."

Char smiled. Brianna had already told him she'd invited her "sisters" to visit. Both girls knew his sister Sheala well since she and Jami were the same age. And Brianna would feel more comfortable having some people she knew around her.

"Brianna certainly puts people around her at ease. You'd think my girls had known her all their lives instead of only a few days. Even Carilin's mother is enchanted," Findal said rearranging the papers on his desk.

Char leveled a stare at Findal. "What about the assassins?"

Findal's eyebrows rose. "What about them?"

"I thought every member of the royal family had an assassin as a guard. Brianna should never have been taken."

A brooding look appeared on Findal's face. "Alalakan don al' Chardadon, even the close family ties you share with us will gain you no knowledge of the Brotherhood. Believe me when I say you were not the only one to miscalculate. It will not happen again."

Char stared at his father's old friend. Finally he nodded, curtly. The Brotherhood was a subject off-limits.

Char changed the subject. Doing some quick calculating he asked, "Did you have a specific departure date in mind for Jami and Vani?"

Findal looked up. "No. What do you have in mind?"

Char smiled. "Dear friend of my father, I would like to borrow the royal shuttle."

Findal' s swift mind had no trouble understanding Char' s scheme. Slowly at first, but then with pure joy, the king began to laugh. When he finally regained control, he looked into Char' s grinning face and said, "Alalakan don al' Chardadon, remind me never to try and outfox you in any business dealings. The Alalakan fortunes are sure to increase under you wardship."

* * * * *

Rodak don al' Bakom was awakened by the incessant buzzing of his telecommunicator. Snarling, he slapped the receiving button. "What is it!"

"It' s Eliana, Doctor. Odam has been arrested."

Bakom became instantly alert. "What? Why?"

"He was implicated in the attempted kidnapping of one of the Hardan royal family, one of the king' s daughters."

"That stupid son of a Varcian whore. How did that happen? My instructions were perfectly clear!"

"I don' t know, Doctor. I' d gone ahead to his room while he met with his contacts."

"Fool! Odam thinks more with his tail than his head. I should not have sent him alone."

"I' m sorry, Doctor."

Bakom snorted. "Where is he now?"

"Police central headquarters. The charges are very solid. There is talk of extraditing him to Mediria."

Bakom frowned, thinking rapidly. "This isn' t good. Have there been any inquiries directed to the Academy?"

"Not yet."

"Well, at least he knows how to keep his mouth shut," Bakom muttered to himself.

"What was that, Doctor?"

"Nothing." Continuing, Bakom instructed, "Any personal inquiries to me, send to my Academy office. As far as you know, I left on a personal retreat to my family shrine yesterday and I plan to be gone at least two months. I want no hints that I am in any way involved with Odam' s illegal activities. Do you understand what I mean?"

"Yes, Doctor. The police already questioned me since I was with Odam the night he made arrangements for the kidnapping."

Sweat began to trickle down Bakom' s back. If both of his personal assistants were implicated, he could expect the police to fetch him from his family shrine. "You are not suspected?"

"No. Neither of the men Odam met with saw me. The police believe I was there for sexual adventure because the inn was not what someone of ' my obvious class' , as the arresting officers said, would frequent for any other reason. I agreed with his assessment of the situation."

"Very good, my dear." Bakom sagged with relief. There was no way he could be connected with Odam now. "We will simply have to cut our losses. Odam understood the risks he faced. We' ll stand back for a time and then seek ways to gain his release. Do you have any questions?"

"Do you wish regular reports sent to you?"

"No. It' s best if I remain completely shut off from Academy business. There will be no way I can be implicated if I have no idea what has been happening for a few months," Bakom answered. "You have cleared my personal papers from my desk?"

"As soon as I left the police station."

"Good. I' ll see you in two months when the Council returns from its vacation."

Bakom ended Eliana' s transmission. He didn' t see the satisfied smile on Lorilana' s face as she locked eyes with her nephew' s sister-in-law.

The shuttle set down on the Alalakan estate' s private airstrip. Once its engines were shut off, wheeled transports rolled out onto the edge of the landing field to take everyone to the main house. Brianna was pleased to have a vehicle to just Char and herself. Sometimes she missed the weeks she had spent in forced isolation on the *Restoration*. Snuggling next to her husband in air-conditioned comfort, Brianna sighed with contentment.

Pulling her close, he kissed her forehead. "Happy?"

Brianna' s answer was to take his hand and place his palm on her stomach. Char felt a very definite kick.

"He doesn' t stay still for very long," she said contentedly.

Char left his hand where it was, smiling at the movements of his unborn child. *My child.* Then. *Bakom is going to make a fool out of himself before the council when they see exactly what his specimen looks like.*

As the vehicle slowed to a stop, Brianna said, "You better get that silly grin off your face. Your parents are waiting for us."

Char' s grin broadened. "I' m sure my grin is no sillier than that of my father when he felt a child of his move."

He did compose himself somewhat, and the smile on his face as he helped Brianna from the car was simply that of a man happy to see beloved parents.

Xdana hugged him close. "Welcome home."

Then she turned to Brianna, smiling broadly at her much-enlarged abdomen. "You are doubly welcome, Alalakan dem al' Brianna."

Before Brianna could reply to her mother-in-law' s greeting, Jamiros swept her up into his arms. "Welcome, Daughter," he said and carried her into the house.

"Is this an old family custom?" Brianna gasped as she wrapped her arms around his neck.

"Old Drakian custom," he answered with a grin. "Centuries ago, if the father of the groom could get his son' s new wife into the house without having her taken from his arms, he had the right to first sex with her."

"*What!*"

Before Brianna could say any more, she was set back on her feet in an opulent foyer.

Xdana gave her husband a playful shove as she shook her head. "Can' t you wait until she is at least in the door, Jamiros?" Turning to Brianna she said, "You may as well prepare yourself. Jamiros is a terrible tease. Don' t believe anything he tells you, especially if he is smiling."

Brianna looked to Char for guidance, but all he did was grin. She was saved from a reply though, by the arrival of the Hardan clan. Both Jamilinlalissa and her sister Vanilinlalissa leaped into Jamiros' arms and were thoroughly hugged.

Xdana greeted the girls warmly but said in a wry voice to Brianna, "My house is not going to be the same after this visit. Sheala has great plans for the three of them."

Barely had those words left her mouth than a younger version of Xdana rushed into the foyer, threw her arms around Char in an exuberant hug, gave Brianna a curious stare and a quick hello, and barreled out through another door with Jami and Vani in tow.

"See what I mean?"

Beti had been in the same car with the sisters. She stood silently inside the doorway.

Xdana greeted her with a smile. "Hello, Beti," she said. "Is Kahn with you?"

Beti nodded once affirmatively and said, "and Dorce, Sloan, and Feni."

Xdana's eyebrows rose. "You remember where the rooms are?"

At Beti's affirmative nod, Xdana continued, "Good. All of the Hardans will be in the blue suite. Char and Brianna will have the heir's apartments."

"And what about me, Aunt?" Bandalardrac asked with a grin as he walked in the doorway. "Do you think you have room somewhere in this great mausoleum for me?"

If Xdana was surprised to see Ban, she didn't show it. Cupping his face in her hands, she kissed first one cheek then the other. "Silly boy, there has always been room for you here. You will be in the heir's guest suite, but," she added with mock seriousness, "I absolutely forbid you to wander around naked! I will never get any work out of the maids if you do!"

Ban was momentarily speechless. He was being given a great honor and he didn't quite know how to react.

Char was equally surprised. *Why did you put him in my suite, Mother? Why put him so close to Brianna?* Unfortunately for him, his mother's wishes overrode his.

Ban grinned and said, "I promise to be naked only under the right circumstances."

"Or on top," Meri grumbled as she entered the house followed by Ademis, who was carrying Celene.

Smiling with delight, Xdana accepted Celene from Adem's arms. The baby chortled happily at the many colored beads she wore.

Jamiros took Brianna' s arm. "Come along, my dear. We have a wonderful lunch waiting."

As his father led Brianna away, Char slowed his mother with a hand to her arm. "Where' s Rodane?"

"Char," Xdana said with complete sincerity, "he wanted more than anything to be here when you arrived, but Todan don al' Upin demanded satisfaction about a bill."

Char grimaced. Todin don al' Upin was the most cantankerous of all the merchants they dealt with. He didn' t envy Rodane his afternoon. Todan would not be satisfied until he thought he' d bested the Alalakans.

"We' ll be lucky if we see Rodane before tomorrow morning," Char muttered mostly to himself.

Xdana chuckled. "He promised to be home for dinner even if he had to give the wool to Todan at a loss."

Char sighed and shook his head. "Todan would still think we were cheating him. No one in the universe is more distrustful."

Xdana patted her son' s arm as best she could while still holding Celene. Ban, Meri, and Ademis had followed Brianna and Jamiros into the dining room. Only they remained in the foyer.

Char placed his hand on her arm. "Mother, how does Rodane really feel?"

"Oh, Char, Rodane told you that he doesn' t begrudge you the status of heir apparent. I think he' s rather relieved, as a matter of fact."

They entered the dining room as Jamiros was holding Brianna' s chair for her. Char had barely reached the table when a voice called to him from the doorway.

"Hello, Char." The lovely young woman sauntered across the room, threw her arms around his neck, and proceeded to kiss him— thoroughly. Nor did he step away from her embrace.

Brianna stiffened and her nostrils flared. *Who the hell is that, and why is Char kissing her?*

Char reached up and pulled the woman' s arms from around his neck and pushed her away. "Hello, Singy. Visiting Crystas again?"

She snuggled closer. "She invited me for Solstice. Then when I heard you' d soon be home, I decided to come early," the woman purred, caressing his arm. "It' s been toooooo long."

Char nodded. "Quite a while, Singy."

"Ahem." Jamiros nodded towards Brianna. She was sitting in her chair, chin up, eyes sparkling, and she was very, very pale.

Char pushed Singy away and hurried to her side. "Brianna, do you feel all right?"

The woman followed him, snaking her arm through his. "A new…guest?"

"My wife. Brianna, this is Molontonon dem al' Singy, an old friend. Singy, my wife, Brianna."

The woman' s shock was apparent to everyone. "Wife!"

"Didn' t Crystas tell you I married?" He kept his attention fixed on Brianna.

Jamiros cleared his throat. "We thought it best to keep the information a family secret until you got home."

Char nodded, but his immediate attention was still on Brianna. She hadn' t greeted Singy yet, and that wasn' t like her. She hadn' t shown any reticence meeting anyone up to this point, but she only stared at Singy. And she was still pale. "Brianna?"

"How do you do?" Brianna finally choked out.

Singy looked down her elegant nose and nodded — barely. Then she turned back to Char, pressing her body against his side.

Unlike Char, Xdana immediately understood her daughter-in-law' s reaction.

So did everyone else in the room, especially Ban. An amused grin settled on his face as he watched the tableau unfolding before him. *I can' t believe you can be so stupid, Cousin. Why even look at Singy when you have perfection in Brianna?*

Xdana handed Celene back to Meri. "I didn' t know you were joining us for lunch, Singy. You informed the kitchen you' d be eating with Crystas and Fio."

Singy kept her attention on Char. "When I heard Char was back, I just had to see him. Sit next to me, Char. Or — we could have a…private…lunch?"

Brianna' s color rose again. She rose to her feet so fast, her chair slapped to the floor. "I' m suddenly tired, Xdana. Show me to my room — please." Her request was more like a command.

Char grasped her arm lightly.

She shook herself free.

His voice sounded worried. "Brianna..."

Her tone voice was icy. "No. Stay with your...friend." Head held high, she swept from the room followed by Xdana, who glared at her son over her shoulder. Both Beti and Kahn followed.

Confused, Char looked from his father to Ademis to Meri. Both Ademis and his father rolled their eyes.

Meri glared at him.

Ban grinned like an idiot.

"Char..." purred Singy, caressing his arm.

"Not now," he said, shaking himself free of her clinging hands. "Father, have lunch sent to our rooms."

Chapter Twelve

Xdana had barely shown Brianna to her suite when Char barreled into the sitting room. "Brianna, what' s wrong?"

Amazed, she stared at her husband. "What' s wrong? You play tonsil hockey with another woman and you ask *me* what' s wrong!"

Xdana withdrew. This was best settled between Char and Brianna.

"Tonsil hockey? Brianna, I don' t understand…"

She threw her braid back over her shoulder and fisted her hands on her hips. "How could you kiss her like that?"

Understanding dawned on Char' s face. "Singy? She was doing most of the kissing."

Brianna' s mouth dropped open. She snapped it shut. "Most?"

Char combed his fingers through his hair. "Well, what was I supposed to do?"

"What were you supposed to *do*? You ass." Jerking her eyes around the room, she spotted a small vase of flowers sitting on a nearby table. One step had her next to it.

Char ducked as it flew by his head, shattering on the wall behind him.

"Damn it, Brianna…" He was faster than she was and wrapped his arms around her.

"Don' t you ' damn it' me! You' re the one who…"

"Kissed somebody else. So?"

"So? So!"

Brianna struggled in his arms, but he refused to release her. "Brianna, stop, you' ll hurt yourself."

She jabbed an elbow into his ribs then cursed when it hurt. "How could I possibly hurt myself? You' re the one holding me. Let me go!"

"Only if you promise not throw anything else. Why did you throw that vase?"

"Why? Why!"

Confused, Char stared into her face. *She thinks I should know why she' s throwing this temper tantrum. Is it just because I kissed Singy? What of it? She' s a past bed partner. I couldn' t just snub her.* Then he thought about the kisses from her point of view. *And how is she supposed to know that? All she' s heard for months is how promiscuous Drakians are. She doesn' t understand.*

Sure now that he understood why Brianna was upset, Char released her, slowly—with an apology. "I' m sorry, Brianna. I forgot you' re not Drakian."

"And what does that have to do with the price of tea in China?"

"Tea? China? I don' t understand."

Brianna crossed her arms over her chest and glared.

Grateful that she was no longer searching for things to throw, Char continued, "Singy isn' t a stranger. She' s a past bed partner. I couldn' t just snub her. Mother taught me better manners than that."

Brianna' s mouth fell open. His explanation was not what she expected. "Past bed partner! Taught you better manners! You fucking asshole!" Whirling, she stomped into the bedroom, slamming the door behind her.

Char heard the lock click.

"I never realized how incredibly stupid you could be, Cousin," Ban commented from the doorway.

Char turned furious eyes on his Medirian cousin. "What the hell are you doing here?"

Ban indicated the door to the suite' s guest rooms with his chin. "I live here, remember? Haven' t you learned anything about Brianna? Do you ever listen to what she says?"

"Of course I listen to my wife," Char snarled. "And our marriage is none of your business."

"You won' t have a marriage if you keep kissing women and introducing them to Brianna as bed partners."

"It' s been almost two years."

Ban sighed. "Damn, but you' re dense, Char. I don' t know why I' m bothering to explain this to you."

Sneering, Char snapped, "I don' t need any explanations from you."

Ban' s own anger surged. "Damn it, Char, Brianna' s afraid."

That pronouncement drained Char' s anger. "Afraid? Of what? Bakom can' t touch her here."

"Don' t you ever think of anything besides Bakom? You no sooner walk in the front door than she sees you with another woman in your arms. Think. And remember, Brianna' s a Hardan princess now. If she wants to leave, I' ll take her."

With those words, Ban strode past a now thoughtful Char and disappeared into his room.

Char turned and stared at the locked door that separated him from his wife. Jealous? Could she be jealous? A slow smile spread across Char' s face. His wife was jealous of another woman.

Brianna lay on the huge bed, curled on her side, silent tears running down her cheeks. Meri had warned her about Drakians. They jump from bed to bed to bed. Char was no different. He only married her to protect her from Bakom. If she hadn' t gotten pregnant, he would have divorced her. She was just another one of his "bed partners". All she had to look forward to was a broken heart. Brianna stiffened at her own thoughts. A broken heart? Oh God, she loved him.

A soft knock. "Brianna, it' s Meri. Let me in. I brought you something to eat."

Brianna' s stomach rumbled.

"If Char thinks he can use you to get me to open the door, he' s crazy!" she shouted.

"He' s not here, Bri."

Fresh tears rolled down her cheeks as Brianna squeezed her eyes shut. He probably went back to — her.

"Brianna, are you all right? Please open the door. I' m worried about you."

After fingering her tears from her cheeks, Brianna pushed herself off the bed and stumbled to the door. A quick turn of her wrist, and it was unlocked. Meri entered followed by Beti, who carried a tray filled with covered dishes.

Setting the tray on the table next to the bed, Beti bowed her head and left.

Brianna' s stomach growled again.

A half-hearted smile appeared on Meri' s face. "Well, you can' t feel too bad if you' re hungry."

Brianna glared at her friend. "There' s nothing to joke about, Meri."

"Well, there' s nothing to pout about either."

Brianna' s nostrils flared and two red splotches appeared on her cheek. "Pout! Do you know what he told me? He slept with her!"

"I doubt that they did much sleeping," Meri answered dryly.

Brianna gaped. "Meri! Whose side are you on?"

"Yours. That' s why I' m here."

Brianna' s shoulders slumped. "Well, it sure doesn' t sound that way."

Meri picked up Brianna' s hand and squeezed it. "Were you a virgin with Char?"

Brianna wiped tears from her cheeks with the other. "You know I wasn' t."

"Then how can you hold his past against him?"

She sniffed. "I' m not!"

"Then what would you call it?"

Brianna jerked her hand free. "Damn it, Meri. He kissed her. Right in front of me."

Meri sighed. "Brianna, you' re on Drakan. It would have been rude of him to just ignore her."

She rose to her feet and began to pace. "He could have just said hello!"

Meri smiled. "She didn' t give him much of a choice."

"Well, he didn' t have to enjoy it so much."

Meri gaped at Brianna. Then she started to laugh. "Would you listen to yourself?" she finally gasped between hiccups. "Not enjoy it? Exactly how would you react if a handsome man kissed you?"

Brianna stopped pacing and stared at the wall. An image of Mel Gibson leaped into her mind. Finally, her lips began to twitch. "I guess I did overreact a little."

Meri nodded. "Maybe a little."

She sank back down onto the bed. "So I made a complete fool out of myself."

"No, you made yourself perfectly clear. Now, though, the last thing you want to do is hide in your rooms and give Singy the idea that you won' t fight for Char."

Brianna clenched her teeth then growled, "Fight for him. Meri, I shouldn' t have to fight for my own husband."

"Wow! Earth must really be different. Men and women there never chase after people married to someone else?"

Cheeks warming, Brianna ducked her head. "They do."

"I thought so. You are human, after all. Remember, Brianna, this is Drakan. Even if Char isn' t interested, other woman will still chase after him. You have to make your claim to him very clear. I' m speaking from experience."

"Char should make it clear himself that he' s unavailable."

"Honestly, Bri, there are women who won' t believe him. There are still women Ademis won' t go near unless I' m right next to him. The prospect of an angry Medirian wife will give any woman second thoughts. And you' re one of the family now."

Rising, Brianna gave in to the demands of her stomach and lifted the lids from the plates on the tray. The food smelled delicious.

"What' s so intimidating about being Medirian?"

"Our assassins, of course."

The lid Brianna was holding clattered to the floor.

"Assassins? The kind that kill people?"

"Of course," Meri answered nonchalantly while she picked among the various plates of food.

"Why didn' t you tell me about them before!"

Meri glanced up at Brianna' s face, surprised at the shocked expression she found there. "I didn' t think it was important. Is it?"

"Yes... Well... Of course... Oh, I don' t know!" Brianna babbled as she sank back onto the bed, her now weak knees refusing to hold her. "I mean, assassins kill people!"

"Doesn' t anybody kill people on your planet?"

"Well, yes, but..."

Meri raised one eyebrow.

Brianna' s stomach growled again, but she still stared at Meri.

"Brianna, the entire population of Mediria isn' t made up of assassins. I don' t even personally know any of them. They' re simply an extension of the palace guard."

Brianna relaxed. The palace guard? Like the Secret Service? That must be it. There must be something in the translation that was mixed up. There was probably no equivalent for the Meridian word for royal guards in English, and assassins was just the closest fit. That was it. Meri and her family were wonderful. They were not cold-blooded killers.

"Brianna, you really need to eat something. You have a big night ahead of you."

"What?"

"Xdana is having a dinner to introduce you to the clan elders."

"Tonight?"

"You really want to sit around and worry about it?"

"No, but..."

"So eat. Xdana wants to give you a tour of the house. Then you' re going to have a nice long soak in the tub. Then we' ll pick out what dress to wear tonight. You carry the Alalakan heir, Brianna. There' s nothing the clan will not do for the mother of its heir, and you' re going to make sure they remember."

Two hours later Brianna gratefully sank into a comfortable sofa next to Meri. After touring the house and its immediate buildings, her feet were killing her. "You have a beautiful home, Xdana."

"Thank you, Brianna. It' s all yours now."

"What?"

"As mother of the heir, management of the household will be your responsibility."

Brianna paled. "Me? But..."

Both Meri and Xdana laughed. "You don' t have to take charge today. We' ll all help you."

Xdana glanced at what Brianna assumed was a watch and frowned. "We' ll have to save introducing you to the staff for another day. Meri said you wanted a nice long soak. You' ve got three hours before dinner. Enjoy yourself."

Meri grabbed Brianna' s hands and pulled her to her feet. "Come on, Bri. Let' s go pick out a dress for you to wear."

With a groan, Brianna followed Meri. She' d really rather take a nap. And where was Char? If he thought she was going to let him carry on with that, that woman, he had another think coming!

* * * * *

While Brianna toured the house with his mother, Char reviewed paperwork with his father. The Alalakan clan controlled a vast business empire, one that would now become his responsibility.

"So there have been no real problems since I' ve been away?"

His father shook his head. "None. Things have been running so smoothly, I was beginning to worry."

Char grunted and wished he could say the same about his marriage. Would Brianna react the same way every time a woman kissed him? "Everything looks fine. If you don' t need me for anything else, I have some errands."

A troubled expression appeared on Jamiros' face. "Char, I won' t meddle in your marriage, but Singy…"

Astonishment leaped onto Char' s face. "Father, surely you don' t think I would crawl into another woman' s bed with my wife in the same house?"

Jamiros smiled sheepishly.

Char grinned back. "If you haven' t noticed, my wife has a temper as fiery as her hair. And, I am not a stupid man. I' ll see you at dinner."

Char left his father' s study through the patio doors. Earlier, he' d gone to the trouble of finding out exactly which guest room Singy had. He planned to stay as far away from it and her as possible. As walked through the garden, he shook his head. He still had to figure out a way to keep Singy away from *him*.

Movement off to his left caught his eye.

Ban lounged against a statue as he gazed out over the huge lawn.

Halting, Char stared at his cousin. Then he smiled. Having Ban around might not be such a bad idea. "I have a job for you."

Ban' s eyebrows rose. "Oh?"

Char grinned. "Singy."

* * * * *

Kahn stepped in front of the woman who appeared in the corridor. "You may not pass."

"Move out of my way," Singy snapped, her tone and attitude condescending.

Kahn' s tone became more patronizing and pompous than Singy' s. "These are the private quarters of Alalakan dem al' Brianna, Princess Hardan. She has not requested your presence."

She waved her hand dismissively. "I' m not here to see her. I want to see Chardadon."

"No."

"You have no right!"

Kahn simply flexed his muscles.

Singy took a step back.

"Problem, Kahn?"

"No, Prince Bandalardrac."

Singy turned and stared at Ban. A crafty look appeared on her face. "Ban, it' s been so long since I' ve seen you. We must talk...somewhere private?"

Ban grinned. His gaze traveled up and down her body.

She preened for him.

Reaching out, he clasped her hand and lifted it to his lips. "Lead on and I will follow you anywhere."

"But your room is so much closer," she purred.

"The suite is off-limits to everyone except immediate family. Your room, however..."

She snatched her hand away. "As if I' d go anywhere with a base half-breed like you!"

Kahn stiffened.

Ban smiled.

Singy whirled around and stomped away.

With noncommittal shrug, Ban nodded to Kahn and let himself into the suite.

Kahn did not fail to note the pain in Ban' s eyes.

* * * * *

Brianna took a deep breath and gazed into the mirror that hung in the sitting room. She and Meri had collaborated a long time on the proper gown to wear. They' d decided on a flowing, floor-length green shift the color of spring leaves, one that left her shoulders bare. With her rampant dragon in full view, there would be no doubt that she was an Alalakan.

Two bands of golden ribbons circled Brianna' s body, one immediately above her breasts and one immediately below. The rest of the green dress flowed from the supple, gold support band underneath Brianna' s breasts. Ribbons of dark green and gold fell from the center of the band. Rather than trying to hide her expanding stomach, the gentle draping of the dress' s silky material emphasized her pregnancy.

She took another deep breath. If only the butterflies in her stomach would settle down.

"You grow more beautiful every day," Char stated from behind her.

Brianna stiffened.

Char had appeared approximately half an hour earlier and disappeared into the bathroom for a quick shower. Now he was dressed in another white uniform.

She met his eyes in the mirror. Anger tinged her voice. "What did you do all day?"

"I reviewed paperwork with my father and completed some errands," he answered as he lifted a box from the table. "I have a gift for you."

"If you' re trying to bribe me..."

A hint of exasperation appeared in his eyes, but he kept his voice contrite. "Please, Brianna, take it."

She took the box he held out to her and opened it. Her eyes widened with surprise. "Char! They' re so beautiful."

Inside the box lay earrings to match her wedding ring. Though women on Drakan did not wear earrings because they had no earlobes, Char remembered the golden studs Brianna had commented on losing when she' d first been brought on board his ship.

Two cascades of red diamonds fell from delicate, red-gold wires. Slipping them on, Brianna sighed with delight as she looked in the mirror. She wore her hair loose, its waves flowing down her back. The earrings fell almost to her shoulders, their sparkling, inner fire highlighting her auburn hair.

Before she could say anything else, however, Char was behind her, gently placing a pendant about her neck. From a delicate chain of yet more red gold, hung a single fiery diamond. Fastening the clasp, he looked into the mirror and met her gaze. His hands came forward and followed the sturdy chain to where the diamond lay on her breasts. "It's the only thing I could find that came close to matching the sparkle in your eyes, my love," he said softly.

He spun her around and swept her into his arms. Lost their mutual passion, it took a few minutes for the pounding on the door to penetrate their consciousness.

"What..." she stammered, her eyes unfocused.

Char rested his forehead against hers and chuckled, "I got the doors fixed. No one will walk in on us again."

Brianna' s equilibrium returned rapidly. "No," she said with a laugh, her earlier anger gone, "they' ll just pound and disturb the entire house until we let them in."

Char' s answering chuckle was downright wicked. "But we don' t have to let them in if we don' t want to, do we?"

Laughing, Brianna turned to unlock the door, but Char clasped her arm gently. "You have more presents. Open them, I' ll get the door."

She looked at the two boxes that still lay on the small table. In the first were two intricately woven bracelets of even more red gold and diamonds. Placing them both on her left wrist, she held them up to the light. Red sparkles lit the room.

When Bandalardrac got a good look at Brianna, he let out a slow whistle. She was certainly beautiful, but he wondered if she realized how much all those red diamonds were worth. "You certainly don' t stint when it comes to your wife, Char."

"No one will doubt the worth in which I hold her."

Brianna turned at the sound of voices and smiled when she recognized Ban. "Was it necessary to break down the door, Coz?"

Ban barked with laughter. "That would take a battering ram. Didn' t Char tell you that it' s a new door?"

Char grinned also. "I told her no one would get in unless they were invited, and you damn well know why."

Even though she blushed at the memory of Ban' s appreciative perusal that day on the launch, she joined in their laughter.

"You still have one more present," Char reminded her.

She grinned ruefully. "I' m almost afraid to open it. The only thing missing is the crown."

Brianna opened the final box. It wasn' t a crown. Holding up the net of finely spun gold and red diamonds, Brianna sighed, "It' s breathtaking Char, but what is it?"

Ban answered for him. "It' s a Medirian bridal net," he replied in an awed tone. "You wear it over your hair like this." Taking the net from her hands, he placed it on her head, adjusting it carefully. When he finished, he turned her to face the mirror. An almost silent exclamation escaped when Brianna saw her reflection.

A woven band of gold fit over her head and behind her ears like an ordinary headband. A very loosely woven net of gold thread and diamond dust fit snugly around her head. Long, shimmering bands of gold and diamonds fell from the sides and back of the net to flow with her auburn tresses. The effect was dazzling. No matter how Brianna moved, sparks of red fire jumped and shimmered about her.

Ban stepped back as he finished adjusting Brianna' s hair. Shaking his head in wonder, he said to Char, "How did you ever find someone to do such delicate work?"

Char admired his wife. Gattan red diamonds were absolutely perfect for her coloring. He was more than pleased to put the collection it had taken him years to amass on display, especially when the setting was his beautiful wife.

Brianna sighed to herself in the mirror and turned to face Char. "I feel just like a princess."

Ban snorted as he took her hand. "You are a princess now, Coz, remember?" Escorting her towards the door, he stopped in front of Char and held out Brianna' s hand. "Yours, I believe."

Char winced. How could Ban say something so stupid!

"I am *mine*, Alalakan don al' Bandalardrac, and don' t you forget it!" Brianna snapped imperiously snatching her hand from Ban' s.

Ban locked his gaze with Char' s and winked. "Said the wrong thing, didn' t I?"

Char nodded and held out his hand to his wife.

With a haughty glance to Ban, Brianna placed her hand in Char' s. "I chose to marry of my own free will. I always had a choice. If you treat women like they' re possessions, it' s no wonder you can' t find one to love."

Turning her back on Ban, Brianna tugged her husband towards the door.

Glancing over his shoulder to his cousin, Char winked back.

* * * * *

Head high, Brianna stomped down the hall. "' Yours, I believe.' Does he really believe that horseshit? What an ass!"

Char chuckled. "I tried to warn you."

Cupping Brianna' s elbow, he slowed her progress. "Easy. You don' t want to fall down the stairs."

She sniffed. "I will not fall."

Pulling her arm free, she placed her hand on the railing and descended the stairs carefully.

Ban caught up with Char at the top of the stairs and flashed a smile. "Singy doesn' t stand a chance."

Because Ban' s remark still rankled, Brianna sailed down the stairway much less intimidated than she might have been by rooms full of people who were all taller than she. That in itself was a unique experience. She was used to being taller than almost everyone else, especially the women. Standing in the receiving line with Char and his parents, Brianna, for the first time in her life, felt short.

As Char and Brianna received their guests, Ban wandered through the crowded house. Char' s bride was the main topic of conversation. Everyone was very curious about her, especially those unmarried women who had been hoping to be in that position themselves. Singy had spent most of the afternoon belittling Brianna in every way she could to everyone she met. Most of the guests, however, had taken one look at Brianna' s exotic beauty, her challenging dragon, and the fortune in red diamonds she wore and had known that Char was more than content with his wife. Singy was a fool if she thought he was still interested in her.

"That should be everyone, Char," Xdana said. "Find Brianna a comfortable sofa."

Sighing, Brianna made herself comfortable. "My feet are killing me."

Meri cocked her head to the side. "What?"

Char leaned over. "Do you want me to get you something?"

Brianna waved him away. "No. Go mingle. Everyone will think you' re afraid to let me say anything without your approval. I' m more than a setting for valuable jewels."

Char grinned. He should have known that anyone who could face down the Dowager Hardan queen would have no trouble with his relatives.

Meri immediately made Brianna stand back up so she could get a closer look at her bridal net. "I have never seen such delicate weaving," she said with wonder. She herself wore her own bridal net, an ancient net of silver and pale emeralds that had been handed down from mother to eldest daughter in her family for generations. "Whoever did this weaving for Char could make a fortune on Mediria."

Brianna smiled to herself. She' d overheard numerous comments about the jewelry she wore, a fair amount of it envious. From what she gathered, Gattan red diamonds were extremely rare and almost impossible to purchase. Char must feel something for her if he gave her such valuable jewels.

Meri and Brianna had just settled themselves on the sofa when Ban sauntered over. Handing Brianna a glass, he said, "Char said this Deslossian red is your favorite. You have to be thirsty after all that hello' ing and how-do-you-do' ing."

Ban' s arrival was a signal for every unattached male nearby to join them. His reputation was well known on Drakian. If the two lovely ladies on the sofa welcomed Ban so openly, perhaps there was a chance for dalliance. After all, Meri' s baby was almost a year old. Brianna' s morals were an unknown element. More than one pregnant wife encouraged attention from other men. And many of their husbands knew about it.

Char smiled to himself as he saw the men gather around Meri and Brianna.

Next to him, Jamiros frowned and took a step forward. Placing a hand on his father' s arm, he said, "No, just watch. Ban will be more protective of his cousins than any Aradab grandmother."

They watched as the men began to rapidly find other, less well-guarded prey. After the last rake disappeared, Ban sent a glance that spoke volumes to Char.

"You didn' t have to chase all of them away, Ban," Brianna muttered crossly. "How do you expect me to meet anyone?"

"Those men are not worth knowing, Coz," Ban answered. "They' re only interested in sex."

Meri had trouble stifling her giggles. "Believe him, Bri, he' s an expert."

"Humph!"

As the hour passed, Char watched as Brianna, Meri, and Ban talked among themselves. Many groups of people watched them furtively, but none other than older men and women made a move to join them. Glancing around the room, his gaze was drawn to a pair of faces wearing satisfied smirks. Singy—and Crystas. They were the reason none of the young women approached Brianna. Could they possibly think he' d dissolve the marriage when Brianna carried the heir?

Sensing a presence next to him, Char glanced over his shoulder and saw his brother' s smiling face.

"How goes the great introduction, Char? Why isn' t your lovely wife surrounded by every rogue in the family?"

"Ban," Char answered. Then he continued in a noncommittal tone, "Crystas hasn' t been introduced to Brianna yet."

Rodane frowned. "I apologize, Char, but Crystas is going to be difficult. She never expected you to come home with a wife, let alone one who is pregnant. She always assumed she' d carry the Alalakan heir."

As Rodane crossed the room to stand next to his wife, Char walked over to stand next to Brianna.

Both Meri and Ban had seen Rodane join Crystas, and both knew what was coming.

Meri leaned closer to Brianna. "You' re about to meet your sister-in-law."

Brianna looked toward the woman who stood next to Singy. So that was Crystas. She' d been here all evening and had made no attempt to introduce herself. Meri had told her some things about Rodane' s wife, but Meri had also told Brianna that she really should form her own opinion.

Crystas was tall and elegant. At six feet six inches in height, she was slender and supple as a willow. Fitting her well-toned body like a glove, the lavender dress she wore had a scooped neck with short puffed sleeves that displayed her slender arms. Her shoulder-length, honey brown hair was pulled back in a severe style that emphasized high cheekbones and almond-shaped eyes. Head held high and shoulders thrown back, Crystas glided across the room on Rodane' s arm.

As Meri gripped her hand and Ban patted her shoulder, Brianna began to feel very uneasy. Then she began to get angry. *Just who the hell does she think she is to snub me? Well, we' ll see just how much the "carrier of the Alalakan heir" can get way with.*

Rodane halted in front of Brianna and bowed deeply.

Conversations ceased. Everyone wanted to observe the meeting between the new sisters-in-law.

"Brianna," Rodane said simply, "I' d like to introduce my wife, Alalakan dem al' Crystas."

Taking the hand Char offered, Brianna allowed him to assist her to her feet. She refused to let this obviously antagonistic woman tower over her more than necessary. "I' m pleased to meet you, Crystas."

Crystas looked down her nose at her new sister-in-law and said nothing.

Rodane glanced at his wife in amazement. This direct snub was unforgivable. He tightened his hand on her elbow.

Inclining her head, Crystas said in a somewhat envious voice, "Rodane did not do your coloring justice. Your hair is certainly...red."

"All the better to display Gattan red diamonds, don' t you think?" Ban asked in a devilish voice. "How are you, Coz?"

Crystas' s voice was tight. "Bandalardrac Hardan, what brings *you* here?"

"Alalakan don al' Bandalardrac," Rodane said in a firm voice, "has come home to his clan."

The whispers that ran through the crowd gave Crystas time to regain her composure and return her attention to Brianna. "So you carry the Alalakan heir. Are all women from your planet so...fertile?" Crystas smiled when she spoke, but her tone of voice left no doubt that the question was an insult.

Brianna was not one to be intimidated. "Do all women on your planet take so many years to...conceive?"

Char hastily stepped from behind Brianna.

At the same time, Rodane' s grip on Crystas' arm tightened.

Eager anticipation shot through the crowd.

Xdana was too competent a hostess, however, to allow a public squabble between her daughters-in-law. In seconds, she was standing between them.

"Brianna, you haven' t met Jamiros' mother, Alalakan dem al' Jenneta."

Brianna broke eye contact with her hostile sister-in-law and turned to face Char' s grandmother.

A wide smile and lively brown eyes met hers.

"Hello, Brianna," Jenneta said, "It' s a pleasure to meet the woman who finally brought an end to Char' s wandering ways. You must be something very special."

Relaxing, Brianna smiled. Char' s grandmother sounded very friendly. "At the time, he didn' t give me much of a choice."

"Char forced you to marry him?" Crystas purred.

"No, he didn' t," Brianna answered flashing a contemptuous glance at her sister-in-law. "No one forced me to do anything. I chose to marry Char."

Jenneta chuckled. "I would be very disappointed in my grandson if he couldn' t convince such a lovely woman to marry him."

"So he kept you in sensual thrall until you agreed to marry him," Crystas interjected snidely.

Sighing, Brianna glanced at the people surrounding her. Crystas just wouldn' t let it go. She could feel Char' s intense outrage and Rodane' s silent disapproval. Only Meri' s hand on Ban' s arm kept him from a scathing retort. Even Jamiros and Xdana were obviously unhappy with Crystas' comments.

Char' s grandmother, however, watched them both intently — as if she were waiting for something.

Brianna sighed and in a determined voice said, "Very well, Crystas, if you want a scene in front of the entire clan, you may have one."

"I have no idea what you are talking about," Crystas said smugly.

Brianna watched the calculated thoughts flash across her sister-in-law' s face. Starting a cat fight would certainly not endear Brianna to the clan. Obviously, Crystas was hoping Brianna would make a fool of herself.

Crystas had miscalculated — badly.

Using a tactic Crystas never expected, Brianna attacked, "I' d like to see your dragon."

"What?"

"Your dragon. All Alalakans wear them. As soon as Char explained their importance, I insisted on one for myself. I was also very specific about the design I chose when Lorilana applied it to my shoulder; its message is quite clear. The fire is mine, and I will fight for me and mine. I repeat, Crystas, where is your dragon?"

No one so much as coughed.

Jenneta' s eyes flashed as brightly as Brianna' s.

Crystas raised her chin, but said nothing.

Rodane answered for her. "Crystas wears no dragon. She chose not to do so until…"

"Until she carried the Alalakan heir?" Brianna finished for him, her hands resting on her protruding stomach. "Well, that' s not going to happen now, is it?"

Crystas glared at Brianna.

Thoughts whirling, Brianna glared back. *It' s so obvious why she hasn' t been pregnant yet. Why haven' t these people figured out Crystas is on birth control?* With a steely voice, she attacked. "Eight years of marriage and no pregnancy? I' m curious, Crystas. Are contraceptives available on Drakan? That' s it, isn' t it? You don' t really want to have a baby, but you don' t want to give up the prestige of being married to the Alalakan heir, do you? Do you enjoy holding the future of the Alalakan clan in your power?"

A shocked look on his face, Rodane turned to his wife, as did every guest in the room. Grasping her upper arms, he spun her to face him. "Is this true?"

"This is not a topic to be discussed in public, Rodane. I can' t believe that anyone would be so ill-bred as to mention it," Crystas snapped.

Anger rippled through Rodane' s voice. "You' re the one who began this with your immediate snub of my brother' s wife, the woman who carries the Alalakan heir. Answer me. Have you been preventing conception?"

She still tried to stall. "How can a woman who hasn' t even been here an entire day make such an accusation? Can it be she who is trying to sow dissension? She is, after all, an *alien*."

The total disgust with which Crystas spoke astonished everyone. Heads turned and murmurs were tossed back and forth. The Alalakans were an extremely open-minded clan in a very open-minded society.

"Well, well, well, the truth is finally becoming known," Jenneta muttered to no one in particular.

Some of the more gullible in the crowd, however, whispered uncertainly. Singy was smiling broadly. Was there something to Crystas' accusation?

Brianna' s husky laughter filled the room. "Why in the world would I want to do that? What could I possibly gain that I don' t already have? I already carry my husband' s child. A husband, I might add, who offered the Alalakan signet he wears and all it entails to Bandalardrac in repayment for saving my life."

Her revelation shocked everyone, including Char' s grandmother. For a woman who seemed to have anticipated everything that had happened so far, Jenneta was just as surprised as everyone else.

Char smiled at the older woman. "Don' t know me as well as you thought, do you, Grandmother?"

"Touché, Char," she said quietly. "First a pregnant bride and now this. You continually surprise me."

Char smiled and nodded.

"And *is* it Char' s child you carry? Not even Medirians get pregnant so quickly," Crystas threw out desperately.

Audible gasps echoed around the room. Crystas had gone too far, questioning not only Brianna' s fidelity but also Char' s integrity.

Char stiffened. "Brianna carries *my* child."

"You haven' t answered me, Crystas," Rodane snapped. "Have you been purposely preventing the conception of my children?"

Looking about the room, Crystas found no Alalakan allies or understanding. Casting discretion to the winds, she spat, "Yes, I have. Why should I be held prisoner to an outmoded tradition with no meaning? Why should I be expected to sacrifice my body to provide a child I don' t want?"

Even Brianna, who had not grown up steeped in Drakian clan tradition, was shocked at her reply.

Disgust filled Rodane' s voice. "So be it. You may not care for clan tradition, but I will honor it to my dying day." Grasping her dress above the right shoulder with both hands, he ripped it to the waist, displaying her right breast and, most importantly, her bare right shoulder. He removed the sparkling bluestone necklace she wore around her neck, the numerous bracelets from her arms, and finally, the wedding ring from her finger.

"The necklace is mine," Crystas said haughtily. "I demand that you return it."

"Wrong," he answered in an icy tone. "It is the necklace of your Matriarchal line. *Tradition* declares that it be passed on down to the *eldest* daughter. Something you have pointed out many times these past eight years you are *not*. This necklace belongs to Fionilina."

Rodane walked across the room and placed the necklace around the neck of a quietly pretty, very surprised Drakian woman dressed in a plain white dress. Only Jenneta' s and Brianna' s eyes narrowed in speculation. Everyone else was too caught up in the unfolding drama.

Returning to the group that stood about Crystas, Rodane handed her jewelry to his father.

"Sell it," he said tightly. "I no longer have a use for it. Char, you are clan leader now that Brianna carries the heir. I request dissolution of my marriage."

The entire assemblage gasped and whispers raced through the crowd. Rodane' s symbolic stripping had declared that he would divorce Crystas, but no one had expected him to state it in public. The dissolution of a marriage was usually a private affair with the announcement made after the fact. Rodane had reached deeply into Drakian clan tradition to sever his bond with Crystas. Tradition demanded that Char, as clan leader, finish what Rodane had started.

"Alalakan dem al' Crystas," Char declared in a tight voice, "your husband, Alalakan don al' Rodane, seeks dissolution of your marriage on the grounds that you refuse to bear his children. Do you contest these accusations?"

Lips pinched together, Crystas glared at Char.

"No answer on your part will not stop these proceedings, Crystas. Do you wish to answer Rodane?"

"No!"

"You bore no Alalakan children nor do you wear an Alalakan dragon; therefore, there is no reason not to grant dissolution of this marriage if neither party contests my decision. Do you wish to remain Alalakan, Crystas?"

"I won' t remain in a clan that breeds with aliens," Crystas sneered.

Brianna snorted inelegantly. "You married into a clan with Medirian blood. Mine is the same as theirs."

"There is no Medirian blood in the Alalakan clan," Crystas snapped. "Like mine, their blood is pure. What lies do you seek to spread now?"

Brianna smiled at her brother-in-law. "Rodane, you never told your wife that your grandmother has Medirian blood?"

Jenneta smiled broadly. "Very, very good, my dear. My mother was Medirian. How did you know?"

Brianna shrugged. "It' s pretty obvious. You have earlobes."

Crystas stared at Jenneta as if she were something slimy that had crawled out from under a rock.

Char' s voice dripped with contempt. "Transportation to your clan' s ancestral holding will be provided. Since you do not wish to fraternize with *aliens*, I suggest you return to your rooms. Maids will soon arrive to help you pack."

Crystas looked about the room. Her pride would not allow her to pull her dress back up onto her shoulder. Walking across the room to her sister, she said haughtily, "Come Fionilina, we are not welcome here."

Brianna jabbed Char in the ribs, and Jenneta sent him an imperious glance. Not obtuse to not-so-subtle hints, he said, "Gerlindenpen dem al' Fionilina is a guest in this house, celebrating the announcement of the Alalakan heir. She need not leave if she does not wish to do so."

Fionilina looked at her sister and shook her head.

Crystas drew her shattered dignity about her and said, "You are no longer my sister." Turning her back on Fionilina, Crystas shot a look of pure hatred at Brianna and then stalked from the room.

"She certainly is a bitch, isn' t she?" Brianna murmured to no one in particular.

"Bitch?" Meri asked.

"It' s a derogatory term used to describe certain women on earth," Brianna answered a bit absentmindedly. "Excuse me. Char?"

Everyone' s attention returned to Brianna. Char' s new wife was providing enough gossip to last until winter.

"Yes?" Char looked at his wife curiously. *What is she planning now?*

"That woman," she stated, pointing to Singy, "has insulted a member of my family. I want her out of here — now."

Char frowned. "What are you talking about?" Surely Brianna wouldn' t make up a lie just because of one kiss.

Brianna tossed her hair back over her shoulder. Flashes of fire sparkled. "She told Ban he was a base half-breed. I will *not* tolerate such an insult to the Hardan royal family."

"She lies!" Singy shouted.

"Would you doubt Kahn' s word, Char? Or that of Ban himself?"

Char glanced at his cousin. "Ban?"

A casual shrug. "I' ve been called worse."

Nervous titters swept through the crowded room.

Char crossed his arms over his chest. "Did Singy insult you?"

Ban grinned. "If Brianna' s insulted, then yes, she did."

Char turned back to Singy. "You' ll leave in the morning."

"Char! You can' t mean that. Not after all that we mean to each other. All that we have together."

"There is no *we*, Singy. The past is the past. You were never more than a pleasant way to pass the time."

A very satisfied smile appeared on Brianna' s face.

Meri, on the other hand, was simmering with anger. "Mondolonton dem al' Singy, do not place foot on Mediria again, or I swear, you will wake up one morning with an assassin in your bed."

Singy blanched, and those who stood near her quickly moved away. Glancing around but finding no support, she burst into tears and ran from the room.

No one followed her.

Char furtively observed a very satisfied Brianna. *She's learned about the Medirian assassins. Meri, no doubt.*

Ban's brow, too, was furrowed. *Kahn told Brianna what Singy said. Does she mean what she says or did she use the "insult" just to get rid of Singy? Either way, Brianna's displayed intelligence worthy of the Hardan — and Alalakan — names.*

The object of the two men's speculation sighed as she sank back down onto the sofa. *Well, maybe this assassin thing isn't so bad, especially if it'll keep other women away from Char.*

She groaned and shifted her weight.

The baby was kicking up a storm.

Meri's tone was worried. "Are you all right, Brianna?"

Char immediately turned to his wife. "Brianna?"

Brianna waved him away. "Oh, stop worrying. I simply need to sit down. The baby is break dancing again,"

"Break dancing?" asked more than one voice.

"You'll get used to it," Char said in a more relaxed tone.

Brianna turned her attention to Rodane. Quietly she said, "Rodane, I'm sorry."

He quickly smiled, bent, and took her hand in his. "Don't apologize to me, Brianna. You did nothing a true Alalakan wife wouldn't do. You defended yourself and your clan. Crystas and I had been growing farther apart each day. What happened tonight would have taken place even if you hadn't married Char."

"But I feel responsible..."

"You are responsible for nothing, except, perhaps, the opportunity to eventually become a father myself...if I can find a woman to love me as you love Char. Now, if you will excuse me, I would like some time alone."

Everyone in the room watched as he walked proudly from the room.

"Well," Jenneta said dryly, "I always said you knew how to throw a party, Xdana. This one will certainly go down as unique in the annals of the Alalakan clan."

From where she sat on the sofa, Brianna was aware of various groups of people still watching and listening. Taking the initiative, she motioned Jenneta and Xdana to stand off to the side so that she had an unrestricted view of the gathering. Raising her chin, she said in a clear voice, "Okay, the show is over. Go back about your business gossiping and eating the wonderful food provided by Xdana. I'm sure you'll have to rehash tonight's event a number of times."

At first absolute silence reigned.

Then Jenneta's hearty laugh cut through the silence. "You are right, Char. I find your wife to be extremely charming."

Char stared at the door through which his brother had disappeared. *Why did Rodane say Brianna loves me? She barely knows me.*

Chapter Thirteen

Ban tugged the arm of the woman at his side. "Come on, Brianna' s back. I' ll introduce you now."

As Ban approached, Brianna looked up.

"Brianna, this is Gerlindenpen dem al' Fionilina. She' d like to speak with you."

Brianna smiled and patted the sofa next to her. "Sit down."

Her eyes downcast, Fionilina said, "I apologize for my sister' s behavior. Ever since the Gerlindenpen clan lost much of its fortune, Crystas has felt that life has been unfair. Even after Rodane and she married, she was dissatisfied with her life. She saw the increasing pressure to bear the Alalakan heir as her way of controlling the entire clan. Then word reached us that Char had married a woman from a newly discovered planet. A few months later, we heard that you were carrying the Alalakan heir."

Fionilina raised her eyes to Brianna' s and continued, her voice bitter. "Crystas hates you, Alalakan dem al' Brianna, more than she has ever hated anyone. She' ll seek revenge."

Her new family members no longer flocked around Brianna. However, one of them was always by her side in case anyone chose to continue Crystas' harassment. So it was Jamiros who answered Fionilina' s warning. "Don' t worry about Brianna. Crystas no longer has any power here, and Brianna will be well protected."

Brianna pursed her lips. *What had Crystas done to Fionilina to make her sound so bitter? Rodane maybe? I bet he married the wrong sister.* "Don' t worry too much about me, Fionilina." Patting her stomach, she continued, "I won' t be going anywhere for a few months. And I have two Aradabs who observe every breath into and out of my mouth."

Ban winked at Brianna and extended his hand to Fionilina. Taking it, she rose to her feet.

Before they could leave, Brianna said, "Would you excuse Ban a minute, Fionilina? I' d like to talk to him."

She nodded and wandered across the room. Ban' s gaze followed her. "I hope this is important, Coz," he murmured. "That is one lady who definitely is in need of comfort."

Jamiros snorted and mumbled something about needing a drink. Catching Char' s eye, he made his way to the buffet table. Char began a meandering course back to his wife.

"You' d think I was made of fine china," Brianna muttered to herself. "What in the world could happen to me while I' m surrounded by Alalakans?"

"You can always pretend we' re worried about the fortune in Gattan red diamonds you wear," Ban teased.

"You' re just as bad as the rest of them."

He shrugged eloquently. "What do you want to talk about, Coz? Has one of these beautiful ladies told you that she finds me irresistible?"

She mumbled a curse. "I' m trying to be serious, Ban."

He grinned and sat down. "Well?"

"I don' t want you to charm Fionilina into your bed."

Ban sighed, but he didn' t even pretend to argue. "You saw it, too."

She nodded. "She wouldn' t be content, Ban. Oh, I' m sure she would enjoy herself. But, you know you' re not serious. She may read too much into any relationship she has with you."

Ban ran his hand through his hair. "The thought had entered my mind. I' ve always been totally honest with the women I love."

Brianna smiled. Char always ran his hand threw his hair when he was thinking, too. Lacing her fingers through his, she said, "You don' t know what it is to truly love a woman, you rascal."

He squeezed her hand. "But I so enjoy trying, Coz."

Shaking her head, Brianna added, "Rodane is still in the library. I' m sure Fionilina would like to talk with him."

"And, I' m sure," Ban added with a wicked grin, "that Rodane would like to *talk* with Fionilina, too."

Char joined Brianna on the sofa after Ban rose. "What was that conversation about?" he asked as he laced his fingers through hers. *And why were you holding his hand?*

"Fionilina wanted to apologize for Crystas," she answered a bit absentmindedly, concentrating on Ban and Fionilina as they walked towards the library.

"Not Fionilina," Char said following his wife' s gaze. *Why are you watching Ban?* "What was so important that you had to take Ban away from a woman he' s spent the entire evening wooing to his bed?"

Still watching the object of their conversation, Brianna answered, "Fionilina isn' t right for Ban. Her feelings run too deep, and he couldn' t give her what she needs."

Pay attention to me, Brianna. "And what' s that?" He leaned closer and nibbled her bare shoulder.

That got her attention.

A seductive smile played across her lips. Her fingers began a delicate dance on his thigh. "She wants to be loved and have a husband and a family. She wants Rodane."

Stretching his arm along the back of the sofa behind her, he pulled his wife closer. Caressing her bare arm, he placed a wet kiss on her neck.

Her breathing quickened and her nipples tightened, straining against the soft material of her bodice.

Char' s low, sexy laughter sent shivers up and down her spine.

She felt her cheeks flush. She could feel eyes darting to and away from them.

"Another of your ' feelings' , love?" he whispered in her ear after he ran his tongue down the length of her neck.

Char didn' t give a damn who was watching them.

"Oh, yes," she purred, her fingers dancing closer to his groin, brushing her knuckles against his erection. As long as he didn' t start making love to her right here on the sofa, two could play this game.

"Aren' t you tired yet?" Char whispered as he nuzzled her ear. "It' s been a long day."

Brianna' s voice was low and seductive. "I' m not tired at all."

"Well, I am." Rising, Char swept her into his arms.

Jenneta appeared beside them. "Char! I haven' t had a chance to talk with Brianna."

"Talk to her tomorrow. We' re going to bed."

Jenneta' s merry laughter followed them up the stairs.

Brianna awoke cradled in Char' s arms. Grimacing as the baby kicked her bladder, she eased away and waddled into the bathroom. After relieving herself, she grasped the headband of her bridal net, tried to remove it, and yelped. During the night, the gold and diamond chains had become impossibly tangled in her hair. Stomping out of the bathroom, she cast a baleful glare at her husband. He was stretched out on his stomach, his arms wrapped around her pillow. Stopping at the side of the bed, she reached down and jerked his tail.

He awoke with a snarl on his lips. "What the hell!"

"' Leave the diamonds, love,' you said. ' Our passion will make the fires in them blaze.' Well now they' re all tangled up! And I refuse to cut my hair!"

Char rubbed the sleep from his eyes.

Brianna' s hands were fisted on her hips, and her eyes flashed with a different kind of fire.

"Sit," he growled.

Leaning over, he pushed a button on the console of the nightstand. "Send breakfast up," he snapped. He' d planned on a long morning in bed making love. Obviously, that plan would not bear fruit.

Brianna turned and flopped—as much as a pregnant woman can flop—onto the edge of the bed and presented her back to Char.

Staring at the tangle of hair, diamonds, and red-gold chains, he realized that she had a point. "I hope you didn' t have anything important to do this morning," he grumbled.

She cursed under her breath. It was her hair that was about to be pulled.

Twenty minutes later, Char threw up his hands in frustration. "I' m sorry, but I don' t know what to do. The strands of gold and diamonds are so fine, I can' t get them untangled."

"What am I supposed to do now?!"

Char was saved from a reply by a knock on the bedroom door. Jumping from the bed, he opened the door to admit Beti and Verna, Brianna' s new maid.

"Char, go put some clothes on," Brianna snapped.

He ignored her. "Beti, how do I get that bridal net off without cutting her hair?"

Beti looked at Brianna, assessed the situation at a glance, and said, "I'll fetch Princess Merilinlalissa."

"Char," Brianna said with her eyes flashing, "you will not walk around here naked when Meri arrives."

Grumbling, he stomped into the bathroom.

"You've certainly got a tangle here," Verna said cheerfully.

Brianna was scowling at her maid when Char walked out of the bathroom wearing a pair of lounging trousers.

Before he could comment, Beti returned followed by Meri who was wearing a tightly belted robe, her dark hair flowing loosely about her.

"I'd stay away from Ademis for a few hours if I were you, Char," she said as she set down a small container.

His voice was indignant. "What did I do?"

All four women looked at him with astonished expressions.

Brianna's reply was icy. "Need you ask?"

"Sleeping in a bridal net had to be your idea, Char. Only a man would have so little sense," Meri grumbled.

"I didn't hear any complaints at the time."

"Probably because you had kissed her senseless," Verna interjected.

Char glared at Beti. "Aren't you going to say something?"

Directing a level stare at him, she answered, "Men lack common sense. It will do no good to berate you for the lack."

Brianna flashed a smile of triumph.

Char was too intelligent a man to stay in a room where he was obviously outnumbered by hostile women. "I'll be having breakfast with my brother," he said as he stomped out of the room.

Meri fingered Brianna's hair. "What a mess."

"You can get it out, can't you, Meri? It's taken my entire life to grow my hair this long."

Meri patted her shoulder. "We can get it out, but it is probably going to take all morning. Verna, fill the tub with water, as hot as Brianna can stand it, and dump that entire container of manis oil into the tub as it fills. Don't forget to add another bath oil, preferably one of a very aromatic musk oil base. We want to kill the fish odor."

"Fish odor!"

Meri ignored Brianna' s outburst. "Beti, go back to my room and tell Ademis he may as well get out of bed. I won' t be back for a while."

"What about Celene?"

"After she' s had her breakfast, tell Feni to give her to my sisters and Sheala. That will keep all of them out of trouble. Celene' s still too small to do anything totally outlandish."

"Judging by the numbers of breakfasts that were ordered to be delivered to rooms this morning, Char' s urge to wrap himself in your hair while it was strung with gold and diamonds is ruining many a plan for a morning in bed," Verna said with a chuckle.

Meri followed Brianna into the bathroom. "Ademis and I are the only ones put out."

Verna trailed after them. "Char goes to his brother, Rodane, who planned to keep Fionilina in his bed all day. She will insist in offering her help to Brianna, the woman who made it possible for Rodane to become hers. When she leaves, the brothers will decide that it' s been too long since they breakfasted with their parents. Therefore, Jamiros and Xdana will be disturbed."

Brianna gasped in amazement. While the idea of Jamiros and Xdana being intimate was not surprising, the nonchalance with which Verna spoke of it did. *Will I ever get used to this casual attitude about sex?*

Brianna dropped her robe and eased into the hot water. "Is there anyone in this house who didn' t plan on an uninterrupted morning in bed?"

"Only me, Coz," answered Ban from where he leaned against the doorway dressed as Char was in a simple pair of lounging pants.

Water slopped out of the tub as Brianna submerged herself to her neck. "What are you doing here?"

"The door was open. So many women' s voices were too much of a temptation," he said as he strolled over and examined her tangled hair. "You certainly have made a mess out of your hair and the bridal net. Do you need any more help?"

He was completely serious.

"No!" she shouted as Meri and Verna laughed. "Get out of here. Go bother the maids or something."

Ban grinned and looked pointedly at the bubbles that completely covered her to her neck. "It' s not as if I can see anything," he teased.

"*Out!*"

Meri grabbed his arm and pulled him towards the door. "Oh, go away, Ban. You don' t have any unattached women here to admire that gorgeous body."

"Speak for yourself, Princess," Verna muttered. "I may be old, but I' m not dead."

Grinning from ear to ear, Ban bowed gracefully and walked out of the room.

Placing her hand on Brianna' s head, Verna said, "Hold your breath." She dunked Brianna under the oily water, effectively cutting off her grumbling about men in general.

* * * * *

Char never paused. When he reached the door to Fionilina' s room, he simply turned the knob, walked in, and threw himself into a comfortable chair.

The scowl on his face brought a grin to Rodane' s. He nudged Fionilina. "Char looks rather disgruntled this morning, doesn' t he, love?" They had just finished their first bout of lovemaking for the day, so Char' s interruption didn' t irritate him as much as it would have half an hour earlier. Fio was snuggled contentedly at his side, her fingers softly caressing his chest and her tail wrapped around his calf.

Pulling her along as he pushed himself into a sitting position, Rodane smiled even more broadly when Char growled something unintelligible at them. "Unlike me, Fio," he said devilishly, "Char is the perfect example of sexual frustration."

Fio chuckled deliciously, not in the least bit embarrassed to be found in bed with Rodane or to sit before Char with the sheets about her waist.

Shooting her a quick glance, Char mumbled something about full breasts, but then his eyes snapped back to her naked torso. Above her right breast rode an Alalakan dragon. When his eyes met hers, Rodane answered his question before he could ask. "I put it there last night. I won' t allow *this* woman to get away from me."

Pushing himself out of the chair, Char walked over to the bed for a closer look. A green and gold dragon hovered with half-extended wings over a nest containing baby dragons. The dragon' s tail, rather than wrapping itself around Fionilina' s upper arm, dipped down around the outside of her right breast. Hugging her chest all the way underneath her breast, the dragon' s tail reached back up her cleavage to have its tip rest casually above her left nipple.

"I didn' t realize you were such a good artist, Brother," Char said as he gently traced the design.

"One of many hidden talents," Rodane answered. "Now, what brings you here to interrupt one of the best mornings of my life?" Then worry crossed his face. "Brianna?"

Char scowled again. "Damn bridal net."

Rodane was confused, but Fio immediately understood. "You don' t mean to say that Brianna slept in her bridal net! How could you let her do that?"

Char shot a very disgruntled look at his new sister-in-law. The official ceremony may not have been performed yet, but the dragon declared his brother' s intentions and Fio' s acceptance quite emphatically.

Practically knocking Char over, she jumped from Rodane' s side. "All that hair!" she exclaimed and headed for the door.

Rodane reached for her but missed. "Wait a minute."

"Fio," Char said before she could get to the door, "you had better put on a robe."

Puzzled, she turned. "Whatever for?"

"Brianna will be embarrassed for you if she thinks you walked all the way to our suite completely naked."

"But, there' s only family here," Fio began. Then comprehension dawned. She jerked open the door to the closet, mumbled something about off-world sexual inhibitions, and wrapped herself in a robe. Then she disappeared out the door.

Char smiled as the door slammed shut. "She has a beautiful body. I never realized before how full her breasts were."

Rodane sighed and sent a dissatisfied scowl in his brother' s direction. "Do you know how long it' s been since I spent an entire day in bed with a woman?"

"Probably since before you married Crystas," Char answered with a grin. "She always impressed me as being rather inhibited."

"She was downright frigid." Rodane swung his legs over the side of the bed and nodded towards Char' s pants. "I take it that Brianna would rather not see you running about bald ass naked either."

"Only if the other people around are women. I can ' run around naked in front of other men, if I want to' she said. And I recommend that you do not wander into our quarters nude either. That is, of course, unless you want to see her blush."

Rodane headed towards the bathroom. "Do you think she' ll always be like that?"

Char shrugged. "I don' t know. I doubt very much if any of us will be wandering about the house naked anymore. Ban and I are working on getting her to relax in our private quarters, though."

Rodane stopped and swivelled. "Ban! You' re letting the most notorious rake on five planets walk about your room naked!"

Char grinned and shook his head. "I' m not stupid. No. He' ll be walking in when Bri' s naked."

Rodane' s mouth fell open. That was even more unbelievable. Shaking his head, he turned back to the bathroom. "I hope you know what you' re doing."

So do I. "Rodane, about Brianna carrying the heir…"

"Char, I' m not lying when I say that I am glad Brianna is carrying the Alalakan heir. I never wanted to make decisions that affected the entire clan."

Char followed Rodane into the bathroom and leaned against the doorway as his brother stepped into the shower. "Is that true? Why?"

Rodane grinned. "Because I don' t want the responsibility. You, on the other hand, revel in responsibility. Take it, with my blessing."

"I can' t do everything myself."

"And I' ll help all you want, Char. Just don' t expect me to make any final decisions where the clan is concerned. My family, even your family, that' s different. But the clan? Too many members are never satisfied. You' re more than welcome to deal with them. Now, do you have any more of those lounging pants? I wouldn' t want to offend the mother of the Alalakan heir."

Laughing, Char turned and pushed the intercom button.

215

When Fionilina left Char and Rodane, she went directly to Brianna's rooms, her glare daring Kahn to try to stop her from entering. Kahn merely nodded his head and opened the door for her. Inside, she found Ban comfortably ensconced in a deep chair watching the morning news video. The remains of a very fortifying breakfast sat on the table beside him.

He looked up when Fio walked in, grinning when he realized that the overly large robe hanging off her left shoulder was all she wore.

"Where's Brianna?"

"In the tub," he answered, and then continued with a suggestive leer, "Want some company? I'm available."

Fionilina smiled even wider and slipped the robe off of her other shoulder. Ban's eyes widened. "Rodane works faster than Char," he muttered. But then a smile crossed his face. "Welcome to the family, Coz."

"Thanks, Coz," she replied over her shoulder. "Now, if you'll excuse me, Brianna needs all the help she can get."

Brianna was soaking in the tub with her hair spread out over the side behind her. Verna and Meri were painstakingly working through it a few strands at a time. Every few minutes, they would dip it into the oily water. Beti stood patiently, holding each strand of gold and diamonds as it was separated from her hair.

All four women looked up as Fio walked over to the tub and looked down at Brianna's hair.

"You really have a mess here," she said, taking charge of the situation completely. "You'll need two days to get that net untangled if you keep working like this. It will be a lot easier if her hair is under the water. Meri, we need to get in the tub."

Dropping her robe, Fio slid into the tub and reached for a strand of hair. "Dip your head under the water again, Brianna. It really should stay oily for this to work properly."

Verna shoved her head under the water.

Brianna came up sputtering after Verna released her head. "You're wearing a dragon," she said wiping oily water from her eyes.

Fionilina smiled a wide smile, her deft fingers untangling Brianna's hair. "And I have you to thank. If not for you, Crystas would still have Rodane in her clutches."

"He certainly didn' t waste any time."

Meri stripped off her robe and slipped into the large tub. "Alalakan men don' t waste time when they know what they want."

"But Crystas hasn' t even left the house yet!"

"She left at dawn. Her father' s shuttle fetched her," Beti said in her flat voice.

Fionilina frowned as she continued to work deftly with Brianna' s hair. "I' d better call my father and mother today and give them the other side of the story before Crystas poisons their minds. Once they find out she was purposely thwarting conception, she' ll get little sympathy."

Meri freed another strand of gold and diamonds. "When will the official ceremony be for you and Rodane?"

"It will take two weeks for the official paperwork declaring the dissolution of Rodane' s and Crystas' marriage to be finalized. We will marry quietly the day after Rodane receives his copy of the papers."

Brianna shifted. "It' s that easy?"

"Crystas agreed publicly. Even if she hadn' t, using birth control without her husband' s knowledge is grounds enough for the dissolution of a marriage," Fio answered. "Crystas won' t want to be publicly humiliated. She' d never be able to make another advantageous marriage."

"You two certainly finalized all of your plans last night," Meri commented as she struggled with a particularly difficult snarl.

Fionilina chuckled devilishly. "We did much more than plan."

All five women in the room laughed.

Brianna had worked through all of the hair strands she could reach, so she leaned back and enjoyed their gentle ministrations. Grimacing, she shifted a little.

"I' m sorry if I pulled your hair," Fio said.

Brianna shifted her weight. "It wasn' t you. The baby has decided it' s time for his morning workout."

"Morning workout?"

Meri smiled. "You get used to it."

Brianna shifted again. "How much longer is this going to take? I' m beginning to feel like a prune."

"Prune?" both Meri and Fio asked.

Brianna chuckled. "Never mind. You'll get used to it."

Ban grinned as Char and Rodane entered the room.

"Comfortable?" Char asked as he threw himself into the chair next to his cousin.

"Quite." Turning to Rodane, Ban continued, "I understand congratulations are in order. You two don't waste any time grabbing onto your women."

Stretching out in another chair and propping his feet up on a stool, Rodane grinned. "It helps keep rakes like you away."

"There are rakes who prefer married women," Ban shot back with a grin just as wide as Rodane's. This family camaraderie was something he'd missed.

"Why did you leave, Ban?" Rodane asked. "We thought you were happy with us."

Though Char was listening to the conversation, he was busy ordering more breakfast from the kitchen. He also took the time to contact Ademis via the intercom and ask him to join them.

Ban leaned forward, clasped his hands, and placed his elbows on his knees. With a somewhat abashed smile he said, "I swore I'd never tell you this, but, since circumstances have changed…"

"Two months after you married Crystas, you made that quick business trip to Mediria. You weren't gone two hours before she was in my bed. At least that's where I found her. I was all of seventeen."

"Crystas was furious when I refused her. She told me that you and Char were making plans to slowly ease me out of the clan since I was a half-blood." Ban smiled. "At the time, I didn't know about Grandmother and her Medirian blood. If I had…"

He shrugged.

Rodane bit out a curse. "So Crystas drove you away with lies."

"I was young and stupid enough to believe her. If not for Brianna and Char…"

"You'd still be devising ways to aggravate Mediria's Dowager Queen," Char finished, "and becoming more and more bitter towards anything Alalakan."

Ban grinned very widely. "Half wrong, Char. I'm still devising ways to aggravate the old witch. I'm just doing it from Drakan."

Both Rodane and Char grinned back. Laughter from the partially open bathroom door drew their attention.

The outer door opened and Ademis entered. "How goes the untangling?"

"Once Fionilina got here and took charge, things seemed to progress much more rapidly," Ban answered. "At least that's how it sounds."

Char rose to his feet. "I suppose I should go see how things progress," he said ruefully.

Ban laughed and stood up. "Wouldn't recommend it, Coz. Meri and Fio got into the tub with Brianna. I really don't think Brianna wants you to see them naked."

Char scowled. Ban had a point. *When will she get over this jealously? Fio's family now, and Meri practically is.*

"Sit down. I'll see how things go with the lovely Brianna," Ban said as he pushed Char into his chair and walked toward the bathroom. "I'm the only one without a naked wife in there. Brianna will be less angry with me than with any of you three."

Ademis' eyebrow rose. "Wife?"

"Rodane and Fionilina," Char answered as he watched Ban enter the bathroom. A sharp jab in the direction of his heart was ruthlessly quashed. So what if Ban saw Brianna naked?

Then, Brianna's indignant yell caused him to wince. "I guess she's still angry," he muttered mostly to himself.

"What are you doing back here, Ban?" Brianna yelped as he entered the bathroom. "We heard the door shut when you left."

"I never left, sweet Coz," Ban answered with a shrug. "I opened the door and let my breakfast in."

Meri and Fio grinned at each other as Brianna sputtered and tried to hide herself under water that no longer was filled with bubbles.

"We're almost finished, Ban," Meri said. "A few more tangles and the net will be free."

"Good. Char ordered enough breakfast for everyone."

"Everyone?"

"Rodane and Ademis are out there, too," Ban answered as he turned to leave. "By the way, Bri," he said as he was ready to duck out the door. "You seem to be putting on a little weight."

Feminine laugher and Brianna' s outraged yelp followed Ban as he hurried through the doorway before the soap bounced off the wall.

At Brianna' s second outraged yell, Char rose to his feet.

Ban slipped through the door and pulled it shut. "Make sure you move fast if Brianna' s ever angry enough to throw things at you. She' s got quite an aim."

I already know that. "What did you say to her?"

Ban grinned more widely. "I mentioned that she looked like she was gaining some weight. "

Rodane and Ademis joined in Char' s laughter.

"Ban has an invaluable place with the Alalakans," Rodane choked out. "Who else would be willing to face Brianna' s temper?"

Ban bowed jokingly to all three men. "I consider it an honor to have three of the galaxy' s most beautiful women angry with me so that their husbands do not suffer. Besides, what woman has ever been able to stay angry with me?"

"One day, Cousin," Char growled, "you' re going to meet a woman who will not think of you as a charming rogue to be petted and cozened. And I, for one, hope to be there to see it."

* * * * *

Sheala grabbed Brianna' s hand and started to pull her across the garden. "Come down to the pool today."

Brianna smiled at Char' s sister. All that energy! "No. I think I' ll see what Jenneta' s doing. The stories she tells about all of you as children are hysterical."

Jami and Vani exploded out of the patio doorway, and all three girls raced towards the pool.

After a leisurely walk in the gardens, Brianna entered the study from the patio to find Char the center of two of the maids' attention. Though he was fully clothed, both of them were naked. And he didn' t seem to mind.

"Char!"

Damn! Why did she have to walk in now? I' d have been rid of them in a few minutes. "Hello, love."

Bright spots of color appeared on her cheeks. "Love! You call me love when I find you with two naked women in your arms? How stupid do you think I am?"

"Brianna, it' s not how it looks."

She shivered and struggled to speak. "Just *how* does it look, Chardadon?"

Both maids smirked. Brianna' s jealously had become the topic of many a conversation and the butt of many a joke. One of the maids went so far as to plaster herself against him and caress his groin. "You are welcome to join us, Alalakan dem al' Brianna," she purred.

Shocked at her audacity, Char stared down at her.

Brianna saw nothing in her husband' s gaze but seeming approval of the maid' s suggestion. Bursting into tears, she fled.

Taking her cue from her compatriot, the other maid slipped her hand inside Char' s shirt and sought his mouth with hers.

"Chardadon! What are you doing?"

Pushing the maid away, Char looked into the furious eyes of his grandmother. "I..."

"You two will leave! Now!" Jenneta snapped.

Both maids grabbed their clothing and practically sprinted from the room.

Eyes flashing, Jenneta rounded on her grandson. "How can you be so callous and unfeeling, Chardadon? How can you shame your family like this? You' re breaking your wife' s heart."

He couldn' t meet her gaze. "Grandmother, I don' t encourage them. I would never have sex with another woman with Brianna in the house. I' d have convinced them to leave in another few minutes. Brianna misunderstood what she saw."

Hands fisted on her hips, Jenneta glared at her grandson. "Misunderstood!" she hissed in a low voice. "She misunderstood nothing. You' ve made no effort to discourage any of the women in this house."

"Grandmother, I won' t be impolite."

"Impolite! Whose feelings are more important, Brianna' s or all the women who' ve shared your bed?"

He opened his mouth, but Jenneta cut him off.

"Don' t say anything you' ll regret. Not now. Brianna carries our heir; yet, if she decided to leave, how would we stop her? She' s a Hardan princess. Ban would take her anywhere she wanted to go, and every Medirian assassin in the galaxy would make sure you never saw her again."

"Damn it, Grandmother, she *is* the most important thing in my life. She carries my child. And she is the key to destroying Bakom. I will *not* allow her to leave."

Anger blazed from Jenneta' s eyes. "Key to destroying Bakom? Is that what she is to you? Brianna is not a thing, you fool. She' s a woman, a woman who loves you. Yet you keep throwing that love back in her face by allowing other women to kiss and caress you."

Char shook his head. "Love! Brianna married me to save herself and her planet from Bakom."

Astounded and aghast, Jenneta glowered at her grandson. Finally she said, "Char, you are an incredibly stupid man." Spinning on her heel, she left the room.

Char cursed fluently — in three different languages. A quick swipe of his hand sent papers flying from the desk. His palms braced against it, he glared unseeing at its surface. Love! Why did everyone keep mentioning love? Of course, he was fond of Brianna, very fond. But they had to destroy Bakom. Why couldn' t they understand? If they didn' t destroy him, all of them would suffer. He would honor Brianna as his wife; she carried his child, the Alalakan heir, but she was now Drakian. She would have to adapt to their sexual mores.

His right hand curled into a fist, and he pounded the desk. Taking several deep breaths, he slowly regained control of his temper. Once it was under control, he retrieved the papers from the floor. Then he grimaced. Jerking the door open, he went in search of his wife. The longer he waited to talk to her, the more upset she' d become.

Sobbing, Brianna raced past Kahn and pushed open the door of her suite only to slam it shut in his worried face. Stumbling to a chair, she slumped into it, her sobs becoming louder.

"Brianna, love. What' s wrong?"

Ban pulled her unresisting body into his arms and sat down in the chair, holding her close, allowing her to cry uninterrupted. Eventually, her sobs slowed. "I want to go home," she whimpered. "I want to see my mother and father. They don' t even know if I' m alive."

"Shhh," he whispered, brushing her hair out of her face, "everything will be all right, I promise."

"No, it won' t," she moaned. "I won' t share with other women. A marriage is supposed to be two people loving each other. Char won' t—can' t—all those other women are always with him, and he doesn' t make them leave. I can' t live like this. Please, Ban, take me home."

When Brianna turned her tear-filled gaze on him, Ban couldn' t resist the misery and longing in her eyes. Lowering his head, he placed a gentle kiss on her lips, a kiss that remained gentle, but became more insistent.

She didn' t fight him.

Ban lifted his mouth from hers and looked deep into her eyes. "Come away with me, love. I' ll worship you for the rest of my life. I will love you as you deserve to be loved. I swear you' ll never be unhappy again."

So intent was Brianna on her misery and Ban in his appeal, neither realized Char stood in the doorway, shock and outrage on his face. Kahn' s heavy hand fell on his shoulder before he could step into the room, and he was jerked back into the hallway.

"Take your hand from me now, Aradab," Char said in a very low, very dangerous voice.

"No."

"She is my wife."

"She is a Hardan princess. She does not wish to see you now."

"I won' t let her fall into bed with Bandalardrac."

"Who is at fault, Dragon of the Alalakans?"

Cursing under his breath, Char turned and strode away. A stairway led to the balcony outside their sitting room. He' d be damned if Ban ended up making love to his wife. Brianna was his!

Brianna pulled her mouth from Ban' s. His kisses were passionate, and he was attractive and sexy, but—he wasn' t Char. "Ban, let me go. Please."

She pushed against his chest.

He released her immediately, and she slid awkwardly from his lap.

A few deep breaths and he was in control of himself. "Do you want to talk about it?"

Fresh tears rolled down her cheeks, but she refused to give in to her anguish a second time. "I found Char with two of the maids. They were naked."

Astonishment leaped onto Ban's face. Char wasn't that callous. He wouldn't shame Brianna in her own house. "All of them?"

"Just the maids."

Ban stared at Brianna. "You didn't jump to the wrong conclusion, did you?"

Appalled, Brianna stared at the handsome man who had just comforted her, who'd offered to love her until her dying day. "Jump to the wrong conclusion! Whose side are you on?"

"Yours, love. But Char wouldn't make love to another woman here in your home."

"And how do you know that?" she snapped.

"Because he's too honorable."

"Too honorable! Ha! You didn't see what I did."

"Brianna…"

"No!" she cried, holding her hands over her ears, pacing awkwardly back and forth, "I don't want to hear about how things are different here on Drakan. I don't care if they're different. I love him, Ban. I can't help it. I don't want to, but I do. And he's breaking my heart."

Ban pulled the unresisting Brianna back into his arms when she passed him. "He doesn't mean to hurt you, Brianna. It's just…"

Finally at a loss for words, Ban simply held her close, giving her what comfort he could, her confession of love for Char destroying any hope that he could lure her away from him.

Stupid bastard. When would he realize how lucky he was?

On the balcony, Char stepped back away from the open door, pondering everything he'd heard. *Love? She loves me? But why hasn't t she told me?*

You are a fool, Char, his conscience said. *What have you done to deserve her love?*

I' ve showered her with expensive gifts. I spend every night in her bed, making love until she cries with the joy of it.

In other words, you' ve treated her like almost every other woman you' ve taken to your bed.

I married her.

To thwart Bakom.

I could have done that without marrying her.

Then why?

I wanted her.

Is that all?

"Damn it," Char growled as he made his way back down the stairway and into the gardens.

He paused next to a small bush covered with fragrant white flowers. A gardener hurried to his side.

"How many blooms could you cut without damaging the plant?"

"Chardadon, this is a linota bush. It' s taken ten years to bloom. Cutting the blossoms could harm it."

"I' ll get you ten more if I have to go to Gattan and dig them up myself," Char snarled.

The gardener took a hasty step back and turned his attention to the bush. Approximately two dozen fragrant white flowers bloomed on its short branches. "Six, I think. I could cut six and not harm the plant."

"Then cut them and see that my wife gets them. And make sure you tell her they' re from me."

The gardener' s lips quirked. News spread fast on the estate, and almost everyone knew about that morning' s encounter. And everyone waited anxiously to see what would happen next. "I' ll do as you say, Chardadon."

Char grunted and walked back the way he had come. The fact that his private life was becoming the main topic of conversation with everyone on the estate was beginning to annoy him. *Damn it! My plans don' t need any complications now. There' s time enough for love after Bakom is destroyed.*

A scowl on his face, Char stopped abruptly when he saw Ban descending the steps from the suite' s balcony. His anger escalated.

Bastard. He' ll never kiss my wife again. Stepping back behind a bush, Char waited until Ban passed. Then, he sprang.

Faster than seemed humanly possible, Ban turned, avoided Char' s attack, and had his cousin immobilized in an Aradab body hold. He relaxed slightly when he realized just who had attacked him. "You stupid fool, I could have…"

"Release me, now, Bandalardrac," Char commanded in a harsh voice.

After a moment, Ban complied.

Char whirled to face his cousin. "Never kiss my wife again." Spinning on his heel, Char strode away.

An amused smile etched itself across Ban' s lips. *Jealous, Char? It' s about time.*

"So, Grandmother' s right."

Ban whirled to face Rodane.

Rodane smiled. "You' re an assassin."

Ban stiffened. Only two other people knew the truth about him.

Rodane' s smile became a grin. "Don' t worry, Ban. I won' t tell anyone."

"How?"

"You were conveniently absent too many times after an assassin had struck after being in the vicinity less than a week before. Grandmother' s never stopped worrying about you, Ban. Her lost grandson, she always called you."

"Will you tell her?"

"That' s your decision. Personally, I' m glad you' re back. You' ve been missed." Rodane turned and strode away.

Ban watched him go. Damn. Rodane knew he was an assassin.

Chapter Fourteen

Brianna stared at the vase of flowers sitting on the table. Their delightful fragrance filled the room. Against her will, her spirits lifted. What was Char up to now? If he thought he could keep buying his forgiveness with exotic gifts, he was wrong.

"Do you like them?" Char asked from behind her.

She inhaled. "They' re lovely. Nothing on Earth can compare."

"Brianna..."

She didn' t give him a chance to finish. "I can' t live like this Char. Maybe Drakian women don' t care if their husbands fool around, but I do."

"Fool around?"

She whirled to face him. "Don' t play stupid, Char. You know exactly what I mean. I won' t share you with other women. If you can' t accept that, I' ll leave."

"You carry my child. I' ll never let you go," he answered sternly as he stepped nearer.

"And that' s all I am to you, a brood mare?"

"No."

"Oh, I forgot. I' m the bait in your trap for Bakom."

"Damn it, Brianna! I came here to apologize." Char pulled her into his arms and lifted her mouth to his.

As always, his kiss was devastating, demanding a response while promising everything.

Brianna melted against him. How could she ever live without this?

When Brianna relaxed in his arms, Char lifted his mouth and looked deep into to her distressed eyes. "Come with me. Mother has gathered the entire staff. Say to them what you will and I' ll support you, no questions asked."

Tensing, she stared back at him. Did he really mean it?

"Mother and Grandmother are waiting with them. You carry the Alalakan heir. You can command anything."

Brianna' s chin lifted and her eyes narrowed. "You better mean what you say, Char, or I' ll make your life a living hell."

As they entered the library, every set of female eyes shifted to Brianna then speculatively back to Char. One of the maids from that morning went so far as to send him an inviting smile.

That smile fanned Brianna' s already smoldering temper. *Bitch. You don' t know who you' re dealing with.* Stepping towards the assembled group, she narrowed her eyes and said very slowly and very emphatically, "Alalakan don al' Chardadon is *my* husband and I will *not* share him with anyone." Fixing her eyes on the two maids she' d found with Char that morning, she continued, "If you have an itch to scratch take it somewhere else."

"An ' itch to scratch' ?" Jenneta whispered to Char.

He shrugged. That was the first time he' d heard that particular phrase.

Several of the maids shifted nervously. Brianna had made her point with them.

The tall maid in front, however, still wore her smug smile.

Brianna attacked. "What' s your name?"

"Kitena," the maid purred her eyes sliding back to Char.

"You' re dismissed."

That got her attention. "What?"

Brianna rested her hands on her abdomen. "You heard me the first time."

"You can' t do that!"

A delicate red eyebrow rose. "Oh? Char, can I dismiss her?"

He clasped his hands behind his back. "You can do anything you like, Brianna. You carry the Alalakan heir."

The entire group shifted uneasily. Both Xdana and Jenneta stood with their arms crossed; their support for Brianna evident in their stances.

"Mistress," the maid said turning to Xdana.

"The disrespect you just displayed towards my daughter-in-law was totally unacceptable, Kitena. If she wishes to dismiss you, she may."

Wringing her hands, Kitena finally turned her pleading gaze back to Brianna. "Please. I' m sorry. I meant no disrespect. It will never happen again."

"Bullshit. I know exactly what you meant; you wanted Char in your bed." Brianna paused and stared at the distressed maid. She couldn' t just throw her out. She was a member of the clan, and had parents and other relatives who could make things harder for Char. "Xdana, are there any other Alalakan estates?"

"There are several. I' ll have her transferred immediately."

Brianna waved her hand dismissively. "Go pack your things. You' ll be leaving before the day is over."

She watched unemotionally as the maid ran sobbing from the room. Then she asked, "Does anyone else have any problems with the thought of living without my husband' s sexual favors?"

A chorus of no' s answered her question. Not a single maid looked in Char' s direction.

Looking towards her mother-in-law, Brianna stated, "I' ve finished now, Xdana."

"I' ll say," Ban stated from the doorway. "Don' t worry, Coz. I' ll protect Char' s chastity with my own body. No maid shall assault his fidelity."

"Shut up, Ban."

He made no attempt to hide the suggestive leers he tossed at various maids, some of whom were returning them cautiously, after furtive glances in Brianna' s direction.

Brianna ignored them. She' d made her point.

Jenneta linked her arm through Brianna' s and guided her from the room. "That was well done. Transferring her will quell complaints. Banishing her might have eventually caused problems."

Sighing, Brianna nodded. "I thought of that. The last thing I want to do is start a feud within the clan. I' m enough of a shock as it is."

Jenneta' s merry laughter trailed behind them. "But you' re such a delightful shock, my dear."

* * * * *

Muttering, Brianna counted again. Again she was one letter short. *How am I going to get these alphabets parallel when Drakian has more vowels?*

Her musings were interrupted when Char walked in.

"Working hard?"

She glanced at him from the corner of her eye. The last few days, he' d gone out of his way to pay more attention to her. And since her speech to the staff, the maids avoided him like the plague. However, houseguests were arriving to celebrate Solstice and Sheala' s eighteenth birthday. She had watched more than one woman flirt with Char. In every case, he had firmly and publicly declined all invitations. Why had he changed all of a sudden?

Char bent, nuzzled her collar aside, and kissed her neck. He placed his hand on her swelled abdomen. "Under different circumstances, love, I' d have you here on the floor right now."

Steadying her breathing, she replied, "No, Char, I' d have *you* on the floor right now."

He scooped her into his arms. "Then perhaps it is best that we do find a bed."

Before he was able to take a single step towards the door, the intercom began to buzz. Muttering an expletive, he set a giggling Brianna to her feet. Reaching over, he pushed the receive button. "Chardadon."

Ban' s voice, sharper than Brianna had ever heard it, exploded into the room. "Get out here to the shuttle pad, Char. There' s a Gattan warbird requesting permission to land."

Brianna placed her hand on his arm. "What' s wrong?"

"Gattan never land at private shuttle pads," he said. Pushing the button, he asked, "Did they identify themselves in any way? The warbird could have mechanical problems."

"' Wendjas has come' ," Ban answered. "I hope you know what that means."

"Find Rodane and tell him to meet me out there," Char ordered without answering Ban' s question, "and inform my father and mother that we may have an unknown number of guests staying for a while."

He glanced at Brianna with a thoughtful look. "You asked once how I got the scar on my chest, and I never got around to telling you. Would you like to meet the man who put it there?"

Brianna nodded. Though this visit was obviously unexpected, Char didn' t think there was any danger. He' d never let her anywhere near that ship otherwise.

Fifteen minutes later, they stood with Rodane and Ban next to the shuttle pad. A door in the side of the sleek ship opened and an automatic stairway emerged.

"What a beautiful ship," Brianna said.

Ban worshiped it with his eyes. "That warbird is top-of-the-line Gattan technology. She' s fully capable of extensive interplanetary flight. I hope these are *good* friends, Char. If we don' t get the Alalakans involved in that technology, their ships will soon be better than ours."

A man appeared at the door of the ship.

"It *is* Wendjas," Char breathed quietly. Jerking his head towards Ban and Rodane, he pulled his shirt over his head. They quickly followed his lead.

Brianna watched them curiously. When Char looked meaningfully at her, she gasped, "If you think I' m taking my shirt off, you' re crazy!"

"Then I hope this isn' t one of your favorite shirts." He ripped off the short sleeve and tore open the shoulder seam so that her dragon was revealed.

"Close you mouth, Coz," Ban hissed, "you want to make a good impression. These are Gattan."

Snapping her mouth shut, Brianna concentrated on the man approaching them. One look told her why the Gattan ambassador to Mediria was so interested in the lion' s picture.

If a full-grown African lion could be reshaped into human form while still retaining its most striking characteristics, he would look like the man who walked towards them. Approximately six feet four, the Gattan wore a full lion' s mane. Thick, golden hair, combed behind pointed ears cascaded down his back. Though he was clean-shaven, Brianna was sure he could sport a full golden beard if he so chose. His nose was somewhat flatter and wider than she was used to but was by no means unattractive. Piercing golden eyes, which moved constantly about his surroundings, missed nothing. His thin lips were drawn back in a wide grin, displaying strong, white teeth.

He glided with the grace of a cat, smoothly and easily. Wearing an open, sleeveless vest, his darkly tanned chest was bare, displaying more than a few white scars, one that matched Char' s almost perfectly. Muscular bare arms displayed more scars. Around his waist, he wore a thick belt of the red gold. Embedded in its elaborately carved buckle was a large red diamond. The dark pants he wore hugged his body, revealing powerful thighs. Boots of the same type of soft, brown leather as his vest reached to his knees. The boot sheath held a dagger with a red diamond on its hilt. All in all he was a very imposing figure.

The lion man stopped in front of Char. "Ho, Alalakan Dragon, I have come as I said I would."

Char crossed him arms over his chest. "I see you, Wendjas Drefeson. What brings you to my home?"

Wendjas threw back his head and laughed. "You haven' t forgotten your stay on Gattan."

Taking his eyes from Char, he focused his attention on Brianna. He moved close enough to trace the dragon on her shoulder.

She felt all three Alalakan men tense.

"So, you' re the woman who conquered the Alalakan dragon and carries his heir. It' s easy to see why. Chardadon has a weakness for fiery hair."

Brianna' s eyebrows arched at his comment.

Lifting her left hand, Wendjas examined her wedding band with a grin. "You told me you would find a good use for the red diamonds, Alalakan."

Still holding Brianna' s hand in his, Wendjas turned his attention to the two men who stood behind her.

Before he could say another word, however, a harsh voice snarled, "Bandalardrac Hardan, Medirian half-breed. What woman do you lust after here?"

Brianna had been concentrating on Wendjas so much, she hadn' t really paid attention to the man who stood close behind him, arms tensed and claws fully extended. From the resemblance to Wendjas, she deduced he was a brother, though he was an inch or so taller and more muscular.

He looked ready to attack.

"Ban is mine!" she declared boldly, wrenching her hand from Wendjas and stepping in front of the angry young man. "He is cousin by both my adopted Medirian family and clan Alalakan by marriage. Ban stands in my defense with my husband and his brother against Rodak don al' Bakom. Do you challenge his right?"

Ever since her puzzling encounter with the Gattan ambassador on Mediria, Brianna had read everything she could find about Gattan and its people—what little information she could find. She had learned that theirs was a race that respected strength and fearlessness in women. A woman who wasn' t afraid to challenge a man was especially honored.

The young man looked down at Brianna furiously.

Before she had time to think about it, Brianna lifted her right hand and grasped his extended claws.

The unexpected pain caused her to gasp and her knees to buckle.

Marljas had not expected Chardadon' s fiery-haired wife to issue a challenge. Nor had he expected her to run her palm against his extended claws. Nevertheless, he was quick enough to catch her before she fell.

For a full five seconds, no one moved. Then pandemonium broke loose.

Rodane didn' t know whether to restrain Char or Ban. The choice was made for him, however, when Wendjas threw his arms around Char and tackled him to the ground, all the while shouting at his brother and demanding an explanation.

Rodane grabbed Ban, fighting his own instincts to leap to Brianna' s defense—and hoping Ban didn' t use his assassin skills to disable him.

Fully conscious, Brianna heaved a sigh of relief as the sharp pain in her palm receded. Struggling against the strong arms that held her, she said, "You can let me up now. I' ll be fine."

Unfortunately, Marljas was concentrating so hard on declaring his innocence to his brother that he didn' t hear Brianna' s soft voice. All five of the men did, however, hear the feminine roar that broke over them.

"Husband, what have you done?"

Elbowing Marljas in the stomach won Brianna her release. Once standing firmly on her own two feet, she turned her attention to the woman who had spoken.

Standing with her feet planted firmly and her arms crossed over her well-developed chest, stood the female equivalent of the lion men.

Svelte, but beautifully proportioned, she was Brianna's height. Her catlike features were more delicate than her husband's, giving her an air of beauty that Brianna had never encountered before. It was her hair, though, that demanded Brianna's attention. Long and thick, it trailed down her back to the middle of her thighs. And it was as fiery as Brianna's own.

Resisting the impulse to stare, Brianna looked to where Char sprawled on the ground with Wendjas on top of him. "Is this the proper way to greet Gattan, Char?" she asked somewhat primly.

Shoving himself free of Wendjas, Char leaped to his feet and jerked Brianna behind him. "You go too far, Marljas Drefeson."

The other men had regained their feet, and even Wendjas looked at his brother with censure in his eyes.

Marljas' anxious gaze leaped from one face to another. "But I did nothing. I would not blood a pregnant woman!"

"Men!" Brianna slipped from behind Char's back to stand before him with her back to Marljas. "Did you, Char," she asked in a scathing tone, "take notice of the fact that I was the one who raised my hand to him?"

She let Char fume and turned to face Marljas. "And you, young man, what gives you the right to go about challenging someone when you're a newly arrived guest?"

Bowing his head submissively, he said, "Forgive me, Lady. My behavior was inexcusable."

"It certainly was. Now what is your name?"

"Marljas Drefeson."

Behind her Char snarled, "Choose your weapons, Drefeson."

Brianna whirled awkwardly. "Stop this right now, Alalakan don al' Chardadon. It's my blood running down my arm, not yours. Marljas' challenge to Ban is answered, and he won't dare issue it again. Will you?" she asked, turning once more to face the young man.

Char, however, gripped Brianna's arm and hauled her around. Angrily he snapped, "How could you chance the life of our child?"

She tried to pull free. "I didn't do anything..."

Wendjas' wife chose that moment to intervene. In a very serious voice, she said, "Hold, Alalakan. This is women's business. Your wife has blooded herself. It will be finished."

Both Wendjas and Char jerked their heads around, Wendjas with shocked surprise, Char with anger.

Rodane's gaze leaped from Denieen to her husband and back again. Why was he listening to her? Supposedly, Gattan men took orders only from their tribal chieftain or their king.

Brianna used the opportunity to slip free and face Marljas once more. She too felt there was something important happening.

Marljas stared first at Brianna then at his sister-in-law. When she frowned and nodded, he raised his left hand. Unsheathing his claws, he drew three of them across his right breast. Lifting Brianna's still-bleeding hand, he matched the furrows on her palm to those on his chest.

"Our blood mingles, Sister. We are one family."

Brianna swallowed uneasily. Somehow she had just lost control of the situation. "Will someone tell me exactly what this means?"

Wendjas' wife walked to Brianna's side and took her hand from Marljas' chest. The bleeding had almost stopped, and the wounds looked like they were already beginning to close.

"These will heal nicely and scar well. I am Denieen Refesdotir, wife of Wendjas," she said with a smile. "Welcome to our family."

"What!"

Behind Brianna, Rodane began to laugh.

Denieen grinned even wider. "It was well done, Alalakan dem al' Brianna. You are now bloodsister to our tribe. Be grateful you used your right hand. If you'd used the left, you'd have another husband instead of a brother."

Brianna gasped and then swallowed as she glanced behind her. Though Wendjas and Rodane were relaxed and grinning, Ban was still angry.

Char was fuming.

Thinking quickly she said, "Marljas is my brother now?"

Marljas himself nodded affirmatively.

Brianna began to smile widely. "What kind of dragon should an Alalakan Gattan wear, Rodane?"

Everyone looked at Brianna in amazement. "Well, if he's my brother, that makes him an Alalakan, too."

Locking her eyes with those of an astonished Marljas she finished, "And you will wear a dragon, Brother. After that, you can settle whatever argument you have with Bandalardrac."

Brianna spared a quick glance for her husband. Though he was obviously angry, there was now a very thoughtful look on his face.

"Ban," she declared quickly before Char met her glance with one of his own, "how in the world did you manage to offend a Gattan?"

"It' s a long story," Ban snapped.

"I expect to hear every bit of it." Glancing back to Marljas, she said just as sharply. "I expect to hear your side of the story too. Then that will be an end to it."

Much of the tension had dissipated, and Wendjas slapped Char on the back. "Very much like my Denieen, a wife to make other men envious."

Both Denieen and Brianna raised delicate red eyebrows.

Char was still furious. The dark stain where her blood dripped to the ground underscored just how important she had become to him. *She could have been killed!*

The belated appearance of Wendjas and Denieen' s sons effectively eliminated any thought of an immediate challenge from Ban or Char. The fact that children were with them proclaimed very strongly how much trust they placed in the Alalakan clan.

Acting more like monkeys than the cats they resembled, both five-year-old boys scrambled into adult arms after their pell-mell sprint across the shuttle pad, one to Wendjas and one to Marljas.

"Our children," Denieen said proudly, "Hendjas climbs upon his uncle and Charjas upon his father."

Brianna smiled at the children' s antics. Hoping she wasn' t being too familiar, she locked her arm through Denieen' s and said, "You must tell me, Sister, how one of your sons came to be named for my husband."

Denieen smiled and nodded. Sending a dismissive glance towards her husband, she commanded, "Bring our sons with you, Wendjas. My new sister and I have much to discuss."

Matching her stride to Brianna' s much slower one, Denieen turned her back on her menfolk and headed for the nearest vehicle.

Char stepped after them. "Brianna," he snarled in a low voice.

"Later, Char," she answered with a wave of her wounded hand.

When I get my hands on her... He was still furious with Brianna for putting herself into such a dangerous position. *I could have lost her. How would I live without her?*

For once, thoughts of Bakom never entered his mind.

Rodane stared after the women. Denieen had been the one issuing commands. Why?

Unaffected by the dampened currents of tension that rolled around them, Wendjas' sons locked glances, nodded once to each other, and launched themselves at the big men who wore dragons on their shoulders. Rodane wasn' t caught totally unawares and was able to brace himself as Hendjas landed on his shoulders. Ban, however, was not expecting an attack from his blind side. He found himself flat on his back staring into merry green eyes.

"Can your dragon really fly?" Charjas asked breathlessly.

Ban was a man who loved children too much to do anything other than grin. "Only in my own ship, fearless one. Perhaps one day I will show you."

"Ha!" Charjas exclaimed as he leaped from Ban' s chest and scooted towards Rodane and his brother. "My dragon man says I am fearless."

Hendjas looked expectantly at Rodane who stared back, obviously at a loss for words. Giving Rodane one last disgruntled look, Hendjas swung his head towards Char, a calculating look in his eye. Char had no doubts as to what his intentions were.

Before Hendjas could leap from Rodane' s arms, Char had grabbed him about the waist and tossed him to Marljas. "That is how to fly like a dragon," he said somewhat gruffly.

Hendjas whooped with joy as he flew through the air into his uncle' s arms.

Charjas quickly changed direction and headed for his uncle also.

Wendjas' loud yell stopped the antics of both boys. "Enough. Is this how a Gattan behaves at the home of a friend? What would your mother say?"

Both boys mumbled apologies, but Charjas had the audacity to look up at his father and say, "But Mother isn' t here."

Even Char had to smile.

Walking over to Ban, Marljas offered his hand. After staring at it a moment, Ban clasped it and Marljas pulled him to his feet. "For the sake of my new sister, I offer truce."

Ban stared at him for a few moments. "For the sake of my cousin, I accept."

"Good," Wendjas said, a hand on each son' s shoulder. "You will take Charjas and Hendjas with you. Chardadon, Rodane, and I will take the other vehicle."

"Perhaps we will be able to keep them from killing each other," commented Wendjas after they left. "My sons will have them fully occupied."

Since Char was staring after Brianna and Denieen, Rodane asked, "How much housing will you require for your crew?"

"There are no other Gattan with us. Marljas piloted the ship."

Char' s mind was pulled from its bloody fantasies. For Wendjas to come alone with his family bespoke trust no other Gattan had ever demonstrated. "I will send people for your things."

"Marljas must accompany them. The ship is set on a defense mode."

An affirmative grunt was Char' s answer.

Rodane asked. "Why are you here, Wendjas?"

"After much thought and reflection, my mother and father decided that trade would be better than war. It' s a much more subtle but equally satisfying way to defeat one' s adversaries."

"Except for Brianna. She can start a war all by herself," Char snarled mostly to himself.

Rodane laughed at the questioning expression on Wendjas' face. "Don' t take what Char says to heart. In his mind, he still sees Brianna lying in a pool of her own blood. My brother just realized just how important his wife is to him."

Damn Rodane. Why doesn' t he keep his mouth shut?

"Marljas would not have knowingly blooded a pregnant woman!"

Char' s tone was caustic. "Perhaps not purposely, but I don' t remember you being very levelheaded either."

Rodane' s eyebrows lifted, but Wendjas was in an affable mood. "Six years ago, Chardadon tried to lure Denieen from Gattan."

To say Rodane was shocked was an understatement. "You courted a Gattan!"

Char shrugged. "She' s quite beautiful."

"What happened?"

Wendjas continued Char' s story when he wouldn' t. "Denieen pretended interest since I was proving too slow to declare my love. She thought a handsome dragon man would spur me on. She was right."

"So that' s how you got the Gattan scar on your chest," Rodane mused. "I always thought you took part in some sort of ceremony to bind our families in trade."

Char snorted. "If you call an angry Gattan trying to claw my heart out a ceremony."

"Denieen didn' t think I' d carry things so far. I' m normally a very even-tempered man."

Char snorted again.

"Denieen stopped the fight?"

Wendjas shook his head. "Once a fight begins, it becomes a matter of honor. Your brother fought well."

"You mean Char could have been killed?"

"Yes."

Rodane rounded angrily on his brother. "And you' re angry with Brianna? Do you realize what would have happened if you had died six years ago?"

Char shifted uncomfortably.

Wendjas continued his story. "Mine and Denieen' s mothers were furious. She' d falsely goaded me into a blood feud. Retribution was necessary."

Rodane contemplated Wendjas. *Their mothers were furious, not their fathers?* "So that' s how you got all those red diamonds."

"And the trade treaty," Wendjas added.

"A treaty that has benefited your family as much as it has mine," Char interjected.

"What caused the dissension between Bandalardrac and Marljas?" Rodane asked.

Char shrugged again. "I have no idea."

Wendjas said, "Last year Bandalardrac appeared on Gattan as a courier for the Hardan royal family. Marljas found the girl he was courting in Bandalardrac's arms, but the Medirian ambassador and the girl's family smoothed things over. She was quite headstrong and not in the least interested in my brother's suit."

"But her family was interested," Rodane guessed.

Wendjas nodded. "Unfortunately, yes. Marljas was too stubborn to listen to me. The girl had no interest in him, and Mother would never have approved the match. However, the day after Bandalardrac left Gattan, the girl disappeared. She hasn't been seen since."

Their mother wouldn't approve? Rodane struggled to keep his mind on the conversation rather than the puzzle turning over in his mind. "So everyone believes Ban spirited the girl away."

"Yes."

Rodane turned to his brother. "Char?"

Char shook his head negatively. "I can guarantee that in the last year, Ban never gave passage to any Gattan. Nor could he have been in the company of one for any more than a few hours if one happened to be in whichever space bar or dive he was frequenting at the time."

"How can you be sure of this?"

"The ship Ban flies is Alalakan built. Its computer sends a steady stream of information back here to our master computer. Ban is Alalakan. We couldn't allow him to roam about unmonitored," Char answered with a satisfied smile. "Whatever happened to that girl, he wasn't involved."

Wendjas looked thoughtful. "I must send this information back to Gattan. Everyone always assumed she left with Bandalardrac. If that isn't the case, there are many new questions to be answered."

They stopped before the house and ceased their conversation. Inside, the women were discussing where to house their unexpected guests.

"Goodness, Xdana. The solution is simple. Put Wendjas and Denieen in the guest quarters of my suite," Jenneta said.

Denieen inclined her head. "I am honored, Matriarch, but do you realize how active my children are?"

Jenneta's dark eyes sparkled. "I raised two boys of my own. Even though yours are Gattan, I doubt there's much I haven't seen. Besides, having me about may dampen their exuberance. If I'm correct, a head of gray hair has that effect on Gattan children. And please call me Jenneta."

Denieen smiled. "Wisdom such as yours is invaluable, Jenneta. We' ll be honored to accept your hospitality."

Xdana sighed with relief. "That means Marljas…"

"…will stay in the other bedroom of the heir' s guest suite," Brianna finished from where she sat on the couch.

Reactions were simultaneous.

"Cousin…" Ban began.

"New sister, I protest," Marljas snarled.

"Brianna, I will not allow…" Char snapped.

"Silence!" Wendjas roared, more to his brother than anyone else. "How can you think to question a breeding woman?"

Caught in an obvious breach of Gattan etiquette, Marljas and Ban had the good graces to look embarrassed.

Char, on the other hand, was no so easily intimidated. "I am the Alalakan," he snarled as he crossed his arms across his chest. "I will say and do what I damn well please."

Jenneta rose to her feet. "Char…"

He spun around, his fury obvious. "No! Don' t say anything, Grandmother. Brianna could have been killed."

With Jamiros' aid, Brianna rose as gracefully as was possible and walked across the room to face her husband. Looking up into Char' s angry eyes and holding out the hand which still showed angry red cuts, she said, "Though it was unintentional, Alalakan don al' Chardadon, I was torn from my family on Earth and brought across the galaxy to an alien planet. Here, instead of the fear and loneliness I could have encountered, I have found the love of not one, but two new families. Now a third opens its arms to me. But, most importantly, your child rests beneath my heart. With such a gift, how can I refuse others?"

Char looked into Brianna' s tear-filled eyes and felt his anger and resistance drain away. Taking her hand, he turned it over and brought her wounded palm to his lips. With a groan he swept her into his arms. Spinning about, he strode out of the room. "Sort things out for yourselves," he called over his shoulder. "I don' t give a damn where any of you sleep."

"A truly remarkable woman," Wendjas said. "Brother, taking such a woman as a sister can bring nothing but honor to our family. Now," he continued, "does anyone know if Brianna has any sisters? My brother needs a wife."

Denieen chuckled and patted her husband' s arm.

The pieces of the puzzle in Rodane' s head fell together. Shock filled his brain. "A matriarchy. Gattan' s a matriarchy. The men aren' t in charge. The women are."

Grinning ruefully, Wendjas glanced at his wife. "Deni warned my parents you would come to realize this very quickly."

Rodane chuckled. "Don' t they control all of us?"

Char kicked the door to their suite shut. Striding across the sitting room, he kicked their bedroom door open, then shut it with a well-placed thrust of his hip. Crossing the room to the bed, he deposited Brianna gently. "Never, ever, place yourself in such danger again," he demanded in a quiet voice.

"But I wasn' t in any danger."

His rage flamed anew. "Damn it, Brianna, they are Gattan. Sneezing at the wrong time can bring on a bloodfeud!"

"They wouldn' t have come here in the first place if they planned on a bloodfeud, not with children!" she snapped back, pushing herself up off the bed awkwardly.

Char raked his fingers through his hair. "You don' t understand…"

She fisted her hands on her hips. "I don' t understand what?"

Char glared at his wife, her anger enhancing her exotic beauty. *I could not live without her.* "I love you."

Brianna was prepared for a good fight. Char' s simple statement took the wind from her sails. "What?"

His voice was still belligerent. "I love you. I couldn' t live without you."

"Why didn' t you tell me before?" Tears in her eyes, she fell into his arms. "I love you, too."

"I know."

Her head snapped up, and she glared into his face.

He pulled her closer. "I was standing on the balcony when you refused Ban. You told him that you loved me then."

"Damn it, why did you wait so long to mention it?"

He stared down at her. "I was waiting for you to tell me yourself."

"You' re such a fool, Char."

"I know, but it' s not a mistake I' ll make again." His mouth descended on hers.

Chapter Fifteen

Brianna and Char were eating a late breakfast when a knock on the door interrupted them.

"Go away," Char yelled.

"Open the damn door," Ban bellowed. "Messengers from the Ruling Council have arrived."

Char shoved himself away from the table and opened the door. "What do they want?"

Ban' s voice was worried. "Brianna."

"Was it a verbal or written message?"

"Written, addressed to Alalakan don al' Jamiros."

Char smiled slowly. "Bakom is a fool. Instead of waiting and gathering information, he petitioned the Council for her immediate return."

"From what your father says, that' s exactly what has happened."

Both men turned to face Brianna who sat contentedly on her chair.

Ban frowned. "You don' t look too worried, Coz."

Fully content for the first time since her hasty departure from Earth, now sure of Char' s love, she shrugged. "Why should I be? I have the Alalakan clan, the royal Medirian family, and now a Gattan brother. What' s more, I carry the Alalakan heir. What can Bakom possibly do to me? One wrong move, and one of you men will tear him to pieces."

Ban only shook his head as Char grinned broadly. "Come, love, let' s go meet these *messengers*. I want to see the look on their faces when you confront them."

"Me?"

"Since you first appeared on my ship, my love, you have returned our cousin Bandalardrac to us and blood-bonded us with a very powerful Gattan family. You routed Crystas and brought my brother the happiness he deserves. And you have won the hearts of my family. Bakom' s messengers stand no chance against you."

Brianna chuckled happily. Surrounded by a loving family, unknown messengers from Bakom did not trouble her in the least. "Very well. Let' s go rout the dastards."

Ban and Char looked at each other. Both shrugged. They were getting used to it.

Char escorted Brianna to the library where his father, mother, and grandmother waited with three strangers. After she had made herself comfortable, Jamiros said, "Char, these are Kadon don al' Meterac, Ruling Council member and messenger, and Sasonit don al' Huwnder and Grovanit don al' Zoterif, Academy of Science guards. They' ve come with a signed order for you to turn over the specimen you unlawfully stole from Rodak don al' Bakom."

He perused the sheet of paper his father handed him. "And if I refuse?"

"You are ordered to appear in person before the ruling council two weeks from this date to defend yourself against charges of treason."

Char cocked an eyebrow. "Treason? Isn' t that charge rather harsh?"

"Probably," Rodane answered as he and Fionilina entered the room. "The legal team is working on it right now." Fio sat down next to Brianna, and Rodane moved to stand behind them.

The messenger had the good grace to look embarrassed.

The two guards were far more belligerent, however. "Enough talking," one of them ordered, "Your cooperation will lead to the charges being greatly reduced."

"Reduced charges for what, Char?" Meri asked as she, Ademis and Bandalardrac entered the library. She settled onto the settee on the other side of Brianna.

Char shrugged nonchalantly. "Treason."

"Oh?" Ademis said curiously. "What did you do?"

Char held out the paper. "I' m accused of stealing one of Bakom' s specimens."

Meri turned to the guard who had spoken. "A charge of treason for the theft of a specimen. Exactly what does it look like?"

"This is not a Medirian matter," the other guard said in a surly voice.

"Is there a problem, Alalakan?" Wendjas asked as he, Denieen and Marljas also entered the room.

All three strangers gaped at the Gattans.

Char grinned. "I've been charged with treason, Wendjas."

The three men in the room did not fail to note that it was Char and not Jamiros who had been addressed as Alalakan by the Gattan.

The two guards quickly realized that there were things that either Bakom did not know or had failed to reveal. Deciding to brazen his way through the current situation, the shorter of the two guards said, "Enough. You won't sway us with off-world contacts. This is a Drakian matter."

"An Alalakan matter?" Marljas asked, softly, dangerously.

"Only an Alalakan matter," the guard answered smugly.

"Very well," Marljas answered in the same dangerous voice. He drew his shirt over his head. On his right shoulder rode a red and gold Alalakan dragon, wings and neck outstretched, flames spouting from its mouth. From beneath the dragon's wings sprang an animal no one but Brianna had ever seen, a snarling lion, jaws agape, forelegs outstretched, slashing claws unsheathed. "I am an Alalakan."

"Rather appropriate, don't you think, Brianna?" Rodane whispered in her ear.

"Ummm," Brianna answered, stifling a giggle behind her hands.

"What is this chicanery?" snarled the larger of the two guards.

Every man in the room stiffened.

The Medirians and Gattans had, with the exception of Marljas, been content to remain silent after their initial comments. The guard had barely finished speaking, however, before every man in the room removed his shirt to reveal his clan totem. Wendjas had no dragon, but his unsheathed claws crossed over powerful, scarred arms were just as clear a message.

"Do you question the honor of the Alalakan clan?" Char asked in a very quiet voice.

The Council messenger muttered an obscenity under his breath. What should have been a simple delivery was getting totally out of hand. "No disrespect is intended, Alalakan don al' Chardadon. If you would please fetch the specimen, we will be on our way."

Since all three men were council representatives, all three wore translators. All three men were shocked when Brianna spoke. "You really should stop baiting them, Char. Why don' t you introduce me?"

Her request eased the tense atmosphere. "Gentlemen, Alalakan dem al' Brianna, my wife and carrier of the Alalakan heir."

The messenger bowed politely. "My congratulations, Alalakan don al' Chardadon."

The two guards stared sullenly.

Char crossed his arms over his bare chest. "My wife is the specimen Bakom wants returned."

"What!" the messenger exclaimed as he turned to the disgruntled guards. "Were you aware of this?"

"We were ordered to return with a humanoid woman who was to be administered the Tests of Humanity. She is from an unidentified planet. It is the right of the Academy to test her."

"She looks *very* human to me," snapped the messenger, "very *pregnantly* human."

"The law states she belongs to the Academy," the guard continued stubbornly.

The messenger hauled himself around to face the guards and snapped, "She' s pregnant. No one has the right to touch her."

"Charges have been made and must be answered," Char interjected calmly. "A suggestion, Kadon don al' Meterac. Return and inform the council that the Alalakan clan will appear on the requested date. To ascertain that the ' specimen' does not flee nor is spirited away, these two Academy guards can stay to monitor her movements. Do you find this solution acceptable?"

The messenger' s answering smile was all that Rodane expected. "It seems to be an excellent solution to me."

"Good," Jamiros answered as he extended his hand. "Come with me to the study, and I' ll write a formal reply to the charges."

Glancing at the guards, Meterac said, "Your orders are changed by my authority as a member of the Ruling Council. You will stay here to guard the ' specimen' until the appearance date set in the original charges."

"You have no right..." sputtered the smaller guard.

"I have every right," he snapped. "The Council rules the Academy, or has a change of which I am unaware been made? I thought not," he continued when no answer was forthcoming. "You will follow my orders or return to your master and explain why he has found himself censured at my suggestion."

Neither man answered.

Sending them a look of pure disgust, the messenger followed Jamiros from the room.

"That went rather well, didn' t it?" Char said. "Now what shall we do with these two?"

Ban slapped the button that opened the intercom, he said, "Have Kahn and his cousins come to the library at once."

Grabbing his shirt, he pulled it over his head. "I hope neither of you were involved in the kidnapping of that Aradab girl. Her relatives are on the way."

Both men paled visibly.

Marljas locked gazes with Ban. "You are not a complete fool, Bandalardrac. Perhaps there is common ground we can find."

Ban simply bared his teeth in his wolfish grin.

The day of summer Solstice dawned dry and clear, and the house and grounds were ready for that evening' s celebration. Not only was it the high point of the summer season, it was also the eighteen birthday of the only daughter of the house.

Sheala stood in the middle of the floor as Brianna walked around her. Her birthday party would begin in a few hours, and she had decided to look different than other Drakian girls. Brianna was from a completely new planet. Surely her sister-in-law would have new ideas for her hair and cosmetics.

Jami and Vani had insisted on accompanying her, and now all three of them waited eagerly for Brianna' s suggestions.

Brianna shook her head at the blue gown that clung to Sheala like a second skin. "That dress certainly doesn' t hide anything, Shea."

Puzzled, Sheala glanced at Brianna. "What do I want to hide?"

Brianna just sighed and said, "Never mind. I' ll get used to it, I suppose. I guess you don' t plan on wearing any underwear."

"Under what?" she asked mischievously as Vani and Jami giggled.

Brianna just snorted and continued her perusal. "Did you ever think of cutting your hair?"

"I used to cut it all the time."

"No, I mean really short."

"How short? I don' t want to look like Rodane."

"No, not like that. I mean cut and styled."

"What do you have in mind?"

Half an hour later, with the help of Verna, who was quite adept at styling hair, Sheala had a unique hairstyle for a Drakian. It was cropped short and tapered in the back, with fluffy bangs covering her forehead.

Sheala loved it.

With her hair cropped short, her graceful neck was displayed to its best advantage. Thick bangs stopped just short of her delicate eyebrows and emphasized the exotic tilt to her velvety brown eyes. Like her grandmother, Sheala had earlobes, earlobes that now displayed a pair of blue Medirian pearls donated by Jenneta.

"I recommend that you have your ears pierced, Shea, but your grandmother' s earrings are beautiful for tonight. I have the perfect necklace and bracelet to match them," Brianna said as she waddled into her bedroom.

In a few minutes, she returned carrying a large box. Setting it on the table, she opened it to reveal row upon row of blue pearls.

"Brianna, they' re beautiful!"

Lifting the necklace out of the box, Sheala draped them around her neck. Shimmering incandescently against the midnight blue of her dress, they fell to her waist.

Brianna gazed at her critically and said, "Let' s try this."

Looping the necklace once around Sheala' s neck, Brianna draped the necklace from the back of her shoulders like a cape. Since the dress was backless almost to the cleft of her buttocks, the soft blue color of the pearls glowed warmly against her bare skin.

Clasping a silver bracelet studded with more pearls around Sheala' s wrist, Brianna said, "That should about do it. What do you think?"

With a stunned expression, Sheala stared at her reflection in the mirror. A stranger gazed back at her. Brianna had applied small amounts of cosmetics earlier to highlight her eyes, high cheekbones, and mouth. The haircut and pearls were the finishing touches. "I don' t know myself."

The door connecting Brianna' s sitting room with that of the guest quarters opened and Ban sauntered in followed by Marljas.

Both men stopped immediately upon seeing Sheala.

Smiling provocatively, Sheala locked her gaze with Ban' s. "Well, Coz, what do you think?"

"I think that if you weren' t my cousin, I' d carry you to the nearest bed right now," Ban said in a very serious tone as he walked completely around her and examined her with a critical eye. "You' re very beautiful, Sheala. Men will ache to possess you. What do you think, Marljas?"

From the moment he' d walked in the room, Marljas had sensed Sheala' s presence. When he saw her, his body' s reaction had been instantaneous. He was very glad he was wearing a tunic or his erection would have been obvious for all to see.

Verna lifted an intricately carved bottle. Removing its stopper, she liberally applied the perfume to Sheala' s wrists. Then she slowly drew the stopper down the deep valley between her breasts.

Breaking out into a sweat, Marljas fled the room muttering something about Denieen.

Char entered with a quizzical look on his face. "What' s wrong with Marljas? He just passed me in the hall looking as if the ghosts of all seven hells were pursuing him."

Ban continued to grin and winked at Verna before he answered. "He forgot about something Deni wanted him to do."

Before Ban could say anything else, Brianna said, "Don' t just stand there, Char, tell your sister how beautiful she is."

Char turned his attention to Sheala. His eyes widened as he stared at her. He circled his sister just as Ban had. "Is that really you, Shea? What did you do to your hair?" Stopping in front of her, he grinned and lifted her into a huge hug. "You are absolutely beautiful."

Grinning from ear to ear, Sheala said, "Come on, Vani, Jami. Let' s go. You two still have to get dressed."

"Only if Verna comes," said Jami. "I want my hair cut like yours."

"But Jami, you' re a Medirian princess!"

Borrowing a comment from Brianna, Jami answered, "What does that have to do with the price of tea in China? I like that hairstyle, and I want it too. I don' t care what anyone says."

Verna shrugged. "I' ll cut your hair, Princess. I' m too old to worry about your parents' disapproval." She led the three girls from the room, Vani arguing vociferously with her sister.

"Guess I' ll go along and try to calm Vani down," Ban said with a wry smile. "She always was a worrier." Leaving the room, he turned and winked at Brianna. "Jamiros wants all of us in the library in an hour, Bri, so don' t go tempting Char with those beautiful breasts of yours."

Char grinned as Ban pulled the door shut behind him. "Are you going to tempt me with those beautiful breasts, my love?"

Brianna scowled—or at least pretended to. "I am going to take a bath and you may scrub my back. I refuse to be late for your sister' s party."

Laughter followed Brianna as she waddled into the bedroom. Her advanced pregnancy had begun to quell Char' s sexual urges. Her company, however, was something he discovered he could not do without. Still grinning, he followed her. He was willing to scrub her back anytime she wanted.

Approximately an hour later, Brianna and Char joined everyone in the immediate family except Sheala in the library. Marljas, Ban, Ademis, and Meri entered immediately behind them.

"Good, we' re all here," Jamiros said briskly. "Now, I don' t really anticipate any problems tonight. Anyone who would have caused problems was simply not invited, but the crowd will be large, and it' s possible for a few uninvited guests to slip in unnoticed. Enough of us are here, however, to make sure Sheala is monitored all evening."

Brianna looked around curiously. "I thought that she was considered an adult now and was old enough to make her own decisions."

Rodane grinned at Brianna. "Do you honestly believe that we would leave Sheala unguarded? She may be old enough to take anyone she wants to her bed, but that doesn' t mean we will allow her to do so. There will be those here tonight who seek to lower Alalakan prestige and power or join with it. Sheala' s an intelligent girl, but she' s still young. She hasn' t yet learned the difference between honesty and ambition."

Jenneta continued, "We don' t seek to keep Sheala from learning the joys of her body, but we will do our best to make sure she' s not used in some plot to bring shame onto her or the Alalakan clan."

"You should be aware, Brianna," Xdana added, "that you' ll receive proposals yourself tonight."

"Me!"

"Yes, love," Char answered with a grin, "most will be for after you give birth, but a few will seek to make assignations for tonight."

Brianna' s mouth fell open. "Why? I look like a beached whale!"

Fionilina smiled and sat down next to Brianna. "Because you are a very beautiful woman, Bri. Your coloring is…exotic. That which is new whets jaded appetites."

"Great," Brianna grumbled, "a mob of horny rakes following me around all night. I think I' ll borrow one of Sheala' s swords."

Marljas walked over to stand in front of Brianna and raised her right hand, the hand that wore scars that matched those on his chest.

"With Denieen at your side, Bloodsister, you needn' t fear unwanted advances. Her claws are sharp."

Brianna' s eyes met Marljas' s, and she acknowledged the twinkle in them. "You' re a very perceptive man, Bloodbrother. Deni asked to stay near me tonight, something about being uncomfortable in crowds."

Marljas smiled. "And you asked that she wear a new dress, I think. Something about standing out in a crowd?"

Brianna laughed outright. "I do think I love the Gattan more every day. When will I meet the rest of the family, Brother mine?"

Marljas' s smile became a grin. "Whenever you' re ready."

Jamiros interrupted. "You two can carry on your family conversation later. Right now we must ascertain that Sheala is always either with one of us or close enough to reach quickly."

Ban had been leaning quietly against the door. "How will Sheala feel when she realizes what we' re doing?"

All eyes turned to Ban.

"It' s her party, after all. If one of us is hovering about constantly, she' ll realize what we' re doing. Sheala has a temper. Do you want a scene tonight? Having two or three hundred guests watching won' t inhibit her."

Char grunted. "Ban' s right. Sheala' ll never forgive us if we hover."

"Don' t hover, then," Meri said. "The area will be well lighted, as will the house. Servants will be everywhere, and most of them are very fond of Sheala. Have them watch her. That way, we can appear at various times to talk to her. Her family members will be expected to dance with her. There' s no reason all of you must dance with her early in the evening. There are also members of other clans and friends whom you trust. Quite a few people want Sheala' s party to be a success. Let them help."

Xdana smiled. "Trust the daughter of a diplomatic queen to be wise. How often is this system used by your family?"

"How often?" Meri answered. "You mean ' how long' . The Hardan family has been monitoring its family members for centuries. We perfected the system. That, and we have Marljas."

"What?" Marljas asked in a surprised voice.

"Most of the guests don' t even realize that there are Gattan here. None of them know of your relationship to the Alalakan clan. Indeed many of them will be afraid of you. Since you don' t really know anyone else who' ll be here tonight other than those in this room, no one will think it odd if you show little interest in any unmarried girls other than Sheala, Jami, and Vani."

"An excellent idea, Meri," Jamiros said, "that is, Marljas, if you don' t mind. I realize your first loyalty is to Brianna. To be perfectly honest, I was very surprised when you agreed to wear a dragon at all, though I am deeply honored that you chose to do so."

Brianna turned and smiled up into Marljas' s face. "You' ll help, won' t you?"

Marljas sighed. "I' ll do my best, Alalakan don al' Jamiros, to protect your daughter from any unacceptable advances. I only hope I' m equal to the task."

Ban grinned and clapped Marljas on the shoulder. His wink was unnoticed by everyone but Marljas.

* * * * *

Brianna stood in the shadows on the stage that had been constructed for the Solstice celebration, admiring the grounds of the Alalakan estate which had been meticulously groomed and decorated for the evening' s festivities. Brightly colored lanterns hung in strategic places, illuminating most of the extensive lawns and gardens behind the house. Drakians being Drakians, however, there were more than enough shaded and dimly lit areas for private conversations and assignations.

"My friends," Jamiros began as he stepped into the spotlight and looked out over the sea of interested faces, "welcome to my home on this Solstice evening. A time of momentous change has come to the Alalakan clan, changes I will share with you tonight."

Murmurs from the crowd reached Brianna' s ears. Rumors had flown about ever since her arrival on Drakan, but tonight, those rumors would be put to rest and everyone would finally learn the truth.

"First, I am more than pleased to welcome back into the Alalakan fold my brother' s son, Alalakan don al' Bandalardrac. Many of you, I am sure, have already made his acquaintance."

Laughter followed as Ban stepped forward and bowed to the crowd, winking and throwing kisses to various women who stood close to the stage.

"Second," Jamiros added, "I am pleased to introduce my son Rodane' s new wife, Alalakan dem al Fionilina."

Escorted to the front of the stage by Rodane who placed her hand in that of his father' s, Fionilina inclined her head graciously to the applauding crowd. Jamiros' s announcement had everyone buzzing. The dissolvement of Rodane' s marriage to Crystas and his subsequent marriage to her sister Fionilina had not been widely known.

After Rodane had led Fionilina back into the shadows and the applause had quieted, Jamiros continued, "My friends, it gives me the great joy to announce the marriage of my son Chardadon to Alalakan dem al' Brianna of the before unknown planet Earth. She is the carrier of the Alalakan heir."

More applause as Chardadon led Brianna forward and handed her to his father. Illuminated by the spotlight, Brianna nodded to the crowd. Flashes of red fire sparkled from the Gattan red diamonds she wore in her hair and on her person. There was no doubt in the minds of most of the crowd that Chardadon prized the exotic woman who was his wife. And it was obvious to everyone that Brianna was very pregnant.

Char grinned to his father and took back Brianna' s hand. Pulling her into his arms, he gave her a kiss that left her breathless, much to the crowd' s delight.

"That should leave no doubt in their minds," Char said as he led her back into the shadows amidst the whistles and cheers.

Grinning, Jamiros bowed to Char and Brianna as they left his side.

"The fortunes of the Alalakan clan are now firmly in the hands of Chardadon," Jamiros announced as he turned once more to face the crowd. "However, wonderful though the announcements have been to this point, the most important reason for tonight' s celebration is the last."

Turning, Jamiros waited as Xdana and Jenneta escorted Sheala to stand by her father.

"My friends, my daughter Sheala celebrates her eighteenth birthday this day and takes her place as an adult in our society. I ask that you celebrate this special occasion in her life with us."

Sheala laughed and waved as the crowd burst into loud applause. She loved being the center of attention, and, despite her father' s earlier announcements, tonight was her night. Murmurs of appreciation about how beautiful she was were easy to hear from many voices in the crowd. Sheala planned to enjoy every minute of her night.

Before anyone realized what he was doing, Ban reappeared from the shadows and swept Sheala into his arms. Planting a huge kiss on her cheek, he took the few short steps to the edge of the stage and tossed her into the air.

Sheala shrieked with surprise as she fell through the air to the strong arms that caught her. Throwing her arms around the neck of the man who held her, Sheala' s locked gazes with Marljas as she slid down the length of his muscular body.

Marljas looked deeply into her eyes and smiled a slow grin, but Sheala had no chance to react before Marljas released her and stepped back.

Hands grabbed Sheala' s, and she was whirled away into the crowd, but not before craning her neck to see the shadowy form next to the stage. Unfortunately, too many people crowded around her as she was whisked away into the crowd so she lost sight of the man who had held her so tightly.

"Why did you toss her into the crowd, Ban?" Brianna asked as the family exited the stage much more sedately by way of the steps.

The orchestra Jamiros had hired began to play.

Ban grinned as he took Brianna's hand and helped her down the last two steps. "It's supposed to be a night for her to remember, and she'll certainly remember flying through the air."

"You're lucky someone thought quickly enough to catch her," Char growled.

"Marl and I had everything planned. I knew exactly where to toss her."

Descending the final steps behind Char and Brianna, Jenneta tried to lock gazes with her rakish grandson as she too placed her hand in his. "Exactly where to toss her, eh?" she said for Ban's ears alone.

Ban's refusal to meet her eyes verified for Jenneta what she had begun to suspect. "Walk with me, my Medirian grandson. It will do this old woman good to be seen in the company of such a notorious rake," Jenneta said silkily, refusing to release his hand.

Knowing when to admit defeat, Ban bowed over Jenneta's hand. "Old! Grandmother, you do not know what the word means."

Soon, both had disappeared into the crowd.

Jamiros and Xdana, joined by Lorilana and Dadon, headed toward the main pavilion, where most of their friends had gathered.

"An interesting way to begin a birthday celebration," Denieen said as she and Wendjas joined Brianna, Char, Fionilina, and Rodane.

Both Rodane and Char took their time admiring Denieen in her new finery.

"Stare at your own wives," Wendjas snarled.

Both men grinned at Wendjas.

Brianna patted him on the arm.

"Deni is lovely tonight, Wendjas. Think how many men will envy you."

"You're not on Gattan, old friend," Char added. "No one here will challenge you for her."

"As if I'd allow it," Denieen teased.

"I don' t think anyone would dare," Rodane dryly. "I' d worry more about someone trying to make off with some of those diamonds you and Brianna are wearing. They' re worth a fortune."

"Humph!" Wendjas snorted. He' d not worn the jacket Denieen had chosen for him. Instead, he' d donned an elaborately embroidered and bejeweled vest that left his arms and much of his chest bare, his white battle scars standing out plainly against his brown skin.

His wrist cuffs contained daggers topped with huge red diamonds.

Deni sniffed. "Judicious displays of claws every now and then will discourage any such thoughts." Locking arms with Brianna and Fionilina, Denieen pulled the other two women towards the dance floor.

"They make quite a trio, don' t they?" said Rodane as the three women sauntered toward the festivities. All three wore red dresses and very expensive jewelry, though Fionilina' s jewels were not red diamonds. Instead, sapphires matched the blue matriarchal necklace Rodane had returned to her the night he refuted Crystas. "Alone, any one of them would demand attention. Together...I hope Sheala doesn' t feel slighted."

Later that evening, comfortably ensconced on a cushioned divan, Brianna watched the continuing festivities. Sheala' s coming out party was an unqualified success. Though many people had presented themselves to Brianna to be introduced, most attention was lavished on Sheala. Nor had the Alalakans had any trouble monitoring her movements. All they had to do was look for the largest group, and Sheala was in the middle of it.

Denieen spent much of the evening with Brianna, Wendjas glowering behind them until Rodane and Char pointed out that many people were afraid to make Brianna' s acquaintance. Wendjas watched as many men admired his wife, but not a single Drakian behaved in what he considered an improper manner. Eventually, he was able to relax and even began to enjoy himself.

As Meri had commented earlier, most of the guests did not know what to make of the three Gattan in their midst, so most tread warily around them. Brianna' s obvious closeness to the female Gattan amazed many in the crowd, and there was a great deal of conjecture about her planet being discovered by the Gattans. Noting how nearly identical

Brianna' s and Demieen' s vibrant colorings were, some hypothesized that Brianna' s race could be closely related to the Gattan.

"Well, Coz, have you saved a dance for me?" Ban asked as he sat and stretched out next to Brianna.

Brianna had danced exactly twice that evening—once with Jamiros and once with Char—slow, sedate dances that did not require a great deal of movement.

"You' ve got to be crazy, Ban. The orchestra hasn' t played anything slow enough for me in at least two hours," Brianna said with a laugh. "Dance with Deni."

He shook his head emphatically. "And find myself facing blood challenge from another Gattan? No thank you!"

Deni' s laughter joined Brianna' s. "He wouldn' t challenge you, Ban. I wouldn' t allow it. However, I don' t know if I want to dance. My feet aren' t used to these Drakian shoes!"

Ban grinned in answer and glanced around. Wendjas was on the other side of the pavilion talking with Char and some of the Alalakan elders, no longer continually watching his wife.

He turned his attention back to Brianna. "The next selection will be much slower because I requested it. I' ll have few opportunities to hold you in my arms, lovely Coz. I must take advantage of them while I can."

As Ban finished speaking, the orchestra finished its number and began a slower, more lyrical tune.

The soft melody rolled across the dance floor and embraced Brianna. "That' s a beautiful song. What is it?"

Grinning, Bandalardrac rose and pulled her to her feet. "It' s the Medirian Wedding March, of course."

Laughing, Brianna allowed herself to be swept into Ban' s loose embrace.

From across the floor, Char answered Ban' s grin with his own and saluted his cousin. Bowing to his grandmother, Char led her onto the floor. Soon other couples joined them.

When the dance ended, Ban returned Brianna to her seat. Winking, he raised her hand to his lips. "Good night, sweet Coz, a lonely widow awaits."

Brianna tried to smother her laughter as Ban strode away, but she was unsuccessful.

"Something amuses you?" Denieen asked as she sat down beside her. She' d danced with Jamiros, and Wendjas had only glowered at her once.

"Ban," Brianna answered when she regained control of herself. "I can' t wait for the day when he finds a woman he can' t charm."

Char settled into the place beside Brianna that Ban had vacated. "Are you enjoying yourself?"

She smiled up into his face. "Hmmm, but I am getting tired. Would anyone notice if we disappeared?"

Char leaned closer. "Probably. Do you have something in mind?"

Brianna chuckled at his suggestive leer. "Yes, sleep. I' m exhausted."

"Has anyone seen Sheala?" Rodane asked as he joined them.

"Marljas just took her some punch," Jamiros answered from behind Rodane, "and Ban is going to gather her up now. Says he hasn' t had his dance yet."

"So much for lonely widows," Brianna muttered.

Rodane rolled his shoulders. "Good. I' m glad the guests are finally starting to leave. Fionilina left half an hour ago. She said she was exhausted. I' m surprised you' re still here, Brianna."

"I took a nap this afternoon."

Char scooped Brianna into his arms. "As long as Ban has Sheala under control, I' ll take my wife to bed."

Wendjas watched Char stride away. "He seems to carry her off to bed quite often."

"How do you think she became pregnant so fast?" was Rodane' s wry answer. "But his idea sounds good to me. I think I' ll join my wife, too."

"Well?" Wendjas whispered into his wife' s ear as Rodane followed Char and Brianna.

Deni laughed seductively as he led her away.

Jamiros chuckled as Xdana joined him.

"What amuses you, Jami?"

"I' m beginning to feel young again, Xda," he answered putting his arm around her and pulling her close.

Xdana laughed quietly. "You may be feeling young again, my love, but we have guests to see to. Now come along."

"Well, I hope they soon go home!"

Ban stood next to the bench under the Chotton bush. Silently, he picked up the blue slippers that sat there. Marljas wouldn' t have left Sheala until he came for his dance. There could only be one reason for them not to be waiting for him.

"Well, Sheala, I hope you know what you' ve gotten yourself into," Ban said lightly.

This was a very interesting development to report!

Much later, in the dim lighting of the captain' s quarters on his warbird, Marljas held a sleeping Sheala in his arms. He' d already made up his mind that he wasn' t going to give her up.

* * * * *

The next morning, Brianna woke to Char' s hands massaging her breasts. Smiling, she rolled awkwardly to face him. An especially strong kick caused her to gasp and she moved Char' s hand onto her stomach. Pressing down on his hand, she removed a small foot from where it pushed against her rib cage.

Her obvious discomfort cooled Char' s ardor quickly. Planting a chaste kiss on her mouth, he murmured, "I will be glad when this baby is finally born."

"No more than I," she answered as she struggled out of bed.

Since his mother' s rib cage had been denied him, her unborn child decided to wreak havoc on her bladder. "Will you call for breakfast?" she called from the bathroom. "I' m starved."

"You' ll have to settle for lunch," he answered. "It' s well into the afternoon."

Brushing her hair, she waddled back into the bedroom. "What I wouldn' t give for some Ben and Jerry' s Cherry Garcia ice cream."

Char grunted. She' d been mentioning foods from her planet for the last three months, and he had no idea what she was talking about. Slipping into the lounging pants she insisted that he wear, he went out into the sitting room. "Put a robe on, Brianna," he called to her. "Ban' s here."

A few moments later, with her hair pulled back and wearing a softly draping blue robe, Brianna entered the sitting room to discover that Jamiros and Xdana had decided to join their son and his wife.

"Good morning, Brianna. How are you feeling?" Xdana asked.

"I' m fine, though I admit I' ll feel better after this baby is born. I' m tired of being fat and running to the bathroom every thirty minutes."

Char chuckled, and Brianna glared at him. "If men had the babies, there would be a lot fewer people in this universe."

Before Char could do so, Ban rose and helped Brianna into his chair. "But, Coz, you women carry pregnancy off so well!"

Xdana' s scowl joined Brianna' s. "I hope your wife has twins when you finally find one, Ban, and she makes your life miserable the entire time she' s pregnant."

Everyone laughed easily. However, before anyone could continue the conversation, Jamiros held up his hand.

"Brianna' s pregnancy is a fascinating topic of conversation, but we are here to finalize the plans for our appearance before the Council four days from now."

Char watched as Brianna tried to make herself comfortable. Then he turned to his father. "Rodane and I thought that leaving for Benishan tomorrow would be best. That will give us two full days in the city before the Council hearing. Findal has already had the Medirian ambassador petition the Federation ambassadors to meet with Brianna and recognize her ambassadorial status from a new human planet."

"They' ve agreed?" Ban asked.

"All Findal had to do was mention Bakom' s name and the fact that Brianna is pregnant with a Drakian child, and they all agreed to the meeting," Char answered. "Federation recognition is another thing Bakom cannot have anticipated."

"You seem to have things well in hand, Son. Which shuttle will you use?"

Char grinned. "None of ours, Father. We will enter Benishan in a Gattan warbird."

Jamiros began to laugh. "You never do anything halfway, my son. If it were possible, I think you' d have Marljas land the *Scrathe* in the middle of the council chamber."

"On top of Bakom' s head if I could manage it."

"I' ll fly the rest of the family in the *Wanderer*," Ban said.

Char continued, "Having the entire immediate family there emphasizes the clan' s support. Brianna is the first widely known ' alien' to carry any clan heir. Bakom may try to convince the Council that ' pure' Alalakan blood would be best."

Xdana' s fork stopped halfway to her mouth. "He wouldn' t dare!"

"Bakom would dare, Mother. I don' t intend to allow Brianna out of my sight again until after the Council meeting," Char stated grimly. "He' ll do anything to get his hands on her."

Placidly, Brianna shifted her weight as the conversation continued around her. She didn' t look forward to confronting Bakom, but knew she had no choice. Her fears had been eased a great deal last night at Sheala' s party. The deference with which she' d been treated because of her pregnancy, even by those whom Ban had identified as some of the worst rakes in the galaxy, had done a great deal to calm her. True, some had sought assignations, but all had accepted her gentle refusals with good grace. She was sure that the Ruling Council would not allow Bakom to touch her. Instead, the Alalakans had to concentrate on saving the rest of Earth from him.

A knock at the door announced the arrival of the meal Char had ordered. Conversation ceased as everyone enjoyed the fine lunch the kitchen staff had prepared.

Xdana and Jamiros left soon after finishing. Orders for readying the townhouse had to be sent and packing had to be supervised. Brianna was ordered to relax. Verna would see to packing whatever personal items she would need.

Ban rose and stretched. He, like Char, wore only loose fitting lounging trousers.

"How is your lonely widow today, Ban?" Brianna asked.

Ban covered his heart with his hands. "Alas, fair Brianna, the lovely widow grew impatient for my return, so sought comfort in the arms of another."

She shook her head. "What are we going to do with him, Char?"

Char rose and headed for the shower. "That, my love, is why the Hardan family was so happy when he decided to come with us. They didn' t know what to do with him either."

Chucking Brianna under the chin, Ban dropped a light kiss on her forehead and said, "It is time to shake Marl out of his bed if he' s still there. We have preflight checks to run on our ships. Enjoy your day, Coz."

Brianna leaned back and mused silently on her current situation. Never in her wildest dreams would she have imagined the life she now led. Even though she missed her own family, she was now the pampered daughter of a powerful and rich merchant clan on a planet across the galaxy from her own, married to and pregnant with the child of a sexy alien who absolutely adored her. She' d been adopted into the royal family of another alien culture and managed to become bloodsister to a powerful family of aliens on yet a third planet. No one was capable of imagining this, not even Hollywood' s best scriptwriters.

Smiling, she pushed herself up out of her chair. She could hear the water splashing from Char' s shower, and she would so like to have her back scrubbed.

Chapter Sixteen

Early the next morning, Brianna climbed the wheeled stairway leading to the open door of Marljas' warbird. Much larger than a Drakian interplanetary or spaceport shuttle, it was still small enough to enter a planet' s atmosphere and land.

"I have room for ten passengers," Marljas told her as he led her to his command center.

Though Char had been uncertain, Marljas assured Brianna that, even though she was almost nine months pregnant, she' d be quite safe and comfortable in the command center of his ship. Char only agreed to her presence there if he could act as copilot. Brianna chuckled to herself. Marljas had been so obviously wary to allow a man as intelligent and space-savvy as Chardadon to see Gattan technology. He had only consented when Wendjas revealed that he had agreed, in principal, that their family and the Alalakan clan would begin a joint venture building interplanetary ships.

Sighing, Brianna shifted as her seat wrapped itself around her. It certainly was comfortable! She watched as Char went through the last preflight checks with Marljas. Wendjas, Denieen, and their sons, as well as Kahn, Beti, Jenneta and Verna, settled into the passenger section of the ship.

As Marljas flipped some switches, she felt a slight vibration through her seat.

"Relax, Brianna, we' ll be lifting off shortly. If we were heading into space," Marljas continued as he monitored his navigational and command computers, "you' d be able to leave your seat and walk around the ship. Since this flight to Benishan will be within the confines of Drakian atmosphere, it will be best if you remain seated. I wouldn' t want an unexpected wind gust dropping you on the floor. A baby has never been born in a Gattan warbird, and I don' t want yours to be the first."

"Don' t worry," Brianna said confidently, "this baby won' t come for at least three more weeks."

Marljas snorted but said nothing. As far as he was concerned, Brianna looked ready to give birth at any minute. Why Char was allowing her to travel and face the Ruling Council at all was a puzzle to him. On Gattan, dealing with Bakom would present no problem. A simple challenge would take care of everything.

Frowning, Ban watched the warbird lift off. He wasn' t happy having Brianna out of his sight, but he couldn' t be in two places at one time. "They' re off, Rodane. Is everyone aboard the *Wanderer*?"

"Everyone but us. We can leave whenever you' re ready."

"Let' s go then. The *Wanderer* is the best we' ve got. Let' s see how she compares to a Gattan warbird."

Rodane laughed with him. "Don' t be too disappointed when we don' t catch her, Ban. That technology of theirs is way ahead of ours."

Ban grinned. "Don' t be too sure, Coz. I' ve made some alterations to the *Wanderer* since she left the Alalakan space yards. I think you' ll be pleasantly surprised."

* * * * *

"Did you enjoy your vacation, Doctor?" Eliana asked as Bakom sat down in the copilot seat of the small shuttle she piloted.

"Quite, my dear Eliana," he answered as he settled himself comfortably. "There' s nothing like a solitary retreat to bring one' s self back into alignment. Now tell me, have our plans born fruit?"

"The Council sent the letter you left with your allies when it was known Alalakan brought the specimen to Drakan. Your handpicked Academy guards accompanied the Council' s messenger."

"Good. The specimen has been returned then," he said smugly.

Eliana took a deep breath.

Bakom in a rage was very unpleasant.

"No, the woman didn' t return with the messenger. The Alalakans have decided to challenge your right to her. Your guards remained at the Alalakan estate to monitor their movements and will return to Benishan with them to stand before the Council."

Bakom was quiet for a long moment. Then he began to laugh.

Eliana turned her head and watched her superior with surprise. This was not the reaction she had expected.

"In my wildest dreams, I had never imagined that the Alalakans would be so stupid," Bakom crowed delightedly. "Not even they have the power to flout Council laws."

"Perhaps they have a plan."

"My dear Eliana, no plan can supersede the laws of the Ruling Council. The specimen is not proved to be human. There' s no way around that simple fact."

Eliana began flipping switches. "Do you wish to be taken directly to the Academy, Doctor?"

Bakom' s laughter had been replaced by a thoughtful expression. "Damn Odam and his choice of accomplices. I could use him now," he muttered. "You' re right. The Alalakans wouldn' t challenge Council laws if they weren' t planning something. But what? I' ve taken every possible move they could make into consideration. There' s nothing they can do. Council laws are clear, with no vague interpretations to support a defense."

He shook himself out of his reverie and smiled. "I must make one stop before we go to the Academy, Eliana. Since Odam was fool enough to get himself arrested, I' m going to rely on you to take his place. You' ve served me well, and now there will be further responsibilities for you. Land at these coordinates," he said as he punched them into navigation.

Eliana nodded but said nothing. The long years with Bakom were finally paying off. Dr. Sendenton would be very pleased.

✳ ✳ ✳ ✳ ✳

Char rechecked his instruments. "That' s interesting."

Marljas glanced at him. "What?"

"The *Wanderer* is approximately fifteen minutes behind us and gaining."

Marljas frowned and rechecked his instruments. "That' s impossible," he muttered. "Even at the subspace speed we' re traveling, he should be at least thirty to forty minutes behind us. Have you been withholding information about your ships?"

Char didn' t miss the suspicious note in Marljas' voice. "I have no idea how Ban has caught up to us. As far as I knew, there was nothing as fast as a Gattan warbird."

"It' s Ban," Brianna interjected. "He told me he' s been modifying his ship ever since he took possession. That' s why he turned down your offer of a new ship."

Char' s expression grew thoughtful. "Ban will have to have some conversations with our engineers. Has he told you anything specific, Brianna?"

Brianna snorted. "Has he told me anything specific? Do you honestly believe I would understand anything he did tell me, Char? I' m a biologist, for goodness sake. What would I understand about the dynamics of interplanetary travel even if Ban tried to explain it to me, probably with words that have no equivalent in my language?"

Char grinned at Marljas. "No help there. You' ll have to wait until we weasel Ban' s modifications out of him."

Marljas grunted. Ban' s modifications were very interesting. If he could make them to his own ship, no one in the galaxy would catch the *Scrathe*.

Char' s voice interrupted Marljas' musings. "We' ll be in sight of Benishan in ten minutes. When do you want to begin prelanding checks?"

"In a few minutes. Benishan tower has us on their screen, but have made no move to contact us."

"They' re sure we' ll be flying on to the Gattan landing near your embassy," Char said with a grin.

Marljas sighed. "I don' t know how I let you talk me into this, Char. The Gattan tower has tried to contact us twice already."

"Why don' t you let Denieen talk to the tower? Won' t there be less of a hassle that way?" Brianna asked from where she sat.

Marljas nodded. "If ' hassle' means what I think it does, that might not be a bad idea. At least they' ll think twice about ordering me there since Denieen is a highly ranked female."

Flipping the switch that opened the intercom to the passenger section of his ship, Marljas said, "Denieen, Gattan tower is demanding an explanation as to why we haven' t filed a landing plan with them and why they had no idea we were coming to Drakan in the first place. Would you like to talk to them?"

"It' ll be my pleasure, Marljas. Send it back to the transmitter here."

Wendjas' laughter was cut off abruptly as Marljas opened a channel to his sister-in-law.

"Can' t we listen, too?" Brianna asked, eyes sparkling.

Marljas grinned. "Sorry, Brianna. I need the other channel to contact Benishan tower. You wouldn' t want to run into another ship, would you?"

She had no chance to answer because Marljas flipped another switch. "Benishan tower, Gattan warbird *Scrathe* requesting landing coordinates."

"Warbird *Scrathe*, this is Benishan tower. Have we heard correctly? You want coordinates here?"

"Correct, Benishan tower."

"Are you experiencing mechanical difficulties? The Gattan landing field is only five minutes beyond us."

"We have no difficulties, nor do we wish to fly to the Gattan field. Will you give us coordinates or not?"

A new voice came out of the communicator. "This is Major Widnasted don al' Patinetr. Who is piloting your ship?"

"I' ll take care of this," Char stated. Flipping the communicator switch in front of him, he snapped, "Major Widnasted, this is Alalakan don al' Chardadon. I suggest you send us those coordinates, or you will experience firsthand just how much damage a Gattan battle laser can do."

"Alalakan don al' Chardadon, I had no idea. We' ll send coordinates immediately."

"The Medirian ship *Wanderer* is approximately ten minutes behind us. I want it berthed immediately next to the *Scrathe*. All other ships are to be kept away. A squad of Alalakan security should be at the field gate. Send them to our pad immediately."

"Yes, Sir. Everything will be done as requested. Benishan tower out."

Marljas eyed Char with new respect. Recognition of his voice alone had gained them what they requested. He flipped a switch and acknowledged the transmission. "Coordinates received, Benishan tower." Flipping the switch off, he continued, "They' re putting us at the far end of the field, Char. I hope you' ve made arrangements. It will be a long hike to the terminal."

"The transports are waiting. We' ll completely bypass the terminal."

"Lifestyles of the Rich and Famous," Brianna mused out loud. "I never pictured myself being whisked away from a private aircraft in a limousine."

Brianna' s comment caused Marljas to glance at Char. "I' ll never get used to it."

While Char was giving instructions to the drivers of the six hovercraft that waited for them, Brianna and the others waited patiently as Ban and his passengers crossed the landing pad to join them. The Medirians, Sheala, Rodane, and Fionilina had flown in with Ban. Char' s parents would shuttle into Benishan on the following morning. Brianna' s "guards" would be released after the council meeting.

"We' ve plenty of room in our townhouse for you," Jenneta said. "Please feel free to accept our hospitality."

"We' re honored by your invitation, Jenneta," Denieen answered. "However, we must go on to the embassy. We don' t want to snub the ambassador and his wife. Marljas will stay with you, if you don' t mind. The wife of the current Gattan ambassador to Drakan was godmother to Sosha, the girl Marljas wished to marry. Both she and her husband blame him for her disappearance."

Jenneta nodded. "He' s one of the family."

Char rejoined the group. "Take the first craft, Wendjas. I' ve instructed the driver to take you to the embassy."

Denieen gave Brianna a quick hug. "I' ll see you tomorrow. Watch Marljas for me. Gattan women keep their men out of trouble."

"How in the world do you manage that?"

Denieen grinned. "I' ll begin your instruction tomorrow."

"Brianna meets with the Federation ambassadors tomorrow afternoon, Deni. I' m afraid you' ll have to put off your visit until the following day," Char said with humor.

Denieen smiled at Char. "I' ll be accompanying Brianna, Char. She is my bloodsister through my husband' s brother."

"A rather tenuous relationship, don' t you think?" Jenneta asked curiously.

Denieen was very serious when she answered. "On Drakan, perhaps, but not on Gattan. Just as Marljas is Alalakan by virtue of his dragon, Brianna is Gattan by virtue of blood rite."

"Enough," Wendjas interjected, "this discussion is better settled in another place. Hendjas, Charjas, come."

With a son on each shoulder, he strode towards the first car.

"The first lesson in controlling men, Brianna," Denieen explained as she moved to follow her husband, "is to let them think they' re in charge sometimes."

Brianna' s clear laughter followed Denieen. That was a lesson she' d learned a long time ago. Her father had been wrapped around her little finger for years.

Char turned to Ban. "Cousin, I' m leaving you in charge. Make sure everything gets sorted out. I' m taking Brianna home."

Ban grinned in answer. As usual, Char had swept Brianna up into his arms and disappeared into one of the waiting hovercraft.

✳ ✳ ✳ ✳ ✳

Brianna waddled from one side of the room to the other.

Denieen' s gaze followed her. "Exercise is good for you, Brianna, but don' t you think you should sit down and rest a little? You' ve been pacing for fifteen minutes."

"Relax, Bri," Meri added with a chuckle. "Sit down. You don' t have anything to worry about. Uncle Kavlalardrac is, what do you say, a pushover."

Brianna blew a curl off of her face. "Uncle?"

Meri draped her arm along the back of her chair. "Father wouldn' t trust just anyone to be the Medirian ambassador to Drakan, Brianna. Kavlalardrac is his younger brother."

Brianna stared at Meri. "Just how many brothers and sisters does your father have? I thought I' d met all of them on Mediria."

"Except for Uncle Kav, Aunt Lindralindra, and Aunt Evileenila, Father' s youngest and oldest sisters, you did. Aunt Evi is the Medirian ambassador on Gattan. Aunt Lini is Ban' s mother."

Brianna flopped back into a comfortable chair. "Why didn' t you tell me there were more uncles and aunts I hadn' t met?"

At that moment, the door opened and Char, Marljas and a young Drakian aide walked in. "Follow me, please. The Federation Ambassadorial Council awaits."

Char squeezed Brianna' s hand encouragingly. "I love you," he whispered into her ear. Lacing his fingers through hers, he escorted her into the council chamber.

Smaller than the regular Federation Assembly chamber, the room where the ambassadors had chosen to meet Brianna and hear her petition contained a semicircular table and a number of chairs set along the walls. One chair sat in the middle of the room, and it was to this chair that Char led Brianna. Before they took more than two steps into the room, however, the Medirian ambassador rose from his seat and met them in the center of the room. Meri flung herself into his arms, making no attempt to hide her joy.

Kavlalardrac' s booming laughter filled the room. He looked much the same as his brother Findal, but his girth was much broader.

"How is my favorite niece?" he asked returning Meri' s hug with one of his own.

"Just fine, Uncle Kav. You really must come to dinner. Celene has grown so much since you saw her. You don' t mind do you, Brianna?"

"What' s another mouth to feed? Of course he' s welcome," Brianna answered watching Kavlalardrac closely. "After all, he' s my uncle, too."

Kavlalardrac' s laughter boomed again as he turned to Brianna. "Findal said I' d like you. Are the dols and orcs really on your planet?"

Brianna smiled and answered that particular question for what had to be the thousandth time. "Yes, they' re there."

"Ha! Findal finally did something right in his old age when he adopted you," he said as he draped an arm over her shoulder. "So, when will I be made an uncle again?"

"If you don' t stop prattling and let us get on with this meeting," said the elegant Varcian woman sitting behind the table, "your next niece or nephew will put in an appearance here."

Chuckling, Kavlalardrac shooed Brianna' s companions to a group of chairs close to the ambassadors' table and led her to the chair in the center of the room. Giving her a quick kiss on the cheek, he waited until she sat and then resumed his place behind the table.

The Varcian woman continued to gaze at Brianna and said, "I know what it is like to carry an active child, my dear. If that chair becomes too uncomfortable, don' t hesitate to mention it."

Brianna inclined her head in thanks. "I' ll let you know if he decides not to cooperate," she said patting her stomach.

"Well then," Kavlalardrac continued, "I' ll take it upon myself to introduce the other members of this council. The woman with whom you' ve been speaking is Chechana Lubineau of Varce. In the center seat and our current chairman is Roth of Deslossia. Next to him is Frenken don al' Markart of Drakan, and finally Mendas Teekeson of Gattan."

Indicating Brianna, Kavlalardrac said, "My fellow ambassadors, I would like to present Alalakan dem al' Brianna, Princess Hardan, carrier of the Alalakan heir, from the newly discovered planet Earth. She is before us to request admission for her planet to the Federation of Planets and appointment for herself to ambassadorial status."

Silence reigned when Kavlalardrac finished speaking, each of the ambassadors watching Brianna and weighing her reactions to them.

Mendas Teekeson spoke first. "How is it, wife of a Drakian, that you arrived in Benishan in a Gattan warbird?" he asked, a belligerent look in his eye. His face was mottled with spots, for he favored the leopard and jaguar species of Earth.

Holding up her right hand so the three parallel scars were visible, Brianna answered, "My brother through bloodbond, Marljas Drefeson, offered to transport me and other members of my family, Ambassador Teekeson."

At that point, Deni and Marljas joined Brianna in the center of the room.

Opening his vest, Marljas revealed the three parallel scares above his right pectoral that matched Brianna' s. "She is my sister by bloodbond, Mendas Teekeson."

Marljas was careful to hold his vest so as not to reveal his new tattoo. A display of the Alalakan dragon on a Gattan shoulder was best still kept secret.

Denieen continued. "The bonding was rightly done, Mendas, in the cancellation of a blood feud. I witnessed and approved."

The Gattan ambassador frowned. Denieen' s outspoken support was unexpected. The fact that Gattan society was matriarchal was kept as quiet as possible. He should have taken the time yesterday to sit and talk with Wendjas and Denieen when they arrived. Unfortunately, he' d had prior appointments. By the time he' d arrived back at the embassy, his wife informed him that their guests had retired for the night. "So be it," he acknowledged with a scowl, "I recognize the bloodbond."

Marljas escorted Denieen back to her chair. Their part in this little drama was now over.

"A Gattan bloodbond, while certainly an honor in its own right," Frenken don al' Markart interjected, "is not reason to grant membership or ambassadorial status to the Federation."

Char tensed. Frenken don al' Markart was relatively new to the role of Federation ambassador. Drakan' s previous ambassador had died unexpectedly, and the Ruling council had appointed Markart to take his place. The Alalakans were unsure where he stood—did he support Bakom or not?

Brianna pushed the foot kicking her rib cage down. "Considering I' m the only inhabitant of Earth here, there' s not much of a choice."

"You' re qualified for this position?"

Brianna took a deep breath. "The position of Earth' s ambassador is not one I would have sought, nor, honestly, even have been considered for under different circumstances," she began. Then she decided a frontal attack was always best. "I' m sure you' re all aware of the fact that the Alalakan clan appears before the Drakan Ruling Council tomorrow. My husband, Alalakan don al' Chardadon, has been charged with treason because he took a scientific specimen from Rodak don al' Bakom, Science Academy First President. I' m that specimen. Bakom demands that he be permitted to perform his Tests of Humanity on me. You cannot fault me for wishing to forego participating."

Char relaxed. Brianna' s mentioning Bakom and his Tests for Humanity would cause the four ambassadors from the other planets to support her request. The Alalakans would have liked the support of the Drakan ambassador also, but a majority would be enough.

"Alalakan don al' Chardadon," Markart asked, "does Bakom know your wife is pregnant?"

Char rose and strode to Brianna' s side. "Brianna' s pregnancy isn' t a closely guarded secret although I don' t know if Bakom is aware of it."

Markart' s eyes narrowed. "Tell us, Chardadon, does Bakom know that you' ve married his ' specimen' ?"

"Markart, I wish to go on record that referring to a Hardan princess as a ' specimen' is completely unacceptable," Kavlalardrac stated flatly.

"Ah yes, she is also now a Hardan princess," Markart continued. "Is Bakom aware of this woman' s adoption into the Hardan royal family?"

Prince Kavlalardrac could be just as haughty and royal as his brother. "Brianna was adopted into the royal family, with a great deal of pomp and ceremony, I might add, because she brought us news of the dols and the orcs, not because we wished to foil the plans of Rodak don al' Bakom. We could have simply kept her on Mediria to accomplish that. Furthermore, news of Brianna' s adoption and the reason for it was broadcast planetwide on Mediria. Did we send a personal message to Bakom? Hardly! Even if the man were not a kidnapper of children, and a criminal on Mediria, we do not inform individual citizens from the other planets of specific actions on ours."

Pushing herself slowly to her feet, Brianna said, "Do you not consider me human, Frenken don al' Markart? Am I wasting my time here?"

Markart was taken aback by Brianna' s question.

Char grinned. "My wife is nothing if not direct, Markart."

"Alalakan dem al' Brianna, one need only look at you to know that you are human. You are carrying a Drakian child," Markart finally answered dryly.

Brianna sniffed. "At least you aren' t questioning my child' s paternity."

Markart smiled wryly, but before he could comment, Chechana Lubineau of Varce spoke. "A full medical report was forwarded to us by Dr. Sendenton dem al' Lorilana, Brianna of Earth. We don' t question the paternity of your child. We question your application for membership of your planet in the Federation and the request of ambassadorial status for yourself. You must admit, your application has been submitted under highly unusual circumstances."

"It' s my understanding that the chief mandate of this Federation is to seek out other human planets and admit them to the council for the betterment of all humanity in the galaxy," countered Brianna.

Chechana smiled. Unlike the Varcian ambassador on Mediria, Chechana did not have a Mohawk-like bony ridge in the center of her skull. Her ridges, dyed a light green, curled over both ears, looking very much like ram' s horns. Like her Medirian counterpart, though, except for eyebrows and eyelashes, she had no hair on her head.

"You' re to be commended on your knowledge, Brianna of Earth. Now tell us why your planet should be admitted to the Federation."

"Am I human, Chechana Lubineau?"

Everyone with Brianna held his or her breath. Acknowledgment of Brianna' s humanity, after all, was the reason behind her petition.

Chechana' s merry laugh filled the chamber. "Though I cannot speak for the others present here, as far as I am concerned, yes, Brianna of Earth, you' re human."

"If I' m human, so is everyone else on my planet. The Federation searches for planets inhabited by humans. Well, you' ve found another one," Brianna countered locking eyes with each individual council member.

Roth of Deslossia finally broke the silence. With a smile he said, "Forgive us, Alalakan dem al' Brianna, but we had to be sure of your motives. Based on your qualifications, we' ve decided against your petition for the ambassadorship, but," he continued holding up his hand when not only Brianna but also all four of her companions would have protested, "the Council of Federation Ambassadors unanimously acknowledges the humanity of Alalakan dem al' Brianna and all other peoples found on her planet. We accept the planet Earth into the Federation of Planets and look forward to welcoming its ambassador once one can be appointed by the proper authorities."

Char smiled broadly. They' d gotten exactly what they wanted. Brianna really didn' t want to be Earth' s ambassador any more than Char wanted her to assume that position. Their child would keep her busy enough.

Roth rose from his place behind the table. Like Qjin on Mediria, he was tall, blue-eyed and albino white. "If you would like to accompany us, we have had a small luncheon prepared to welcome you."

Brianna stared at the ambassadors suspiciously. "You knew exactly what you were going to do before we even arrived!"

Chechana Lubineau smiled. "Never before in the history of Mediria has the royal family adopted a being from another planet. That, in and of itself, was enough to impress upon us the necessity of granting your planet membership in the Federation. We did wish, however, to learn what the woman who had married into the Alalakan clan and become the adopted daughter of the Hardan royal family was like. You always have been an ambassador of your planet, Brianna, and it should be very proud of you."

"Oh, come on, Bri," Meri said tugging her hand. "Don' t start an argument now. I' m starving. I was so nervous this morning, I couldn' t eat a thing!"

Brianna looked from Char to Meri. "Well, I guess I could eat a little."

Marljas bark of laughter filled the room. "A little, Bloodsister! I' ve seen you eat as much as one of the Gattan royal guards."

Brianna scowled at the grinning Marljas. "Ever since you and Ban settled your quarrel, you' ve been acting more and more like him. I think I liked you better when you wanted to rip out his heart."

"Ban? Bandalardrac Hardan?" Mendas Teekeson roared as he rose from his seat and stalked around the table. "He' s here in Benishan?"

"Now, Mendas," began Kavlalardrac.

"Alalakan don al' Bandalardrac, accompanied by other members of the Alalakan clan, arrived in Benishan with us yesterday, Mendas Teekeson," Brianna answered coolly. "The blood feud has been satisfied. Do you question the word of a Gattan bloodsister?"

Mendas' eyes bulged.

"But..."

Denieen slipped her hand under his arm. "Come, Mendas, much has been revealed in the last few weeks. I had a long conversation with your wife this morning."

"Do you think there will be any problems with him?" Char murmured in Marljas' ear.

"Not if Denieen talked with his wife this morning," Marljas answered, slipping Brianna' s hand under his arm. "Come, Bloodsister, if your husband will not feed you, I will."

Brianna, Char, and Marljas had just returned from their meeting with the Federation Council when Jami and her sister burst into the room. "Have you seen Sheala?" she asked in a vexed tone. "It' s not very funny of her to leave us waiting for her downtown."

"A package from one of the infant' s shops was delivered about an hour ago, but we haven' t seen her," Xdana answered. "It' s not like

Sheala to just leave you. I know she's got a playful streak, but she never purposefully causes undo worry. When did you last see her?"

"It has been over three hours, Alalakan dem al' Xdana," Feni answered from where she stood by the door.

Worried looks appeared on everyone's faces. Marljas' nostrils flared.

Xdana glanced at her husband. "Where do you think she could be?"

Brianna cleared her throat and all eyes leaped to her. "Are people kidnapped on your planet?"

Char said only one word. "Bakom."

A vicious snarl erupted from Marljas' throat as he ripped the arm from his chair.

* * * * *

Eliana grimaced as Bakom fondled her buttocks. "Are you finished with the entries my dear?" Squeezing her breast, he clamped his mouth on hers.

Eliana pretended an interest she didn't feel, grateful when he pulled away.

"Come, we have much to do tonight."

Fifteen minutes later, Bakom landed the unmarked shuttle on the roof of a building in downtown Benishan.

Eliana didn't have to look at the navigation control to know it was the same place she had left him two days ago. He led the way to the elevator that, interestingly enough, was waiting for them, the doors open.

"Now pay attention, my dear. Any time you come here, press the gray panel underneath the basement button. This is an Academy building, but most of the floors contain residential apartments. The bottom two floors contain shops, and all of the rents are used to help fund various Academy projects. However, the three levels below the basement are where you will want to go."

As the elevator began its descent, he continued, "Very few people know of the existence of these laboratories. You'll tell no one else."

"Of course, Doctor, you can rely on my discretion," Eliana murmured as he caressed her breasts.

"You' ve proved your loyalty on more than one occasion, Eliana, and you' ll be rewarded for that loyalty. I' ve decided you shall be one of the women who will bear my children."

He' s mad. "Doctor, I...I' m speechless."

"An unexpected honor, I know," he answered and pulled her one-piece uniform from her shoulders. Soon she was naked from the waist up, but the opening of the door halted further sexual progress.

Bakom grabbed Eliana' s arm and pulled her through a dimly lit corridor and down two flights of stairs. "Another time, I' ll show you the experiments on those floors, but tonight our destination is the bottom level." Pushing open a door, he led her into a large, brightly lit laboratory.

Eliana followed Bakom deeper into the laboratory. Though she longed to, she hadn' t bothered to cover her upper body. Bakom would become suspicious. As she followed him, her sharp eyes darted around the cavernous room, memorizing all the details she could.

The laboratory was filled with various pieces of equipment resting on both the floor and tables. The eight large cages against the back wall, however, drew her attention. Only two were occupied, one with an unconscious Drakian woman, the other with a Gattan female obviously in thrall to the drug mithrin. Both women were naked.

Bakom stopped before the Gattan woman' s cage. "Interesting specimen," he said as he absentmindedly stroked Eliana' s breast. "We' ve discovered that the Gattan can become addicted to mithrin. Once addicted, they are subject to very painful withdrawal symptoms if the drug isn' t administered on a regular basis. According to her chart, Sosha received her last injection an hour ago. From ongoing observations, we' ve learned that she' ll be sexually insatiable for two hours. Then, as the drug begins to wear off, she' ll regain control of her body. For approximately two hours, she' ll be as sane and levelheaded as you and I. Then her body will begin to demand the drug until she' s mindless with pain. Only another injection will relieve her."

Eliana was very adept at hiding her disgust. "Very thorough, Doctor," she murmured. "But are you sure she' s safe? What about her claws?"

Bakom' s breathing became harsher and his tail began to jerk as he watched the Gattan' s writhing body. "She' s quite safe now, my dear. She craves sexual satisfaction and is very receptive to anyone who cares to mount her. Odam enjoyed her body quite often. And we removed her claws."

"Doctor, I didn' t know you arrived."

Gathering himself, Bakom said, "Eliana, meet Gothran, Odam' s brother. He' s as well endowed as Odam."

Gothran grunted, his eyes fastened on Eliana' s breasts.

Eliana heard a door open and shut, and a slender woman joined them. With a smile, she walked into Bakom' s arms, her mouth seeking his.

"Eliana, this is Tetiras," Bakom said when the passionate kiss ended. "You must get to know her better."

Tetiras turned to Eliana and smiled.

Eliana smiled in return as Tetiras cupped her breast. Aware of the ultimate objective concerning Bakom, she was ready to do almost anything to aid in his downfall.

Bakom caressed Tetiras' buttocks and said, "Not now, my dear, we have other things to do." Turning to Gothran, he said, "What surprise do you have for me?"

Opening the door to the other cage, the other man gathered the unconscious woman into his arms and carried her to an examining table. "Alalakan dem al' Sheala."

Chapter Seventeen

Chaos ruled the Alalakan townhouse. Xdana had been put to bed with a sedative while Jenneta and Fionilina sat with her.

Brianna remained downstairs with the men. "Bakom would never have taken Sheala if it weren' t for me," she said with tears in her eyes. "Perhaps it would be best if…"

"Don' t complete that thought, Brianna," Jamiros snapped. "You' re married to my son and carry my first grandchild. You are just as much a part of this family as Sheala. You will go *nowhere* near Bakom. Do you understand?"

Gritting her teeth, Brianna nodded. If only she weren' t so pregnant and could move faster.

Ban dropped a hand on her shoulder. His tone was sharp. "Do you really think Bakom would give Sheala back if he got his hands on you?"

Before Brianna could answer, a very loud commotion in the street drew their attention. Looking out the window, Rodane said in an astonished voice, "Someone' s landed a shuttle in the middle of the street!"

Before anyone else in the room could comment, he leaped away from the window and through the doorway into the hall. In what seemed only seconds, he returned, his hand clamped around the upper arm of Bakom' s assistant, Eliana.

"I know where he has her!" she called as she stumbled through the doorway.

Growling, Marljas leaped to his feet, claws extended.

Char laid a restraining hand on his arm. "Wait, she' s one of Bakom' s assistants." He directed his next comment to Eliana, "How do we know this isn' t another trap?"

"Dr. Sendenton," Eliana gasped, "I work for her. Cindar is my sister. Now hurry! There' s no time!"

With those words, she jerked free of Rodane and ran back the way she'd come.

Marljas wrenched his arm free of Char's grasp. "Trap be damned! I go with the girl."

Ban rose and followed Marljas.

"Char, Rodane," Jamiros commanded, "go with them. If this is a trap, I promise you, I'll pull the Academy down around Bakom's ears."

Brianna pushed herself to her feet. "Char!"

Taking the time to sweep her into his arms, he kissed her hard and said, "I'll be back, love. Don't worry." Then he too was gone.

Tears rolled down her cheeks as Brianna planted her fists on her hips. "'Don't worry,' he says. What does he expect me to do?"

When Jamiros put his arm around her, she buried her face in his chest.

* * * * *

Eliana had barely set the shuttle down when Marljas jumped out. "Wait," she called after him. "You don't even know where you're going. This way."

All four men followed her to the elevator. After Marljas made sure no one was waiting inside, they crowded in.

Char clamped his hand around Eliana's upper arm.

"It's not a trap!" she exclaimed in frustration as she pushed the correct panel and the elevator began its descent. "Bakom has secret laboratories below this building that I only found out about tonight. He's never trusted me with this secret before."

"If you're lying..." growled Ban.

Marljas flexed his fingers. Four-inch claws appeared. "I'll rip your guts out while you watch."

She ignored their threats. "The elevator will open onto a dimly lit corridor. I don't know what experiments Bakom is performing on the first two levels, but Sheala is being held on the third. There's a stairway at the end of the corridor; follow it all the way to the bottom. There's only one door that I saw. Sheala's in that laboratory."

The hand clasping her arm tightened. "Laboratory?"

Eliana flinched but swallowed her pain. "You' d best prepare yourselves. I don' t know exactly what her physical condition will be."

Char loosened his grasp—a little. "Are there any guards?"

"No, but two of Bakom' s assistants were still there when we left. One of them is Odam' s brother."

There wasn' t time for any further questions. The door of the elevator opened, and Marljas sprinted down the corridor.

"Marljas, wait," Char called.

The other three men kept Eliana with them and followed more slowly, still suspecting the possibility of a trap.

Ban glanced towards Char and Rodane. "Now may not be the best time to mention this, but Marljas and Sheala..."

Marljas burst through the door of the laboratory as Gothran crawled off Sheala' s naked back. Both of Bakom' s assistants whirled about as the door burst open.

Seconds later, Gothran lay against the wall, slit open from throat to groin. Tetiras made a beeline for the door. Marljas ignored her. Instead, heedless of the blood that stained him, he went to the table where Sheala lay sobbing and gathered her into his arms. "Shhhhh, you' re safe. It' s me."

Sheala buried her face in his chest and sobbed harder.

"I' m here," Marljas whispered as he hugged her to him. "I promise no one will ever hurt you again."

"I waited and waited," she sobbed in a voice hoarse from screaming, "but no one came. They, Bakom, he..."

Tears slid from Marljas' s eyes. "Hush, love, I' m here. No one will ever hurt you again."

Sheala looked up into his face. "Promise me," she hissed fiercely between her sobs. She held out her left hand. "Promise me."

Marljas unsheathed the claws on his right hand. "I cannot do this for you. You must do it yourself."

Eliana, Ban, Char, and Rodane entered the lab as Sheala pulled her left hand over Marljas unsheathed claws.

Releasing Eliana, Char leaped toward them. "Sheala, no!"

But it was too late. Marljas ripped his vest open and pulled his claws down over his pectoral below his tattoo. Lifting Sheala' s still bleeding hand, he held it against his open cuts. "Blood to my blood, heart to my heart, we are one forever."

As he placed a gentle kiss on Sheala's lips, she fainted.

Lifting his head, he looked squarely into Char's eyes and said, "She's mine now, Alalakan."

Ban broke the silence. "No more than you're hers, Marl."

Marljas refused to reply.

"Help me," came a faint feminine voice from the back of the room.

"He treats humans like animals," Rodane said in disgust when he saw the cages against the back wall. "Free her and I'll go back and pick up that woman you knocked out, Ban."

"Best idea at the time," Ban answered as he and Char headed to the back of the room.

"Gothran has the keys," Eliana said in a helpful voice.

"Who? Oh," Ban said as he looked at the bloody body on the floor. "You definitely don't do anything halfway, do you, Marl?"

Marljas remained leaning against the table, Sheala cradled in his arms. "He raped her! What would you have done?"

Ban's answer was terse. "With your claws, castrated him and shoved his balls down his throat."

Marljas said nothing, but there was approval in his eyes.

Bending over the body, Ban sighed with relief. The force of Marljas' attack had thrown the keys clear of the body. He grabbed them and joined Char, where he got his first good look at the woman in the cage. "Sosha!"

Marljas looked up when he heard the name. Still cradling the unconscious Sheala in his arms, he joined Char and Ban.

She was naked, her body battered and covered with both fresh and healing bruises in a kaleidoscope of colors. She moaned and tried to cover herself. "Please, get me out of here."

Marljas snarled. "Sosha, what has been done to you?"

"He addicted me to mithrin," she sobbed as they opened the door to her cage. "I've been used as the sexual plaything of Bakom and anyone else he brought here."

Ban lifted her into his arms and cuddled her against his chest.

Sosha lay listlessly in his arms.

Eliana tugged Char' s sleeve. "We' ve got to get out of here. I don' t think Bakom plans on coming back tonight, but I' m not sure."

Hope leaped into Marljas' eyes. "Then he is a dead man."

Sosha struggled in Ban' s arms. "The files. Bakom kept notes on everything. There are also videos."

An ugly smile appeared on Char' s face. "Where are they?"

She pointed to a spot on the back wall. "In the wall safe, behind that cabinet. Be careful, it' s set with a chemical dissolvent. The wrong number code will trigger it."

Char muttered a blasphemy. "Without the correct code, those files may as well be on Gattan.

Sosha' s voice was bitter. "Six, two, three, seven, four."

Char looked from Sosha to the wall. "Are you sure of that? If you' re wrong…"

"I am sure," she answered even more bitterly. "Bakom would often recite it in my ear when he mounted me. A game he played. He thought I would not understand because of the mithrin."

Rodane shoved the cabinet out of the way. "There' s only one way to find out."

In a few short minutes, the safe was open.

"Hurry," Marljas snarled. "We must get the women to a doctor."

Char tossed a blanket to Ban for Sosha, then rummaged through the equipment and other items lying on tables. "Just put everything in a case or sack or something. We can go through it at home. Marljas is right. We need to get to Lori."

Rodane found a large box and a sack and emptied Bakom' s safe.

Char picked up the boxes. "The authorities have to be notified. Rodane, see if you can shake that other woman awake enough to walk to the shuttle. If you can' t, you' ll have to carry her. Eliana, can you get yourself home from here? We' ll take care of the shuttle."

She handed a slip of paper to him. "I' ll manage. This is the name and address of the shuttle owner. Bakom never uses an Academy shuttle when he comes here."

Marljas and Ban carried Sheala and Sosha toward the door.

Rodane slung the sack over his shoulder and followed them out.

"Where will you take them?" Eliana asked Char.

"We' ll take them home. Lorilana is probably there already."

Char clasped her arm when Eliana turned to walk away. "The Alalakan clan is grateful for your help tonight, but you do realize that there will be a great deal of explaining to do if you lied about Lorilana' s patronage."

Eliana grinned. "Then I have nothing to worry about. If Dr. Sendenton doesn' t acknowledge me, Cindar will make Miklan' s life a living hell."

Char smiled. That was the one answer from Eliana that he totally believed.

She nodded her head towards Gothran' s body. "What about that?"

His lip curled. "We' ll take care of it and the woman. Go home before you' re missed."

"With what you got out of that safe," she said as they left the laboratory, "you aren' t going to need any more help."

When they arrived home with the Sosha and Sheala, Lorilana sedated the two women and made sure they were tucked into beds.

Informed of their goddaughter' s rescue, Mendas Teekeson and his wife Pikeen Sodasdotir arrived a bare ten minutes later. They remained upstairs with her.

Restless and angry, Marljas, prowled Sheala' s room. Only Brianna and Jenneta had the courage to demand that he wash the blood off of himself.

Brianna he ignored.

Jenneta proved to be more intimidating than any Gattan matriarch.

Brianna walked into the breakfast room as the family was engrossed in the new plans for that afternoon' s meeting before the Ruling Council.

"There' s no doubt that Bakom will be held criminally responsible for his actions," Jamiros said as he steepled his fingers together. "We only have to decide how to go about revealing his crimes to the Council."

Char leaned back in his chair. "Bakom' s downfall will be much more effective if we let him believe he' s in control. Brianna' s obvious pregnancy and her marital status will certainly cause him problems. I' d like to see just how he reacts."

Jamiros frowned. "Is that wise?"

Char nodded. "If we hadn' t discovered Bakom' s secret laboratories, that' s the position we' d be in. What' s more, we need to discover which members of the Council knew about the laboratory. Sosha said that Bakom would give her to others when she was under the influence of mithrin. If any Council member ever entered that laboratory, he or she is just as guilty as Bakom and should be punished and censured accordingly."

Jamiros turned to Brianna. "What do you think?"

She shrugged as she ate her breakfast. "I' ll go along with whatever plans you devise since the baby won' t be in any danger."

A concerned Jenneta interrupted. "Will Sheala or Sosha have to be there?"

"No, Grandmother. Sosha may be called upon another day to identify any other Council members who were in Bakom' s lab, but the ' scientific records' that Bakom filmed will condemn him as far as their rapes are concerned."

Xdana winced and fresh tears began to flow at the word *rapes*.

Char patted her arm. "I' m sorry, Mother."

Xdana waved him off. "It' s not your fault, Char. It' s just that Sheala didn' t deserve the treatment she received from that animal."

Jamiros rose and walked around the table to his wife. Taking her hands, he lifted her from her chair and pulled her into his arms. "No one deserves what happened to Sheala and Sosha. Now we must help them. As long as Sheala has us to love her, she' ll be fine."

Ban had remained silent during the discussion. Now, however, he spoke. "Don' t forget Marljas. You can be sure he intends to be part of any plans concerning Sheala."

Jamiros frowned. "We' re going to have to decide what to do about Marljas."

Brianna' s head snapped up. She had just finished the substantial breakfast and now turned her attention to the family discussion. "Do something about Marljas?"

Everyone looked at her.

"We are discussing my brother."

Xdana' s voice was sharp. "Do you expect us to accept this marriage?"

Brianna nodded. "Yes. Mine and Char' s marriage began under similar if less violent circumstances."

Ban grinned. "She has you there, Aunt. And you' re discussing Sheala as if she has no say in the matter."

Jamiros shook his head. "Sheala was hysterical. She didn' t know what she was doing."

Jenneta spoke for the first time. "Why don' t we ask Shea when she wakes up?"

Jamiros stared at his mother, his surprise obvious. "You think we should honor this marriage?"

Jenneta pursed her lips. "If my information is correct," she said, nodding in Ban' s direction, "Sheala spent Solstice night with Marljas on his ship and the night before last in his room here. She must have some feelings for the boy."

Brianna snorted inelegantly. Only Jenneta would call Marljas a boy.

Jenneta ignored Brianna and continued, "We can be very grateful for Marljas. If Sheala had still been a virgin when Bakom and his assistants raped her, the mental damage would have been much more profound. As it is, it may take years for her to recover from this experience. This marriage to Marljas may aid in her recuperation. We must think very carefully before we try to deny them."

"Marljas would just take her to Gattan anyway," Brianna muttered.

Char gazed at his wife thoughtfully. "Brianna' s right. We all know Marljas is impulsive. Right now he' s convinced he loves Sheala. Maybe he does. At this point, it will harm no one to agree with them. Later, if one or both believes there' s been a mistake, well, there was no formal marriage. They can walk away from each other."

Brianna stared at Char as if he' d grown another head, but she kept her thoughts to herself. From Denieen, she' d learned that nothing on Gattan was as binding as a bloodbond. Sheala and Marljas' blood had mixed on his chest and her palm. To the Gattan, they were as married as married could be.

Jamiros sighed and patted his wife's shoulder. "Then we'll bide our time with Sheala and Marljas. As for Bakom and this afternoon's hearing, we are in agreement?"

Affirmative nods answered his question.

"Good. We'll meet together again in four hours to leave for the Council building. Until then, I suggest we make sure everything is ready."

As everyone was going his or her separate way, Brianna said, "I am expecting Denieen soon. Please have her brought to my room when she arrives."

After Brianna left, Char turned to Ban. "What are my wife and Denieen planning?"

Ban stared at the doorway Brianna had just disappeared through. "I haven't got the vaguest idea but knowing Brianna, whatever it is will make an impression."

Char started towards the door. "That's what I'm afraid of. We've got Bakom right where we want him. I don't want Brianna to ruin that, nor do I want her in any danger of any kind."

Ban's hand on his arm stopped him. "Don't. You know Brianna. If she doesn't want you to know what she's doing, she won't tell you and you'll both only become more upset. Brianna won't do anything to endanger her baby. Leave her be. What could she possibly do, anyway? We'll all be there to stop her."

After a short pause, Char nodded. Ban was right. What could she possibly do with all of them there? Findal surely had assassins somewhere. The members of the royal family always had at least one guarding them at all times. Char cursed mentally, wishing he could recognize the assassins. Not the Aradabs. They'd never shown any interest in the Brotherhood. Damn, but he had to talk to Findal. Brianna was *his* wife. He deserved to know what the assassin guarding her looked like.

Ban stared at the wall. Brianna would do as she damn well pleased and not even he would be able to stop her. Shaking himself out of his reverie, Ban rose. He too had things to do before the meeting.

* * * * *

Bakom awoke refreshed. The Alalakans were exactly where he wanted them. Unfortunately, late-night planning had caused him to sleep later than usual, and he wouldn' t be able to stop at the secret laboratory before the Ruling Council' s hearing. A session with the Gattan would have been so invigorating.

Charging Alalakan don al' Chardadon with treason had been a stroke of genius, Bakom admitted to himself. He only needed the agreement of ten other Council members to register that charge, and he' d had little trouble finding ten members who hated the Alalakans enough to agree. The fact that treason was normally leveled against only those who compromised the security of Drakan in some way didn' t matter. He, Bakom, was or soon would be the ruler of Drakan. Anyone who went against his wishes was a traitor. Soon he' d have not only the Alalakan daughter but also his stolen specimen back.

Slipping into the official yellow robes of Academy President, Bakom chuckled gleefully. These robes would bolster his argument by reminding everyone of his position. And anyone voting against him would be marked and remembered.

After checking his appearance one last time in the mirror, Bakom left his bedroom. Calling to his housekeeper to bring his breakfast, he made his way to his study. Sitting down before his computer, he checked his agenda. Shrugging away the irritation he' d experienced earlier because he wouldn' t have time to stop in at his secret laboratory, he checked the time. He had one hour until he had to meet with his primary allies on the council to review their strategy. Two hours after that, he would break the back of the Alalakan clan.

Taking a deep breath, Eliana pressed the code that would connect her with Bakom' s personal computer. The early morning call she received from Alalakan don al' Chardadon had been very clear. The longer it took Bakom to reach the Council chamber, the better. She knew exactly what they were asking her to do.

"What is it, Eliana?" said Bakom' s voice from her communicator. "There isn' t a problem at the lab is there?"

"No, Doctor," she answered as she pushed a button. "I know you' ll be busy this afternoon and this evening. I was hoping I could congratulate you on your victory while there was time."

Bakom stared at the viewing screen on his computer. The image of Eliana was very clear. She stood before her screen practically naked. A small scrap of sequined leather barely covered her pubic region and two sparkling nipple tassels were strategically placed on her breasts. He watched as she took her tail in her hand and began to rub it over her body. His breath quickened and his pupils dilated.

"Forget the breakfast," he yelled to his housekeeper. "I am leaving now."

His allies knew his plans. He could talk to them later.

Chapter Eighteen

Char squeezed Brianna' s hand. "Remember, you need only answer the questions asked by Council members. You don' t have to speak to Bakom at all."

Brianna craned her neck and tried to look into the room. "Well, at least I' ll finally get to see what he looks like."

Silence spread across the room as Alalakan don al' Jamiros entered.

Bakom was already seated in the chair reserved for the accuser, arriving barely five minutes before the hearing began. The hour he' d spent with Eliana had been well worth the delay.

Nodding to friends and acquaintances as he crossed the floor, Jamiros bypassed the chair reserved for the accused and took his customary seat among the counselors.

A shocked silence seemed to echo throughout the hall as Bakom smiled with glee. This slap in the face to the Council was more than he' d dreamed of.

The Council president cleared his throat and said, "Alalakan don al' Jamiros, do you remember why this session of the council was called?"

"Of course I do, Mr. President. I' m not senile."

"Why then have you taken your customary seat? As head of the Alalakan clan, you are required to answer the accusations made against your clan member."

Jamiros made eye contact with a smug Bakom and chuckled. "But Mr. President, I am no longer head of the clan. That honor now belongs to my son."

Bakom scowled but then his countenance cleared. Rodane was no smarter than Jamiros.

The president smiled briefly. The Alalakan clan had waited a long time for Rodane and his wife to conceive. "My congratulations, Alalakan don al' Jamiros. Your son is here?"

"Of course, Mr. President. The Alalakan clan would certainly never ignore a summons from the Ruling Council. My son is simply waiting for the accusation to be placed before the Council and acknowledged as legitimate."

Many members, especially Bakom's allies, grumbled. They'd expected a quick session. The Alalakans were demanding formal procedure.

The president frowned and sighed. He'd spent most of his career on the Council struggling to remain neutral between Bakom and his allies and the Alalakans and theirs. "Very well, Jamiros. Madam Speaker, please read the accusation placed before the Council."

A woman, much stouter than the usual Drakian, rose and began to read. "The accusation as placed forth by Dr. Rodak don al' Bakom, First President of the Academy of Science and Ruling Council member, against Alalakan don al' Chardadon is as follows: Know then that Alalakan don al' Chardadon did knowingly and maliciously steal a hitherto unknown animal specimen native to a newly discovered planet from the presence of Dr. Rodak don al' Bakom. While Dr. Bakom is willing to acknowledge Captain Alalakan's reasoning that the specimen needed medical attention, Dr. Bakom does remind the Council that he is a fully qualified medical doctor. Furthermore, after medical attention was no longer necessary, Captain Alalakan removed the specimen from the medical section of his ship to his private quarters, denying Dr. Bakom all access. The specimen's human-like characteristics demanded that it be given the Tests of Humanity. Captain Alalakan willfully disregarded Dr. Bakom's claim. Dr. Bakom therefore enters the charge of treason against Captain Alalakan don al' Chardadon on behalf of the Drakian Academy of Science. Will the Head of the Clan Alalakan acknowledge this claim of treason?"

Chardadon strode onto the chamber floor and took his place next to the chair allotted to him. "The head of the Clan Alalakan hears the accusation and answers."

Bakom leaped to his feet. "What perfidy is this?"

The President turned to Jamiros and said, "This isn't amusing, Alalakan don al' Jamiros. What game do you play?"

Jamiros met the President's questioning gaze with a stern stare. "No game, Mr. President. My son Chardadon now heads our clan. His wife carries the Alalakan heir."

"The Council was unaware of Alalakan don al' Chardadon's marriage."

"As Head of the Clan Alalakan, Mr. President, I demand that you address your comments to me," Char said in an icy tone. "And since when has it been necessary to inform the Council when one marries?"

"It's a lie," Bakom snarled. "He's spent most of the last fourteen months in space or on Mediria. He didn't have enough time to court and marry, let alone impregnate, a woman."

Char's smile was anything but pleasant. "That's assuming my wife is Drakian. Mr. President, there is no law that requires me to marry a Drakian, is there?"

The president grimaced. He was being maneuvered into a corner and there was nothing he could do about it. "No, Alalakan don al' Chardadon, there is no law requiring you to marry a Drakian."

"I will not tolerate this!" Bakom shouted. He was beginning to get an inkling of what Chardadon was about to reveal. Now he understood why some of his allies were so upset about his late arrival. Rumors of Chardadon's marriage must have been circulating.

The President pounded his gavel. "I will have silence from you, Dr. Bakom. Your accusation has been made. The Alalakans have the right to answer."

Char smiled and bowed his head towards Bakom. Then he turned back to the Council. "Ladies and gentlemen of the Ruling Council, in the interest of time and to help expedite matters, I would like to introduce to you my wife, Alalakan dem al' Brianna of the previously unknown planet Earth, Bakom's so-called *specimen*."

Char held out his hand towards the door he had entered. On cue, Brianna swept into the room on Rodane's arm followed by Bandalardrac and Ademis. All three men, as had Char and his father, wore jackets with heavily embroidered representations of their dragons on the lapels. Brianna, on the other hand, bared her flaming dragon with its implicit challenge for the entire Council to see.

Brianna was dressed in a flowing white dress that bared her right shoulder, her dragon shimmering in the lights of the Council chamber. Her hair flowed down her back, held in place by her bridal net of red diamonds. Red diamonds also sparkled from her right wrist, fingers, and ears. On her left forearm, she wore a Gattan wrist sheath of beaten red gold covered with even more red diamonds. Denieen had delivered it that morning with very specific instructions on how to use the razor-sharp knife that rested in the sheath.

To say Brianna dazzled those sitting in the Council chamber would be an understatement. Seeing her, every member there could understand why Chardadon had married her — and why Bakom wanted her back. More than anything else, though, her pregnancy was obvious to everyone.

Taking Brianna' s hand, Char helped her into the chair he stood beside. Turning to the Council, he asked in a challenging tone, "Are there any questions?"

By rights, the President should have called an end to the meeting right then and there. However, Bakom was not about to give up, something Char and his family had counted on.

He rose from his chair and beat his fist on the railing before him. "This is ridiculous! How do we know she was not pregnant when she first boarded the ship?"

Char stepped forward and handed a folder to the president. "Medical records from Dr. Bakom' s own computers detailing his initial physical examination of my wife. As you can see, it is stated quite clearly that she was not pregnant at that time. Also included in the file are records from Brianna' s latest prenatal examination. Blood tests performed by Dr. Sendenton dem al' Lorilana prove quite conclusively that she carries a Drakian child."

The President didn' t bother to open the folder. He had no doubt that everything Char said was true.

As Bakom snarled and sputtered, a loud pounding from the doors at the back of the Council chamber interrupted the preceding. Motioning the guards to open the heavy doors, the President sighed again. Obviously the entire Council session was being very carefully orchestrated and manipulated by the Alalakans. Bakom had finally gone too far.

The doors were barely open when the Medirian ambassador strode down the aisle to the center of the Council floor.

The President rose to greet him. "Prince Hardan, we are honored by your presence, but surely this is not a Medirian matter."

"Since when is the demand that a Hardan princess be turned over to your Academy of Science as a *scientific specimen* not a Medirian matter?" Kavlalardrac snapped in a very icy tone. "I' m here to inform you that the Hardan royal family will not forgive this insult to its honor.

Failure to dismiss all charges against my niece's husband will result in an immediate cancellation of any connections between Mediria and Drakan. Have I made myself clear?"

The President paled and shot a venomous look in Bakom's direction. "Your Highness, please, there must be some misunderstanding."

Bakom's fists pounded the railing again. "It's a lie. The Hardan family is in collusion with the Alalakans!"

Gasps of dismay filled the room. Even Bakom's staunchest allies would not go so far as to anger the Medirian royal family. Too many of them would be financially ruined if Mediria severed all contacts with Drakan. And there were the assassins to consider.

Kavlalardrac became even more icily royal, if that were possible. "Brianna was adopted into the Hardan royal family months ago because the dols and orcs reside on her home planet. That is all the explanation my brother wishes to provide. I trust that I can inform him that this has all been a terrible misunderstanding?"

"Rest assured, Prince Kavlalardrac, that the Ruling Council of Drakan has no wish to bring any insult to the Hardan royal family."

"You fools!" Bakom howled. "Can't you see that the Alalakans are manipulating you? Who is in charge here?"

Brianna had had enough. "God, what an asshole."

Rising slowly, she left her seat and stepped up onto the platform before the Council members. Char placed his hand on her arm, but she shrugged it off. Her head high, she brushed her hair back off of her shoulder so that her flaming dragon was fully visible to everyone.

"I've had enough of this bullshit," she said in a voice that carried clearly.

"Bullshit?" flew around the chamber in whispers from mouth to mouth.

Both Char and Ban stepped onto the platform but were halted by Council guards as Brianna waddled purposefully towards Bakom. Fists clenched, she stared at the man who had given her nightmares for months. *Bakom's just like Gustovson, interested only in himself, and he doesn't care who he hurts to satisfy his own ambitions. Well, he picked the wrong person to mess with.*

Halting three feet from her nemesis, Brianna drew the knife from the wrist sheath. Very deliberately and very slowly she drew the sharp blade across the fleshy part of her lower arm. Blood rolled down over her hand and dripped to the floor. With a quick flick of her wrist, she buried the knife in the floor in front of Bakom.

"I, Alalakan dem al' Brianna, call bloodfeud on Rodak don al' Bakom," she stated in a clear voice that seethed with anger.

Pandemonium broke loose.

As soon as she threw the knife, Council guards grabbed Ban and Char.

"Brianna!" Char bellowed as he struggled against the two guards that held him.

She ignored him.

Eventually, the pounding of the president' s gavel and his shouts for order silenced most of those present.

"Alalakan dem al' Brianna," the President demanded, "you are not a Gattan to call for bloodfeud."

Flexing his shoulders, Ban tensed to throw off the two guards who held him.

Marljas' shout halted him.

Every head turned to the Federation balconies that lined the walls around the Council chamber.

Marljas' voice rang clearly from the Gattan balcony. "I, Marljas Drefeson, answer my bloodsister' s call."

Leaping from the balcony, he landed as lightly and gracefully as any cat. Rising, he strode to Brianna' s side. Muscles rippled on his bare arms and chest. The Alalakan dragon and an unknown beast that resembled Marljas closely were bared for everyone to see.

Standing before Bakom, whose eyes widened at the sight of the dragon, Marljas unsheathed the claws of his right hand and drew them across his left forearm, one at a time, reciting each accusation against Bakom clearly. "Rodak don al' Bakom, I call bloodfeud," he snarled as the first rivulet of blood began to flow down his arm and drip to the floor, "for your harassment of my bloodsister, Alalakan dem al' Brianna and your failure to honor her humanity.

"I call bloodfeud," he continued, "for the kidnapping and rape of my wife, Alalakan dem al' Sheala."

Audible gasps filled the Council chamber as the second rivulet of blood flowed down Marljas' arm. A Gattan-Alalakan alliance of marriage would have profound interplanetary trade implications.

"Finally," Marljas finished with a roar, "I call bloodfeud for the kidnapping, rape, inhuman scientific experiments, and addiction to mithrin of Sosha Kanicsdottir, a Gattan citizen!"

Loud voices demanded explanations as the third rivulet of blood joined the other two. Only the light pressure of Brianna's hand on his arm kept Marljas from attacking Bakom.

"How do you answer these accusations, Rodak don al' Bakom?" Brianna spat in a voice heard above the growing uproar. "Tell the members of your government how you and your friends use women as sexual slaves."

"Lies! All lies!" Bakom shrieked. "I know nothing about those women! How dare you accuse me, the First President of the Academy of Science!"

Brianna simply turned to her husband. "Char?"

Jerking free of the guards, Char glared at Brianna then picked up a sealed envelope and walked to stand in front of the Council president. "Mr. President, would you care to view the rape of my sister and of the goddaughter of the Gattan ambassador by Bakom and his assistants now or later? We obtained enough evidence to support these and many other accusations when my family rescued the two women from a secret laboratory Bakom had for his private use. Even now, the police are combing through files and samples taken from three separate floors where he performed experiments secretly."

All eyes in the room turned to Bakom.

"Well, Dr..."

The Council President never finished. Bakom sprang from the platform and fled across the room much more rapidly than anyone thought possible.

Snarling, Marljas leaped to the knife embedded in the floor and jerked it free. His catlike reflexes sent the blade flying after Bakom, who screamed and tumbled to the floor.

"Guards!" shouted the Council President, "arrest him!"

Council guards streamed into the chamber, fighting against the stream of Council members trying to leave.

However, before they could reach the door, guards wearing the uniform of the Medirian royal household filled the doorways and refused to allow anyone to leave.

Disgruntled and panicked Council members milled about the room. Some returned to their seats. Others scuttled from one door to another, seeking escape.

Rodane' s sharp eyes noted each and every one.

Pounding his gavel, the President eventually restored some semblance of order. "Prince Kavlalardrac, Medirian guards have no place in the Council Chamber of Drakan."

Kavlalardrac bowed. "My sincerest apologies, Mr. President. My guards must have heard the commotion and feared for my safety. I will dismiss them immediately. I would suggest, however, your own guards man the doors. Perhaps there were others here who joined in Bakom' s perfidies."

Howls of outrage greeted that statement. Council members rose to their feet, some shaking their fists at being so accused. Others loudly swore their innocence. All of them looked to the package that lay on the President' s desk — the one that held the lab videos.

"Wait until they find out there are fifteen more recordings and the police have made copies of all of them," Rodane muttered to Ban. "Not to mention the copies we made for ourselves."

Again the President pounded his gavel to bring order. "Sergeant, take Rodak don al' Bakom into custody until the police arrive. And set guards at the doors on your way out. No Council members are to leave without my permission."

The Medirians melted away from the doors as the Council guards hustled Bakom from the chamber.

The President turned to Chardadon. "All charges brought forth by Dr. Rodak don al' Bakom against the Alalakan clan are dropped."

The blood had stopped flowing from Brianna' s arm, for she had been very careful to make sure the cut had been shallow. Nevertheless, Char was furious. "Bandalardrac," he said in a tightly controlled voice, "take Brianna to the shuttle."

Crossing her arms over her breasts, she glared back at Char.

"Bandalardrac," Char snarled, "you heard me the first time. Take Brianna to the shuttle."

Shrugging, Ban grinned lopsidedly and presented his arm to Brianna.

She chose to ignore him and turned to a still fuming Marljas. "Brother, I wish to go home now."

Snarling once more at the door where Bakom disappeared, Marljas turned his surly expression on Char and said, "Come, Bloodsister. My *wife* has need of me."

They both ignored everyone else as they left.

The Council President locked his eyes with Char's. "Are you sure, Alalakan don al' Chardadon, that your wife is not Gattan?"

✳ ✳ ✳ ✳ ✳

When he entered his family's townhouse, Char stalked toward the jubilant voices coming from the drawing room. He was going to shake Brianna until her teeth rattled. How could she endanger herself like that? If Bakom had grabbed her, he could have used her as a shield. Jamiros grinned and raised his glass when he saw his son standing in the doorway.

"Congratulations, Char. Bakom is finished."

Char accepted a glass from his smiling mother and acknowledged his father's salute. Lifting the glass, he tossed its contents down his throat. The coughing and gasping that resulted had a laughing Wendjas pounding on his back.

"What is this?" He'd been expecting his favorite Deslossian red.

"A very old vintage of *troctikoc* brandy, my friend," Wendjas answered. "Denieen insisted that we bring it with us. Be honored. It is very rare and complicated to brew. Gattan drink it only on momentous occasions, the birth of a child, the defeat of a blood enemy."

"Give that to your enemies and you won't have to worry about blood feuds," Char growled when he regained his breath. He gaze jerked around the room. She wasn't there. "Where's Brianna? I'm surprised she's not here sipping this swill with you."

Coming from anyone else, Char's comments would have begun another bloodfeud. Wendjas, however, grinned more widely.

Chuckling, Xdana said, "Brianna swept into the house with Meri, as regal as any Medirian princess, and informed us that she was going to her room because she was 'fatigued'. The only other person she wanted to see was Denieen because she owed her bloodsister an explanation and profound apology for misplacing her ' first blood' knife. Denieen is with Meri and her now."

Char threw his glass into the fireplace. "Not for long."

Still grinning, Wendjas said, "An angry man does not interrupt three women who wish to be alone with their thoughts."

Char shoved Wendjas out of the way. "Stop spouting Gattan proverbs at me. She' s my wife, and I want to talk to her."

Ban took a step towards Char, but Fionilina reached her brother-in-law' s side first. Placing her hand on his arm, she said, "I' ve never seen you so angry, Char. Your temper will do Brianna no good now."

Char muttered an expletive as he shook off her arm. However, Wendjas and, interestingly enough, Marljas moved quickly to block the doorway.

With an exasperated shrug, Fionilina returned to her chair.

Hushed silence filled the room as Char faced the Gattans. "You are blocking my way," Char snarled in a dangerously low voice. "I suggest you move. Now."

Everyone in the room shifted uncomfortably as Ban hurried to his side and grasped his arm.

Char jerked free. "Leave off, Bandalardrac. Brianna is my wife, and she behaved totally irresponsibly today."

"She acted in true Gattan fashion, Alalakan," Marljas countered, obviously offended.

"Gentlemen, please..." began a now alarmed Jamiros. The unprecedented ties that had been forged with this Gattan family seemed to be on the brink of severing.

Char' s anger had not abated. If anything, it had grown hotter. Ignoring his father, he eased out of the embroidered jacket he wore. "Move now, Gattan, or I will move you."

Xdana pushed herself out of her chair. "Char!"

The tension eddied about the room, and Ban' s gaze leaped from face to face. Now was not the time to reveal that he was the most dangerous man in the galaxy.

Concern, fear and anxiety were clearly visible on the faces of all present—except one.

Ban' s eyes snapped back to Fionilina' s and the amused and exasperated expression on her face. Fio wasn' t worried? What did she know that no one else did?

Ban searched his memories of all that happened in the Council chamber. Char had the right to be angry. Brianna *had* acted irresponsibly. Then he remembered a surprised expression that had appeared on Brianna' s face during the chaos that exploded after Bakom' s capture.

Realization dawned.

Ban' s bark of laughter cut through the tension. Delivering a staggering punch to Char' s shoulder, he said, "Think, man. Fio said Brianna didn' t need an angry husband *now*!"

Char threw his angry gaze at his cousin, but the subtlety of Ban' s remark began to register. His eyes widened and he returned his gaze to the grinning Gattans.

"I told you we only drink *troctikoc* brandy on special occasions," Wendjas said. "Denieen insisted we bring a few bottles over with us."

Shoving the now cooperative Gattan out of his way, Char bolted out the door.

The other inhabitants of the room stared at each other. Then all gazes locked on Ban. A broad smile on his face, he shrugged, sauntered over to the sideboard and poured himself another glass of brandy.

Xdana glared at Ban' s back. "Well, I never."

A puzzled frown lay on Jenneta' s face. Then her eyes widened. "Brianna' s having the baby."

The silence was shattered almost instantly.

Lorilana rose. "I must go…"

"Why didn' t she…?" Xdana said as she also rose.

The general exclamations of joy and surprise were hushed as the two Gattan once again barred the exit. "You will wait here," Marljas said crossing his arms.

"I beg your pardon, young man," Lorilana said haughtily, "but I am her physician."

"She didn' t ask for you," Wendjas answered. "She wishes to be attended only by Denieen and the Princess…and by the Alalakan."

"Char!" Xdana exclaimed. "What does she want him for?"

Ban answered from across the room where he had gone to stand beside an equally amused Fionilina. "Custom on her planet, perhaps?"

"That' s what she told me," Fio answered from her seat. "Brianna expects Char to be with her when the baby is born."

"Well, what are we supposed to do?" asked a miffed Xdana. "Tradition demands that women of the clan be present."

Ban chuckled. "Surely you' ve realized by now, Aunt, that Brianna doesn' t give a damn about tradition, at least not all of it. How long," he asked, turning to Fionilina, "were you going to keep quiet?"

Fionilina smiled triumphantly. "Brianna told me not to say anything until Char came."

Xdana, Jenneta and Lorilana bent accusing gazes on her.

"And you agreed?" Lorilana snapped. "What if there are complications?"

"Denieen is a competent midwife who' s experienced enough to know if something is going wrong. An emergency minishuttle is standing by, just in case," Fio answered smoothly. "I see nothing wrong with granting Brianna' s wish. My mother told me how much she hated having so many people gawking at me when she gave birth."

Jenneta glanced at the two grinning Gattan in the doorway. "Well, what are we supposed to do now?"

Rodane smiled broadly as he refilled his glass and sat down next to his wife. "I' m afraid you' ll have to do what the men of Drakan have done for generations, Grandmother. You wait."

The three older women threw scathing looks at Rodane as he pulled his wife close.

Wendjas and Marljas laughed uproariously.

Supported by Denieen, Brianna walked back and forth across the room.

"There has to be…an easier…way…to do this," Brianna groaned, gritting her teeth against another contraction.

"If we were on Mediria, you' d be in a birthing pool," Meri said. "If you were home on the estate, you could relax in your tub, but this one is simply too small."

Denieen pursed her lips thoughtfully. "Giving birth in water, how interesting. Less trauma for the baby. I' d like to come to your planet to observe this, Meri."

"You' re welcome any time, Deni," Meri answered with a smile. "Mother will be more than happy to show you our maternity hospitals."

Brianna' s contraction passed, and she shook herself free from Denieen. Taking a deep breath, she grumbled, "That one was strong. Char better get his ass home soon."

Meri and Deni smiled at each other behind Brianna' s back. Both had been in her confidence and so knew that her labor had begun that morning before the Council session. Luckily for Brianna, she' d had no strong contractions until Marljas was bringing her home. After he' d dropped her off, he' d fetched Denieen. Brianna had been adamant about not having all of Char' s female relatives present at the birth of her child. Therefore, Denieen had been very specific with her instructions to Marljas and Wendjas. Earlier Fionilina, who had happily agreed with Brianna' s wish not to be the main attraction of a three-ring circus—whatever that was—agreed to send Char up as soon as he returned.

Another stronger contraction rolled around Brianna' s stomach, and she would have fallen if Meri and Denieen had not each grabbed an arm. A rush of water pooled at their feet.

"It won' t be long now," Denieen said as Brianna moaned. "Chardadon will miss the birth of his child if he doesn' t soon come."

Brianna struggled to regain her composure as her friends helped her to the bed.

Then the door slammed open, and Char stomped into the room.

He' d only taken four or five steps into the room when Brianna had another contraction. Blanching, he watched the muscles on her stomach contract and take control of her body. He broke out in a sweat when he heard her moan with pain.

"Brianna!"

Gritting her teeth, she spat, "Damn it, Char, it' s about time you got here. What took you so long! Your son isn' t going to wait much longer."

"It' s going very well, Brianna," Denieen said. "You are one of the lucky women who will give birth relatively easily."

Brianna clenched Char' s hand as another contraction took control.

"Easily!" he exclaimed between clenched teeth as Brianna' s grip tightened.

Both Meri and Denieen laughed.

Meri plumped some pillows behind Brianna' s back. "My labor lasted almost twenty-eight hours."

Char gave Brianna his other hand as he shook feeling into the hand she' d just squeezed. "Can' t you give her something for the pain?"

"I' m not taking anything unless I can' t stand the pain," Brianna panted. "If I...can get through this...so can you."

"But, Brianna..."

"Don' t ' but Brianna' me, Char," she snarled through clenched teeth as another pain struck. "I' m the one having this baby, and I' m going to do it my way whether you like it or not!"

Denieen glanced between Brianna' s legs. "Push with the next contraction, Brianna."

Helpless, Char watched as nature took control of his wife' s body. He' d seen videos of birth and helped in the birthing sheds of the clan' s herds. However, he' d never been emotionally involved before. His anger evaporated with her painful moans. He had never felt so helpless in his life.

"Help her up a little, Alalakan," Denieen said. "That' s it, sit behind her and support her back. I can see the head."

Char slid onto the bed next to Brianna, and pulled her up against his chest. Tears fell freely from his eyes as he felt her shudder against the pains that racked her body.

"Damn it, Char..."

"That' s it," encouraged Denieen. "One more push."

Brianna screamed, and her son slid from her body.

"It' s a boy," Meri said as she laid the baby Denieen had handed her into Brianna' s arms. "A fine, big boy. Congratulations, Char."

Tears of joy were streaming from Brianna' s eyes as she reached for him. "Connor, Char, his name is Connor."

"Whatever you want, love, it' s yours," he answered. He stared over Brianna' s shoulder at the small being who stopped crying when he was laid in her arms.

"He's got a tail," Brianna continued.

Char smiled and gently hugged her. "Good. Ban would never let us hear the end of it if our son were tailless."

Denieen smiled at their banter as Brianna delivered the afterbirth with no trouble. This was one of the easiest births she'd ever attended. "But he will have a head of flame as does your wife. He will truly be a Dragon among the Alalakans."

Brianna sighed. Exhaustion was finally taking control.

"Hand Connor to me, Char," Meri said. "He needs to be cleaned up and Brianna needs to rest."

Slowly Char eased from behind his wife and very carefully, as if he were carrying the most fragile glass, lifted his son from Brianna's arms.

"I love you, Char."

Depositing Connor gently in Meri's arms, Char turned back to his wife. "I have loved you all of my life, Brianna, even before I met you," he answered. "You are the other half of my soul." Easing himself down onto the bed, he gently pulled her into his arms and cradled her against his chest.

Soon her even breathing told him she was asleep.

Meri placed Connor in the baby cot that had been dragged over from the nursery. Then she and Deni left the room.

Char leaned his head back and closed his eyes.

A cheer from downstairs slipped beneath the closed door and he smiled. Connor's relatives had been informed of his arrival.

Char shifted Brianna so she'd be more comfortable, then buried his face into her fiery curls and inhaled her special fragrance. Finally he was home.

About the author:

Living in a small town in Central Pennsylvania, Judy Mays spends the time she isn' t teaching English to tenth graders as a wife and mother. Family is very important to Judy, and she spends a lot of time with her husband and children. Judy' s pets are a very important part of her life, and she' s had many over the years. Currently, Zoe the cat and Boomer the Lab mix help keep things hopping around the house.

Judy loves reading—especially romance, the spicier the better. After reading for more years than she cares to admit, Judy decided to try her hand at writing romantica—and her wonderful husband of seventeen years provides plenty of motivation and ideas.

In the upcoming months, the tales by Judy Mays will contain werewolves, vampires, witches, and aliens from five planets on the other side of the galaxy. All of the heroes or heroines will fall madly in love and demonstrate their love in so very, very many ways.

Enjoy Judy' s books, and after you' ve read one, she would love to hear what you think. Either stop by her website at www.judymays.com and sign her guest book or contact her directly at writermays@yahoo.com. She can' t wait to hear from you.

Judy welcomes mail from readers. You can write to her c/o Ellora' s Cave Publishing at 1337 Commerce Drive, Suite 13, Stow OH 44224.

Why an electronic book?

We live in the Information Age — an exciting time in the history of human civilization in which technology rules supreme and continues to progress in leaps and bounds every minute of every hour of every day. For a multitude of reasons, more and more avid literary fans are opting to purchase e-books instead of paperbacks. The question to those not yet initiated to the world of electronic reading is simply: *why?*

1. *Price.* An electronic title at Ellora' s Cave Publishing runs anywhere from 40-75% less than the cover price of the <u>exact same title</u> in paperback format. Why? Cold mathematics. It is less expensive to publish an e-book than it is to publish a paperback, so the savings are passed along to the consumer.

2. *Space.* Running out of room to house your paperback books? That is one worry you will never have with electronic novels. For a low one-time cost, you can purchase a handheld computer designed specifically for e-reading purposes. Many e-readers are larger than the average handheld, giving you plenty of screen room. Better yet, hundreds of titles can be stored within your new library — a single microchip. (Please note that Ellora' s Cave does not endorse any specific brands. You can check our website at www.ellorascave.com for customer recommendations we make available to new consumers.)

3. *Mobility.* Because your new library now consists of only a microchip, your entire cache of books can be taken with you wherever you go.

4. *Personal preferences are accounted for.* Are the words you are currently reading too small? Too large? Too...**ANNOYING**? Paperback books cannot be modified according to personal preferences, but e-books can.

5. *Innovation.* The way you read a book is not the only advancement the Information Age has gifted the literary community with. There is also the factor of what you can read. Ellora' s Cave Publishing will be introducing a new line of interactive titles that are available in e-book format only.

6. *Instant gratification.* Is it the middle of the night and all the bookstores are closed? Are you tired of waiting days—sometimes weeks—for online and offline bookstores to ship the novels you bought? Ellora' s Cave Publishing sells instantaneous downloads 24 hours a day, 7 days a week, 365 days a year. Our e-book delivery system is 100% automated, meaning your order is filled as soon as you pay for it.

Those are a few of the top reasons why electronic novels are displacing paperbacks for many an avid reader. As always, Ellora' s Cave Publishing welcomes your questions and comments. We invite you to email us at service@ellorascave.com or write to us directly at: 1337 Commerce Drive, Suite 13, Stow OH 44224.

Discover for yourself why readers can' t get enough of the multiple award-winning publisher Ellora' s Cave. Whether you prefer e-books or paperbacks, be sure to visit EC on the web at www.ellorascave.com for an erotic reading experience that will leave you breathless.

WWW.ELLORASCAVE.COM